LIVING WITH MONSTERS

Fig. 1. Detail from Hieronymus Bosch, *Ship of Fools* (1490–1500)

First published in 2023 by punctum books, Earth, Milky Way.
https://punctumbooks.com

ISBN-13: 978-1-68571-082-8 (print)
ISBN-13: 978-1-68571-083-5 (ePDF)

DOI: 10.53288/0361.1.00

LCCN: 2023934594
Library of Congress Cataloging Data is available from the Library of Congress

Book design: Hatim Eujayl and Vincent W.J. van Gerven Oei
Cover image: Rebecca Dagnall, "Paradise #6" (2009) from the series *Paradise in Suburbia*. https://www.rebeccadagnall.com/.

spontaneous acts of scholarly combustion

HIC SVNT MONSTRA

Living with Monsters

Ethnographic Fiction about Real Monsters

Yasmine Musharbash &
Ilana Gershon (eds.)

p.

Contents

Acknowledgments

This book was conceived on a dark and stormy night, about three minutes into a cab ride from a restaurant to a conference hotel (thank you, Minnesotan cabbie!). Ilana was working on her second edited volume of ethnographic fiction; Yasmine was working on her second edited volume of monster anthropology… and voilà: let's do an edited volume of ethnographic fiction about monsters! A trilogy of sorts for both of us — so simple, so elegant!

Who do we know who might be interested to write something for such a volume? Turns out, quite a few people. Surprisingly quickly, we found critical mass, and the contributions started to come in. Those were exciting times. Every week or so another chapter arrived: inventive, thought-provoking, beautifully crafted (thank you, wonderful contributors!). Each so unique, and together they began to form a volume that simply charmed.

We were enamored with our edited book, the proposal to send the volume off to the publishers almost wrote itself (thanks, proposal!). And with that we had burnt through our reserve of good luck and had to wait for it to replenish. Neither Ilana nor Yasmine ever before received so many rejections, yet such kind and supportive ones. We might get one ecstatic review and one cautious one. Absolutely love the manuscript, but we are not the right press. Or not fictional enough, not academic enough. And so on. This grinds you down (thank you, contributors for sticking with us through thick and thin!).

Enter punctum books! They get us, and they get the book. They get the book! (Thank you, punctum and especially Vincent, Eileen, and Lily!)

Along the way, many people helped and encouraged, and we would like to especially thank Fran Benson, Jane Blackwood, Stuart McLean, Chris Marcatili, Anand Pandian, and Janelle Taylor. (Thanks also to all the chocolate makers whose good work propelled us forward after every setback).

Yasmine would like to thank the Australian Research Council for Future Fellowship FT13010041 which gave her the freedom to experiment, the University of Sydney for bankrolling the *Living with Monsters* Symposium, and the Australian National University for time to work on the manuscript. Ilana Gershon would like to thank Indiana University for having the good taste to hire some of the contributors to be her colleagues.

Massive thanks to Rebecca Dagnall for allowing us to use one of her fabulous art works on the cover.

Dedicated to our nieces and nephews:

Yasmine — Tilly, JJ, Wissou, and Fatou

Ilana — Colin, Lila, Lily, Mira, Nina, and Shai

Here Be Monsters

Yasmine Musharbash and Ilana Gershon

When I return to Saibai after some time away the spirits of the dead inhabit my dreams at will. They hitch a ride inside, have a little fun, a bit of a yarn, then tootle-doo off.

The villagers won't like it if you cross the river because you will bring back "bad things" to our village. Maybe your soul is strong, and you won't suffer harm. But the evil will follow you, it will attach to you. Those who are weak, like us children, are in danger if you behave irresponsibly.

If you can see them, Kurdaitcha look like humans, like Yapa, but with even darker skin, red-ochred dreadlocks, and big half-erect cocks. "Their feet must look like human feet," he thought. "Surely, this is why they use the feather shoes when on the prowl." That is why they had smoothed the sand, so they could see the tracks appear while they were waiting for the attack.

Sakawa boys scare me. They scare lots of Ghanaians.

Only now, after all these years, do I see how my work has been shaped by the monstrous beings that have been haunting me since childhood.

"Did you hear a single thing Uncle said to you, Sarah? A single damn thing?" Marvin shook his head in exasperation. "Don't go looking for things unless you want them to find you."

These quotes are extracts from some of the chapters that follow, and they superbly condense what we mean by *Living with Monsters*. There is a fundamental distinction between the monsters you will meet on these pages and the ones you may have met already on film and TV screens or on the pages of books, comics, and zines. The latter are usually fictional. Everybody agrees that they are metaphors or symbols, that they "stand for" something else. Take zombies for example. Not only are they one of the most prolific monsters of contemporary popular culture,[1] but they have been interpreted to stand for anything from labor exploitation, the appropriation of female bodies, drug epidemics, the horror of killing during the Vietnam War, mindless consumerism, brain-washing, and the threat of contagion to apocalyptic visions including Y2K, nuclear disaster, alien invasion, and climate change.[2] The monsters of popular culture are devices employed artistically to express contemporary concerns in a particular genre — horror first and foremost but often mixed with other genres from romance and comedy to western.

Monsters in anthropology have much in common with their fictional cousins, but they are also distinctly different. A major aim of this introduction is to contour these differences in more detail. In a nutshell, though, we understand monsters as

---

[1] For the sheer numbers of zombie movies — and these are pre-*The Walking Dead!* — see Dendle (2001, 2012b).

[2] The literature on zombies is vast. For some overviews, see Bishop (2010); Hubner, Leaning, and Manning (2015); and Vervaeke, Mastropietro, and Miscevic (2017).

non-human social actors who are other-than-the norm, always contingent on the humans they haunt, the times and the places in which they operate, and with a profound awareness of social rules, taxonomies, and classificatory schema that they then subvert — including, naturally, this very definition. (Musharbash 2021)

Crucially, the monsters our authors are concerned with, for the most part, are understood to be real by those they haunt. When anthropologists are doing fieldwork, they often meet people who are living with monsters. This brings with it difficulties for the people themselves, who need to figure out how to live their lives alongside often terrifying and meddlesome beings, and quite a different set of difficulties for the anthropologists. Living with people who live alongside monsters is a poignant example of how participant observation often entails studying people who see the world differently than you do. It illustrates beautifully how fieldwork encourages anthropologists to start noticing things they had previously overlooked. For example, an anthropologist might learn to worry when they see a shadowy solitary figure in the distance, feel a sudden breeze, or hear a particular bird. The anthropologists in this volume are experimenting with ethnographic fiction to share these experiences with you. Writing fiction gave each author the freedom to explore the topic outside of the usual academic constraints. Moreover, it allowed them to creatively capture the essence of what it means to be in a world populated with monsters too.

Living with monsters is all too often living in a world of as-ifs. For anthropologists, it can mean experiencing how those they live with and study are confident that they exist alongside beings that anthropologists are not always certain are even real, as Lynch describes in her ghost tour of an old New England mill. Yet even if the anthropologist is convinced the monster exists, this may be something they are only willing to admit to a select few people. It may cause some serious moral and ethical issues for the anthropologist and their hosts to resolve, as Davis describes in his piece; or it can hit home in the most intimate, painful, and unexpected ways as Bastian narrates.

Anthropologists are often caught — determined to respect their fieldwork interlocutors who live in a world populated with different beings or unable to admit to their colleagues that they have joined this world too. To be respectful and act with integrity to those whose lives they study, they have to live as-if monsters interfere with people's daily lives. Or they have to live as-if these monsters don't exist when among their colleagues. Monsters make the relationship work at the heart of anthropology into the work of living in the as-if.

This is the third collection in a series of ethnographic fiction that follows a collection of imagined job manuals (Gershon 2015) and imagined animal guides (Porter and Gershon 2018). Approaching jobs and animals through the lens of ethnographic fiction opened a different set of possibilities for the authors than writing about the monsters who dwell in their fieldsites. Being asked to write imagined job manuals encouraged the authors to critique the standardizing impulses and expectations inherent in the concept of the job manual. Those authors showed how culturally specific it is to imagine jobs as work bound to roles, bound in ways that can be made explicit, and taught through standardizing guidelines for set practices. Turning to animals opened another set of conversations and encouraged authors to engage with the advantages and limitations of being human when writing about interactions across species. While many contemporary ethnographies reflect on this, ethnographic fiction gave the authors a different purchase in part because they were free to write from the perspective of another species (and had to weigh whether they wanted to). Writing ethnographic fiction about monsters offered a different set of challenges and allowed people to engage with a generosity of spirit simultaneously towards those who know monsters exist and towards those who are skeptics. Ethnographic fiction about monsters enabled these authors to write about complicity and ambiguity with a sophisticated unsettledness that ethnographic writing alone elides. It opened the door for our authors to write in the space of multiple as-ifs — how interactions take place when some people act as if something doesn't exist and others as if it does, as well as allowing this multiplicity to exist for readers as well.

It is not only anthropologists who are drawn into as-ifs by monsters. And monsters are not the only key to unlock a world of as-ifs. Most of us are constantly living with as-ifs. We communicate with others in contexts where there are multiple ways to communicate, and thus we tend to interact as-if the communication we settled upon was appropriate and intelligible. We operate in contexts where we could slip into other social roles, where we have multiple ways of being with others in any given situation, and thus we act as-if we were one role and one role only for that moment, for the efficacy of that interaction. We sometimes work with friends, and different contexts will shape whether we are interacting as friends or as co-workers, and we might act as if we aren't friends in a workplace meeting, or as if we aren't colleagues at a birthday party. Or, in the example that first encouraged us to think along these lines, as Barbara Yngvesson (2008) points out, when you are adopted, you act as if your adoptive parents are your family, and when you go to visit your birth family, you act as if these people are your family as well. They are all your family, of course, but there is always an as-if element because, for the families she studies, adoption is not the default way to form families. Monsters make explicit a different as-if, an as-if not of default social roles, but of default ontology. Monsters are beings in some people's worlds, but not everyone's worlds. This is why thinking with monsters is such a great way to analyze how to live in an ontological state of as-if.

But, hang on, what exactly are these monsters? you may ask, and *what is it that makes them monstrous?* And, also probably, *what exactly do you mean when you say "living with"?* In this introduction we tend to these questions, and then turn to a final one (our favorite!): "What can we learn from looking at monsters?"

What Are Monsters?

The monsters of this volume include a smorgasbord of evil spirits, ghosts, demons, aliens, and fairies, and there are also great number of locally named and highly specific monsters, including Ali, Anito, Chinka, Huldufólk, the Jersey Devil, Kaji, Kappa, Kurdaitcha, Markay, Mini, Mr. Top Hat, Muniswarar, Muruyg, Nyukur, Sakawa Boys, and Sasquatch. Although wildly different from one another, they also have much in common, which is why we refer to them collectively as monsters. That is to say, we use the term "monster" as an umbrella term to refer to socioculturally specific beings who are "other than" — neither human, nor fauna or flora[3] — and who in one way or another live up to the term's etymological meaning. The noun "monster" comes from the Latin *monstrum,* which combines two verbs: *monere* (to warn) and *demonstrare* (to reveal). This might indicate that warning-revealing, to monsters, is an action, force, movement, response. In this vein, monsters have often been understood as beings who signal danger; both in the sense of "there be monsters," a warning when venturing into the perilous unknown, and in the more conceptual sense of flagging strangeness, difference, liminality, category confusion, and illicit boundary crossing.[4]

Let's explore the monster's liminality, that is, its neither-here-nor-there-ishness, first by looking at their bodies. The monstrous body always crosses or combines categories that are otherwise distinctly separate.[5] Take some of the undead as an example: a ghost, a vampire, or a zombie is neither exactly dead (i.e., the former person disintegrating, their body rotting, their spirit departed) nor exactly alive (i.e., their biological functions differ, inability to eat, digest, and defecate the way humans do).

---

3   If you are wondering about monstrous plants, look no further than Miller (2012).

4   This is received wisdom in monster studies. See, amongst many others, Asma (2009); Cohen (1996); Dendle (2012a); Mittman (2012); Picart and Browning (2012); Weinstock (2014); Van Duzer (2012).

5   See also Musharbash (2014, 8–11).

The bodies of ghosts, vampires, and zombies are "unnatural" or monstrous because they combine categories that are otherwise mutually exclusive by being *both* dead and alive or, depending on how you look at it, *neither* dead nor alive). You will encounter many monsters straddling the dead-undead divide in this volume, in the chapters by Bastian, Davis, Funk, and Lynch and Coppola. Other monsters embody their liminality in different ways; some, for example are of human-like appearance but with more-than human powers, such as being able to shapeshift, turning invisible, flying, and so on, as Mabefam and Alexeyeff's, Lepselter's, Hawkins and Onnudottir's, Manning's, and Musharbash's chapters demonstrate. Others again merge human and non-human attributes and characteristics, much like classical monsters such as werebeings, both human and animal, or the devil with his horns and hooves, as Arumugam's, Foster's, Murray's, Tolbert's, and Tomlinson's chapters show. Some conjoin animal and non-animal characteristics, as Foster's, Hawkins and Onnudottir's, and Tomlinson's chapters explain. Or, in the case of the Icelandic Nykur, dangerous monster-horses described in Hawkins and Onnudottir's chapter, their monstrousness is indicated through combining opposite directionalities: "their feet are monstrous, back to front, with the hoof pointing toward the tail and the fetlock to the front. Such ugly feet, and so dangerous!"

In short, the bodies of monsters are anthropological fare *par excellence,* and in Mary Douglas's (1969) terms the very fact that they cross categories gives them meaning. That is to say what it is to be human becomes highlighted in the monstrous figure that is more-than-human, less-than-human, or other-than-human. As Cohen (1996, 4) said: "The monstrous body is pure culture," and it is pure culture because the ways in which it exceeds or recedes from being human is always done in a culturally intelligible way for that community. Even when it violates classification, it violates culturally specific classifications, and it violates in a way that makes sense in a culturally intelligible way.

In each case, the particular ways in which the monstrous body is fashioned is loaded with meaning for the people interacting with that body. This is how the uncut hair and nails of Manning's Georgian goblins signal their wildness (vis-à-vis humans; they are quite civilized in their own monstrous ways when at home in their lair); much in the same way that the semi-erect penis of the Kurdaitcha, as Musharbash demonstrates, signify theirs. Such signs of other-than-human sociality — or in contrast to human sociality, their wildness — are also found among the Kappa, as Foster explains, but in this case, it is precisely these signs that change over time to make it easier for those monsters to live alongside humans. And, of course, this bodily signal becomes amplified morally. This is beautifully illustrated in Mabefam and Alexeyeff's tale of a young man so poverty-stricken that he is desperate enough to join the Sakawa boys. The rituals of joining those magically powered criminals irreversibly turn a formerly moral human being into a corrupt, immoral, and heinous version of his former self — a monster.

The locations where monsters dwell and haunt, customarily, are liminal as well: in the shadows, on the margins, around ruins, at crossroads, and so on. Many of the monsters in this volume are quite traditional in this sense. Lynch and Coppola's ghosts in the old mill, say, or Arumugam's Mini spirits around the pond next to the shrine, Foster's Kappa under bridges, and pointedly, the lack of monsters at Lake Hopatcong. As Tomlinson explains, "Lake Hopatcong can't possibly host a monster. It's a perfectly nice body of water, but it's kind of small, and really suburban." Mind you, some of the chapters illustrate that it is also tremendously significant when monsters do *not* dwell where they are expected to, most aptly captured by Lepselter's Reptilian Alien Lacerto:

> Lacerto has suddenly materialized beside Aline. The audience blinks. […] Where did he go? I'm not sure. He could be among you; maybe he vanished.

There is something especially terrifying about the thought of a monster out of place, about monsters who walk *among* us —

unrecognized. It is also telling that monsters seem to haunt out of place more these days than they used to as Foster and Tomlinson demonstrate on monsters adapting to the times.[6] As the world has become more porous, filled with more and more translocal connections, monsters have become more mobile, too. So much so that they now also prowl in virtuality, as Tolbert's chapter showcases.

Something similar is going on with the temporality of monster appearances. Traditionally monsters are "creatures of the night," and prone to appear on inauspicious dates such as Halloween or Friday the 13th. This makes it particularly interesting to think through the meanings of the different "whens" in the pieces in this volume. Some of "our" monsters stick to custom: at night they appear in dreams in Davis's chapter, or as ghosts in Bastian's, and Lynch and Coppola's chapters; and night is the only time some of them can walk around freely, like the trolls do in Hawkins and Onnudottir's; and it is when the Georgian goblins are most active, like in Manning's; and night-time is when they conduct their abductions, like aliens and fairies do in Lepselter's. Implicitly, Tolbert suggests connections between nighttime, Halloween, and monsters, and the Minis in Arumugam's piece capture their human lovers on Tuesday and Friday nights. Sakawa boys appear at rituals and festivals, bridal showers and christenings and *shower* all presents in dirty money. There is always meaning associated with the timing of hauntings, but it means one thing if they are regular and predictable and something quite different when they are sudden and unexpected. Simply put, the less predictable the temporal and spatial anchoring of a monster, the bigger its impact on those it troubles. This is perhaps most strongly expressed in Funk's piece, which presents a child's view and explanation of just how deeply, relentlessly, and strongly the scary Anito pervade the lives of Tao people. So, much like the ways in which different zombies

---

6   And have a look at Musharbash and Presterudstuen's (2020) volume on
    the anthropology of change and social transformation explored through
    ethnographies of monsters.

adjust to the meanings they are meant to express (for example, being slow and mindless, or fast and vicious, raiding a deserted house in the countryside or a shopping mall, being night-active or on the hunt 24/7) the monsters in our book come in a great variety of bodies, and haunt a multitude of spaces and places, and at different times. *What do they* do, *though,* you may ask, and *what does it all mean?*

What Do Monsters Do?

As our authors illustrate, monsters do more than terrorize people, scaring them, making them tremble, and sending shivers down their spines. The monsters in these pages protect, seduce, sigh, moan and groan, feed, eat with others, get fed, possess, appear in dreams, drive around in spirit cars, use computers, learn languages, come for a yarn, help, teach, exploit, adapt, adjust, die, get captured, abduct, drive into madness, forewarn, have sex appeal, live, love, grieve, and kill. Our contributors show again and again that monsters, much like humans, are relational beings. Monsters are connected to others through control, respect, ties of obligation, and even kinship as well as rich monster-to-monster sociality. But not all monster relationality is the same. Sometimes the monsters are complex, nuanced beings; sometimes they are mortally dangerous like the Kurdaitcha or slightly less so like the Sasquatch; or they can become flatly cute for humans, as Foster depicts in the graduation speech at the Kappa academy. Sometimes the monsters are such threats that they affect the ways that humans interact with each other at all times or the threat that keeps children from crying and adults from expressing anger on Lanyu Island. Through the eyes of an Icelandic mare, monsters often remind humans that they can be prey as much as predators, that there are threats out there they can try to avoid or appease, but in ways that only reiterate the vulnerability of being alive. Yet just as often, monsters are sleeping next to humans, crafting domestic relations with humans, only to fracture these relationships when their other abilities or forms are revealed. Monsters always exist in relation to other beings, but what those relations can be — that reveals the power of monsters.

What Is Talking about Monsters Good For?

Each of the monster encounters contained in these pages emphasizes that much as the monsters themselves, the relationship between them and their hauntees is always distinctive; or to express it more generally, monsters enact their terror, or even their cuteness, in socio-culturally appropriate ways. Each monster is paired with a specific people, in our volume these include Ghanaians, Indian villagers, us Americans, Japanese, Tao people, settlers, Native Americans, Aboriginal Australians, Icelanders and their horses, Georgians, and blog visitors. Monsters will haunt their people in specific ways which make the problems that everyday interactions can throw up sharper and more tangible. Thinking with aliens allows people to reflect on their contemporary anxieties about migrants and even migrants who *seem* to have a different biology. In this way, talking about, for example, alien hybrids becomes a more palatable, less fraught way of talking about people with different and often mixed racial backgrounds. Moreover, focusing on other-than-humans allows people to discuss different ways of being domestic and explore what it means that there is no one way to carve out a domestic life with people who have different customs and different expectations. And new internet monsters allow people to engage in not so well-disguised ways with the sense that new media unsettle the more familiar techniques people have for evaluating how typed assertions link to what is actually happening. Monsters become useful for thinking about strangers and strange practices, functioning as powerful beings who encapsulate danger and otherness in a guise that can be less messy and less ambiguous than the otherness of an in-law or a racially or culturally different neighbor.

Some of the relations the monsters in this volume condense are part and parcel of capitalism. Indeed, read together, the chapters openly engaging with capitalism offer different takes on what it means to live alongside monsters in this capitalist moment. Lynch and Coppola reflect on how the ghosts that haunt old textile factories are the ghosts of capitalisms past — the sounds of earlier migrant workers whisper in empty rooms, the time disciplines of previous decades turn into today's rubbish. Ghosts here are partially, but only partially, allowing people to express nostalgia for older forms of work and criticize the contemporary market pressures that limit how long well-established textile mills can stay in business. While Lynch and Coppola's chapter turns to the local costs of increasingly globalized supply chains, Mabefam and Alexeyeff's piece invites us to reflect on the uncertain possibilities that globalization offers, the chances to tap into the mysterious flows of capital that circulate through the internet. The Sakawa boys are magically compelling, able to turn strangers into cash-cows by sending miraculously enhanced enticements through the internet to the randomly found Westerners they can now reach. Powers that used to be limited to local wealth now can stretch across vast distances, just as capital flows do. Tomlinson's chapter also explores a question that only contemporary capitalism with its emphasis on marketing and branding would raise: How should one best brand a monster? Tomlinson parodies the assumptions of contemporary capitalism, that everything can and should be turned into a marketable commodity, that even the horrific can have its commodified place and appeal in the contemporary marketplace, managed properly. In short, these are pieces that turn to monsters as lens for how people experience changes in capitalism, remembering older forms of factory work or ways of accumulating wealth and wrestling with the new consequences of globally intertwined markets.

Monsters alert us to other issues impacting people's lives as well, such as settler colonialism and cultural appropriation in the chapters by Davis, Murray, and Musharbash, for example. In his piece on possession and the cultural variances between different kinds of demons and spirits, Davis also contemplates the thorny problem of how to deal with being the anthropologist and friend the spirit has chosen to visit, when this spirit *should* have visited his own actual family. With panache, Murray draws the reader into a scenario that first follows in detective-like fashion, and then perpetrates, the thoroughly colonist misdeed of doing what Indigenous people warned against — with grave consequences. Musharbash, in turn, twins a monster whose sole purpose in life is to rape, ensorcell, and kill an Australian Aboriginal people with a naïve, non-Indigenous newcomer, highlighting the destructiveness they share.

In the very ways they haunt, then, monsters accentuate what it is that haunts people: next to post-capitalist and neo-colonial malaise, a focus on monsters pinpoints all sorts of inequalities (gendered, aged, raced, classed) and insecurities (about home and the planet, climate, nature, or food). In short, monsters are "good to think with," to use a well-worn anthropological phrase. The works of ethnographic fiction contained in this volume invite you into the realm of monsters and their hauntees, then, not just for the chilling thrills and the delicious dread that monster stories bestow, but also to invite you to contemplate difference, to understand inequality, and to see the world from new angles.

Enjoy! But also: Beware! Here be monsters!

References

Asma, Stephen T. 2009. *On Monsters: An Unnatural History of Our Worst Fears.* Oxford: Oxford University Press.

Bishop, Kyle William. 2010. *American Zombie Gothic: The Rise and Fall (and Rise) of the Walking Dead in Popular Culture.* Jefferson: McFarland & Company.

Cohen, Jeffrey Jerome. 1996. "Monster Culture (Seven Theses)." In *Monster Theory: Reading Culture,* edited by Jeffrey Jerome Cohen, 3–25. Minneapolis: University of Minnesota Press.

Cohen, Jeffrey Jerome. 2012. "Undead (A Zombie Oriented Ontology)." *Journal of the Fantastic in the Arts* 23, no. 3: 397–412. http://www.jstor.org/stable/24353082.

Dendle, Peter. 2001. The *Zombie Movie Encyclopedia.* Jefferson: McFarland & Company.

———. 2012a. "Monsters and the Twenty-First Century: The Preternatural in an Age of Scientific Consensus." In *The Ashgate Research Companion to Monsters and the Monstrous,* edited by Asa Simon Mittman and Peter Dendle, 437–48. Aldershot: Ashgate.

Dendle, Peter. 2012b. *The Zombie Movie Encyclopedia,* Vol. 2: *2000–2010.* Jefferson: McFarland & Company.

Douglas, Mary. 1966. *Purity and Danger: An Analysis of Concepts of Pollution and Taboo.* London: Routledge & Kegan Paul.

Gershon, Ilana, ed. 2015. *A World of Work: Imagined Manuals for Real Jobs.* Ithaca: Cornell University Press.

Hubner, L.M. Leaning, and Paul Manning, eds. 2015. *The Zombie Renaissance in Popular Culture.* London, New York: Palgrave Macmillan.

Miller, T.S. 2012. "Lives of the Monster Plants: The Revenge of the Vegetable in the Age of Animal Studies." *Journal of the Fantastic in the Arts* 23, no. 3: 460–79. https://www.jstor.org/stable/24353087.

Mittman, Asa Simon. 2012. "Introduction: The Impact of Monsters and Monster Studies." In *The Ashgate Research Companion to Monsters and the Monstrous,* edited by Asa Simon Mittman and Peter Dendle, 1–14. Aldershot: Ashgate.

Musharbash, Yasmine. 2014. "Introduction: Monsters, Anthropology, and Monster Studies." In *Monster Anthropology in Australasia and Beyond,* edited by Yasmine Musharbash and Geir Henning Presterudstuen, 1–24. New York: Palgrave Macmillan.

———. 2021. "Monsters." *The Cambridge Encyclopaedia of Anthropology,* October 15, 2021. DOI: 10.29164/21monsters.

Musharbash, Yasmine, and Geir Henning Presterudstuen. 2020. *Monster Anthropology: Ethnographic Explorations of Transforming Social Worlds through Monsters.* Abingdon: Routledge.

Picart, Caroline Joan S., and John Edgar Browning. 2012. "Introduction: Monstrosity and Multiculturalism." In *Speaking of Monsters: A Teratological Anthology,* edited by Caroline Joan S. Picart and John Edgar Browning, 1–12. New York: Palgrave Macmillan.

Porter, Natalie, and Ilana Gershon. 2018. *Living with Animals: Bonds Across Species.* Ithaca: Cornell University Press.

Van Duzer, Chet. 2012. *"Hic sunt dracones:* The Geography and Cartography of Monsters." In *The Ashgate Research Companion to Monsters and the Monstrous,* edited by Asa Simon Mittman and Peter Dendle, 387–435. Aldershot: Ashgate.

Vervaeke, John, Christopher Mastropietro, and Filip Miscevic, 2017. *Zombies in Western Culture: A Twenty-First Century Crisis.* Cambridge: Open Book Publishers.

Weinstock, Jeffrey Andrew. 2014. "Introduction: Monsters are the Most Interesting People." *The Ashgate Encyclopedia of Literary and Cinematic Monsters,* edited by Jeffrey Andrew Weinstock, 1–7. Farnham: Ashgate.

Yngvesson, Barbara, and Susan Coutin. 2008. "Schrödinger's Cat and the Ethnography of Law." *PoLAR* 31, no. 1: 61–78. DOI: 10.1111/j.1555-2934.2008.00001.x.

1

Don't Say His Name

Cailín E. Murray

Sarah sat at her desk and sighed, running one hand through spikey blond hair. From her small window on the second floor, she could see the employee parking lot, and if she cranked her head sideways, the residence wing where an oversized rhododendron bush framed a window. She had arrived at the clinic as a new doctor of psychology earlier that year and her imposter syndrome was still fresh. Now it had been triggered into high gear by the lack of progress on the new case. Earlier during morning rounds, when asked by her supervisor Dr. Ortega if she had anything to share about the new patient, Sarah had to admit she did not.

"Has he spoken yet?" Dr. Ortega asked, his mouth set in what Sarah thought of as his "no bullshit" face.

"No, not yet. He's had Group twice since he was admitted. He just sits there, staring."

"Where was he found again?"

"The Hoh Rainforest, in the Olympic National Park. "

"So, what's his story?"

Sarah leafed through a blue patient folder, searching for a better answer then shrugged. "This says some hikers on the Hoh River Trail found him unconscious with a goose egg on his forehead, near a river crossing. Rescue rangers humped him out and then he was medevacked to Harborview Medical Center. He regained consciousness that night but never spoke. He recovered fairly quickly from a concussion, some bruised ribs, and a sprained wrist so there was no reason to keep him, he'd been there a week. His doc called me and asked if we had a bed for him. That was two days ago. There is no physical explanation for his loss of speech. I think he is choosing not to speak to us, but he seems to understand." Dr. Ortega raised a questioning eyebrow. Sarah paused a moment then added, "It's just a hunch. When I ask him a question, he focuses on my face. He's cooperative. If staff hands him a towel and soap, he takes a shower. He just won't speak," she sighed.

"Do we have a name?"

"No. He came to the emergency room wearing, let's see, an REI fleece jacket, beige hiking pants, and trail boots. No pack, no wallet, no phone, not a granola bar or a water bottle. Park rangers did not find an unclaimed campsite. He looked pretty rough, like he'd been in the backcountry for a few days. He probably was sleeping outside of an approved camping ground. That's pretty wild country and its huge, it would be easy to miss someone whose gear was stowed off trail."

Dr. Ortega looked skeptical. "Are you telling me we don't have a name? Not a relative or a friend or a co-worker? Doesn't *anyone* know this guy has been missing from his life now for three damn weeks?"

Sarah shrugged her shoulders. She understood these were rhetorical questions; Dr. Ortega knew as well as she did that the man the staff had nicknamed "John Hoh," was as much a mystery today as he had been when he arrived at Harborview in late August.

"Maybe we should dig a little deeper," Dr. Ortega said.

"What do you mean, sir?"

"What else do you know about the Hoh Rainforest?

"A little," she said, "I did research out there one summer, for my MA." Dr. Ortega rubbed his chin for a moment, "Great, see what you can dig up."

***

The man called John Hoh sits on a hard-backed chair in his solitary patient's room. He has bright copper hair, gray-blue eyes, and pale, lightly freckled skin. The four walls surrounding him are a buttery shade of cream. His room is furnished with a bed, a small desk, a color photograph of a nameless beach and the chair he occupies for most of the day, except when he is prodded by the clinic's staff to leave his room. This morning they tell him no more meals in his room, he must go to the common dining room if he wants to eat.

John Hoh does not care about that, any more than he cares it is also lunchtime and his stomach is rumbling. Instead, he watches the window. His fingers are so tightly entwined that they are turning white at the knuckles. The window is firmly locked with an elaborate safety latch. Still, he wishes the building had multiple stories and that he was on a top floor. He imagines the smooth comfort of black-top pavement and the security of skyscrapers. Outside the window is a giant rhododendron with forest green leaves and bright yellow blossoms. He watches the large leaves and their rippled shadows for sudden movement. So far, nothing. His eyes remain fixed on the dark-green leaves. He is afraid, but he cannot pinpoint what scares him so. He just knows the large plant makes him anxious.

He remembers disconnected semblances — thumbing a ride from Bremerton, the weight of a pack, a red camera and a silver water bottle, wooded silence on an empty trail. But his actual name and the details of how he came to be a patient remain shadowed. Sitting quietly in his chair he does not remember where he was lost, or who might have lost him. He sits. He waits. He wonders when he will be found. If he is found, he feels certain the window with the elaborate safety latch will be no match for anyone seeking a way inside. His hands hurt as his knuckles grow whiter still.

***

Since she had been a master's student at the University of Washington, Sarah always enjoyed the majestic interior of Suzzallo Library's reading room. There was something about the arched Gothic windows, rows of oak desks, and brass reading lamps that imposed a sense of significance on her own intellectual pursuits. Later, as a medical student, she had used the Health Sciences Library more often, but found she missed Red Square where Suzzallo fringed its eastern edge. As a graduate student in Anthropology, she had spent many quiet hours there researching and writing papers.

It was a rare sunny day in early Autumn. The kind of day in the Pacific Northwest when the Puget Sound sparkles with all of the promise of a freshly washed morning. Sarah slid her aging Toyota into a narrow spot on a little-known side street near campus, silently thanking the Parking Gods. She walked past used bookstores and Asian food joints and smiled at the homeless teens parked on the sidewalk. In Red Square, students were taking advantage of the bright morning. She climbed the steps to the library entrance and paused while security personnel rummaged through her bag. She glanced hopefully at the espresso counter but kept moving when she saw the sinewy line of students and professors waiting for their morning fix.

Sarah climbed the stairs to the Reading Room and found a seat at the end of one of the long desks. After her computer hummed to life, she created a file on her desktop labeled "Hoh Rainforest Research." From there she clicked her way to the library's online catalog. In a few moments, the screen began to fill with titles and Sarah bent forward to read.

Two hours later she paused to massage the back of her neck. Glancing at her notes, it seemed like a lot of work with little to show for it. The Olympic National Park was created in 1938, is a UNESCO Biosphere Reserve and World Heritage site, frequent sightings of deer, elk, bobcats, black bears, and cougars. She pondered her patient's physical injuries once again. He could have had an altercation with a wild animal, or possibly another hiker. But even a close encounter with a bear or cougar, or an unhinged human, apparently had not resulted in significant injuries. It was John Hoh's refusal to speak that suggested a far more traumatic turn of events. She glanced at her short list of materials, realizing she would have to visit special collections. She packed up her computer and headed towards the stairs again, this time passing by the main floor on her way to the basement and the Pacific Northwest Collection and Archives.

Sarah opened the glass doors and approached the counter to hand her belongings to a bored student worker who then buzzed her through a locked gate and into the reading room. She found an empty chair and grabbed a small pencil to fill out call slips, handing them to the archivist commanding the round counter in the center of the room, who then disappeared behind the door leading to the closed stacks. He emerged a few minutes later with books and a gray box on a small cart, which he pushed to Sarah's table. She reached for the nearest book, a battered history of the Olympic Peninsula, and began to read.

1915 — Elks Club in PA held a 3-day circus, July 1-3. "Among the sideshows advertised for the event was 'The Wild Man of the Hoh'— at this time he is practically a captive in his remote lair and will be secured and prepared for transportation to the city and exhibition as soon as the exhibition cage can be built and conveyed to and from the wilderness."

Sarah approached the resource desk, "Pardon me," she said to the archivist, who glanced up from his keyboard to peer at her, "could you help me understand what I am reading here. It doesn't really make sense." The archivist turned the laptop to read the screen. He chuckled. "It was a hoax for a circus side show." He keyed in a few search terms and handed back the computer. "See?" He pointed to a grainy black and white photo that shimmered onto the screen. Sarah saw a large woman, dressed in a white wig with a fake snake wrapped around her shoulders. "The lady snake charmer of the Zanomi Elks Circus, Port Angeles, Washington, 1915," she read out loud. The archivist continued, "Local communities did these kinds of events all of the time. I don't have a photo of the 'Wild Man of the Hoh,' but he was probably about as real as that snake." Sarah pondered the photograph. "I understand a lady snake charmer. Where did the Wild Man idea come from?"

The archivist clicked out of the screen with the snake charmer and entered new search terms. "You've heard of Bigfoot, right?" Sarah nodded, "Of course, I was born in Seattle. Should we call him Bigfoot or Sasquatch?" The archivist found a reference and continued to speak as he wrote down the citation. "Neither, really. The tribes around here all have their own names for that particular creature. Those stories have been around for thousands of years if you ask the elders. But even white settlers told stories about the Wild Man. Here, I'll have two more books brought up for you."

A few moments later, Sarah was reading the correspondence of a nineteenth-century missionary to the Northwest; her eyes widened as she entered notes into her computer.

They [Spokane Indians] believe in the existence of a race of giants which inhabit a certain mountain, off to the west of us [probably the Cascade Range]. This mountain is covered with perpetual snow. They inhabit its top. […] They hunt & do all their work in the night. They are men-stealers. They come to the people's lodges in the night, when the people are asleep & take them & put them under their skins & take them to their place of abode without their even awakening. When they awake in the morning, they are wholly lost, not knowing in what direction their home is. […] They say their track is about a foot & a half long. […] They frequently come in the night & steal their salmon from their nets & eat them raw. If the people are awake, they always know when they are coming very near, by the smell which is most intolerable.

Sarah did not believe in monsters, and this research more and more seemed a waste of time. On the other hand, John Hoh's concussion and bruised ribs suggested he had been startled by something, imaginary or otherwise. Sarah knew how human minds sought pattern recognition. John Hoh could have convinced himself of practically anything on a lonely trail in the middle of an overgrown rainforest. Dark thickets full of old logged-over stumps covered in moss could certainly spook a person into thinking there was something out there. She sighed and turned to the next volume; regional oral histories collected by federal employees during the 1930s. She continued to make notes.

> *Before the white people came to this country, a big Skookum, or hairy man, came and drove the Indians away that were living on the Pe Ell Prairie and the Indians never went back there to live until after the Roundtree boys took up claims there and went there to live.*

Sarah flagged the archivist again. "Excuse me, do you know what this means? What is a *Skookum?*" He removed his glasses to clean them and said, "That's a Chinook Jargon word, you know, the trade language?" Sarah nodded. "It was pretty common in these parts. It was a lingua franca that borrowed words from different languages. So, in Chinook Jargon, salt water becomes salt chuck. Skookum usually means 'big' or 'oversized.'" So, the Skookumchuck River literally means, big water river, that tells you something about its physical geography. He squinted at the passage. "I would say the person who told this story was referencing how the creature appeared."

Sarah thanked him and stood to collect her belongings. Whatever had silenced John Hoh, there were no more answers to be found in the library. She retrieved her belongings and drove to a gas station to fill her tank and check oil and tires. While waiting, she left voicemail for Dr. Ortega, "I will be heading to the Olympic Peninsula, to see if I can find someone who knows something, anything that might help." She opened Google search engine and found the morning ferry schedule.

***

The next day, as Sarah rises in the dark to catch the ferry, John Hoh is dreaming. His sheets are damp and tangled around his legs. He is walking on a dirt trail. It is a darkly shadowed path, but he also sees sunlight breaking through green boughs far overhead. The air is sweetly scented with the smell of warm cedar. His camera dangles from his neck, a shiny red Nikon digital. The lens cap is tightly secured, and he sees nothing he wants to photograph. He is thirsty so he slows his pace to reach for his water bottle and take a swig. He screws the cap back on and stuffs it into the back pocket of his pants. He unties a worn blue cotton bandana from around his neck to wipe his face. The air feels heavy this day and his face is damp with sweat. He hears something moving through the brush, on the left side of the trail. He turns fast enough to catch tan and dark brown moving in the forest. "Elk," he says to himself. He thinks about removing the lens cap from his camera then changes his mind. By the time he is ready to snap an image, the creature will be gone. He is not here to photograph elk. "One for the memory banks." John Hoh continues to walk. This is where his dream becomes strange. The trail is no longer familiar beneath his feet and sunlight no longer dapples through the upper canopy of the trees. It is dark, too dark, even for the rainforest. A breeze whispers close to his ear carrying with it a foul stench that smells like death. Something to his right whistles low and for a moment the sound resonates, as if bouncing off of the trees. John Hoh turns over in his sleep, and then opens his eyes. It is still dark outside his window. He thinks about what is outside. He wonders what it smells like. He stays awake while the dark turns to gray light and the clinic staff begin their morning bed checks. An orderly, whistling a cheerful tune, knocks on his door. "You awake?"

***

It was still early enough for breakfast when Sarah arrived in Port Angeles. She drove the familiar curving road, ignoring the tattered John Birch Society sign and the postcard view of the Straits. Instead, she kept driving, past the Walmart and the tourist motels. The peaks of the Olympic Mountains, glistening with ice and snow, rose to greet her. When she reached the downtown harbor, she pulled into a parking lot and grabbed her phone. Sarah breathed in the intoxicating smell of salt water, fish, and cool mountain air as she punched in a familiar number, "Hello?" a voice boomed. "Marvin? Its Sarah Fields, I'm in PA, can I buy you breakfast?"

"Heck yeah. I'll meet you at Pete's."

Some minutes later, she stood in front of a shabby diner window clouded by steam. "Hey, White Girl," a familiar voice called from half a block away. Sarah turned to see an olive-skinned man with a black beard streaked with silver, angling down the street towards her. He wore neatly pressed utility pants and a cotton t-shirt emblazoned with "Just for the Halibut." "That's Dr. White Girl," she laughed. Marvin approached and wrapped her in a bear hug. "It's good to see you, Doc."

Marvin ushered Sarah through the door and caught the eye of the waitress, who gestured towards a table by the window still fresh with grease from the breakfast rush. "Coffee?" She waggled a silver carafe at them. They both nodded and she returned with two thick brown ceramic mugs. They ordered food and sipped coffee as they waited. "It's been a while, Sarah." Marvin studied his friend's face, noting she was thinner than he recalled and her hastily applied makeup did little to conceal the pale blue circles under her eyes.

The food arrived and the two began to eat, in companionable silence. Finally, Marvin dabbed a bit of egg yolk from his dark beard and sat back. "So, what brings you here, Sarah?"

Sarah hesitated, weighing her patient's confidentiality against learning his story, then pulled out her phone. She swiped through photographs and stopped at an image of a pale white man with red hair. She handed her phone across the table. "Have you ever seen this man in town before?" Marvin studied the photograph of John Hoh. "Can't say I have," as he returned her phone. He waited patiently for Sarah to continue. "He's one of my patients. He was found out by the Hoh River by hikers, injured. They sent him to Harborview and then to our clinic. His physical injuries are healing but he's not said a word in in almost two weeks. We don't know why. He seems traumatized but is not telling us anything."

Marvin looked up, "the Hoh?" Sarah nodded. "In the park, up-river. We don't know what happened and frankly, we are out of ideas. I did some research yesterday." Sarah handed Marvin her notes. He scanned them. "There is not much there to explain what happened to John Hoh." Marvin raised an eyebrow. "That's what the staff is calling him, we don't know his name. I don't know how to help this man." Sarah raised her shoulders in a helpless gesture and peered out the window. "Well, how about you and me head out to the reservation and see what we can learn?" Sarah smiled gratefully at Marvin, "I'll drive."

***

The drive across the Peninsula to the Hoh River Indian community took a couple of hours. Marvin spent the time rereading Sarah's notes. Finally, he set them on his knee and asked her, "What do you know about the wild man?" Sarah stared ahead at the road, "Bigfoot? Not much. I've seen the pictures of fake footprints, and I watched the Patterson film, that footage shot back in the 1960s in California? I think it was fake too. What else is there?"

"Well, for one thing, we don't call him Bigfoot."

"Okay, what do you call him?"

Marvin hesitated then spoke a word in Coast Salish. Sarah tried to pronounce the word but stumbled over the unfamiliar sounds.

"Don't sweat it. We don't say his name much, anyway."

"Why not?" Sarah asked.

"Because it calls him. If you say his name, he hears you, and he comes."

"Is that a bad thing?"

"Depends on who is calling and why. But it ain't anything to do for no reason, that's for sure."

"How would you know he's here?" she asked.

Marvin glanced away, clearing his throat before he answered her. "First, there's the smell. He smells terrible to humans — like shit and something dead blended together. People smell him more than anything. Second, he makes a lot of noise. Once, my cousins got chased by him at night, down by the mouth of the river, on those fishing trails. They never saw him, but it was like he was crashing through the woods, to get after them. No matter how fast they ran, he was always right behind them. You know he is giant, eight feet tall maybe, and covered in long tangled black hair. He has kind of a monkey face. But most of all, there are his eyes. Scariest eyes. I can't explain it. One of the weirdest things I ever heard was from one of our cousins, over there in Canada, on the Island. She said he could shift."

Sarah was puzzled. "Shift, how?"

"Into different forms, in and out of places and back and forth. He can mess with your head, make you see things that aren't there. It is like time does not work the same for him. Like if you were to see him, one minute he would be up close and the next second he would be far away. Back and forth, as if he could cross miles in seconds."

Sarah was quiet, considering her words carefully, not wanting to offend her Klallam friend. Still, she was too practical to simply accept his words without a challenge. "Okay, but these are just stories. I mean, there are no stinky, giant ape men running around the woods, not really, right?"

"Old people have a lot of stories," Marvin said, then grew silent.

"Do white people ever see him?" Sarah ventured after a few minutes.

"Sure, but it makes them crazy. No teachings, *enit?* My dad was a logger, right?" Sarah nodded. "Well, he told me that back in the 1970s or so, a bunch of white men came over from eastern Washington, all the way out to the Peninsula with cameras and camping gear. They were 'hunting for Bigfoot.' They set up cameras and trip wires and all kinds of gear. During the day, they would go for hikes looking for evidence. At night, they took turns standing watch, hoping to catch a glimpse. Talked real big about how they were gonna kill a Bigfoot and bring back its carcass for the world to see, prove he was real. Anyway, one day, they were gone. Left all of their gear behind, even the cameras. Got in their car and drove away. Never saw them again. Dad said served 'em right for trying to see what was not meant for them."

***

After breakfast and a group session the man called John Hoh retreats to his room. Fog shrouds the window, so he curls up on top of his blankets and falls into a restless sleep. Like a staccato beat, pictures flash in his head: a dirt trail with dappled sunlight, the red camera in his hand, the shadows moving behind a deadfall and a thicket of ferns. Thrashing. A black and brown creature. The sounds, a silver water bottle, the elk, the red Nikon, these things are real, he is certain of that. The air becomes thicker. An odor grows stronger, despite the damp breeze. Something is close. He gags as he raises a sweaty blue bandana to his nose to block out the stink. And then the light simply vanishes. He stops walking, gagging into his bandana again, and reaches for his water bottle. Off to his right there is a sound, much louder now, like a rhino crashing through the dense patch of trees. He wants to run but can't move. He fishes in his pocket for his phone and taps the screen awake. A random song from his play list thunders out heavy metal lyrics. The crashing noise stops. He freezes, then quickly mutes the phone and holds his breath, one count, two count, finally exhaling. The quiet is like nothing he knows, no birds, no wind, no insects, it is the sound of nothing.

***

An hour and a half later, Sarah turned onto a reservation road dotted with newer homes in cheerful shades of blue and burnt brown. "Uncle's place is that second one with the porch." Marvin bobbed his head in the direction of a newer one-story home with a fishing boat dry docked in the yard. Gear was spread across yellowed grass.

"So, I guess he's a fisherman?"

Marvin laughed. "Yep."

Sarah pulled onto the weedy driveway as a Native man with a shock of white hair came outside, a barking German shepherd by his side.

"Hush, now," he ordered the dog. "We got company. Hey, nephew!"

The two men embraced. "Missed you, Uncle Skeet."

"Who's this?" Skeet asked, looking at Sarah, "Geez boy, you finally getting married?" Marvin laughed, "not today, Uncle. This is Sarah Fields. She's a shrink from Seattle, looking for stories." The three entered a tidy front room with a glowing woodstove. Marvin and Sarah sat down at the kitchen table and watched Skeet pour water into the coffee maker and Italian roast into a paper filter. A plate of fresh cookies appeared along with three mugs, spoons, cream, and sugar. "Uncle was a cook in the Army, good cookies," Marvin told her. Skeet shot his nephew a look and joined his guests at the table. He stirred cream into his mug, took a sip, and then looked at Sarah. "What kind of stories you hunting for?"

Sarah helped herself to a cookie, breaking it into smaller pieces on her napkin. "I'm not sure, here's what I know." Skeet listened intently. When she finished speaking, he leaned back in his chair, crossed his thick arms across his chest and looked out the window, towards the woods before finally glancing back and uncrossing his arms.

"Sounds to me like your guy saw something he did not understand. That could make a man go quiet. Had a young fella here last month — came from somewhere south, said he wanted to take pictures of 'Sasquatch,' you know what some of them people call 'Bigfoot.' Asked me if I knew any old stories that would help him find 'evidence.'" Skeet spat the word "evidence" out to make certain Sarah heard his disapproval. "White people don't understand. We did not make him up, like some old fairy tale. If a person isn't careful, he might just eat their spirit. Ever seen a person walking with no spirit? Not dead but not alive either?

"I told him he wouldn't find any evidence. It's not an animal, you see. It is more like a spirit, a powerful one too. When we see him, it means something — maybe it means change is coming, maybe he's come to warn us, maybe he is there to help someone find his way. Sometimes, he just shows up because he wants something. My grandma said one used to take fish from her cleaning table, if she did not clean Grandpa's catch fast enough and left her salmon untended. He's been known to steal laundry right off the line, and people too. One girl, a real beauty, used to catch one peeking in her bedroom window at night. I guess he was in love that time." Skeet laughed. "He comes and goes. If we see him, it is because he has something to teach us."

"How do you know he is there?" Sarah asked, curious if Marvin's uncle had information that was different.

"Smell, sound, way things feel kind of different, eerie like."

"What sounds does he make?"

"Well, his kind doesn't talk like humans. They whistle. Its why the old people told us to never whistle outside in the dark. He carries a walking stick too, knocks trees over, real noisy I guess." The old man paused to sip his coffee before continuing. "He was always here, since the Animal People, since before us. He'll be here when we're gone. My grandpa would say, 'Don't say his name. He'll come if you do.' One time, when I was young, I wanted to hike up to the river's headwaters, look for him or whatever else is up there. My grandpa told me to be careful because I just might find something. Told me to wait a few years before I looked for him." Skeet looked down at his calloused hands, "I never did take that trail. All I know is what grandpa told me, 'Be careful with that power because he always expects a trade too.'"

Skeet and Marvin exchanged a look, and the older man chose his next words cautiously. "That young fella asked me what its name was in 'my' language. I said to him, 'Man, I speak English just like you.' But I was just playin' with him. I told him the word and I warned him too. I said, 'don't say his name. He'll come if you say it.' I gotta hand it to him, he sat right there and said it over and over until he got it right, and it is not an easy word for you white folks to learn."

Sarah pulled out her phone and opened the photograph of John Hoh. "Was this the man you spoke to last month? Skeet nodded. "Hair was buzzed pretty short but yeah, that's him."

Did he mention his name?"

"If he did, I can't recall it now. We didn't talk long. He didn't believe me. Last thing he said is he was heading into the Hoh Rainforest to camp out. Said he was using his leave to hunt for Sasquatch. I told him to be careful. He might just find him."

Once they were back in the car, Sarah turned to Marvin, "I still don't know what happened, I need to see that trail for myself."

***

John Hoh is unaware of shadows moving outside the window. He is crouched deep into a corner of his room, sounds gush from his mouth, suspending words in the air like a river carries dark sediment in its rush to the sea. He is back in the forest. Everything goes silent. John Hoh stands still too, like a statue, and then slowly turns. He aims the camera in the direction from where he had heard the noise and peers anxiously into the viewfinder. He hisses in frustration when all he sees is an old logging stump, covered in long tendrils of dark moss. Then he remembers the word the old man taught him, and his warning. "Fuck him," John Hoh mutters to himself. "His rules not mine." First, he whispers the word, then he says it louder. Finally, he shouts it into the dark, heavy, smelly silence that surrounds him. The stump moves.

***

The next morning, Sarah recalled Marvin's parting reminder, "Don't go looking for things unless you *want* them to find you."

She shot back heated words, "This isn't about me. It's about my patient. I have to help him, isn't that what good people do, help?"

"Wild Man doesn't care if you are bad or good, Sarah. He's not Santa. We didn't create him, he's part of the mystery and he's not going anywhere, he's here." She tried again to explain, "I'm not 'hunting Sasquatch,' I'm searching for evidence that will help my patient find his voice."

She exhaled and refocused on her surrounds. The sky was bright blue and dotted with soft white clouds, unusual for the Hoh Rainforest in autumn. If nothing else, Sarah enjoyed the feeling of the trail beneath her feet. The rainforest was a bit eerie, but sunlight dappled through the upper canopy. By noon, she was ready to stop for water and a snack. She found a dead fall to sit on and opened her bag. As she unwrapped a protein bar, she glanced around, wondering if an animal had died nearby. As she started to look, she caught a stream of light glinting off a shiny surface, beneath a bracken fern. Sarah reached for the object; it was a red Nikon 35mm camera. As she pressed the power button, the air became still and then silent.

***

"Has she spoken today?"

"No, Dr. Ortega, not a word. I think she understands me, but she refuses to speak."

"What were her injuries again?"

"Um, let's see; a pretty good bump on her head, a hairline fracture, and abrasions on her upper back, like she'd been dragged, maybe by a predator? Although that does not make a lot of sense, given her other injuries."

"Why not?"

"No bite marks. How would a cougar wrestle then drag a human and not leave marks?"

"Why is she mute, do you think?"

"Well, it wasn't the concussion or the fractured wrist or any bruises or abrasions, all of those are healing nicely."

"I suppose it could have been much worse. She's lucky she filed a day plan with that park ranger, or she may have died out there from exposure."

"Yes, she certainly is lucky. Now, we just need to figure out what she ran into that caused her this much psychological trauma." Dr. Ortega closed the folder on his lap.

Bibliographic Note

During the Elwha Klallam Tribe's fight in the 1990s to remove two hydroelectric dams from the Elwha River, multiple sightings of Wild Man were reported on the reservation. As their elected leaders brokered partnerships with state and federal agencies, tribal citizens found ways to engage with natural and sacred spaces by entwining cultural and environmental restoration goals (Wray 2003). While not all tribal citizens at the time interpreted encounters with Wild Man positively, correlations were made nonetheless between the monster's emergence from the shadows and Salish cultural survivance (Murray 2019).1

Tribal stories shared with me as factual accounts shared similarities with variations of the Wild Man motif found across North America (Buhs 2009). I wanted my fictional story to reflect how conflicting worldviews spark dialogues and disagreements similar to those I write about here. Indigenous encounters with the strange are often overshadowed by settler colonial debates about the paranormal (Bader et al. 2017; Boyd and Thrush 2011). Wild Man accounts, along with plaster casts and fuzzy images become part of an ambiguous physical record pitching Western science against anecdotalism (Daegling 2004; Halpin and Ames 1980). These unreconcilable positions then compete with Indigenous voices struggling to be heard, even though regional Wild Man stories are rooted in their cultures (Robinson 2000).

In the twenty-first century, Native North Americans continue to engage in political and cultural struggles to protect natural resources and sacred sites identified with their beliefs (Estes 2019; McCloud and Abbe 2001). Often these are one in the same. Private property rights and increasing demands for access to public lands and natural resources means tribes remain vigilant within the long shadows that settler colonialism casts.

---

1   The Anishnaabe scholar Gerald Vizenor coined this neologism to blend Indigenous survival and resistance.

Bader, Christopher, F. Carson Mencken, and Joseph O. Baker. 2017. *Paranormal America: Ghost Encounters, UFO Sightings, Bigfoot Hunts, and Other Curiosities in Religion and Culture.* New York: New York University Press.

Boyd, Colleen E., and Coll Thrush. 2011. *Phantom Past, Indigenous Presence: Native Ghosts in North American Culture and History.* Norman: University of Nebraska Press.

Buhs, Joshua Blu. 2009. *Bigfoot: The Life and Times of a Legend.* Chicago: University of Chicago Press.

Estes, Nick. 2019. *Standing with Standing Rock: Voices from the #NoDAPL movement.* Minneapolis: University of Minnesota Press.

Halpin, Marjorie, and Michael Ames. 1980. *Manlike Monsters on Trial: Early Records and Modern Evidence.* Vancouver: University of British Columbia Press.

McCloud, Scott, and Jessica Abbe. 2001. *In the Light of Reverence.* Oley: Bullfrog Films.

Murray, Cailín. 2019. "Locating the Wild Man: Rain Forest Enchantments and Settler Colonial Fantasies amid the Ruins of the Anthropocene." *Journal of Historical Sociology* 32, no. 1: 60–73. DOI: 10.1111/johs.12224.

Robinson, Eden. 2000. *Monkey Beach.* Boston: Houghton Mifflin Press.

Wray, Jacilee, ed. 2003. *Native Peoples of the Olympic Peninsula: Who We Are.* Norman: University of Oklahoma Press.

2

Advice for the Apparitionally Challenged: A Ghost (Hunter) Story

Misty L. Bastian

"I don't ordinarily consult on a case like this one," the ghost hunter smiled, looking around at her surroundings. "Most people are interested in finding a way to get rid of the spirits in their houses, or else to learn to live with them without having to spend much time in their company."

Admittedly, I was not "most people," and my colleague the ghost hunter was very aware of that fact. "Call her a paranormal researcher," I reminded myself, silently. That's what ghost hunters prefer, since serious ones like Katie spend most of their time researching the past and don't particularly enjoy the metaphor of hunting spirits. Of course, everybody in the field sometimes slipped and talked about ghost hunting, as it was the name of the first, really popular North American book on the subject, Hans Holzer's *Ghost Hunter,* and also the name of most famous of the many North American television shows, *Ghost Hunters.* Truthfully, almost all the paranormal researchers I had met thus far loved the show and had read the Holzer book often, and when they were kids. There are a lot of other books now, and a plethora of television and live streaming programs. Katie had even been on a few of those; she was pretty well known in the whole mid-Atlantic region of the para-community.

"You're sure you want to talk to this ghost or whatever it is?" Katie was skeptical, even though she regularly talked to spirits of all kinds. Like many paranormal researchers, she had been fascinated with spiritual communication all her life. Unlike most, she was also a medium — a person who can see ghosts (a clairvoyant), hear them (a clairaudient), and sometimes sense them in other ways (a clairsentient). It wasn't talking to my ghost that Katie considered a problem. It was the fact that I wanted to interview the spirit for my ethnographic research. As she had already pointed out, most spirits are unaware of anthropology as a field of study. Most ghosts would resist being interviewed, as well. Katie should know. She'd tried often enough to convince spirits to hold conversations with her.

"If it's a ghost, it won't have much of an attention span," Katie grinned. She had been grilled, by me, over several hours in formal interviews; she was dubious that a spirit would have the patience for that sort of intrusive activity. "We might be able to ask it a few questions, like what its name in life was, or when it died. It might not know it's dead, though, so that can make it freak out and cut off the conversation. It might not even be a human spirit. What kind of questions are you going to ask something like that?"

Again, I had to concede Katie's wisdom on this matter. Paranormal researchers spend a lot of time asking hopeful questions to apparently empty space, often in the middle of the night. They are accustomed to disappointment with the paucity of answers. As I tried to explain to Katie, though, anthropologists also spend a lot of time asking hopeful but ignorant (and sometimes impertinent) questions to reluctant, busy people, at any time of the day or night. We are accustomed to the same disappointment. "Yeah," she said, "but at least you know if the person you're talking to is actually in the room with you." I decided not to get into a discussion with Katie about how people can appear to be in a room but aren't really there at all. She's a human being. She knows what that's like already.

Part of the problem was that I wasn't really sure if there was a true haunting in my house. Oh, there had been signs: the low murmur of a conversation when there was nobody home but me; hearing a piano playing in a room where there was no musical instrument at all; those pesky, bloody footprints that appeared under my kitchen table that time; the way the cats liked to stare off into the shadows in the hallway as if somebody was standing there; the usual things. I had not, however, seen any full-body apparitions — or even partial-body apparitions, which, Katie assured me, were a lot worse. Mostly it was just a feeling of presence where no presence ought to be, but not any strange temperature fluctuations or being touched by a spectral hand in the middle of the night. Katie was hoping we might elicit that sort of thing if we were going to go to the trouble of investigating the house and trying to convince a ghost to talk into my digital recorder.

"Are you sure you want to stir up whatever this is?" Katie was more than a bit dubious on this point. Most paranormal researchers refuse to investigate their own houses, even when they felt there was a possibility of a ghostly presence. "You have to live here, you know. What if you piss it off?"

These were valid questions. I did, of course, live there in what I called my "1900 house," a three-story row home built at the turn of the last century, and none of the signs of haunting had been so bad or intrusive that I felt threatened or even that uneasy. From what my many friends and colleagues in the paranormal research field had told me, it could be a bad idea to stir up a spirit. Researchers posit that the majority of domestic hauntings are not what they would call "intelligent" hauntings; that is, the ghosts are usually going about their mundane, repetitive business, not noticing that they are dead, and certainly not noticing that they are sharing their spiritual space with living, material creatures like ourselves. In attempting to contact such spirits, one might negatively gain their attention and cause them to try to push back against the intrusion. Some ghost hunters even suggest that, in cases like these, we are haunting the dead — popping up out of nowhere, acting in unfathomable ways, shouting at them about incomprehensible technologies ("Talk into the red light!"), and generally annoying them. Stirring up the dead could center their attention on us and make things a lot worse — for us.

Another possibility, though, would be that we would gain the attention of an "intelligent haunting," one that is very well aware that it is no longer a living person (or never was a living person) and possibly one that is not that happy about the fact. Spiritual entities like these are tricky, according to paranormal researchers. Such knowing ghosts like to play games, and they are easily offended. The intelligent haunt can be malevolent, and it can also take its time, once awakened, in gaining revenge on the person who dares to challenge it. After all, it's already dead or in some other less understandable state. It can afford to wait you out, letting you think that it isn't around or has forgotten about you altogether. Paranormal researchers' stories about intelligent hauntings frequently end badly for somebody, often the unfortunate living person who decided to call the entity out.

"Maybe you should just let sleeping dogs lie," Katie cautioned me. "Or maybe we can go to a place where the ghosts are used to researchers talking to them."

As I knew by now, there were many such places. Paranormal researchers sometimes refer to them as "paranormal playgrounds": well-known and much investigated haunted houses or businesses with interesting histories, like a nineteenth-century tavern we had researched a couple of years back, or the preserved battlefield at Gettysburg, which is a public heritage site and therefore open to discreet investigation year round, at least in the daytime. Private houses were investigated quietly, by established research teams, and on the invitation of the homeowners. Needless to say, most homeowners chose to invite in the ghost hunters only if they were feeling overwhelmed by unexplainable things happening in their houses. A paranormal playground might have ghosts that would be amenable to interview, unlike the shy or angry entities one would be likely to find in an ordinary home.

The thing was, though, that I didn't want to talk to men who died in a famous Civil War battle or who chose to haunt their favorite, local watering hole. I wanted to know who I was sharing my house with, if anyone, and I wanted to open a channel of communication that might be more ongoing. Like many paranormal researchers, I wanted what anthropologists call a "key informant" in the other realm — someone who could give me a privileged window into the past or who might be able to explain what things were like once people had been transformed through death. Maybe I just desired a reason to believe in an afterlife, which is what a number of ghost hunters had told me over the years had motivated their own search for connection to the spirit world. Mostly, though, what was behind this need for investigation was the same motivation that had led me to become an anthropologist in the first place: I wanted to know more about the human experience, and the best way to do that was to talk with other human beings and observe them doing ordinary things. According to my friends in the para-community, the dead were just that — ordinary people, who happened to be in a circumstance that only seemed extraordinary to *us,* the living.

"No," I told Katie, "I'm sure. This is what I want to do. Let's set up some equipment and see what happens."

Paranormal researchers have a growing array of equipment to make contact with the dead and spirit entities. Just about any ghost hunter I met during my lengthy fieldwork owned a rifle case or two full of digital recorders, cameras, tripods and other stands, as well as infrared, motion, and sonic sensors (originally these cases were made to transport weapons). The researchers also routinely carried what seemed like miles of cable, several power strips, numerous chargers, and bags of batteries to keep these electronics up and running during their investigation. If the researchers were, like Katie, psychic mediums, they might have a secondary arsenal of crystals, pendulums, dowsing rods, holy water, and other blessed objects used to focus psychic energies. Most paranormal research groups with whom I've worked were made up of a mixture of both technological researchers and mediums, so those investigators tend to bring at least some of all these tools of the trade along with them.

Because we were setting up an investigation in my house, Katie had brought her standard kit: a couple of digital recorders, a tool known as a "Frank's Box," a K-2 meant to measure fluctuations in electromagnetic energy, a digital camera, a pair of dowsing rods, and her favorite pendulum. She also had an LED flashlight and spare batteries for everything that required them. (One pro tip from the world of real ghost hunters is that you can never bring enough batteries. The night you forget is going to be the night that every device that needs them will fail.) I had a similar kit, although with only one digital recorder, a much less sophisticated digital camera, and a cheap infrared point-and-click camera. Since I ordinarily spend as much time researching the researchers as I do hunting ghosts, I had long since decided to keep my equipment on the minimal side, although I always enjoyed learning about and playing with others' more specialized technology. The communal ethos that reigns in investigations means that everyone borrows and works with everyone else's tools during the evening, although some objects, notably digital recorders, cameras, and pendulums, are seen as more personal than others. We'd use our own recorders and cameras for this investigation, but we'd share the more specialized Frank's Box, the dowsing rods, and the K-2.

The Frank's Box is my favorite oracular tool of the contemporary ghost hunter, mainly because it seems such an unlikely one. The first Frank's Boxes — and I've seen a few of those still owned and lovingly maintained by paranormal researchers who have been in the field for decades — were hacked Radio Shack transistor radios. Basically, these devices scan through AM or FM radio frequencies and stop randomly to tune in signals. During a typical Frank's Box session, one hears a bit of music, lots of garbled talk, even more hiss, and sometimes a word or phrase that is pulled in with clarity. Those words or phrases may appear to answer questions that have been put to the Frank's Box;

sometimes they even give verbal shape to a spectral presence that has been teasing researchers for hours.

It was just after dark, but Katie was not quite ready to get started. Before we could go "lights out," she and I sat down at the kitchen table, and she asked me to talk to her about what I had experienced in the house. She'd heard these stories before, but only as stories, not as a briefing to begin a formal investigation. She listened carefully, asked some clarifying questions, and took a few notes — all of which made me feel rather like the ethnographic tables had just been turned.

For this moment, I was the "homeowner," which is a formal status in any paranormal investigation that takes place inside a private residence. The homeowner is the provider of information about any potential haunting but not necessarily a trustworthy one. My report was therefore treated skeptically, and alternate theories were presented to me to explain what I had experienced, or thought I had experienced. After this interview, Katie asked me to remain in the kitchen while she took a walk around the house, using her mediumistic senses to locate areas of potential interest for the investigation. She decided to begin on the third floor and to work her way down. I could hear her walking around, talking quietly to my cats who were unhappily imprisoned in the second floor bathroom, and speaking at intervals below her breath to whatever she sensed was present.

After about thirty minutes, Katie returned to the kitchen and told me that we were ready to turn off the house lights. She wished to start the investigation on the second floor in my bedroom because she had a feeling that there might be activity there, which was not, exactly, a comforting thought for this particular "homeowner." The beginning of any investigation, after the initial walk through, is meant to set parameters for the researchers. Particular spaces are singled out for attention, and something like a schedule is developed for work in those spaces. The lead researcher decides where to begin, although he or she might defer later to others on the team who have some specialized knowledge or an intuitive feeling about activity in other parts of the space being investigated. In a private investigation, which technically is what this one would be, the homeowner is treated respectfully and may come along with the investigators but does not really have much status in the work of the group. I was rather different from the usual homeowner because I had worked with Katie on various investigations and was no longer considered a "civilian," in the militarized terminology of ghost-hunting teams.

After we made sure that all the lights were turned off in the house, Katie suggested, "Let's sit down here on the bed and do an EVP session. I feel like there's something going on in here." After sitting, we put our digital recorders on the bed beside us and turned them on. Their red lights were the only internal illumination in the room, although a little light leaked past the shade on one of the windows from my neighbor's backyard. Darkness is not a prerequisite for paranormal investigation, but it is considered a beneficial atmosphere conducive to research success.

We sat quietly for a moment, accustoming ourselves to the ordinary noises of the old house and allowing our eyes to adjust to the semi-darkness. An electronic voice phenomena (EVP) session is one of the standard tools of paranormal researchers, and can also be one of the most meditative experiences in the field. In an EVP session, the participants ask questions of any putative spirit or spirits in the space of investigation, giving time for the digital recorders to record what seems to be the silence in between questions. After the investigation is completed, the researcher will sit and "review evidence," including these recorded sessions, attempting to hear any responses that might have been made along the way. For reasons that researchers debate among themselves, sometimes there are whispers, noises, or even startlingly clear EVP responses in these digital recordings — a few of which are difficult to explain in ordinary terms. Paranormal researchers use the EVP session much like the old-fashioned séances of the nineteenth and early twentieth centuries, as a way to gain the attention of entities and as a primary method of spirit communication.

"If you make a noise, be sure to mark it on the digital," Katie reminded me, "and if you hear something, speak up and mark that, too."

"Of course," I replied, jokingly. "Remember how my stomach growled during the first EVP session at that brewery? Marty was running a real-time EVP and thought he'd caught a demon, for sure." We both laughed. Jokes about the very material embodiment of researchers are common among teammates, as are jokes about how ghosts sometimes emit echoes of their former embodiment. Inappropriate stomach growling on EVP recordings is a perennial favorite story among ghost hunters, as are comments about other, even lower comedy body emissions. Descriptions of ghost farts, for instance, are always good for a chuckle.

Having set the scene and made ourselves comfortable in our current roles as research teammates, Katie and I settled into the work. For the next fifteen minutes or thereabouts we took turns asking questions of any spirit that might be in the room with us, all the same time paying close attention to the sounds of our breathing and the sensations of our bodies. While researchers enjoy working with the technological objects they bring to their investigations, everyone agrees on one, salient fact, that the most important tool any researcher has is their body. While it is rare to see a spirit, it is not rare to feel as though one has been touched by an entity or to hear something that might be a disembodied voice or some other, phantom sound. It is even fairly common to catch a scent that seems out of place in the space being investigated. Indeed, one of the reasons why researchers go "lights out" is to allow the team members to extend their sensorium outwards and to discover what sounds or smells seem to be associated with the space, without the distraction of sight.

Not much appeared to happen while the EVP session was going on. My bedroom just felt like my bedroom to me. There were no cold spots forming — a sure sign, according to some researchers, of paranormal activity, which was no surprise since it was actually the middle of summer and the central air conditioning never worked that well in the room. Neither of us felt like we had been touched or otherwise communicated with; neither of us saw shadows moving out of the corner of our eyes; both of us, however, heard the cats trying to scratch their way out of the bathroom next door, which might have sounded pretty eerie in reviewing evidence later if we had not recognized what the noise was and marked it on the EVP recording. ("That sound is just cats scratching on the bathroom door," Katie remarked into our recorders. "They're really loud.") By mutual agreement, we turned off the digital recorders and considered what to do next. The cats offered a few, yowled suggestions. We ignored them.

Katie still felt, through her psychic senses, that there was something in the room with us and that the spirit might be amenable to communicating with us via one of our other technologies. She gave me her K-2 and pulled out the dowsing rods, saying we should both stand up and see which could give us a better response. The K-2 is a small, hand-held device with a rainbow series of lights at its top. If electromagnetic energies fluctuate in its vicinity, the lights brighten or dim in response. According to paranormal research theories, ghosts or other spirits cause such fluctuations, and they will sometimes become interested enough in the lights to play with them by drawing nearer to the researcher holding the device.

Katie's copper dowsing rods worked in a similar fashion, pointing towards entities or spinning away from them in a prearranged type of message. Before we could begin, therefore, Katie had to ask the dowsing rods to show her their most basic, binary code, that is, what motion from the rods signaled an affirmative answer and what motion signified a negative one. In this case, crossed rods seemed to signal a yes and rods that moved away from each other seemed to signal a no.

I began this part of the investigation, asking any spirit in the room with us to come closer to the green light on the triangular box in my hand, explaining that the lights might change to record its presence. Nothing much happened, although the lights on the device did flicker a little. There is an art to holding dowsing rods, as I had learned over the years: too tight and they never move; too loose and they simply spin about. Katie held the dowsing rods loosely, extended them before her, and asked if anyone was with us in the space. What, I wondered idly, would it mean if the rods signaled no to the question of presence. Fortunately, I didn't have to consider this ontological problem further at the time, as the rods crossed immediately and with a certain, definitive quality, suggesting that we were not alone.

Shaking the answer off the rods, Katie then repositioned herself and requested the rods to point towards the location of the spirit. The thick copper wires pivoted to the left, towards one corner of the bedroom. Katie and I walked over to that spot, and I once again held the K-2 out in front of me, explaining about its lights. As noted above, researchers never imagine that ghosts have much of an attention span, especially about contemporary technology. This time, the lights surged once into the amber, and twice all the way into the red, and then they went back to the steady green.

"I think we have it cornered," Katie grinned from the shadows. She held out the dowsing rods once more and started to ask yes or no questions. Was the spirit a woman? (Yes.) Was there more than a single spirit present? (No.) Was this room the spirit's room when she was alive? (The rods flew wide apart, as if in an emphatic negation.) Had the spirit seen me before? (A tentative crossing, as if the spirit was not sure, but maybe.) Would the spirit like to talk with us further? (Another no.) Was the spirit aware that she was dead? (The rods did not move at all.) Katie sighed, "Uh oh. I don't think she liked that question. She's gone. Pfft, just like that." The K-2 continued to glow green, undisturbed by anything in the corner.

That was our luck throughout most of the rest of the evening, as well. Katie and I tried various rooms of the house, as well as the basement, and we would gain intimations of an elusive presence only to have it hive off just as we felt we were establishing communication with it. We even tried the bedroom again, only to decide that there was now no sign of whatever we had contacted in our first foray. As much as I wanted to speak with my spectral cohabitant, it did not seem that she(?) wanted to speak back — or, perhaps, understood what the terms of this mediated communication were. In this, it was a typical investigation. We pursued and cajoled and even flattered any spirits that might take notice of us, and they gave us ambiguous hints of response or no response at all. After working with paranormal researchers for several years, I could not really be surprised. For the para-community, the thrill was always in the courtship of the spirits, and any suggestion that the quarry had been even temporarily within reach constituted the researchers' main pleasure.

"I'm afraid you're out of luck." Katie and I had returned to the kitchen, now fully obscured by darkness, and resumed our seats at the table. "She's around. I can feel her. But I don't think she wants to play."

"Yeah, I guess so," I responded. "But we haven't tried the Frank's Box tonight. Why don't we run a session with it in here?"

Today one can buy an inexpensive app for one's phone that will do much the same thing as a Frank's Box, and there are very sophisticated boxes that sell for over a hundred US dollars that can be adjusted for scanning speed and sensitivity to radio signals that the original tool, the Shack Hack as it is affection-ately known, could never match. There is something endearing, though, about the old Shack Hack, with its blundering through the radio dial, catching a momentary note of music here and a fragment of electronic sermonizing there. It seems a fine repur-posing of an older technology — not simply of the transistor but of radio itself, which had appeared both magical and spectral to listeners in its earliest years. The Shack Hack is also emblem-atic of the early years of modern ghost hunting, when people with a desire to communicate with something felt but not seen could reimagine and fashion a cheap piece of electronics that was meant to entertain into a tool for reaching across time itself to resurrect the dead.

Katie didn't have a classic Shack Hack, but she did have a modern Frank's Box that I had given her as a gift at one of the several moments when I thought I was finished with doing my ethnographic fieldwork and was preparing to cease participant observation. The Frank's Box wasn't her favorite technology, but she always brought it along when I was part of her team. The device represented our now years' long friendship, our shared experiences in the field, and our work together as ethnographer and research-collaborator. In that sense, as all heartfelt gifts are, it was a Maussian prestation, the gift that references the giver's self, the collective past of giver and gifted, and an object that speaks to the continuing, connected future of the relationship being referenced. Doing a Frank's Box session was something that Katie and I often attempted at some point during an investigation. It was our tradition, and it felt right that we should honor that tradition here at the end of this frustrating, albeit typical, evening's work.

So Katie brought out the Frank's Box from her bag, set it up on the table, checked the batteries, and turned it on. We kept it on the AM spectrum, which was a mutual preference, since there is less music there and much more talk. As the box began to cycle through the dial, what we heard was exactly what we might expect — mostly hiss and the squeals of the machine passing over weaker signals. We asked the box if the woman we thought we had communicated with earlier was present. If she was nearby, we explained to her that she might speak through the box by causing it to stop on significant words. Nothing much happened at first. We asked the female ghost her name, and there was a brief pause, almost as if the box was taking a breath, but then it continued on its cacophonous way. We asked if others besides the woman were present, and we thought we might have heard a sibilant, drawn-out, "yes." That was a positive sign. Katie and I nodded to each other, and I asked, "Who's there? What's your name?"

The box cycled through again and, suddenly, a man's voice said, "John." Of all the names in the world, that was not the one I wanted to hear. Startled, I looked up at Katie, whose face my dark-adjusted eyes could just make out in the ambient light from the kitchen windows. Without asking for my permission, my friend reached out and switched the Frank's Box off.

We had a deal, Katie and I, made almost seven years before. The deal was that Katie would never tell me if she sensed, or saw, or spoke to the presence of my dead husband — and I would never ask. My ethnography was not to be about me or about my personal experience of death. It was to be about social class, gender, and spirit communication in the twenty-first century, a set of topics I had chosen when my husband was alive and seemingly well. My John was no great believer in any religious dogma nor in anything he could not empirically verify in the world. However much I missed him, it seemed to me wrong to entangle his memory in something of which he would not approve. Katie respected that, as she respected our friendship, and she kept quiet about whatever contact she might have with a person she had known in the flesh and had come to enjoy while she had known him.

"It's time to put the lights on," Katie told me, all of the reasons for that left unsaid. I got up and went over to the switch, flooding the kitchen in artificial illumination. We both blinked and then smiled at one another.

"Typical that he'd choose the Frank's Box," I laughed. "It's always the radio with him, although it's usually music." I hadn't told Katie about the way that certain songs seemed to come on the radio just when I really needed to hear them, or how I'd walk into a local coffeehouse and a song that meant a lot to us would suddenly start to play, or how the only time I thought I'd seen John since his death was in the crowd at a Bruce Springsteen concert, walking away from me with his usual, slightly bow-legged gait. "I suppose he's around, then."

"He's always around," Katie agreed. "That's the way it is."

"So I guess I live in a haunted house."

"We all do, honey," Katie smiled at that. "Isn't that great?"

"Do you have any advice for the, um, apparitionally challenged, then, Katie?"

"Just keep the peace with your ghosts, and never, ever investigate your own house. Why would you need to do that, anyway?" Katie came over and gave me a hug. "You already know your own ghosts. Make some new friends in the afterlife instead." Words to live by.

Bibliographic Note

This piece is meant as a hybrid: not quite an ethnography, not exactly a fictional account. I never meant to write extensively on North American ghosts and ghost hunters, but the project ended up being both long-term and very meaningful to me. After looking for hauntings around the American mid-Atlantic region, I find that I can never quite think about regional history or the movement of memory in quite the same way that I had done in my previous, decades-long work on southeastern Nigeria and its colonial past. I certainly did not expect to confront the profundities of everyday grief and working-class nostalgia for an elusive past in what was meant to be a lighthearted project in which I could engage undergraduate anthropology majors and demonstrate ethnographic field methods near our college. I really did do a bit of paranormal research in my then-home, a 1900-era town house in Lancaster, Pennsylvania, but this chapter is meant to inform the reader more about what I learned about ghost hunting in the twenty-first century than to represent an actual ghostly encounter in that home. Nonetheless, the ending of the piece is as true as I feel I want to make it, and I'm sure that "Katie" will recognize herself and her excellent advice in the piece when she reads it, even though I conflated several encounters between us into one here. Under the influence of "Katie" and her compatriots, I can now say that death may be a monster, but I'm not entirely convinced ghosts are anything but deeply human.

On the paranormal:

Bader, Christopher D., Joseph O. Baker, and F. Carson Mencken. 2010. *Paranormal America: Ghost Encounters, UFO Sightings, Bigfoot Hunts, and Other Curiosities in Religion and Culture.* New York: New York University Press.
Hanson, George P. 2001. *The Trickster and the Paranormal.* New York: Xlibris.

Hill, Annette. 2011. *Paranormal Media: Audiences, Spirits and Magic in Popular Culture.* New York: Routledge.

Kripal, Jeffrey J. 2010. *Authors of the Impossible: The Paranormal and the Sacred.* Chicago: University of Chicago Press.

Northcote, Jeremy. 2007. *The Paranormal and the Politics of Truth: A Sociological Account.* Charlottesville: Imprint Academic.

On ghosts and hauntings:

Bennett, Gillian. 1999. *Alas, Poor Ghost! Traditions of Belief in Story and Discourse.* Logan: Utah State University Press.

Blum, Deborah. 2006. *Ghost Hunters: William James and the Search for Scientific Proof of Life after Death.* New York: Penguin.

Dickey, Colin. 2016. *Ghostland: An American History in Haunted Places.* New York: Viking.

del Pilar Blanco, María, and Esther Peeren, eds. 2013. *The Spectralities Reader: Ghosts and Haunting in Contemporary Cultural Theory.* New York: Bloomsbury.

Davies, Owen. 2007. *The Haunted: A Social History of Ghosts.* London: Palgrave Macmillan.

Gordon, Avery. 1997. *Ghostly Matters: Haunting and the Sociological Imagination.* Minneapolis: University of Minnesota Press.

Howes, David, ed. 2009. *The Sixth Sense Reader.* Oxford: Berg.

Hanks, Michele. 2015. *Haunted Heritage: The Cultural Politics of Ghost Tourism, Populism, and the Past.* Walnut Creek: Left Coast Press.

3

A Mare's Field Guide to Monsters in Iceland

Mary Hawkins and Helena Onnudottir

One Morning at Brekka Farm, Dalasysla, West Iceland

The foal was born early, while there was still snow on the ground. Her dam nudged at the parcel of limbs, flesh, and fur, gently licking the foal's eyes open, using her warm tongue to clean and coax the foal into full life. When at last the foal stumbled to her feet and stood, swaying slightly, the mare looked her over closely, assessing her head, her body, her long trembling legs. Satisfied, she drew the foal to her, snuffling the foal's neck, breathing encouragement into the foal's ears. This was a strong, bright-eyed foal, who should do well when later they went as a company of horses to the mountains. Thinking this, the mare raised her eyes to the distant peaks. It was mid-morning, just light, and a heavy mist was weaving itself around the mountains. The mare thought she saw something move far off, where land and mist merged, and wondered if it were one of the monsters that had harried the horse company last summer. She would need to prepare her foal for such encounters, and soon, before they left the farm. Now, however, she could see the farm humans crossing the big field, stopping to speak to the other farm horses. In a minute they would come to the small field set aside for her birthing, where they would greet the new foal and make much of the mare. She whinnied and tossed her head proudly. This was her seventh foal, and she was a highly valued mare.

Four Weeks Later, at Brekka

It was June, and summer had arrived in the valley. The melting snow had left wet marshy patches in the fields, which the foal delighted in. The mare watched her foal gambol and spook when a plover took flight from the grass. Many of the mare's sister horses had foaled by now, and her foal joined the others to race, tussle, and rear up at each other in mock combat. The mare knew that they would soon be going to the mountains and decided that this morning she would begin to teach her foal about the creatures of the mountains and mists. Raising her head, she neighed in the direction of her foal, who trotted over accompanied by two other young ones who were followed by their dams. The horses put their heads together and turned their rumps out, forming a tight circle against the stiff spring breeze, and the mare began to speak.

"I have spent many summers in the mountains, and I have seen many things. Soon you all will follow me there, and we will discover spring flowers, and the juiciest of new grass, together. The days will be filled with light, and the nights short. You foals will grow your bodies strong there, and you will learn our land. But remember, it is not home land," and here she tossed her head to indicate the fields and farm houses around them. "In home land we live with humans. We help them, and they help us. In the mountains, we are a company of horses, but we are not alone. Other creatures live there too. Some we may not see, only feel as they pass by. Others may appear and disappear. Some are ugly, some as beautiful in their own way as us. Many will not disturb us, but some are dangerous. One such creature is the *nykur*." At the mention of *nykur* one of the older grey-chinned horses grew anxious, shuffling her feet and rolling her eyes. The mare said, "Yes, you, like me, have seen the *nykur* and foals, it is likely you will see *nykur* too. Wherever there is water, a river or a lake, there are *nykur*. Some call them *nennir* or even *vatna-hestur* (waterhorse), but all are the same, whatever their name. They look rather like us, usually with a grey or dark brown coat, but their feet are monstrous, back to front, with the hoof point-ing toward the tail and the fetlock to the front. Such ugly feet, and so dangerous! Once there were four children playing on the sand, near a lake not far from here — we will pass it when we are in the mountains. They saw a grey horse and went to meet it. One of the children jumped on the horse's back, and then invited the others to join him. Two did so, but the fourth hung back, saying he could not be bothered — the word he used was *nenna* (I cannot be bothered). Hearing *nenna* spoken, the horse startled, and ran into the lake, with the children on its back. This is well known, that if you name a *nykur* in its hearing it will take refuge in the nearest body of water. As for the children, they were never seen again. So you see that our humans need help with these creatures, it is up to us to identify their dwelling places, so that when we ride with humans we may avoid such places." The foals were disturbed by this story, and one asked, "Are there *nykur* foals, like us?" The mare replied, "Yes, *nykur* do foal. Some of these foals are themselves *nykur,* others are like us. Some say these foals join us when we come down from the mountains before winter, and that the foals are just like us, stronger even than us, but do not believe that. The foals of *nykur* all have a fatal attraction to water, they are drawn to it and want to lie down in it, even if they have a human on their back. You must learn to recognize *nykur* and their foals, and avoid them, especially when you are with humans. Be wary of all lakes. Even frozen lakes may contain a *nykur,* which will scream if a horse or human passes across the ice." The foals, who had not yet seen ice, looked confused, and the grey-chinned horse said, "Enough for now. We will tell more stories when we travel."

Two Weeks Later, Leaving Brekka for the Mountains

One sunny morning, a small group of horses and a couple of accompanying humans left Brekka for the mountains. The mare and her foal were among them, the mare traveling paths she knew very well, the foal skittish and excited by her novel surroundings. After a few hours, when they had left the valley and begun to climb into the mountains, the humans turned back, and the horses continued, lead now by the mare and other experienced horses. They were aiming for a high valley which at this time of year was lush and green, but they were content to move slowly, allowing the foals to explore and learn. In this way the horses strayed off their usual path, and the mare, realizing this, looked to the sky. The sun was still high, and birds were circling. Let the foals have their heads, she thought, there was ample time to find their way back to the known route, and there was plenty of new grass here. The company settled in for a time of snuffling grasses and pulling at the tiny and tasty purple flowers that were everywhere abundant.

One foal, a very handsome colt, was so excited and so impatient that he quickly grew bored and left his dam's side, racing off towards a narrow pass which he entered and was then lost to sight. The mare, who had seen the colt disappear from view, neighed in warning to the colt's dam, and together they trotted to the pass, followed by a number of curious foals. The pass was rocky, damp, and strangely silent, as if the horses were walking not on rock but on snow. All the birds overhead had suddenly fallen quiet. The horses pressed the foals between them and surged forward, anxious to be out of the pass. They rounded a sharp turn and saw opening before them a small valley, hardly big enough to contain the whole company of horses, but more verdant than any the mare had ever seen. On the opposite side of the valley was the colt, preoccupied at that moment with investigating a bright green hillock that was dancing with butterflies. Just then a man stepped out from behind the hillock. He carried in his hands a bridle, but this was no ordinary leather or rope harness, nor was he any ordinary human. The bridle dazzled like sun on ice, and the man holding it was very tall, his body finely shaped and his bright clothing made of the stuff that the mare had seen worn only once or twice a year, when the humans gathered together to eat and drink and dance into the night. The mare was momentarily entranced, but as the man approached the colt, holding the flashing bridle in front of him, the mare became alarmed. She saw now that there was nothing behind the hillock, just a sheer wall of rock, earth, and grass: this was no human! She neighed loudly, and the colt's dam joined her. The colt spooked, rearing up and twisting to one side in order to avoid the bridle, before galloping towards the horses and foals and plunging through them and out of the pass. As one, the mare, the colt's dam and the foals turned and fled, gathering the rest of the company of horses in their flight. They did not halt until the mare, recognizing that they had regained the familiar path, slowed to a trot and led them to what she knew was a safe place of grasses and small bushes beside a clear stream.

For a few minutes the horses and foals rested, letting the sweat dry on their flanks and their breathing slow. The thirsty foals drank from the stream, shying at a small shoal of fish that swam past, but soon, being young creatures, their curiosity overcame their fear, and they stamped their hooves, demanding to know what it was they had just seen. The mare looked to the grey-chinned horse, the eldest of the company, who began, quietly, to explain.

"What you have just seen is one of the Huldufólk, the hidden people. Some call them elves. They live within the mountains and the hills, and they pass in and out of the mountain rock as you might move in and through this stream. They have fine clothes, and many fine things, and they are themselves fine looking. That small valley is beautiful because it is theirs." The grey-chinned horse paused and looked at the colt, saying, "When you came into their valley the *huldumaður* (male, hidden person) saw you. You are a fine young creature, and the elf wanted you. If the elf had managed to put that bridle on you, you would have been bound to the elf, and you would never have been able to escape. We horses must be wary of magic bridles. Once I saw a hideous creature fly past. It was mounted on a long bone that it commanded with a bridle that flashed like the one we have just all seen. That hag was followed by others, riding jaw bones, even shoulder blades. It was said they were on their way to sup with the Devil himself. And those bones, well, they were from a horse." At this the foals trembled, and even the horses rolled their eyes in some alarm. The grey-chinned horse turned to the foals and continued, "Remember, the hidden people look like humans, but they are not like our humans. Some may do you no harm, but if you come across a particularly lush hillock, it is best to avoid it. An elf may live there, and if you are carrying a human rider, know that the human cannot see the elf and may be in danger. Human young can see elves, but as soon as human young receive a name, baptism they call it, their eyes are closed to hidden people."

The mare interrupted then, saying "but my old human can see hidden people. Foals, some humans can see elves, but they are few. Stay away from elf places and keep your humans away from these places as well. There is likely nothing good there. But now the wind is building, and the light is low. Let us find a more sheltered place to pass the night."

Midsummer, the High Valleys

Every day the foals grew sturdier. The horses had completely shed their thick winter coats and were now glossy, glowing bay, dun, and chestnut in the sun. The colt who had encountered the elf was grey, with an unusually long white mane. For some time after that incident, he had been subdued, but over the last days he had become more confident and was almost back to his brash, young self. When the horses crossed a lava field, carefully making their way over a path that some of them had taken many times over many summers, the grey colt wandered off to poke at the soft green moss, nudging at it with his nose, and snorting in alarm when the moss broke to reveal a narrow, deep crevice. His dam whickered to him, exasperated, but also proud. If he could but mature, he had all the makings of a top horse, one the humans would select for special care. As a top horse he would be given the best food and the best rider, he would be taken to meet other horses far away, and the top mares would bear his foals. That is, of course, thought his dam, if he didn't fall and break his leg on the lava first.

It was an unusually warm and often wet summer, so grass as well as mountain flowers and herbs were plentiful. Often the horses came across bilberries, crowberries, blueberries, and brambleberries, even wild strawberries. As they roamed across valleys and past lakes, the foals learnt to drink from the clear rivers and avoid the grey, turbulent, glacier waters, to give a wide berth to caves that might hold trolls or other monsters and to recognize elf dwellings. Sometimes they spied groups of human riders and walkers in the valleys, smelt the food they grilled in the evening, and heard them singing at night. Often, they passed small families of sheep, usually an ewe with two or three lambs. The horses had no more meetings with monsters. Once the mare and her foal were passing a lake and saw, far off, what might be a horse, lying half in the water. "*Nykur,*" murmured the mare and urged her foal away from the water. The *nykur,* if indeed it was that, did not follow, and the day passed peacefully. This, thought the mare, is a good summer.

Late Summer

It was now nearly three months since the company of horses and foals had left Brekka, and the days were growing shorter. The wind was sharper, and there was often a damp mist lying low over the land. Enough grass remained, but it had lost its freshness. There were far fewer birds and fewer humans, whether riders or on foot. Soon, thought the mare, our humans will come for us, so let us find our last valley, down the mountain, and wait for them there.

The paths to the last valley of the summer lead past craggy outcrops and many caves. The mare knew the path and had never encountered any creature on it other than horses and occasionally humans, but as they set out this day, she was uneasy.

The sun had not yet fully risen. Her foal was unperturbed, and the colt, trotting ahead of the company, was full of spirit, but the mare noticed that the other horses were wary like her. They formed a close group and moved swiftly, but as they approached one particularly steep scree slope, above which a cave mouth gaped open, mist descended, and the path disappeared. At the same time, rumblings, followed by a loud cracking sound, could be heard from above, and then thuds, one after the other, and coming closer. A moment later, the mist parted, and the horses saw a monster descending the slope, huge, ugly, with enormous teats. There was no need to warn the foals: all sprang forward and galloped, necks stretched out, hooves pounding the earth. As the rhythmic thuds continued behind them the horses and foals moved faster, and faster, their flanks wet and heaving and their manes flying. It was a long time before they no longer heard the monster behind them, but even after that they kept on. When finally they came to a halt, on a sunny and open plain that afforded no hiding place for monsters, the horses were exhausted, and the foals could hardly stand. It was many minutes before they calmed. The colt's dam was the first to speak, saying, "But why was she there; in that place? I have never seen her there, and it is not her place."

The grey-chinned horse said, "I have never seen her before, but I have heard of her, as have you, from the horses who came with their humans from the North. That was Kráka."

"Kráka?" asked the mare. "Then her human must have asked for a foal. Perhaps for one in particular."

"What?" whinnied several of the foals, in some terror. "What is that monster, and why does she look for foals?"

"I will tell you," said the mare, "But let us keep moving while I tell this tale." So the horses and foals drew breath and paced forward, slower now, and the mare began her story.

"We horses have heard of a troll called Kráka, who lives in Bláfjöll Mountains, near the great Lake Mývatn, far to the north of here. Trolls are very strong, but they are not as clever as horses or humans. Some of them can only go about at night, and in the day must shelter in a cave, away from the light. If they venture out during the day, they will turn to stone. We have already passed a couple of these troll stones, when we were running from Kráka: they cannot hurt you. Kráka is of a different troll company, those who are not affected by either light or dark. She is, as you have all seen, of immense size, and hideous. She takes and eats sheep from the farms around Mývatn, even horses who cannot outrun her. And she has a liking for humans, for human men, not to eat but to keep as company. Once she abducted a shepherd called Jón, and took him to her cave, where she made much of him, giving him all the food and drink that she thought humans most liked. But Jón would not eat. After some days, he said he would eat, but he must begin with *hákarl* (fermented and cured shark), that had been cured for twelve years. Foals, you would not like *hákarl,* it smells like the piss of a sick horse, but many humans prize it. Hearing this from Jón, and knowing that she could find *hákarl* of that age in the far north, Kráka left Jón in the cave, but came back a few times to check that he was still there, as she was afraid he would trick her and run away. Each time he was still in the cave, so she was finally satisfied and set off to the north. Jón waited until he thought she was far away, then ran off to his home. When Kráka returned and found the cave empty, she chased after Jón, crying out that she had for him not just twelve years cured *hákarl,* but *hákarl* of thirteen years vintage. She reached Jón's village to find him cowering behind the local blacksmith, who took a red-hot iron from the furnace and brandished it at Kráka, threatening to spear her with it if she did not quit the village forever. Kráka had no choice but to do so, but sometime later she ventured out again, and took another shepherd. He asked for goat, and although this time Kráka rolled a stone over the doorway to her cave, intending to imprison him while she went for goat, she left in the cave a sword, which the shepherd used to carve an opening through the rock and escape. Trolls are not very bright, are they? I think that this time Kráka has taken a human who has asked for foal. That surely is the only reason she is this far south, and following us."

"You are probably right," said the colt's dam, "but let us move quickly to the last valley of the summer. And let us hope that no other company of horses encounters Kráka."

The day was long, and when darkness finally came the horses rested, huddling together against a chill breeze. The foal, still nervous, leant against the flank of the mare, and asked, "Are there no good trolls? Do all the hidden people want to trick us?"

The mare thought long, and then replied, "The Devil is always evil, but I have not heard of him coming among horses. Ghosts, well, they are often spiteful, but they tend to dwell near humans. We have not seen a ghost in the mountains, but you might well see one when we are home at Brekka. As for the others, elves and trolls, and other monsters, they are neither all good, nor all bad. I have heard of humans who have been brought up by hidden people, and when these humans return to the farm of their people, they are as other humans, sometimes even more gifted. I have also heard of a human who fell deathly ill but was cured by a potion brewed by an elf. We horses often come across dangerous monsters because we roam in the mountains, where the monsters live. Once, though, and this is a story my own dam told me, a troll did help a foal. The foal had been playing with other foals on a bank overhanging a river and had stumbled and fallen into the river. The river was swift and freezing cold, and the foal might have died, but a troll uprooted trees and flung trees and boulders into the river, making a dam, and the foal crossed the dam and was saved. So, there are a few good trolls. You need not always be afraid."

Returning to Brekka

The horse company had now reached the last valley of the summer. They rested, ate, and rested some more. The foals, much bigger then when they had left Brekka some months past, wrestled with each other, and explored the valley, but they drank from the stream rather than go near the lake, and kept away from the cave on the far side of the valley. Late one morning the mare was grazing, pulling up the last of the summer flowers, when she heard the sound of human voices, and horses' hooves. Lifting her head, she saw riders approaching, led by her own old human from Brekka, who was riding the mare's first foal, now a ten-year-old horse. The ten-year-old's mane and tail was the same white gold as the old human's hair, and for a moment the mare thought she was seeing a mounted elf, so fine did the pair, human and horse, look. But then both human and horse called to her and the mare, accompanied by her foal, and with the company of horses following behind, whinnied a reply and trotted to greet the humans. Winter was coming, and she was going home.

Bibliographic Note

Horses are perhaps more vulnerable to monsters than are humans. For sure, there are many monsters, ghosts in particular, that haunt places of human habitation. But the most monstrous — trolls, including Kráka of this story — live in the mountains and valleys, far away from humans but not from horses. When in the summer months horses roam the uplands, they are bedevilled by trolls and taunted by elves. In this manner horses learn and take their knowledge of monsters home, so that they may keep their humans safe. Horses and humans are symbiotic. The Icelandic film *Hross in Oss* (2013) describes just this relationship — "the horse in me." The primary source on Icelandic monsters and their relationship to humans is undoubtedly Jón Árnarson's *Íslenzk Æfintýri* (*Icelandic Folktales*), originally published in Iceland in 1852, and his expanded collection *Íslenzkar Þjóðsögur og Æfintýri* (*Icelandic Folktales and Legends*), published in two volumes in 1862 and 1864. An abbreviated version of the 1,300-page original has been translated into English as *Icelandic Folk and Fairytales* (2000).

On people and horses in Iceland, past and present:

Einarson, S. 2010. "The Role of the Icelandic Horse in Icelandic History and Its Image in the Icelandic Media." BA Thesis, University of Akureyri.

Sigurdardóttir, I., and G. Helgadóttir. 2015. "The New Equine Economy of Iceland." In *The New Equine Economy in the 21st Century*, edited by Céline Vial and Ryse Evans, 223–36. Wageningen: Wageningen Academic Publishers.

On Huldufolk (Elves) and Trolls:

Árnason, Jón. 1852 & 1864. *Íslenzkar Þjóðsögur og Æfintýri.* 2 Vols. Leipzig: J.C. Hinrichs.

———. 2000. *Icelandic Folk and Fairytales.* Reykjavik: Iceland Review.

Árnason, Jón, and Magnús Grímsson, eds. 1852. *Íslenzk Æfintýri*. Reykjavik: E. Þórðarson.

Jónasdóttir, Erla. 1983. *Grýla the Mother and the Murderer: Cautionary Tales and Fairytales* Reykjavik: University of Iceland.

Puhvel, Martin. 1987. "The Mighty She-Trolls of Icelandic Saga and Folklore." *Folklore* 98, no. 2: 175–79.

Sigmundsdottir, Alda. 2015. *The Little Book of the Hidden People: Twenty Stories of Elves from Icelandic folklore.* Reykjavik: Enska Textasmidjan.

4

On the Prowl

Yasmine Musharbash

"Almost like another planet," thought Justin, eyeing the world unfolding beyond the windscreen, the corrugated road snaking through endless red sand dotted by mulga, witchetty bushes and spinifex grass. Towards the horizon two red, rocky outcrops shimmered like mirages as if they were floating just above the earth. Everything so still, even the leaves of the bushes and grasses stencilled into the air silent and unmoving. Then he saw the dust devil. It came from the right, twisting and turning out of nowhere towards his car, running a parallel path for a bit, then loping behind the car and spiralling towards him from the left before at last spinning off into the distance. "Eerie," thought Justin. He shrugged and continued on his way to his new job, hell, his new life, as program design trainer with the community radio station of Wurrukangu, a small Aboriginal settlement out here in the middle of the Australian desert and a very, very long way away from Sydney.

"That Kardiya arrive yet?" asked Walpa.

"Yuwayi, he's here," answered Old Makita.

"What's he like?"

"Ah, you know they little bit all the same them whitefellas. Might be, he's alright. Might be."

Walpa was excited about her new job at the radio station, but she was also worried. She had not really had a job before, not a proper, paid one anyways. She had helped her sisters with their kids, and sometimes she had helped out at the old people's center, getting work-for-the-dole money for cleaning and making cups of tea. There was going to be training at the radio job, and maybe she could travel for conferences and courses like her aunty. All the Yapa with good jobs traveled. They went to places far away and met strangers at meetings and brought back nice things from the shops in the big cities. Traveling would be nice. "I hope, I'll get along with that new Kardiya," thought Walpa.

"Oh, come on, Old Man," she begged. "You know I will have to work with him! Tell me something!"

But Old Makita had said all he would, he creakily got up and slowly shuffled away towards the post office, where his cronies sat in the shade, chewing tobacco and gossiping.

Justin trudged from his accommodation block towards where, he hoped he remembered correctly, the Media Building was. The cul-de-sac that led from his place towards Wurrukangu's main street (if you could call it that) was a double row of quiet fenced-in houses with lockable cages for cars in their tidy yards, closed front doors, and curtained windows. "This is where you Kardiya live," Old Whatshisname (Ryobi? No! Makita!) had told him. The main street was something different all together, a wide strip of bitumen, flanked by a variety of buildings from an old corrugated shed ruin, a brightly colored higgledy-piggledy assembly of structures that Old Makita had said was the Wurrukangu school, to the state-of-the-art design council chambers. All of them were covered in the ever-present red dust, yet the street had been teeming with life.

As Justin turned the corner, he thought, "Curiouser and curiouser!" Where yesterday, there'd been Toyotas parked outside all the buildings, and Toyotas had been driving up and down jam-packed with Aboriginal women in colorful clothes, snotty-nosed kids, and solemn men in cowboy gear and where groups of teenagers had huddled in the shades of buildings, today there was nothing. Instead of the cacophony of Aboriginal voices calling out to each other from one slow driving car to the next, from cars to groups sitting outside in the shade or slowly ambling up or down the street, the Aboriginal music blaring from car stereos and the riotous barking of the countless dogs everywhere, there was silence. Towards the end of the street a dust devil crossed out of the school yard towards the police station, carrying with it some desolate chip packets swirling around almost gleefully. Even the dogs were gone. Well, one old dog was left, over there in the shade, scratching himself and looking as deserted and lost as Justin felt.

Walpa had scrambled out of the radio studio and sprinted to Bottom Camp as soon as she had heard the news: Kurdaitcha were trying to kill Keziah, her brother's daughter. Now she was sitting with the other women surrounding the child, everyone was here — all her mothers, aunties, sisters, and cousins. Towards the west stood her grandmothers and the old men, yelling at the Kurdaitcha. Keziah was lying on a pile of blankets, shivering, with her eyes looking haunted and her skin dull and scary looking, breathing shallowly. Wankati, her sister, whispered into Walpa's ear what had happened. Keziah had told Wankati that she had seen a man with matted hair all caked up with red ochre standing on top of the sand dune beyond the houses where the kids often played. He had waved her over, and as she strolled towards him, she had heard a strange whistling and then felt tugging on her arms and feet, like from invisible ropes. Frightened, Keziah had staggered back home, found her auntie, and after telling her what had happened, she collapsed. Wankati had yelled out for their grandmother, who had identified the Kurdaitcha attack.

Justin arrived at the Media Building to find its doors open and all offices and studios deserted by Aboriginal workers. Only Tilly, the Kardiya bookkeeper, was in the back office.

"Where is Walpa?" he asked her. "We have our first training session scheduled to begin in five minutes."

Tilly rolled her eyes and said, "She's run off to Bottom Camp, everyone has."

For entirely different reasons, Justin rolled his eyes at Tilly. This was not going well. Nothing was going as planned in this place. Yesterday he had waited for two hours before Old Makita had showed up and given him his induction. How could he do his job if his trainees weren't here? He thought about what to do. Wait? Again? Take action? How? He sighed. "Tilly," he said, "I don't know where Bottom Camp is. Could you take me there, please?" Now Tilly sighed, but she grabbed the Toyota keys and got up.

They drove past the shop and the football oval and along a bit of dirt road when he spotted few rows of dilapidated houses, and right at the end, in the yard next to the last house, two large groups of people and what must be all of the dogs of Wurru-kangu. One group of people was a huddled mess of bodies, the other a row of figures gesturing and screaming into the desert that lay beyond the houses. He could spot Old Makita among them. He could not see Walpa. Tilly stopped the car maybe fifty yards away from the house with the huddle of people in the yard and sat silently in her seat.

"What now?" asked Justin.

"Better leave it alone," murmured Tilly. "This is not for Kardiya, this looks like Yapa business."

Old Makita spotted the Media Toyota driving towards them, and when it — thankfully! — stopped, he put it out of his mind. He concentrated on the Kurdaitcha out there beyond the sand dune. He could see Keziah's foot tracks. From how she had dragged her feet, he could tell how much she must have fought against the pull of the Kurdaitcha to make it home. Brave little kid. Him and the other senior people had raked the sand around Keziah's tracks, hoping to spot the Kurdaitcha's tracks should it try to come nearer.

He remembered his grandfather telling him a long time ago when he was a little boy, and they were still living out bush: "You can't see their tracks! Kurdaitcha wear special shoes, feather shoes, to mask their tracks so we don't know they are here, stalking us." Old Makita knew that if you can see Kurdaitcha, and most people can't because Kurdaitcha can make themselves invisible, so only medicine people and crazy people and children can see them, but if you can see them, Kurdaitcha look like humans, like Yapa, but with even darker skin, red-ochre dreadlocks, and big, half-erect cocks. "Their feet must look like human feet," he thought. "Surely, this is why they use the feather shoes when on the prowl. Because we would notice their foot tracks. Yapa would spot them immediately, familiar tracks since they are human-footprint looking but at the same time the tracks of strangers; not the tracks of anybody who lives in our camp; not Old Wirliya's wide, almost square tracks with the big toe on the left foot strutted to the right; not Nangala's flat, waddling tracks; not Mimpi's tracks, the right one always a bit deeper than the left; not Wamuru's tracks, so certain, so straight, every toe print clear and the heels, too; and certainly not any of the children's tracks." He sighed and continued his thoughts. "So when they come across us Yapa, when they circle our camp, looking for a victim to ensorcel or kill or rape, they wear feather shoes."

Old Makita knew that the Kurdaitcha's feet don't touch the ground, the warm, red, desert sand. Their feet have interwoven layers of grass and feathers and hair-string bound to them and through their soles Kurdaitcha feel not the sand but the prickling of the dried grasses, the tickling of the feathers, and the coarse softness of the hair-string. And through the grass-feather-hair-string their feet leave on the ground: not a footprint — toes, arch, heel — but a mirage of untouched sand. The feather shoe tracks blend with the rest of the ground, they continue the teeny rifts, rims, and ripples made by the wind. Bits of grass spike down and create imitations of burrows by tiny insects.

The feather shoes cushion the steps of Kurdaitcha. The sound of their steps is not like the comforting quiet crunch of the top layer of dry sand when it is hot, nor the satisfying low squelchy sound feet make each time they touch and then again when they leave the soft wet ground after the rains. Their steps are quieter, still, a rustling that blends in with the rustling of the desert, with dry eucalyptus leaves falling on hard ground, light sun-bleached twigs scraping on rocks, the wind being caught in spinifex grass.

That is why they had smoothed the sand, so they could see the tracks appear. And while they were waiting for the attack, they yelled at the Kurdaitcha, telling him to turn away, to go hunt else-

where, to leave them alone, that they had done nothing, that they would defend their own, get more medicine men and medicine women. They were the old people now, singing out the same words to ward off the Kurdaitcha he had heard old people sing out when he was just a little boy. Always, the Kurdaitcha had tried to hunt them down, but things had gotten worse since everybody moved into the settlements. The Kurdaitcha didn't even need to look for them anymore, they knew where to find them: right here at Wur-rukangu, in this spot chosen for a settlement by the missionaries, with its brick walled houses and bitumized roads, never-moving.

Closer to the house, Walpa was softly crying with the other women while holding Keziah. She was so frightened. Keziah looked so weak and vulnerable, every so often her little body would buck up, being pulled by the Kurdaitcha's invisible strings. Walpa thought of her brother who had been killed by Kurdaitcha, same as her cousin, and her auntie. So many people had died. She was so worried. One of her aunties poked her softly in the ribs and pointed her nose south. She followed her glance and saw the Media Toyota. Damn! That Kardiya had come to get her for that training. But she couldn't leave. She'd explain when Keziah was safe. Oh, please, let her be safe, she prayed.

Justin had spent most of the day familiarizing himself with manuals and office procedures, bored senseless and itching to get started on the radio work. It was almost knock-off time and, really, he had not achieved anything all day. Frustrated, he went outside for a smoke. He sat on a painted rock in the Media Building's yard and looked dourly at a dust devil rotating past in the distance carrying with it some plastic shopping bags and what looked like a pillowcase.

Walpa was exhausted. All night long the Kurdaitcha had at-tacked again and again. They heard whistling when it happened, Keziah's body would jerk and she'd breathe, "he's pulling me, he's pulling me," before sinking back onto her pile of blankets. Walpa and the women had held her, and the old people would begin their barrage against the Kurdaitcha anew. Throughout the night, Ke-ziah's skin had become ever duller and blacker. Walpa could not go to work now.

A week had passed, and Justin was almost senseless with boredom. Nobody but Tilly had come to the office, and all she had said in explanation was that "they are all busy with that Kurdaitcha haunting them." Whatever that meant. Justin had nothing to do, he had not even met any of his neighbors. They all seemed happily busy during the day and then locked themselves in behind their doors in the evenings, while he kept himself amused, barely, with the books his predecessors had left behind in his accommodation block: lots of anthropology, some geology, philosophy, a native flora guide, and one single detective novel that he had devoured on his first night at Wurrukangu. "Really, there is nothing to do but watch dust devils here," he thought morosely. This is not what he had pictured when he left everything behind in Sydney, his failed relationship, his failed dreams, his dull job at a commercial radio station.

He had set out looking for adventure and excitement, and, he admitted to himself, under the assumption that here, in the red heart of his country, he would stop being himself, start being someone he liked better. Training Aboriginal people had seemed an incredible opportunity to perhaps make up a little for the unspoken and suppressed guilt that sometimes stabbed at him. Plus, Indigenous Media after all was where it's all at. He'd had such high hopes for making cutting-edge community radio, maybe even winning prizes.

And here he was, in a lavishly equipped radio studio with nobody to make programs with, and from what he could tell, nobody who'd listen to them even if they were broadcasting. All the Aboriginals were still in Bottom Camp. He hated not knowing what was going on. He hated not understanding.

The next day, the studio door creaked open and Old Makita stuck his head in. "You there, Justin, my boy?"

Justin jolted out of his seat. "Yes! Come in, Old Makita!"

Old Makita shuffled inside, bowed and grey looking. "Finished," he said, gravely.

"Finished?" queried Justin, hope rising that it was all over, that everybody would finally come to work.

"Finished," nodded Old Makita. "They took her," he said, and walked away.

Another week went by, everybody in Bottom Camp seemed to be involved in funeral preparations, and nobody spared radio work a second thought. Justin felt near catatonic with inaction. There weren't even dust devils to watch any more, everything was even stiller than before.

The next Monday, Walpa was in the studio waiting for him when he arrived for work. Justin was surprised by how excited he felt and how angry—how could she not have come to work for so long?! He allowed the excitement to take over, and he swallowed his admonitions.

"Let's get started then," he babbled. "Our first show, what shall it be about, do you have any ideas? I have lots of ideas. But let's hear from you first. Once we have an idea, we can nut out the technical bits and do some learning on the go, right?! It'll be great! It'll be fun! Let's do it, let's start! What do you reckon?!"

Walpa looked down and said nothing. Justin waited. Nothing happened.

"Okay, then," he finally said, "how about we make a show about Kurdaitcha?" Walpa slowly got up and without looking at him, strode out of the studio.

Towards the horizon a sand devil was forming, then another one. Justin sat on what by now he considered his stone, deeply inhaling his cigarette. He stared into nothingness, feeling numb.

"What…?" he could not even formulate the question properly. It was all too much. Old Makita was tottering towards him and sat down on the ground next to his stone.

"You gotta smoke?"

"Yeah, Okay," grumbled Justin, and passed one and the lighter to the old man. Then, "Old Makita, tell me, what did I do wrong? I want to work with Walpa on that radio show, but when I asked her to start, she just walked away."

The old man sighed. "You bin ask her about that monster that took her niece. She got sad." And a little while later, he added, "We don't like talking about them. They hear us, and they come. And then they take more."

The next day, Justin went to see Old Makita at his camp. As Tilly had suggested, he brought a tin of tobacco, a frozen kangaroo tail from the shop, some oranges, bread, tea, and sugar. The old man invited him to sit down next to him on a rickety bedframe covered with a thin foam mattress. Justin gingerly did and hoped none of the old man's fierce looking dogs would come too close. They both smoked. Then Justin gathered his courage and asked, "Those monsters, the ones we were talking about yesterday, the ones you don't like talking about because they might hear you — could you talk about them in the studio? It's soundproof. Nobody can hear what you say in there."

Old Makita thought for a long while and then nodded, "Yuwayi, I will come tomorrow and tell you."

The following day, in the studio, Justin made an on-the-spot decision: he turned the desk mic on. As soon as Old Makita left, frenzied with momentum he began working on his piece. Recording different voice overs to frame and interpret Old Makita's story, he commenced his piece in a "Thunder Throat" imitation: *"In remote Australia, deep in the desert, Aboriginal people say that monsters are real. One such monster is called the Kurdaitcha."*

Cut to Old Makita's voice: "Kurdaitcha, they are invisible, only clever people can see them, and mad ones and children. Whitefella can see them, too. They look like us, only different. They are crafty, hiding their tracks with feather shoe. We can't see them, but they come for us. They make Yapa sick, sometimes they kill us. That's what they like doing, kill Yapa. They have always been here, same as us, same as the Dreaming, jukurrpa. They hunt us. They steal women."

Over to hipster-philosopher voice: "If being invisible and stealthy wasn't cruel enough already, Kurdaitcha can also fly. Aboriginal people say about Kurdaitcha that 'they can fly fast as a bullet.' Try imagining Kurdaitcha flying. They have no wings, so, I guess, they don't fly like birds: not high up into the air, riding the winds, gliding, sailing, zooming around. No, they fly like bullets, and I imagine they fly in straight lines. Birds in flight tip forwards, they move their bodies from the vertical to the horizontal, look-ing down or ahead when flying, with their bodies behind them, their wings stretched wide out of their line of sight. I can't see Kurdaitcha flying like birds, transforming their view of the world, their perspective on it in flight. I think they stay upright. I think they just lift above the ground, a little, not much, creating space between the soles of their feet and the sand and then they zoom forward, fast. Or maybe, the ground underneath them zooms backwards, fast, while they hover slightly above, still. Like when a plane leaves the dock at the airport, and you are not sure if the plane is moving or the airport. That's how I imagine Kurdaitcha flying — only much, much faster. Like the earth spins underneath them, hurtles through space as it does, until they sat down, and now they are somewhere else: fast as a bullet."

Back to Old Makita's voice: "They whistle. That's how we can tell they are here, when we hear that whistling. Sometimes they gotta bird, too. We know his song. And when we see dust devil go-ing strange ways, we know there is Kurdaitcha traveling.

Pretending to be an anthropologist with a plummy, Attenbor-ough accent: "In the central Australian desert, when Aboriginal people hear a strange noise or see an odd weather phenomenon, they know it is probably a monster. And they say this is what kills them, these monsters. Not a car accident, not alcohol, not pro-cessed shop-bought food, but inexplicable monsters. How can we understand this? I think it is important to note that either way, whether wearing feather shoes or flying: Kurdaitcha don't touch the ground. Next to their assumed intentions and, too often, ac-credited actions, to rape and murder, this is what makes them monstrous. Local Aboriginal people say about themselves 'waly-angka nyinami.' Walya- means sand, ground, earth; -angka means on, in, upon; and nyinami is a verb meaning both to sit and to be. It has been translated in many ways ranging from Nancy Munn's coinage of 'We are the people who live on the ground' to Michael Jackson's, the anthropologist, 'at home in the world.' Clearly cen-tral is the connection of people to the ground, to earth, the world. Kurdaitcha don't touch the ground, at least not when they are at their most monstrous, when they are on the prowl, when they *wear their feather shoes or fly. Not touching the ground, not being in touch with the ground, with earth, with the world underscores their monstrosity in exactly the opposite way to how Lévi-Strauss defined Oedipus as autochthonous — of the earth — through his swollen foot. 'In mythology,' he says, 'it is a universal character of men born from the earth that at the moment they emerge from the depth, they either cannot walk or do it clumsily'."*

Back again to Old Makita's voice: "The old people showed us how to chase them away, but sometimes we don't spot them early enough, like when my nephew was killed. Sometimes, they win, even though we all try together to chase them, like when Walpa lost her niece. We sing out to them to go away. And the clever men and clever women can sing them away. And they don't like our dogs. The dogs can hear them, and the dogs help us chase them."

"Thunder Throat" voice in closing: "And so some traditions remain strong in the magical wonderland of the outback." Here the voice blends over into Old Makita singing a traditional song from a recording Justin had found in the studio's archives. He superimposed this with digeridoo music. Over the next days he worked on the soundtrack. To illustrate whistling, Justin used bird recordings he took in the bush surrounding Wurrukangu. He added the sound of a sand devil he had recorded as it twirled through his very own backyard. When he was done, he sent the clip to a radio station in Sydney.

Maybe a month or so later, one morning as Justin walked into the Media Building's yard on his way to work, he notices some of his Aboriginal colleagues scuttling away as they spotted him. When he entered the office, Tilly averted her eyes and scampered into the next room. Then Jakamarra, the local Media organization's board member strode towards him and said in a flat voice: "Justin, you gotta pack your things and leave. Now. You are not working here anymore." Stunned, Justin stumbled home.

From his front door, Walpa stepped towards Justin. "You should not have done that," she said quietly. "We heard that radio show. We tried to tell you. Now you must go." She turned away from him and walked towards Bottom Camp with slumped shoulders.

He packed that same night and left at sunrise. Wurrukangu was a long way behind him before he noticed the sand devils trailing him. He felt as if the earth was spinning underneath him, like being hurtled through space, and knew that soon he would be somewhere else: fast as a bullet.

Bibliographic Note

I am continually struck by the significant similarities between the monster I write about here (Kurdaitcha) and some non-Indigenous Australians in central Australian communities. The narrative format allowed me to look at this from more angles than I am usually able to in my academic writing. I especially like how fictionalizing allows the reader to first identify with and then to judge Justin. He is the figure through which I portray some of the many levels on which non-Indigenous Australians deny the dangers that monsters — and they themselves — pose. I believe this denial of danger lies at the heart of the contemporary settler-colonial state and giving it narrative shape hopefully makes it easier to see. Contrasting Justin's view with those of Walpa and Old Makita, then, gave me the chance to not only contrast the Indigenous view with the non-Indigenous view but remind the reader that there are not just gendered and aged differences but also differences due to personality and attitude. Additionally, it made it easy to show that some notions are shared by Warlpiri people despite internal differences, chief among them the appreciation of the seriousness of monsters.

On walking, feet, and techniques of the body:

Catenaccio, Claire. 2012. "Oedipus Tyrannus: The Riddle of the Feet." *The Classical Outlook* 89, no. 4: 102–7. https://www. jstor.org/stable/43940190

Ingold, Tim, and Jo Lee Vergunst, eds. 2008. *Ways of Walking: Ethnography and Practice on Foot.* New York: Routledge.

Lévi-Strauss, Claude. 1955. "The Structural Study of Myth." *The Journal of American Folklore* 68, no. 270 (October–December): 428–44. DOI: 10.2307/536768.

Mauss, Marcel. 1973. "Techniques of the Body." *Economy and Society* 2, no. 1: 70–88. DOI: /10.1080/03085147300000003.

On Warlpiri people and some of their monsters:

Jackson, Michael. 1995. *At Home in the World.* Durham: Duke University Press.

Meggitt, Mervyn J. 1955. "Djanba among the Walbiri, Central Australia." *Anthropos* 50: 375–403. https://www.jstor.org/stable/40451033.

Munn, Nancy. 1973. *Walbiri Iconography: Graphic Representation and Cultural Symbolism in a Central Australian Society.* Ithaca: Cornell University Press.

Musharbash, Yasmine. 2014. "Monstrous Transformations: A Case Study from Central Australia." In *Monster Anthropology in Australasia and Beyond,* edited by Y. Musharbash and G.-H. Presterudstuen, 39–55. New York: Palgrave Macmillan.

Thurman, Joanne. 2020. "The Nine-Night Siege: Kurdaitcha at the Interface of Warlpiri/Non-Indigenous Relations." In *Monster Anthropology. Ethnographic Explorations of Transforming Social Worlds,* edited by Yasmine Musharbash and Geir Henning Presterudstuen, 143–57. New York: Routledge.

On settler-colonial relations in Australia:

Watego, Chelsea. 2021. *Another Day in the Colony.* St Lucia: University of Queensland Press.

Wolfe, Patrick. 1999. *Settler Colonialism and the Transformation of Anthropology: The Politics and Poetics of an Ethnographic Event.* London: Cassel.

Wolfe, Patrick. 2006. "Settler Colonialism and the Elimination of the Native." *Journal of Genocide Research* 8, no. 4: 387–409. DOI: 10.1080/14623520601056240.

On Yapa-Kardiya relations, specifically:

Biddle, Jennifer. 1997. "Shame." *Australian Feminist Studies* 12, no. 26: 227–39. DOI: 10.1080/08164649.1997.9994862.
Musharbash, Yasmine. 2010. "'Only Whitefella Take That Road': Culture Seen through the Intervention at Yuendumu." In Culture Crisis: *Anthropology and Politics in Aboriginal Australia,* edited by Jon Altman and Melinda Hinkson, 212–25. Sydney: University of New South Wales Press.

5

"Keep Off the 'Bad Things,' Uncle!": A Tao Child's Perspective on Anito Monsters on Lanyu Island, Taiwan

Leberecht Funk

At home we are three siblings: my elder brother, my elder sister, and me. Elder brother lives in Taiwan where he attends high school. He only returns to Lanyu during summer vacations. I miss him a lot! Maybe he will come home for Chinese New Year, but we don't know yet, because mother doesn't have money to pay for the flight. Elder sister is just one year older than me. She doesn't always treat me nicely. Yesterday she said something nasty to me.

We live together with our paternal grandparents. They are very strict, we are not allowed to talk back when they tell us things. Grandma works in the taro fields. She has a lot of work to do. She has to weed the fields every day and check if there is enough water. She said next year when I graduate from elementary school she will take me to the fields. We children are not allowed to go to the fields by ourselves. The elders say there are "bad things" in the mountains that will snatch our souls.

Grandpa doesn't go fishing very often anymore. He drinks a lot of alcohol. The preacher said it is not good to drink alcohol, it will destroy your body and mind. We should only drink things that are good for us, like water. When I grow up I will never drink alcohol. It doesn't smell good. I'm afraid of Grandpa when he is drunk. Once he took a knife and threatened to kill everyone. We ran away from him and didn't come back until the next morning. When Grandpa is drunk, Grandma will ignore him. Then he talks and talks, but Grandma will not listen to him.

I miss our mother a lot. She left for Taipei to start a new job. She is working in an office, but I don't understand what she is doing there exactly. Sometimes we talk on the phone with her. She said that she will bring us lots of sweets when she comes home.

Father is already living in another world. Mother said his soul flew straight to heaven. His soul is now with Jesus, we don't need to worry.

I'm in third grade of the local elementary school. Our class teacher is really nice, she encourages us to learn every day and almost never scolds us. All of our teachers are Chinese. They live in separate buildings on the school grounds. We get a free lunch at school, it's really nutritious and tastes good!

Soon there will be exams. The teachers say we will only have a bright future if we concentrate on our studies. They help us to do homework in the activity center. My mother said she will buy me a mobile phone if I get best results in the final exams. But I'm not sure if I can manage. Last year I only got eighty points out of a hundred.

When I'm grown up I also want to become a teacher. I want to learn the Tao language and teach children about our traditional culture. Grandpa says young people have forgotten the laws of the ancestors, they have become like the Chinese.

My best friend is Enqi. She is my second cousin, her grandfather is the younger brother of my grandmother. We are like sisters. She also goes into third grade.

You ask what we like to play? Most of the time we hang out with the other children. We like to play The Ghost Is Catching You. This is a funny game, you have to play it in a tree, like the big one behind the school building. Someone is the ghost, he has to touch the others. You can move everywhere on the tree but jumping off is forbidden. In summer we have a lot of fun. Every day we go to the *vanwa* for bathing and swimming. We only come home for meals when we are hungry. Once Grandma scolded me because I came home late, it was well after sunset. The elders say that at dawn the Anito will awake and try to harm people.

I save all my money for later. When I go to Taiwan I will be able to buy whatever I want. On Lanyu there are not many ways to spend money. We can buy snacks at the village shop or play computer games in the *wanka*. Some children always want to play computer games, they even steal money from their parents. My mother said she doesn't want me to go to the *wanka* so I don't go there.

***

You have such a strange name. Fengke [Funk] just sounds like Vonkow — one of our fiercest monsters. The old people say it lingers around in the mountain forests. You actually speak like a ghost because your pronunciation is strange. Sometimes you say things I don't understand. I don't know if I can trust you. It is good that Enqi is around. Then nothing can happen to me.

I know you are interested in our monsters. But I will not talk about these things with you. Nobody will. Don't you know that they can overhear human conversations? Nowadays they can even understand Chinese since there are also graduates from Chinese schools among them. No, don't make me think too much about Anito, who knows, maybe they are able to read my thoughts? I will better go now.

***

You haven't returned to your European country yet? You must like it over here, even though I can't understand why you like this place. We don't have attractive beaches like the ones they show on television, the beaches on Lanyu are all rocky and dangerous.

Where are you heading to? To the river? This is not a good idea. Don't you know that on the other side of the river there is our graveyard? They bury "those who have already left" in the thicket near the coast. We never go there, it is a place where many "bad things" gather. Only brave men go there for funerals when someone died in the village. They wear helmets and armors to keep their souls attached to their bodies, they carry daggers and spears to ward off the evil. Children and women are not allowed to watch them, but of course we all know what the men do on these occasions.

The soil at the burial ground is very dirty, the men get sick and die if they don't wash it off properly. The worst thing you can do to your enemies is to throw a handful of this dirt on the rooftops of their houses. Their fortune will change for the worse, there will be accidents, mishaps, and deaths occurring.

When there is a typhoon the waves will nag at the shore and wash out bones from the graveyard. It is really a frightening place! The villagers won't like it if you cross the river because you will bring back "bad things" to our village. Maybe your soul is strong, and you won't suffer harm. But the evil will follow you, it will attach to you. Those who are weak, like us children, are in danger if you behave irresponsibly.

If you go there sudden high waves will tear you into the deep water. Earlier this year the youngest son of the shop owner almost died. He didn't pay attention to what the elders said and went swimming at the beach. The current pulled him out to the ocean, he almost drowned. In the last moment the men of the village rescued him. They brought him to the hospital on the west coast, from there he was flown to Taiwan. He drank almost five liters of sea water. He still feels anxiety from time to time. His brain suffered from lack of oxygen. On Lanyu people say that the Anito are still clutching to him. Let's change subjects…

***

This is the younger brother of my cousin Enqi. He is very cute, he is only two years old. I bought him cookies because he was crying. His mother left for her taro field, but he didn't want to stay behind. He threw a tantrum, and everybody was laughing at him. Small children are sweetest when they are crying. They are so babylike, they don't understand the proper ways of human behavior!

You want another cookie? Come over here to the shadow, let's talk with uncle. You don't need to be afraid of him. Sit down and don't touch the ground. It is very dirty.

Do you easily get angry? We on Lanyu are a peace-loving people. We are calm and friendly and don't speak with loud voices. It is not good to become angry. When I get harassed by the other children I just run off. Grandma told me that it is forbidden to beat anyone. She also told me that I shouldn't make use of bad language. When you are angry you say sometimes words that are not true. This is very dangerous because they will fall back on you.

My elder brother once had a fight with another boy. The other boy said that my brother was "useless" because he didn't know how to fish. Since we don't have a father and Grandpa is always drunk, there was nobody to teach him. My brother got very angry and hit the boy with a stone. The other boy was injured, blood was dripping from his wound. The boy's father was very angry with us. He demanded a taro field for compensation. Grandpa gave him two pearls because we need our land and can't afford to give it away.

I almost never cry. If I really can't suppress my tears I go and hide somewhere. Last time I cried was when I hit my head against the table. I was so much in pain that I couldn't help it. You see the little scar on my forehead?

You are in danger when you get angry or cry out loud. The Anito will approach you and steal your soul. You are an easy prey for them. When you are in a rage you behave stupidly because you are not able to think clearly about what you are doing. You hurt others or get hurt by yourself. Sadness weakens your body, you don't care anymore about what will happen to you.

You can only become a little bit angry or a little bit sad. If you manage to control your heart and your deep inside the Anito can't affect you.

Our monsters are not like us. We get up at sunrise, they get up at dusk. We go to school and work, they are just lazy creatures who like to steal food or whatever they can get. While we wash our bodies and comb our hair the monsters let themselves go. When there is a rotten smell you can be sure that monsters are around. They delight when our bodies suffer, when we are sick and in pain. When we feel weak, they feel powerful. We have to be strong and fierce and impress them with our threatening appearance. Then they don't dare to come closer.

When small children are upset we have to make them stop crying. If they continue crying for a long time their souls will eventually fly away. It is important that small children stay calm. Then their souls are firmly attached to their bodies and the Anito cannot cause them any harm. But if their hearts beat faster and faster and if they are out of breath then their souls lose grip, they will start floating. The souls are scared, they are in a panic because they are still unknowing. They are not yet familiar with this world, so they are easily confused and frightened. One little irritation and they are gone. Unknowing souls have no orientation. They will get lost in the mountain forests or linger around at the coast not finding their way back to the settlement.

You know that children suffer from soul loss when they cry for a long time and there is nothing you can do about it. When this happens the parents will go to the sea shore very early the next morning to call back their souls. The souls will recognize their voices and happily follow them home where they will reattach themselves to the children who carry them.

When small children cry we usually give them sweets to soothe them. Or we laugh so that they feel happy again. The Anito don't like it when we laugh because then they know that we are not afraid of them.

We have to go home now. The little boy is tired, he wants to have a nap. Enqi, wait, I come with you!

***

Uncle, don't touch this! Don't do it! Don't pay attention, this thing is evil. Let's just continue walking and leave this thing alone.

You are right, it looks like a beautiful butterfly, but the elders say it is the soul of the Anito. It is playing tricks with small children, trying to lure them away from the settlement. The children are fascinated by its beauty, by its aimless and fluttering movements, they want to catch it and start following it. Suddenly they find themselves in the jungle and realize that they have lost their way. Then they experience great anxiety and are paralyzed with fear. The evil thing rejoices for it can grab their souls.

The owl is another monstrous creature. It is able to talk but only with a ghostly voice. Its call sounds like "human being, come and find me!" It sits in the forest preying on human souls.

There are evil and benevolent creatures all around us. You need to know about them, otherwise you better stay in the village. It is only thanks to our ancestors that we can distinguish edible plants and animals from poisonous ones. The ancestors had a daring heart and tried all the different things in the forest and in the sea. In this way they made a sacrifice for later generations. We will always feel gratitude towards our ancestors because they put their bodies at risk to enable us to have a pleasant life on the island.

Children should remain in the safe area of the settlement until they graduated from elementary school. Only then are their souls strong enough for them to work on the fields and to go fishing at the shore.

***

We laugh at you because you slipped, uncle. Everyone laughs when someone stumbles or falls down. Don't be angry with us!

When elder brother climbed a tree and fell down, he broke his arm. Grandpa was angry with him because he didn't listen. He said, "Who told you to climb this tree? It serves you right!"

Then we all laughed. Elder brother was in pain because of his arm. Eventually we had to bring him to the hospital.

On our island we believe that a person has many souls. They rest in the head and in the joints, that is in your shoulders, elbows, and knees. Adults normally don't stumble because their knee souls have already learned to be attentive. They guard your steps so that nothing will happen to you. But if you don't have your mind set, it might be that your knee souls are absent. They fly around in the vicinity because they are distracted by other things. It is not good to be too curious about everything.

Uncle, you see the old man over there? You see how he is pulling his leg after him? His knee soul got caught by a monster, now he cannot move his leg properly anymore. When someone is crippled or not able to move anymore the souls in the joints have already departed.

It is good to be always careful and attentive. If you are happy, uncle, just laugh for a short moment. Otherwise the Sky Gods will be offended. They constantly watch what we are doing down on Earth and if they dislike what they see they will become angry. They will think: "What!? He is laughing all the time?! Wait, we will teach him about who he is." The Sky Gods are powerful, they can give orders to the Anito who will make something bad happen shortly afterwards.

It is not good to be too proud. We on Lanyu don't like proud people. For younger persons it is better not to talk too much because there are many things they don't understand yet. Grandma never praises me because if others listen to her words my fate will change for the worse. Our Chinese teachers behave differently. When we perform well in school, they might even say "Cool!" or clap our hands and give us five.

It is not good to talk about yourself. Your own concerns should stay in your deep inside, don't let them affect your behavior and choose words carefully. People should be humble and modest, they should be able to endure hardship.

In the past we here on Lanyu had difficult lives. We didn't have clothes to wear, it was freezing cold in winter. From time to time we were facing food shortages, not everyone could eat his fill. When people are hungry they are easily upset because their insides are bad. When there is not enough to eat, people will start to fight.

***

Today I'm not feeling well, uncle. I have a cold, my nose is running, also I'm feverish. When you are sick it is better not to let yourself go. Grandma doesn't like it when I stay in bed after sunrise. She will scold me. Only lazy people and those who are about to die stay in bed during daytime.

The old people always go to work in their fields no matter how they feel. Grandma has swollen and painful knees, but she never complains. She says it is important to always have a good inside. Don't pay attention to the "bad things." If your inside is bad, you have to pull the bad seeds out, just like weed. The old people on Lanyu are very strong, they are afraid of nothing. Don't worry, uncle, tomorrow I will be fine. It's just a little cold.

***

Mother came home yesterday! She took a train from Taipei and came here by ferry boat. See my new sweater? Mother bought it for me. She also bought me a jacket for the winter.

Grandpa went fishing yesterday, he caught a lot of fish. Grandma went to the reef to catch crabs. Many people came to have dinner with us.

There are fish for women and fish for men. Women can't eat men's fish, but men can eat everything. Men's fish usually smells strong and has many bones. Men can eat it because they are stronger and tougher than women. Women prefer mild tastes. The elders say that women will get sick if they eat men's fish, also they will develop skin rash. Some people say this is superstition, but Grandma wouldn't let me eat men's fish. So I never have tried it.

It is the same with goat meat. Goats roam freely on the island but they are owned by men. All goats receive ear marks by their owners, so there are no arguments about to whom a goat belongs. When men prepare goat meat it really stinks badly, the smell is very intense. Goat meat is like a medicine because all what the goats do is to feed on wild plants. If the men eat goat meat it helps them to regain their strength. Men are stronger than women, they have to be brave and enter the mountain forests to cut wood for their canoes. A man cannot be afraid of monsters, he has to show off his strength to keep the Anito at bay.

Have some sweets, uncle, mother gave us a lot. You have shared your candies with us, now it's my turn to share.

***

This man is dangerous, don't say anything when he passes by. He will get angry, he will throw stones after you. He is crazy, he suffers from insanity. People give him cigarettes because he likes to smoke. His relatives bring him food. He lives alone in a hut close to the fields. Grandpa says he used to be normal but about ten years ago his problems started. Don't look into his eyes, there is something bad about him.

He is possessed by a really fierce monster, he doesn't act like a human person anymore. He never washes himself and let his hair grow. He goes nowhere to work, he is completely useless. He doesn't like children. When he throws stones it really hurts, uncle!

Some people in the village are in the clutches of the Anito. Don't look at them, otherwise you will be polluted by bad things. If they start cursing you better run away, don't let their words enter your ears. The Anito want to destroy human bodies to catch hold of the souls. They whisper "bad things," they want you to go to dangerous places where you get injured and die. They tell you to drink alcohol as they rejoice when you get drunk and start a fight with someone. They tell small children to go to the forest where they get lost, and their souls fly away in panic. Never pay attention if you hear voices from within!

It must be very dangerous to live in your Western countries because you have so many madmen over there. They just take a gun and shoot. I have seen all this in movies. I'm glad I live here on our island where life is more peaceful.

***

Look there are Enqi and little brother, let's scare the little boy, let's have some fun! Little brother doesn't hear me as I'm approaching him from behind. Don't tell him that I'm already close.... No, he doesn't shrug his shoulders, he already knows how to behave. Little brother, you don't get scared, do you? Little brother's soul stays fixed in place, soon he will run around with his little friends.

It's fun to tease little children, they are so innocent. Everyone thinks old people are particularly good in making jokes with young children. They pinch them in their legs when holding them on their arms or show them their ulcers. Also, they make fierce faces and threaten to beat them. Young children cannot tell the difference between real and fake behavior, they are afraid of old people.

Children and old people, we have a special relation here on Lanyu. Elders need to be respected but when they become really old it is better to avoid them. This is especially the case when they start forgetting things, when they have problems walking and when it is difficult for them to reach the toilet. They are already too weak to ward off the monsters, they start to smell bad and say confusing things. The Anito feast on their bodies, they cause some old people to have bad insides. Then the old people are jealous of the young and heathy bodies of children. If the old people find themselves alone in old age they are envious of others because they have children and grandchildren when they do not. They might send a curse because they can't bear it that others are happy while they themselves are miserable. Children shouldn't stay in the same room with old people, it's best if they turn away from them.

***

Today everyone is in a good mood, the whole village will have a barbeque in the afternoon. There will be lots of meat, everyone can eat his fill. Also, there will be a boat race, even women are allowed to row! You can also take part in the race, uncle, if you want.

The village feast is sponsored by the local nuclear waste disposal site, they give money every year to all the villages on Lanyu. If they wouldn't give money there wouldn't be any resources for cultural activities, sport events, for nothing.

Many men in the village work at the waste deposit, it is very difficult to find a job here on Lanyu. You can sell souvenirs to the tourists, get a government paid job or work at the nuclear waste disposal site, there are no other options for earning money.

Some people say there is a leakage, that the environment is contaminated because of the nuclear disposal side. Scientific measurements have shown that land and sea areas are affected, that it is not safe to eat taro from adjacent fields. One of the best places to fish is next to the waste disposal. Men from all villages go there for fishing. My uncle has caught fish with bent backbones near the disposal site, they look strange and rather terrifying. He said this is because of all the "bad things" that are now in the waters of Lanyu. But the government always says that the waste storage is safe and that we don't need to worry about it.

When the government built the site they didn't tell us what they were planning to do. There were even rumors that they were building a fish cannery. It took some time until people on Lanyu understood what was going on. When they learnt that they had been fooled by the government they became very angry. The men from all villages took their spears and went to the waste site to oppose the evil. There have been many protests since then, even in Taipei. The government now wants to find another place where it can dispose its nuclear waste, there already have been negotiations with North Korea and other nations.

It makes me upset to see all the plastic in the sea today. After a storm the coast is full with plastic bottles and flip flops. The villagers have to clean the coast several times a year to make it a good place to live, without rubbish everywhere. We children also take part in this activity, last week our teacher took us to the beach to collect rubbish.

There are many "bad things" in the waters. Uncle, when you go swimming at the *vanwa* make sure that you take a shower afterwards to wash off the dirt.

***

You better go home now, don't stay on the streets. Haven't you heard about it? Something bad has happened in the village. Just half an hour ago someone died. Now the ancestors will gather at the *vanwa*. They will come to his house, they want to receive him because he is now one of them. They can smell his blood as it flows out from his body. This is a very dangerous situation, you better go home where you are safe.

Our ancestors do many good things for us, they give us their blessing so that the fruits on the fields will flourish and that everyone can lead healthy and happy lives. But if they have only recently died, they might not feel this way. They have not yet fully transformed themselves into an ancestor, they still remember their former lives as human beings. They miss their wives, husbands, their children und friends. If they are selfish they might inflict diseases upon those they used to be in close contact with while living among us. We have to draw a line between them and us, we have to tell them to return to their world because this is where they now belong.

Once the soul has left the body forever, the body is no good. Soon it will start smelling, it is entirely helpless, it cannot stop the rotting process, it cannot comb its hair anymore nor is it able to brush teeth. The dead body is very dirty, it has become an Anito. There are different kinds of Anito. There are those of the ones who have nurtured you, they will not do you any harm because they truly love you and they will continue caring for you. Who will be afraid of the ghost of one's own mother? But there are also the ghosts of those who had anger, envy, and greed in their deep insides when they used to be human. With them it is different, they will become fierce Anito after death, they will become monsters that try to kill you. We cannot know about the deep insides of people but most of them have bad insides, at least this is what my grandmother told me.

The elders say that children should stay at home when death has occurred in the village. The souls of young children are still so fragile, they can easily be taken away by malicious Anito. Infants and toddlers have to stay inside, it is better to close the door. My sister and me are already old enough to sit in front of the house, but we are not allowed to roam the streets together with our friends.

You better go home, uncle! Don't make any loud noise for this will offend the spirits.

***

I know that you are leaving the island tomorrow. You will go home to your country and write your book. Even though I like you, I won't come to say good-bye. It is better to walk off casually, don't make a fuss out of it. We never say goodbye when we depart, that is the way of Chinese and Western people. It is better if my soul stays with me, I will miss you, but I won't think too often about you. The people who have left the island are in some ways like the dead because they have gone to another world and we don't see them anymore.

Bibliographic Note

In 2010 and 2011 I stayed for one year on Lanyu in order to do field research about the socialization of emotions. I wanted to understand how local Tao children learn the emotional repertoire of their society and which emotions play a leading role during the socialization and ontogeny of emotions. Many children between the ages of four and twelve years soon became my friends. They were interested in me as a stranger and might have spent time with me because they were simply bored. In my chapter I recall the many conversations and events I had with Tao children while I was hanging out with them. The main protagonist — a nine-year-old girl — was inspired by a real person. Many episodes really happened with her in the way I describe them. Other occurrences, however, are taken from interactions with other persons, mostly children.

My story is confusing in several ways. For one thing, it lacks a narrative arch. This is due to the fact that I am mostly concerned with sharing glimpses of everyday life with my readers through a series of exchanges with the Tao girl, the central figure of my narrative. By meeting her again and again it becomes clear that Anito monsters pose a constant danger to the Tao and that they have to cope with them in culturally specific ways. For another thing, I want to tell a story according to local standards and not necessarily one that is in line with Western storytelling conventions. As you might have noticed, the girl is quite often changing topics, apparently for no reason. She *needs* to do this in all situations, which are somehow connected to the Anito because otherwise the monsters would gain power over her. For instance, when the girl mentions her deceased father she can do so only very briefly. For the same reason moments of emotional significance are glossed over. Sadness weakens the mind and the body, expressions of intensive joy are dangerous as others (humans and spiritual beings) might turn against the offender.

On the Tao People and Anito of Lanyu Island (Taiwan):

Benedek, Dezső. 1987. "A Comparative Study of the Bashiic
    Cultures of Irala, Ivatan, and Itbayat." PhD Thesis,
    Pennsylvania State University.
Funk, Leberecht. 2014. "Entanglements between Tao
    People and Anito on Lanyu Island, Taiwan." In *Monster
    Anthropology in Australasia and Beyond,* edited by Yasmine
    Musharbash and Geir Henning Presterudstuen, 143–59.
    New York: Palgrave Macmillan.
Yu, Guanghong. 1991. "Ritual, Society, and Culture among the
    Yami." PhD Thesis, University of Michigan.

On anxiety as a socializing emotion among the Tao:

Funk, Leberecht, 2022. *Geister der Kindheit: Sozialisation von
    Emotionen bei den Tao in Taiwan* [*Ghosts of Childhood:
    Socialization of Emotion Among the Tao in Taiwan*].
    Bielefeld: Transcript Verlag.
Röttger-Rössler, Birgitt, Gabriel Scheidecker, Leberecht
    Funk, and Manfred Holodynski. 2015. "Learning (by)
    Feeling: A Cross-Cultural Comparison of Socialization and
    Development of Emotions." *Ethos* 43, no. 2 (June): 187–220.
    DOI: 10.1111/etho.12080.

*On the anthropology of emotion, the anthropology of childhood,
and psychological anthropology:*

Briggs, Jean L. 1998: *Inuit Morality Play: The Emotional
    Education of a Three-Year-Old.* New Haven: Yale University
    Press.
Lancy, David F. 2022. *The Anthropology of Childhood: Cherubs,
    Chattel, Changelings.* Third edition. Cambridge: Cambridge
    University Press.
LeVine, Robert A. 2010: *Psychological Anthropology: A Reader
    of Self in Culture.* Chichester: Blackwell.

6

Hunting for Monsters (and Gods): The Making of an Anthropologist

Indira Arumugam

I am an anthropologist.

For this, I blame my mother.

Her stories, especially those about monsters and apparently monstrous gods, are why I do ethnography in the way I do — pursuing stories and pestering storytellers. When I began my fieldwork, I thought my quest was about migrations from my field-site in Vaduvur, a village in central Tamil Nadu, South India to Singapore, mirroring the journey that I myself had taken years ago. While I was doing the fieldwork itself, I thought my project was about the interactions between rituals and politics. When I was writing, I thought my thesis was about how ordinary people theorize politics. Only now, after all these years, do I see how my work has been shaped by the monstrous beings that have been haunting me since childhood. My project has morphed into a hunt for the monsters looming large in my mother's stories.

During the course of my fieldwork, I found myself chronicling the sacrificial rituals dedicated to a குல தெய்வம் *kula teyvam* (tutelary deity), முனீசுவரர் Muniswarar. His devotees had built Muniswarar a new icon and temple. To consecrate this complex, they enacted a sacrifice. The நாட்டாமை *nāṭṭāmai* (headman) told me about the rituals preceding this sacrificial worship called கிடா வெட்டு *kiṭā veṭṭu* (goat-cutting). Blood from a sacrificed goat was mixed with rice, rolled into balls, and flung up into the trees for the மினி Mini spirits. The moment I heard this prelude, I immediately recognized the numinous beings he was describing.

Throughout my childhood, my mother had mentioned these mysterious Mini. Everything grew still for a moment. I was barely listening to the rest of the description. I remember breaking into a wide grin. All the pieces fell into place. The Mini were actually here. They would be there tomorrow. I had been looking for these spirits all these years without actually realizing it. The monsters that had haunted me for decades would now step out of my mother's stories. I would be able to encounter them for myself. Or if not, at least finally see tangible traces of them.

Long before, I went there for fieldwork, Vaduvur was already an intimate place for me. My father's father had been born there. He had grazed cattle amidst the thorny grounds of the Sivan temple. He had been forced to work from dawn to dusk to repay the debts accrued by his family. On a nearly empty stomach. To escape this debt bondage, he had fled to Singapore.

My mother is also from Vaduvur. She had lost her own mother when she was just seven years old. To look after the family and the farm, she had been forced to stop schooling. When she was eighteen years old, a marriage had been arranged between her and my father, who is born and brought up in Singapore. Soon after her marriage however, she was left behind in her father's house. My father did not have the funds to pay for her to immediately join him in Singapore. Married but parted from her husband, my mother endured pregnancy, childbirth, and the torments of her new sister-in-law. It was nearly four years before we were finally reunited with my father. All of my mother's family — brother, sister, nephews, and nieces — still live in Vaduvur.

Vaduvur is my birthplace too. My mother was too busy with the farm and too distraught over my father's absence to spare much time for me. I did not mind. I toddled from one house on my street to another, readily welcomed and endlessly fussed over. Spending most of my time with neighbors and extended kin, I returned home to my mother only to eat and sleep. I had never met my father. I did not know where Singapore was. Whenever I was asked where my father was, I would reply "up in my nose." For all I knew, he could very well have been up there. We left Vaduvur when my father was finally able to finance my mother's and my journey. I was nearly three years old by the time we arrived in Singapore. Since I had only ever lived in Vaduvur, away from my father, the first time he came near me, I burst into inconsolable tears. This tall, curly-haired man with a large moustache was a stranger, a frightening monster.

My siblings and I may have grown up in Singapore. But to my mother, it was not our "real" home. Vaduvur was home. Intimacy with our village was fleshed out in and given life to through stories. When my siblings and I begged, my mother did not tell us, as most Indian mothers would, about Sita or Draupadi or Kannagi from the great Indian epics. What she did narrate was her life in Vaduvur. About her home, family, village and the life that she still missed. We had heard her stories so many times that we had memorized them. We prompted her when she forgot minute details and corrected her when she deviated from previous recitations. We could parrot her own stories back to her. Yet, we still clamored for her to tell the stories again, in her own words, just one more time.

Tell us the one about your goat that died. The beautiful kid that got so thirsty one day. So thirsty that it gulped down most of the peanut oil you had set out to dry in the sun. You had to kill it because it was bleating with abdominal pains. But it had the most deliciously tender meat. Because it was still so young...

No! No! No! Tell us the one about when grandfather would be out in his fields overnight irrigating the crops. You would bring him dinner. It would be very dark. And you were very afraid, walking all alone, along the deserted paths late at night. Until you glimpsed the light from your father's lantern. Even though you had already eaten, you father would share his food with you. You would wash up and fall asleep together under the inky sky and endless stars.

My mother spun compelling stories from the most innocuous incidents. The specific details that she remembered about her long-dead kin.

…My mother had long, thick, dark hair. She wore it carelessly bunched up onto her head. But it was so beautiful. I don't know how she achieved it. I can still smell the intense fragrance of the pandanus flower she threaded through her hair. Pandanus flowers are rare. People destroy the bushes because they harbor snakes. They say snakes love that scent.

…I still remember the song my grandfather always sang whenever I visited him, "On the day Manga (my mother's pet name) was born, the jasmine vine blossomed…"

…My elder brother loved simple dishes. The freshest moringa leaves, sauteed with grated coconut and served hot. He could finish a whole pan of them. He always teased me about what I would serve him when he came to give me the obligatory gifts after my marriage — chicken rumps…

These stories were not grand epics. They did not have any structure or even a proper beginning or end. They were just impressions, digressions, memories, and trivial incidents. But we could not get enough of them.

We may have been growing up in a thoroughly urban, cosmopolitan, and hyper-competitive city-state. But my mother's stories made the village, which I may have been born in but barely remembered, come alive. We knew about the shifts in the weather in Tamil Nadu, the qualities of the soil, the temperament of the crops and the rhythms of the agricultural year. We were familiar with the characters of the villagers and the idiosyncrasies of village life. Most of all, we were familiar with the various ghosts, spirits, demons, and monsters that populated Vaduvur.

> They say people in the past had been able to detach and reattach their heads whenever they wanted. Women would unclasp their heads, place them on their laps and thoroughly groom (wash, delouse, oil, comb, plait) their long hair. Once they were done, they could simply fasten their heads back onto their necks. One day, a woman had just unfastened her head when she heard her baby cry. In her haste to check on the child, she forgot about her head.... A dog snuck in grabbed the forsaken head and ran off into the night.... And this is why heads are no longer detachable.

Vaduvur seemed an amazing place where extraordinary things happened routinely. Snakes should never be killed. They remembered wrongs done to them and would relentlessly hunt you down to wreak their terrible vengeance. Suicides were not relieved of their desires even after death and became ghosts haunting tamarind trees. People who died because of epidemic diseases such as small-pox, measles, mumps, cholera, and even chickenpox were buried instead of being cremated and became gods to be venerated at their tomb and temples. Gods themselves were not ensconced in temples but roamed freely through the land. Nor were they unreservedly good. They relished blood and promised grisly punishments. Vaduvur pulsed with a mystery and a magic that eluded us in staid and successful Singapore. In Vaduvur, a sort of wilderness still existed, full of unexplained phenomena and untold possibilities.

The story that really shaped my imagination was about the Mini. Mini are spirits that reside in the branches of large trees and haunt ponds. As fertility spirits responsible for the yield of the land and the waters, they must be regularly appeased with sacrifice. Only then would they ensure continued agricultural productivity.

> Once a year, you would harvest the fish from the pond. You would wait until summer when the pond waters would have naturally receded. The men would take several days to fish for all the large enough fish. But the first fish and also the biggest fish from the very first day's work, they would have to leave aside. You also have to do this on the last day of fishing. You have to keep it separate. They would cook these fish and some rice and offer prayers. To the Mini.

> They would cook, offer the fish to the Mini, and eat the now sacred offerings and wash up. There and then by the shores of the pond.... This fish is the pond's share, the Mini's share. You have to give the Mini their share or else the fishing would fail, your harvest would be poor.... You have to do this so that the fish will be there the next time. And the fish will be fat.

Along with fish, the Mini are also offered blood sacrifice. The Mini live around the lands owned by the Mannaiyar lineage. The tutelary deity of this lineage is Muniswarar. Muniswarar is a vegetarian and largely benevolent deity. Muniswarar keeps the unruly Mini spirits in check, more or less. Every five years or so, the Mannaiyar lineage enacts a worship culminating in sacrificing roosters and goats to their Muniswarar. Each household from the lineage saves for months in order to afford the goat to sacrifice to the deity. These individual and household goats can be offered only later. The first goat sacrificed is a communal one, paid for by contributions from and offered on behalf of the entire lineage. As my mother then related,

> Once this first goat has been decapitated, some of its blood is mixed into cooked rice. This blood-tinged rice is rolled into huge balls. The rice balls are picked up and brought out to the

trees on the fringes of Muniswarar's shrine. One by one, they are then flung high into the branches.

And they would not fall back down. The bloody rice balls would disappear.

The Mini would have caught them. And eaten them.

We pestered my mother with relentless questions.

What are these Mini, Amma?
What did they look like? Did you see them?
Why do they live in trees?
How would they catch the rice balls? Did they have hands?
How did they eat them? With their mouths?
How is it possible, Amma?
How? How? How?

But she did not know. So, she offered yet more stories. About how the Mini lured people to their deaths.

You know Devi grandmother.... She lives a few houses down the road from your uncle's house. Voluptuous and fair-skinned, she was a very beautiful woman. She used to sleep with the door open. The Mini always used to seize her.... On Tuesdays and Fridays she used to be visited by the Mini. Sometimes, her husband would get frustrated. He would lock her inside the house. But she would rattle the doors and windows. She would scream and shout "I will come! I am coming! Let me go! I am coming!"

Her husband would be outside. He would pace up and down in front of the doorway. He would brandish a broom or sometimes a slipper and hit the porch floor with it. He would shout, use expletives, and scold the Mini and ask them to get out. If you scold the Mini with vulgar words and ask them to go, then it will go. But only if you use curse words. But sometimes even he would get tired, frustrated or he would have other things to do and then the Mini would get her.

The Mini would look just like her husband. It would assume her husband's form. Then it would call her. Standing outside her door, it would call her. She would come outside and go with the Mini. The Mini would sweet-talk her. They would talk, joke, and laugh. They would behave just like a married couple. They would walk out of the house. On their way to the pond. They would walk to the pond. And then into the pond. Her head would be pushed into the water. She would then wake up, wet, spluttering, and very frightened. Shivering and sobbing, she would make her way home.

My mother had never seen these Mini. She did not know what they looked like. All she knew was their terrible effect. Intimately so.

Your father himself got caught by a Mini. Just a few days after our marriage. There was the deity's procession near the Red Pond. Someone had got possessed by the Ellai Satti Mini. Your father grabbed the man to try to stop the possession. You are never supposed to touch a Mini-possessed person. You have to let the possession take its course. Otherwise, the Mini will leap into you. Your father was seized. He had a high fever and shook with chills for days. We were all so worried. Luckily, he recovered after a week.

She also knew that the blood-flecked rice balls that had been thrown into the trees had never come down. And for years, the rice-balls' apparent defiance of gravity haunted me. All these stories flashed through my mind as I heard the headmen explain about the ritual prelude to Muniswarar's sacrifice. I could barely contain my excitement as I waited to finally see the rice-balls disappear as the Mini grabbed them.

But it was not to be. They did not appear. At least, they did not appear that year. The blood from the sacrificed goat had been mixed with the rice. The bloody rice had been rolled into balls. The rice balls had been thrown up into the trees. But as soon as they had been flung up, they had fallen back down. They had smashed uselessly onto the ground. The Mini had not grasped them.

The headman demurred:

The huge groves have been removed as people extend their fields. Huge branches hang over the crops blocking the sunlight so there is not as much yield. So people have cut the massive trees down. But this means there is nowhere for the Mini to take shelter.

… Also, it is not as dark any more. In the past, we only had weak kerosene lamps and flickering fire. Today, there is steady electricity and lots of light. There is no true darkness for the Mini to be in.

The eerie milieu that had harbored these numinous entities has been compromised. The spirits were no longer as present or compelling. Wary of light, people, and development, they had retreated even deeper into mystery. Once again, the Mini had eluded me. They had refused to leave the realm of stories. And so, I pursued them to where they clearly preferred to remain. I chased them deeper into the stories about them.

To do this also meant grappling with how Vaduvur itself had been constituted. Not so much through maps, statistics, and official histories but as a storied place, even a mythic one. Vaduvur is a palimpsest of tales that are not just multiple and diverse but also often contradict each other. Each tale-telling is an assertion of the right to be part of Vaduvur. Not just to live in the village but to be the first to or indeed the only ones who should live there. Not just by living, loving, laboring, and dying do people inhabit Vaduvur. They make Vaduvur theirs by filling its nooks and crannies with their gods and monsters.

The origins of Vaduvur are swathed in epic — specifically the *Rāmāyana*.

At the end of his fourteen-year exile in the forest, the god-king Rama, his beauteous wife Sita, and his loyal brother, Lakshmana, prepared to return to his kingdom, Ayodhya, and resume his reign. On their way home, they passed through Tamil Nadu.

Some say it was actually much later, after the great war between godly Rama and the demon Ravana.

Ravana was the ten-headed ruler of Lanka and great scholar who abducted and imprisoned the virtuous Sita. Laying siege to Lanka, Rama eventually defeated and killed Ravana and rescued Sita with the help of his divine monkey devotee, Hanuman. On the way back to Ayodhya from Lanka, Rama had tarried in Tamil Nadu. His erstwhile companions, the sages who shared his woodland exile, were loath to part with Rama. They asked that he remain with them forever, and Rama promised to fulfil their request the next day. In the meantime, Rama made an idol of himself and placed it in front of his lodging. When the sages came to see Rama in the morning, they were arrested by the idol's alluring beauty. They lost themselves in the statue's enigmatic smile. They desired to keep it for themselves. A knowing Rama asked the sages if they preferred the idol to himself. The mesmerized sages nodded yes. Rama left the statue with them and returned to Ayodhya.

Then the statue gets lost, even to myth. A thousand or so years pass. It then remerges. A story, even a glimmer of a history, surfaces. To protect it during a foreign invasion, the idol was buried in a nearby village called Thalai Gnayiru. The statue remained buried for a thousand more years. But it wanted to be found.

Rama himself appeared in the dreams of King Serfoji, the Marathi ruler of the nearby Thanjavur region. The god directed the king to build him a temple and also indicated where his idol was buried. Having retrieved the idol, the royal entourage was on its way back to Thanjavur when it took a respite, in Vaduvur. The people of Vaduvur saw the statue. They too were captivated by the icon's charming smile. They begged the king not to take the statue away and leave it with them. The king refused. The Vaduvur villagers all threatened to climb their main temple's central tower and jump down from it, that is, commit mass suicide. This threatened collective sacrifice persuaded the king to leave the statue behind. The hitherto predominant deity was side-lined. Rama's statue was installed in Vaduvur's main temple.

Vaduvur then became renowned for its Rama temple and particularly, the enigmatic smile of its Rama icon.

Or so those of the elite Brahmin caste said.

But other villagers, of other castes, had other stories. Of different gods. Older gods. More hot-blooded gods. Gods who had prior claims to Vaduvur. A longer association. And a deeper affinity with its soil and its people. அய்யனார் Ayyanar is the காவல் தெய்வம் *kāval teyvam* (guardian deity) whose temple is older even than Rama's. It sits on the banks of the Vaduvur Lake. This Ayyanar is a harbinger of doom.

> If ever the lake waters were to rise to the level of Ayyanar's nose, then the levees would be broken. Vaduvur itself would be thoroughly submerged under the floodwaters.

Or the goddess Pidari who is also a guardian, specifically of boundaries. Her temple is now in the middle of Vaduvur's market district with houses and shops crowding around it. In the past however, it had been surrounded only by deep forest.

> At this temple, there had once been a massive Banyan tree. The headmen would gather under it for their assembly. All

the gods would also gather here. They would sing and dance. You could hear the sound of the bells on their anklets. They would bathe and wash their clothes here because all temples have ponds. You could hear the sounds of splashing water and the pounding of wet cloth on a wash-stone. They would sing, dance, play, and then go to sleep. They liked it there. The place was secluded. They would not be disturbed by the sound of pounding grain, that is, human habitation.

Stories about the Muniswarar at whose sacrifice the Mini are supposed to swoop in and snatch the rice balls were legion. He has a particularly fearsome reputation and is known to quickly take offence at infractions, especially those deemed to compromise caste purity.

At a sacrifice for Muniswarar, his lineage congregation had bought a perfect sacrificial specimen from a nearby village. One of their daughters who was married to a man from this village, promised to hire a man to ferry this goat to Vaduvur. On the way, however, the goat broke away and ran off. Despite searching high and low, the goat was not to be found. Another goat was brought from within Vaduvur itself and the sacrifice was performed. Right at the end however, the missing first goat suddenly turned up. When Muniswarar's சாமி-ஆடி *cāmi-āṭi* (medium, lit. god-dancer) was consulted, he thundered that the "bringer [of the goat] was not right." When they investigated further, the daughter admitted that she had sent the goat with a Paraiyar [also referred to as Untouchables and despised as the very essence of caste impurity in the Tamil social sphere]. Muniswarar had intervened to prevent a ritually polluted animal from contaminating his sacrifice.

Muniswarar punishes caste infringements very severely.

A lower caste laborer was working in the rice fields near Muniswarar's temple. Having finished his work, he had taken a bath and sat on the embankment near Muniswarar's temple. He soon developed terrible stomach pains. When he went to the hospital, doctors diagnosed him with dysentery. Despite the medicines, his stomach pains did not stop. Until, that is, he was taken to Muniswarar's priest and was given some holy ash to smear on his forehead.

His wrath at those who do not uphold caste discipline by only marrying members of their own caste is even more terrible to behold.

A lower caste man from the neighboring village had come to Vaduvur to work in the harvest. During this time, he developed a relationship with an upper-caste woman belonging to Muniswarar's lineage. The lovers eloped and set up home in the man's village. The man soon developed crippling stomach pains and eventually died. His upper-caste lover committed suicide thereafter.

Even his own congregants are not spared his ire. The primary role of any tutelary deity such as Muniswarar is to safeguard the interests of their own lineage. Muniswarar secures the productive success — biological, agricultural, and economic — of his congregants and defends them against existential threats including the forces of chaos and evil. Indeed, it is Muniswarar's one and only function. However, when they do not adhere strictly to his ritual protocols, Muniswarar also punishes them spectacularly.

The deity Muniswarar is made manifest through the medium of a god-dancer. The god-dancer is the ritual specialist who will ritually get possessed by the deity as part of worship. The god-dancer himself was punished by Muniswarar. He is also the one who drinks the goat's blood at Muniswarar's sacrificial worship. When he drank the blood at the last sacrifice, he became severely sick. He drank too much of the rich blood. He had a heart attack and died.

Another god-dancer had been responsible for Muniswarar's statute being built improperly. It was a brand-new statue. But the statute fell. When Muniswarar's statue fell, so did his god-dancer-*cum*-priest. He has been motionless since then. The standing statue fell backwards. So did the priest. He fell and had severe fits. Now he is bedridden and has to be looked after.

Even priests who perform the worship and decapitated the goats and roosters at the ritual sacrifices are not immune.

Several of the priests who had done the worship got sick within a year of the sacrifice. Got sick and died. You have to be scrupulously clean... not drunk.... Or else Muniswarar will punish them.

So much so that the local priest, who presided over the last sacrifice, refused to perform any more Muniswarar sacrifices.

He is still alive. But he was too afraid. He did not want to come this time. We had to get a foreign priest. From a distant village. We did not tell the new priest too much about our Muniswarar and his fastidious and fearsome reputation. But this priest is also a very brave man.

As I delved deeper into Muniswarar's sacrificial cult, the thread that had drawn me to Vaduvur in the first place reemerged. The Mini were inseparable from Muniswarar. The monsters were sometimes even indistinguishable from the gods. I had pursued the monsters that my mother had captivated me with right into their lair. The gossamer threads from my childhood tautened and also thickened.

It emerged that my aunt — my mother's elder sister — had also personally encountered the Mini.

Your uncle had left on an errand. I was in the kitchen. I heard your uncle call my name. I was a bit surprised because he had just stepped out. But there it was again, my name. I went to the door and there your uncle stood. He asked me to come along with him. I asked why but he would not say. Just insisted I come with him. I asked him to wait while I changed my saree. I went back inside. When I went back outside, he was gone. A few minutes later, your uncle stepped foot into the front yard. I asked about him not waiting for me to change. He looked at me without any understanding. I described what had happened. He said he had just that minute come back from his errand. Only then did I realize that it was the Mini that had come to my house. The Mini had looked like your uncle. The Mini had called me. Luckily, your uncle came back in time. Otherwise…

I could even follow some of the original story strands. Devi grandmother's Mini encounters were repeated and added on to.

Your grandfather has seen her this way. He was coming back from his fields late at night, holding only a machete and a hurricane lamp to light his way. It was on a Friday or Tuesday. He was frightened. Tuesdays and Fridays are when Mini are supposed to walk about. When he was coming, he saw Devi grandmother smiling and laughing and going to the pond. But he could not see who she was with. He immediately stepped into the rice field and hid. If you catch the victim or interrupt them, then the Mini will seize and try to kill you. He hid there until she had gone by. He rushed home and told Devi's husband.

Even more significantly, the story was also concluded, albeit tragically.

Devi really hated being seized by the Mini. She was so frightened that the Mini would kill her. They tried everything to try to bind the Mini so that it would stop possessing Devi.

They went to many priests and ritual specialists. All of them said that they could not do anything. If the Mini had captured Devi as a mother or a sister then, then it will abandon them midway. But because Devi has been seized as a wife... The possession had actually only started after her marriage. The Mini liked her much too much. It will never let her go... Unless there is a flaw. In her mind and body. Then the Mini will voluntarily release her.

The Mini did eventually let Devi go. The possessions did stop... when Devi developed breast cancer. And she had to have one of her breasts surgically removed. She was no longer perfect. And the Mini let her go.

And even though I myself never saw one, I finally had an answer to what a Mini looked like. One of the பூசாரி *pūcāri* (ritual priests) who performs animal sacrifices:

My grandfather has seen one. He said, it was immensely tall. It was all white. But he could not really make out its face. Very huge. As tall as a palm tree... stretching between the sky and the earth.

Unknown and unexplored territories, in medieval maps, were often denoted with mythological monsters. Here be dragons! Here be sea-serpents! Vaduvur, despite being my birthplace, had been a similarly uncharted realm for me when I started doing fieldwork. What had been the map to and indeed the territory itself have been the stories. My mother had populated the land, the remembered and the unknown, with her stories of gods and monsters. Tales of a village and the kin she loved and still longed for. Tales of a humid place with deep dark nights and endless seemingly empty fields. Tales of a people whose gods and monsters may not be all that different.

These narrative skeins had stretched across the years and the oceans to wind around my days and become entangled in my dreams. Where mere facts had become dust and been forgot, the tales had not just endured but also lured me back to their lair. Where there are monsters, there are mysteries. Where there are mysteries, we are always compelled to ask, "And then what happened?" This question, haunting for years, the places in my mind that I rarely visit, pushed me to return to Vaduvur for fieldwork. To hunt for the monsters or at least gather even more stories about them. In the name of anthropology.

For which I thank my mother. She gave me the stories in the first place.

Bibliographic Note

In popular Hinduism, the distinctions between gods, monsters, and humans, are porous, negotiable, and at times even nonexistent. Monstrosity and godliness do not describe supernatural beings or ethical standards as much as articulate a specific hierarchy of power. From a philosophical standpoint, gods and monsters and strangers encapsulate alterity. Exceeding the human grasp, gods and monsters are ultimately enigmatic.

Stories do not simply communicate experiences or represent events. Building worlds, stories actually constitute reality. Keeping memories alive across space and time, stories make a place and a people vivid. Stories are the main data generated through ethnographic fieldwork. As a means to excavate deeper philosophical and anthropological meanings, storytelling is also a form of analysis.

Sacrifice forges tenuous connections between the terrestrial and the celestial. In agricultural milieus, the gods ultimately arbitrate the success or failure of farmers' productive and reproductive labors. To acknowledge their debts to the gods and secure their blessing for future efforts, animals are ritually killed and offered. Sacrificial animals are tithes; they are forms of libations.

Arumugam, Indira. 2020. "Gods as Monsters: Insatiable Appetites, Exceeding Interpretations, and a Surfeit of Life." In *Monster Anthropology: Ethnographic Explorations of Transforming Social Worlds through Monsters*, edited by Yasmine Musharbash and Geir Henning Presterudsteun, 44–58. London: Bloomsbury Academic.
———. Forthcoming. "The Sacred Unbound: Insufficient Rituals, Excess Life and Divine Agency in Rural South India." *Hau: Journal of Ethnographic Theory.*
Benjamin, Walter. 1968. "The Storyteller." In *Illuminations: Essays and Reflections,* edited by Hannah Arendt, 83–110. New York: Schocken Books.

Girard, René. 1977. *Violence and the Sacred.* Baltimore: Johns Hopkins University Press.

Hubert, Henri, and Marcel Mauss. 1981. *Sacrifice: Its Nature and Functions.* Chicago: University of Chicago Press.

Kearny, Richard. 2003. *Strangers, Gods and Monsters: Interpreting Otherness.* New York: Routledge.

Mines, Diane. 2005. *Fierce Gods: Inequality, Ritual, and the Politics of Dignity in a South Indian Village.* Bloomington: Indiana University Press.

Nabokov, Isabelle. 2000. *Religion Against the Self: An Ethnography of Tamil Rituals.* Oxford: Oxford University Press.

Rosaldo, Renato. 1989. *Culture and Truth: The Remaking of Social Analysis.* Boston: Beacon Press.

Taussig, Michael. 2006. *Walter Benjamin's Grave.* Chicago: University of Chicago Press.

7

How to Domesticate a Georgian Goblin

Paul Manning

It was a dark and stormy night in a remote inn in the mountains. Because there were not enough beds in the inn, I found myself spending a sleepless night talking with the other inconvenienced travelers. In the early hours of the morning, the packer, who had been delayed on the road with the luggage, finally arrived.

He knocked, we opened the doors for him, we looked at him: a young man, very pale in color, holding a big rifle in his hands. As soon as he came in, he called out, "In my entire life I have never experienced such difficulties as these, what devil made a fool of me, that I spent the night in such a cursed place! The whole road, I swear, I didn't take a breath, the whole time I was looking this way and that and I had my rifle at the ready in my hands; and God protected me, if he hadn't, then, as you also well know, these forests and cliffs are full of devils and witches."

"There," he continued, "where there is a lovely meadow, there I encountered a lovely woman. I called out to her: 'Who are you, tell me, a Kaji or a human?' She mumbled something incomprehensible and didn't answer me and followed me for about forty strides and then, when I looked, she was no longer there. I crossed myself and cried out, 'Fie on the devil!' I made sure the devil had vanished and went on my way."

Many in the room crossed themselves, and I observed many had their hair standing on end. I made a mental note to ask more about what a ქაჯი Kaji was.

"Worse could have happened to you, child," one traveler, apparently an impoverished aristocrat from his dress and patronizing tone, told him, "if you say a word to a witch, you'll turn mute instantly, and if its beauty seduces you, you'll fall down and become crippled without any chance to recover. My brother has a man who was turned speechless like this by a devil. Worse could have happened to you."

"Now, there are Kajis and witches in our land," the same man began, "more than are found anywhere else. There where there are caves in the cliff, from there a Kaji threw a rock at me and nearly broke my head open. As I passed by again a little later and under the clear, star-studded sky a devil threw water and snow at me from the cliff!"

"Really, I swear," added another traveler, "the Kajis know how to do marvels. If it is good weather, they throw snow at you and if it is bad weather they pelt you with dry earth and rocks!"

"What exactly is a Kaji?" I asked since we were on the subject.

"A Kaji is a Kaji, isn't it? I am not one who has seen one," answered an Imeretian traveler, who, like an attorney, sometimes pointed his finger at the assembled group, sometimes pointed it upwards and waved it this way and that, "but in our village a man had a Chinka, and this I know for a fact." He told his tale. Apparently a man had caught a ჭინკა Chinka in the forest, and he clipped its nails, and he made it help him as a servant at home. On one Sunday, when the owner of the house had gone to pray, this Chinka tricked his son into telling him where the clipped nails of the Chinka were hidden. The Chinka took out his nails and he pasted them back on his own hands and feet and supposedly this made his strength come back, and he stole off. The child, on the other hand, was supposedly thrown into boiling water by the Chinka. "So I heard, I wasn't there to witness it myself." Our traveler finished his story. Earlier he had been trying to convince us that supposedly he had seen a Chinka himself.

Of Chinkas

"What in the world is a Chinka?" I asked, since apparently we were now talking about Chinkas.

Another traveler, a man named Toma, answered, "what's a Chinka? They come, they call out your name, they pester you, they make fun of you, but you mustn't speak in response, or they will drive you crazy. I'm not kidding. With my own ears I've heard the Chinkas, calling out 'Toma, Toma!' But of course I didn't answer them."

Another man added, "I've heard a similar story about Chinkas calling out to a man sleeping outside by a campfire in the woods, 'Are you sleeping, Tsikuro? Are you sleeping?' And they raked the coals until he woke up. When he woke up with a start and rushed at them, they ran off crying out 'You woke up, Tsikuro, you woke up!'" He paused a moment, and then added thoughtfully, "of course the name was different because in this story the man was named Tsikuro, not Toma."

Toma gave him a long indecipherable look and then went on. "It's really creepy how they always know your name. I've heard another such story. Once, apparently, a certain Jamu was walking down the road. Some Chinkas were following him calling him by name 'You, walking there, are Jamu!' Then they called out to Jamu using a second name, 'Kosta': 'Kosta! Where are you going?' It turns out that Kosta was Jamu's baptismal name, which even his own parents didn't know! It's a mystery how Chinkas always know these things."

"What does a Chinka look like? Where do they live?" I asked, fascinated by this new creature.

Toma, apparently the resident expert on Chinkas, replied, "I never actually saw one but I hear they are really small, they have the form of a human, and they are always naked. They can be either boys or girls. As to where they live, no one really knows, I suppose they must live in the woods, where your Tsikuro," here he nodded to the second man, "ran into them, and you can encounter them on roads, like Jamu. They seem to like to hang out around humans, though, you'll find them sitting on carts and you'll find a lot of Chinkas in flour mills. Apparently they like to eat the flour." He paused. "Or at least that's where I heard them, when I was spending the night in the mill with my uncle."

Another traveler added, "they also seem to have a penchant for home invasion. I heard such a story, in a village near my own, from a man named Markoz Parulava, who lived alone in a mud wattle hut. One night, Markoz had buried the coals of his fire in the hut and went to sleep. At some point while he was half asleep, Markoz apparently saw that someone had opened the door of the hut, had sat down by the hearth, and begun to rake the coals. When the fire had rekindled, it was light enough and Markoz recognized that it was a Chinka. He thought 'I will catch it!' and leapt to close the door. The Chinka beat him to it and fled. Then the Chinka tormented him by calling out his name from outside "Markoz! Markoz!" Finally, Markoz threw a burning log at it and it fled for good."

"Chinkas seem to have a thing about campfires but also seem to be afraid of being burnt. I know a similar story about a man named Badvra who also fell asleep by a campfire, and the Chinkas came to him and called him by name: 'Are you sleeping, Badvra?' Badvra leapt out of bed and flung a burning log at them, and they fled, crying out 'You have burnt us, Badvra, you have burnt us!'" This from an unkempt ragamuffin who was squatting by the hearth, poking the embers obsessively.

I offered a synthesis. "Well, as Toma said, Chinkas seem to generally be found in the vicinity of human homes, and we use the term 'hearth' — after all, the center of the house — in an extended sense to mean also 'home' and 'family.' And what is a campfire but a temporarily constructed hearth in the woods? The Chinkas' apparent obsession with raking the coals at night, whether the fire is in a hearth or campfire, is easily explained by their general affinity for human domesticity."

Of Kajis

There was a pause. Finally, it appeared, we had heard all that was known about Chinkas, so maybe it was time to talk again of Kajis. "What is a Kaji?" I asked.

Toma, the resident expert on Chinkas, turned out to be a bit of a natural historian of all the goblins of the land. He responded in the manner of a lecturer. "A Kaji, according to all I have heard, is like a Chinka, similar to a man in appearance. Unlike a Chinka, which is generally small, it has an enormous body. It is ugly to look at, it even expresses horror itself at its own appearance! It has a body covered in hair, and, of course, does not wear clothing. On its chest it has spines, which, when it becomes angry, it releases."

"I had always heard that a Kaji had horns, like a goat," another traveler interjected, "hence the expression used to reprimand obstreperous children, თხა და კაჯი *tkha da kaji!* (goat and Kaji!)"

"I heard they had wings and could also walk on water!" another offered.

Toma nodded as if all these contradictory descriptions somehow added up to one fantastic creature.

"How does a Kaji differ, from, say, a Chinka?" I asked.

Toma answered, "the Kaji is very distinct from the Chinka. The Chinka is more like a domestic creature and does harm to domestic animals, objects, and furniture. The Kaji, however, is wild, it does not come near the house and does not harm anything domestic; it harms the man himself, if a Kaji runs into a man on the road, it begins to wrestle with him, if it defeats him, it doesn't kill him, but it really gives him a good thrashing."

"I heard you say that the Chinka probably lives in the woods, but you seemed somewhat doubtful, where does the Kaji live? Does it also live in the woods?"

"I suppose we say a creature lives 'in the woods' when we don't really know where it lives. No one really knows where the Chinka lives, for example, but the Kaji lives in cliffs, caves, and deserted places, in creeks, and in water. According to place of habitation, there are two kinds of Kaji: one dwells in water, and the other dwells on dry land. Since the Kaji resembles a man in many respects, we call these two kinds of Kaji 'water man' and 'forest man.' Kajis of the two breeds walk about on the earth from twilight to the cock's crow; afterwards they hide themselves in their own places. At night they wander about here and there and avoid people. If a Kaji of the dry land runs into a man, then he begins to fight with him; the water Kaji does not fight much with men, and I have never heard tell of a water Kaji fighting with a man."

"Perhaps the water Kaji doesn't bother people because it doesn't share a common place of habitation with them?" I offered.

Another added thoughtfully: "When you think about it, only the Kaji really has a home of its own. Chinkas and Alis wander the forests, but Kajis, your 'Kajis of the dry land' anyway," here he nodded to Toma, "live in caves, hollows in cliffs, and in ruins."

I made a mental note to ask what an 𐎂𐎂𐎂 Ali was.

Another added, "in Kajeti, the land of the Kajis, the Kajis do everything backwards, they speak backwards (if one tells the other to destroy a house, the other immediately starts building one). Their feet are also backwards. A Kaji can appear to a human in the form of a beautiful woman or as a horrifying monster. Kajis live in caves, in rock dwellings in cliffs. Kajis also live in the old ruins of houses and abandoned villages and fields. Passing such places at night, a man might be attacked by Kajis. Unseen voices will address the man, calling him by his own name. They can drive a man crazy or throw him from a cliff. At night a passing traveler might see a campfire in a meadow or in the middle of the woods. Around the campfire appear shadows like those of humans."

"This talk of Kajis calling out to you with your own name seems a bit more like something a Chinka would do." I objected and was met with a series of blank stares. I changed the subject. "So there really are two kinds of places where Kajis live, in natural rock dwellings, caves, where saints and holy hermits often live, and old abandoned human dwellings that have reverted to nature, like ruins, while all the other creatures, the Chinka and the Ali — whatever that is — wander the forests without any permanent or specific home."

"Kajis live primarily in caves in cliffs." This from the traveler who thought Kajis were winged. "They have wings so they can fly from cliff to cliff. They can pounce on a man from above and carry him off flying. They have black hair, some with long hair, others with short hair. They have hands and feet like humans. They have children. Their leaders — heads of households — can be male or female Kajis. You can't domesticate a Kaji."

"Now that's interesting. We have spoken of domesticating Chinkas by cutting their nails, why can't you domesticate a Kaji in a similar manner?"

Toma replied, "even though a Kaji can be caught, still it cannot be domesticated, that is, it cannot be kept at home by cutting its hair and toenails, as for example with a Chinka. I can't remember a single example of anyone managing to domesticate a Kaji. Whoever catches a Kaji, it is said, that Kajis will never again come near anyone of their surname."

"One wonders why you can domesticate one and not the other. The Chinka is a bit like a homeless or orphaned child wandering the woods, you can tidy it up by cutting its hair and nails and domesticate it. After all, it seems to want to hang around your house anyway, why not bring it indoors? But Kajis are a different matter entirely. How else can you protect yourself from a Kaji, other than never leaving your home and setting foot on the road?"

Again Toma: "With wine. Look, some Kajis actually pursue humans, you don't always run into them accidently on the road. In such circumstances, if it has caught up with you, you must pour wine for the Kaji, and, because it likes wine a lot, and wine has a greater effect on it, it will not refuse and it will soon become drunk. The moment it gets drunk it falls asleep. Then a man can easily save himself."

I offered a summary: "So while Kajis have homes of their own, you primarily encounter them like any other stranger, on roads, while the Chinka seems to come to your home. One might say that the Kaji is a *stranger* spirit, and the ways of dealing with it are those one uses to deal with strangers, since, after all, drinking wine together, by Georgian custom, is how we turn strangers into friends, and wine is legendarily the stuff of Georgian hospitality, and Georgians will often bring wine with them when traveling to visit friends and relatives. You could say, by contrast, the Chinka is a *familiar* spirit, since it haunts the house and its grounds, perhaps overly familiar, since it always seems to know your name and comes as an uninvited guest. The Kaji isn't so much a *wild* spirit as it is an *alien, foreign, "outsider"* spirit, since we use the term გარეული *gareuli* to mean all these things, it is a haunter of roads and woods, and the Chinka is a *domestic, tame* spirit, a *familiar,* or rather *interior,* spirit, since here we use the term შინაური *shinauri* to mean all these things, it is a haunter of domestic animals, mills, and houses. We fear Kajis on the road in the way we fear strangers, outsiders, in such places, and when at home, we fear the overfamiliarity of Chinkas, who seem like creepy, abusive forest children invading our homes. The Kaji has a home to go to, the Chinka seems like a homeless child living on the margins of your own home. But I digress. Are there any other ways to protect yourself from a Kaji in a chance encounter on the road?"

Again, Toma provided a ready answer. "Well, when we meet strangers on the road, of course we greet them in the usual Georgian fashion: The first to speak says გამარჯობა *gamarjoba!* ('victory!'), and the second must reply, გაგიმარჯოს *gagimarjos!* ('victory to you!') Now when you are out walking on the road at twilight, you see a figure in the gloom, you may well wonder, 'is this a human, or a Kaji?' Then you must beat the Kaji to the punch and greet it first. If it is a human, you are simply defusing the tension with a polite greeting. If it is a Kaji, and if the Kaji forgets itself and answers with the usual response *gagimarjos!* then, as the words themselves imply, the Kaji will lose any subsequent fight. If, however, the Kaji remains silent, the matter of victory in the fight remains in question. Similarly, if the Kaji manages to greet you first, then you must not reply. Kajis seem to be literalists."

"So there are three ways to defeat a Kaji on the road: by offering them wine, an act of hospitality; by greeting them, an act of sociability; and by actually beating them up rather than being beaten up, an act of violence. All of these are things one might do meeting a human stranger on the road, depending on the context. But I had another question: the Chinkas seem to lack homes, and also seem to lack societies, but the Kaji, who has a house of its own to return to, also seems to have a head of the household. Are Chinkas then individual creatures, and the Kaji social creatures?"

Toma answered authoritatively. "Like Chinkas, Kajis physically resemble people, aside from their spines or horns and general horrific ugliness. Like humans, and unlike Chinkas, the Kaji has customs, for example, there are many tales of Kajis lamenting the dead. Kajis even have a political order and social life, too. They have the very same sort of elders as in the society of humans, all members of the household pay deference to the head of the household, who, as we have seen, unlike among us, can be male or female, and they have one main elder, whom all Kajis pay respect to."

"So, while Chinkas seem to be individual unwelcome invaders of human homes and society, living on the margins, in the woods, what makes a Kaji strange is precisely that they are strangers, outsiders, with homes and a whole society of their own, both similar to our own, and also reversed — a human social world turned upside down. Like members of other distant human communities, we meet them as strangers on the road, and not as guests, welcome or otherwise, in the home." Everyone seemed satisfied with my summary.

Of Alis and other female sprites

"I have heard mention of Alis, what's an Ali? Since, like a Chinka, it seems to be a homeless creature wandering the woods, can it be domesticated and provided a home?"

One traveler recited what amounted to a catechism: "An Ali is a young woman of eighteen years of age. She has long, black hair, which reaches her ankles. She doesn't wear any clothing. She's always found standing in water. Sometimes she sits on a rock and combs her hair. If someone manages to steal upon her and cut her hair with scissors, she becomes like an ordinary woman. One can even marry an Ali whose hair has been cut. Nevertheless she always seeks vengeance in the end. If she finds her hair or snippets of her fingernails, she kills the members of the family and flees."

"Has anyone heard any actual stories about Alis being domesticated?"

One traveler had. "I heard a story of a neighboring village where once they stole the hair of an Ali. This made her powerless, so that they could make her do everything. But you had to tell her what you want her to do backwards. If you wanted her to bring something you had to say, 'take it away!' Once the Ali and a child were left alone in the house. The Ali, with the help of the child, found her hair. The Ali threw the child into the middle of the fire, apparently, and then fled screeching."

At this point, another traveler objected to the first man's description of an Ali. "Now what you say about domesticating an Ali is true. Alis have rules. As long as someone has their hair and nails hidden somewhere, they search for them like a precious treasure. If they can't find them, then they submit to their fate and stay with that man, but if they find them, they snatch them and instantly return to the forest. But as far as your description of appearance and habitat, you seem to have mixed up the Ali with a 'water mother,' who, as her name suggests, lives in the water deep in the forest. They are never seen during the day, and they bathe only at night. The water woman has white skin, black hair. Her hair is very long, her body is strikingly beautiful, and she has gold teeth. This creature pursues men, particularly unmarried men. If a man takes up with a water woman, she drives him mad and destroys his family. If a man meets one, he should not speak to her. She will laugh, trying to stun him with her beauty, but he must say nothing to her."

His objection met with another objection from a Mingrelian traveler: "Your 'water woman' is clearly nothing other than what we call in the Mingrelian language a ნყარიშმაფა Tsqarish-mapa, which you could translate into Georgian as 'მაფა *mapa* (queen) of the ნყარიშ *tsqarish* (water).' The დედა *deda* ('mother' of 'water mother') is probably just a short for the Georgian word დედოფალი *dedopali* (queen), but we Mingrelians call her მაფა *mapa* (ruler), which is your Georgian word მეფე *mepe*, the same way that Georgians call their ancient queen Tamar, Tamar *mepe* (King Tamar) because she ruled Georgia in her own right as a king, so the Tqarishmapa rules her watery domain. I have never heard of an Ali with combed hair, but a Tsqarishmapa is always found in the water, combing her long hair which reaches her feet. If you steal the hair of an Ali, as we have said, you can bring her into your home as a wife, but in the case of the Tsqarishmapa, you must steal her comb to achieve the same effect. In either case, it usually ends badly. In the story I heard, the man who married her and had children with her, for some reason one day said to the Tsqarishmapa, 'Why do you want this old comb anyway?' and threw it into the fire. The Tsqarishmapa started shrieking, killed all the children and cursed his family name."

Here Toma interjected. "Seemingly you can achieve power over any female goblin through its hair. Kajis, as is well known, can take the form of beautiful females as well as horrifically ugly monsters. Once, apparently a woman caught such a female Kaji sleeping with her husband. While they were both asleep thus — twined together in the Kaji's long unruly tresses — she put the Kaji's hair in curls. When the Kaji woke up, she was pleased and swore never to bother this man again. But again, a Kaji, even a beautiful female Kaji, is still a Kaji, you cannot domesticate it by putting its unkempt hair in curls or any other way, the best you can hope from a Kaji is that it will leave you alone."

Another traveler, also apparently from Mingrelia, added: "Tsqarishmapas are well-known to treasure their combs, but I have also heard that you can domesticate a ტყაშმაფა Tqashmapa by cutting their hair, much the same as an Ali. I also have never heard of Alis being naked. All such female forest goblins seem to have long hair down to their ankles, whether combed or unkempt, but Alis, generally speaking, are dressed in rags, while a Tqashmapa, for example, is usually dressed in white."

"What is a Tqashmapa?" Toma asked.

"Just as there are land Kajis and water Kajis, so there is the Tsqarishmapa which lives in the water, and the Tqashmapa, Mingrelian for 'forest queen' or 'forest ruler' which lives in the woods alongside other forest creatures like Chinkas. A Tqashmapa is, like an Ali, a beautiful, long-haired woman, but with completely white skin, like your 'water woman.' She is dressed in white, her hair is red and she has eyes that flash like the sun, or a glow-worm. As far as grooming, I've never heard of a Tqashmapa having a special comb, but I do know they wash their hair with milk, so I've always assumed they kept their hair combed, unlike an Ali. However, I've always heard that she actively pursues handsome, young men. If she speaks to you, you must not answer, or you are utterly lost. But you cannot refuse her lust entirely, you must hold up a number of fingers, showing how many years you will live with her. You see, a man can pursue and capture an Ali and bring her home as a wife, but a Tqashmapa instead pursues and captures an attractive, young man and brings them home to live with her as a husband instead."

It seemed we were getting off topic with all these Mingrelian succubae, so I steered the conversation back to Alis. "I have one last question. There seems to be a great deal of disagreement: do Alis have combed hair, or tousled? Are they naked, dressed in rags, or white dresses? Perhaps we can appeal to the authority of an eyewitness account to resolve this. Has anyone actually *seen* an Ali?" I asked.

One man answered. "When I was a child I was always told 'Don't go into the vineyard of Tsibo Lagurashvili, or the Alis will take you away.' 'What's an Ali like?' I asked. They answered me, 'a woman with long, tousled hair.' 'Why are they in the vineyard?' 'They have become accustomed to Tsibo's vineyard, and they refuse to vacate the premises.'"

"I myself have seen an Ali with my own eyes," said another man. "In a neighboring village I had an aunt. I went up there to visit, and in their vineyard, I saw three Alis preening, they wore white dresses, they had tousled hair, their hair reached their feet. I had thought they were young women of our village. When I realized they were not, I became frightened. My aunt told me, 'don't be afraid, they live here.' They vanished presently."

I thought it interesting that Alis seemed to like to hang out in vineyards, much as Chinkas liked hearths and mills, but said nothing.

Another man offered the following account: "Once I myself saw five Alis in the woods outside our village. It was evening. Suddenly, from a nearby ridge, I heard strange peals of laughter and noise. I became interested and went towards it through the woods. When I got close, I saw five women dressed in rags with tousled hair. One was clapping her hands, another was drumming her hands on a large rock, and the other three were leaping here and there, emitting peals of laughter and calling out to each other. The sun had just set. I watched for a while and when I was convinced they were Alis, I got scared and fled."

After this story was told, the sun was rising, and it was time for us to part ways. For a time, the lad accompanied me on the road, and we talked of various things. At some point I realized he was calling me by name, and I turned to him and asked "I don't believe we have been introduced. What is your name? And since we are on the topic, why do you think Chinkas like to poke embers in fires, since you know so much about it?" He shrugged and said, "why does anyone do anything?" and vanished laughing into the woods. I too departed the roads into the woods, and presently came to the home of my queen, who sat combing her beautiful long red hair. "What are the humans saying about us?" you asked with a smiling voice and flashing eyes, and I began, "it was a dark and stormy night…"

Bibliographic Note

The dialog above is constructed out of pieces of real folklore. For the most part, I have left the original voices of the other travelers exactly as they were in the original texts. The frame narrative is drawn directly from a Georgian newspaper account from 1868 of travelers at an inn telling stories of goblins. Most of the additional tales are drawn from the Georgian folklore collection of 1992, Toma's longer speeches from an early Georgian folklore newspaper article of 1888.

This discussion is inspired by a canny observation by Diane Purkiss about fairies:

> What there are is hundreds of different fairy names, and thousands of different fairy stories, but only a few really significant types of fairy in popular culture. [...] There are fairies with *their own household* — who might entertain you or take you as a servant — and fairies *who live in yours*, and who might act as your servants. [...] Both these roles are analogous to human social structures: early modern people knew what it was to be a guest, to be an apprentice in a larger household, to be a servant and to have a servant. Fairy beliefs are filtered through the commonsense of everyday social relationships. (Purkiss 2007, 17, emphasis added)

Like fairies, Georgian goblins are social creatures. They each embody anxieties about specific human social relationships. The Chinka resembles a rude, disobedient, human child, like an adopted orphan or a child taken in as a resentful servant or apprentice in the household. The Ali is a beautiful young woman, basically a walking, talking bundle of male fears and fantasies about female sexuality, strongly resembling ancient Greek nymphs (Vernant and Doueihi 1986) and modern Greek neráïdes (Stewart 1991; 2014).

Again, like fairies, some Georgian goblins have their own homes, and others can end up living in yours, sometimes as an unhappy prisoner, sometimes as an unwelcome intruder. Both Chinkas and Alis lack a specific home, they are said simply to wander the forest, and sometimes they are found in the vicinity of homes of specific people, including mills and vineyards. Both of these are creatures who lack a home of their own but can be forced into resentful servitude in the human home. The hearth and fireplace, in Georgia symbols of settled domesticity par excellence, often play a key role in these narratives; under the hearth is where one hides valuables, including the clippings and hair of the enslaved goblin, and Chinkas seem obsessed with the fire as if it symbolized the very opposite of their forest abode. The Kaji, however, has a home and even a society of its own. It resembles a stranger one meets on the road. Because it has its own home, it can never be domesticated, the ways one deals with it are the ways one deals with strangers one meets on the road who might wish one harm, and the best one can hope for a Kaji is that it will go on its way and bother someone else.

Placing different descriptions of the "same" monster side by side reveals immediately that all folklore is variable. But from these examples, one can see the bodies of monsters vary more than the relationships one can have with them (sometimes Kajis have wings, spines, horns, and so on) but they are always aggressive and cannot be domesticated. But the monstrous form of these bodies, too, can be narrative clues or cues about the kinds of relationships one might have with them (Fogelson 1980; Brightman 1993, 2015; Weismantel 2001, 2005). The Kaji is like many European monsters in that it has affinity with goats, the least domesticated of all domestic animals, both having horns like a goat and the personality of a goat: restless, aggressive, aggravated. The Chinka and Ali are less monstrous, they often have primitivist features, either being nude or dressed in rags, with long unkempt hair, and, presumably, long fingernails. These features are cues that they can be domesticated by grooming them, cutting their hair and nails. The Tqashmapa is in this respect completely unlike the Ali. She has her own home, she is well-groomed, and she takes humans as unwilling husbands but is never taken as an unwilling wife.

"It was a dark and stormy night…" is a conventional or formulaic framing sentence for some North Americans at least (Leguin 1980), that alerts the listeners that this will be a spooky story of ghosts and ghoulies, a campfire story, just as "Once upon a time…" introduces a fairytale. For such a ghost story to be spooky, it has to be told as (if it was) a true story, localized as reasonably contemporary events that happened in the next village down the road, witnessed by the narrator or heard from someone known to the narrator. This is what folklorists call a "legend" as opposed to a "myth" (i.e., stories that take place a long time ago, before the world was as we know it now), nor of "folktale" or "fairytale" (i.e., stories of "once upon a time"). For a classic treatment of how genres of folklore include within them conventionalized "spaces" and "times" see Bascom (1965); for ways that all spooky stories in any media form share these generic properties with legends, see Stewart (1982). Goblins not only have particular times and spaces of haunting (from dusk till dawn, forests, lakes, ruins, mills, vineyards), but they also have narrative space-times. Every culture allots its monsters to different genres, just as it allots them different haunts. Some monsters live only in the distant past of myths, some monsters live only in the other worlds of fairytales, and some monsters, like ghosts, live in legends, that is, "not far from here, but just down the road."

In addition to my work on Georgian goblins, I suppose it's fair to collect here a related set of papers I have written on Transatlantic spectral migrations of ghosts, fairies, and goblins (2005, 2016, 2020), haunted houses and haunted landscapes of the New World (2017), and the "domesticated spirits" of the North American Spiritualist Séance (2018, 2021).

When I wrote this, I decided to treat the project as a kind of Bakhtinian puzzle: how could I suture together the scattered voices of a bunch of folkloric narratives collected at different places and times into a dialog? For the spooky setting of this dialog, I plagiarized a frame narrative of exactly such a dialog of travelers telling ghost stories gathered around a fireplace in a remote mountain inn. In addition, I borrowed a later authoritative ethnographer's voice — Toma is the quoted voice of an actual Georgian ethnographer — summarizing and systematizing such variable and conflicting voices and narratives into a coherent cosmology. These are all standard actors and elements of the folkloric or ethnographic encounter, but here their voices are all equal as guests in the same inn, even the monsters. (I allowed a Chinka to be one of the guests.) I changed some things, the original frame narrative had a dismissive skeptical "scientific" narrator, here I changed the narrator into a "curious" one, but I also made him an unreliable narrator, a spy. The story itself begins and ends with a notorious cliché, indeed, some claim it is the most cliché of all clichés: this is deliberate. The phrase "it was a dark and stormy night" has moved from literary cliché, emblematic of the worst excesses of purple prose, to become the conventional introduction to a "campfire story." My inspiration for using it as the opening and closing is more personal. My own father used to tell such a story around the campfire: "It was a dark and stormy night. Three bandits sat around a campfire. One of the bandits said, Jim, tell us a story, and Jim began, 'it was a dark and stormy night....'"

Bascom, William. 1965. "The Forms of Folklore: Prose Narratives." *The Journal of American Folklore* 78, no. 307 (January–March): 3–20.

Brightman, Robert. 1993. *Grateful Prey: Rock Cree Human-Animal Relationships.* Berkeley: University of California Press.

———. 2015. "And Some Guys Dream Bad Things." *Semiotic Review* 2. https://www.semioticreview.com/ojs/index.php/sr/article/view/23.

Fogelson, Raymond. 1980. "Windigo Goes South: Stoneclad among the Cherokees." In *Manlike Monsters on Trial: Early Records and Modern Evidence,* edited by Marjorie Halpin and Michael M. Ames, 132–51. Vancouver: University of British Columbia Press.

Khalvashi, Tamta, and Paul Manning. 2021. "Human Devils: Affects and Specters of Alterity in Eerie Cities of Georgia." In *Modern Folk Devils: Contemporary Contructions of Evil,* edited by Martin Demant Frederiksen and Ida Harboe Knudsen, 63–79. Helsinki: University of Helsinki Press.

Le Guin, Ursula K. 1980. "It Was a Dark and Stormy Night; Or, Why Are We Huddling about the Campfire?" *Critical Inquiry* 7, no. 1 (Autumn): 191–99. DOI: 10.1086/448094

Manning, Paul. 2005. "Jewish Ghosts, Knackers, Tommyknockers, and Other Sprites of Capitalism in the Cornish Mines." *Cornish Studies* 13, no. 1: 216–55.

———. 2012. *Strangers in a Strange Land: Occidentalist Publics and Orientalist Geographies in Nineteenth-Century Georgia.* Brighton: Academic Studies Press.

———. 2014. "When Goblins Come to Town: The Ethnography of Urban Hauntings in Georgia." In *Monster Anthropology in Australasia and Beyond,* edited by Yasmine Musharbash and Geir Henning Presterudstuen, 161–77. New York: Palgrave Macmillan.

———. 2016. "Pixie's Progress: How the Pixies became Part of the 19th Century Fairy Mythology." In *The Folkloresque: Reframing Folklore in a Popular Culture World,* edited by Michael Dylan Foster and Jeffrey A. Tolbert, 81–103. Logan: Utah State University Press.

———. 2017. "No Ruins. No Ghosts." *Preternature* 61, no. 1: 63–92. DOI: 10.5325/preternature.6.1.0063.

———. 2018. "Spiritualist Signal and Theosophical Noise." *Journal of Linguistic Anthropology* 28, no. 1: 67–92. DOI: 10.1111/jola.12177.

———. 2020. "Goblin Spiders, Ghosts of Flowers and Butterfly Fantasies: Lafcadio Hearn's Transnational, Transmedia and Trans-species Aesthetics of the Weird." *Japan Forum* 32, no. 2: 259–83. DOI: 10.1080/09555803.2019.1676291.

———. 2021. "Spectral Aphasia, Psychical Ghost Stories, and Spirit Post Offices: Three Modern Ghost Stories about Communication Infrastructures." *Signs and Society* 9, no. 2 (Spring): 204–33. DOI: 10.1086/714424.

Purkiss, Diane. 2007. *Fairies and Fairy Stories: A History.* Stroud: Tempus.

Stewart, Charles. 1991. *Demons and the Devil: Moral Imagination in Modern Greek Culture.* Princeton: Princeton University Press.

―――. 2014. "The Symbolism of the Exotika." *Semiotic Review* 2. https://www.semioticreview.com/ojs/index.php/sr/article/view/21.

Stewart, Susan. 1982. "The Epistemology of the Horror Story." *The Journal of American Folklore* 95, no. 375 (January–March): 33–50. DOI: 10.2307/540021.

Vernant, Jean-Pierre, and Anne Doueihi. 1986. "Feminine Figures of Death in Greece." *Diacritics* 16, no. 2 (Summer): 54–64. DOI: 10.2307/465071.

Weismantel, Mary. 2001. *Cholas and Pishtacos: Stories of Race and Sex in the Andes.* Chicago: University of Chicago Press.

―――. 2005. "White." In *Fat: The Anthropology of an Obsession,* edited by Don Kulick and Anne Meneley, 45–62. New York: Penguin Books.

8

A Kappa Manifesto

Translated by Michael Dylan Foster (Human)

EXPLANATORY NOTE

The following is a transcript of a commencement speech given at the 2022 graduation ceremony at Kappa University of Kappa Universal Knowledge, widely recognized as the foremost tertiary educational institution for Kappa in Japan. The address by Dr. Gamishiro-Kawappa-Garappa, a leading Kappa historian and evolutionary theorist, has already assumed legendary status because it neatly summarizes evolutionary history of Kappakind and simultaneously serves as a rallying cry for young Kappa to develop innovative strategies to perpetuate the species.[1]

---

1   Translator's Note: I have studied the secret culture, history, and language of Kappa for over twenty years. Kappa rarely share their writings and philosophies with non-Kappa, so I was surprised when this manuscript, including the opening explanatory note, appeared in my inbox. Though the anonymous senders did not explain their intentions for leaking the document, they urged me to translate it into an appropriate Human language for publication. My only modification was to add several images to further elucidate Dr. G-K-G's argument. I should also note that many *yōkai* mentioned in the Manifesto do not have standardized kanji associated with their names; to avoid confusion I have not included Japanese script.

My fellow Kappa, I congratulate you!

There is a strange old expression in the world of Humans whereby people say they are green with envy. Well, like most of you, I am literally green. But I am also figuratively green with envy — of your youth, your achievements, your potential. You will pave the road for future generations of our species.

And that's what I would like to talk about today: *the future.* Today I want to present you with what I am calling a *manifesto* — a reminder of who we are and how we got here, and with it, a call to act for the continued proliferation of our species. I myself am too old to enact what I am calling for here, but I hope that you will take it to heart and learn from the experiences and wisdom of our ancestors so that our descendants will prosper. Now that you are about to enter the world at large, the future of our species is in your webbed hands. I urge you to be bold.

But before thinking about the future, we must consider the present and the past. Let's begin with color. We are mostly green, a bright green, almost florescent. Certain body parts — like our beak-like mouths — are pastel yellow or some other playful hue (fig. 1). This is how we Kappa have evolved, particularly over the last several decades. We have become cute brightly colored things, employed as mascot characters for towns and businesses, and logos for local rivers and hot spring baths. We are featured on advertisements for shops — banks, dry cleaners, restaurants, you name it. We are clean, and soft, and cuddly. We have become clipart! We smile a lot. I am cute, and so are you.

In other words, these days the popular image of the Kappa — nay, our reality — is that Humans cherish us. We have insinuated ourselves into everyday Human life, even in small ways, such as the Kappa roll at the sushi shop — which is of course named for our love of cucumbers!

But practically speaking, most of our old traits have been forgotten. Sure, many Humans still associate us with rivers and ponds, and remember that the word *kappa* comes from the Japanese meaning "river child" or "river urchin." Some people vaguely remember we have an indent on top of our heads in

Fig. 1. Contemporary Kappa posing as clipart.

which our strength-giving fluid is contained — one spill, and we are bereft of power. For the most part, though, Humans these days don't really care much about our habits and history, our rich Kappa heritage.

But as you know, our Kappa ancestors were very different. We were dangerous water goblins, grotesque and monstrous, green yes, but slimy and mottled like frogs. We lurked in ponds and rivers, ready to drown unsuspecting Humans. Not surprisingly, a lot of old-timers who remember our old ways tend to bridle at the cartoonish characters, the lucky-charm figurines, into which we have mutated. They claim we have let Humans domesticate us, allowed them to strip away our powers as *yōkai* — monstrous creatures from folk belief. Now we are nothing more than playthings for Human children, loveable mascots, or malleable advertising icons for Human businesses. Humans have de-monsterized us, sapped us of agency, made us into objects. We are no longer "authentic" or "real" monsters, no longer the authors of our own futures.

This is the conventional wisdom.

So what I will say today may seem subversive because, I argue, we are just as authentic now as we have ever been. Like all monsters, like all Humans for that matter, our species is a work in progress, endlessly evolving. Most importantly, I argue, Humans have *not* manipulated us; rather we Kappa have taken advantage of Human culture to keep our species alive, indeed, to thrive in this monster-eat-monster world. By closely reading the desires and needs of our Human host society, as fickle as it may be, we have triumphed in the evolutionary battle against many of our rival *yōkai*.

When we consider our past, we need to remember the original source of our power: long ago we were really scary. We were *deadly*. We had to be, because those were violent times, and violence was the only way to grab Human attention. Our first mention in Human documents was in the *Nihonshoki* of 720, the second oldest Japanese book. In the year 379, that book explains, there was a creature called a Mizuchi living in a river in Kibi Province. It was a lethal troublemaker: "Now when travelers were passing that place on their journey they were surely affected by its poison, so that many died." (I quote here from the very atmospheric 1896 English translation by W.G. Aston.)

A Mizuchi is one of us, an early form to be sure, but a clearly identifiable ancestor of the modern-day Kappa. That was how we made our formal entrance into the Human arena — as a despised and murderous water monster. Hah! And if you read that document carefully, you get a sense that this was not the first time such a thing had happened. Kappa — or rather Mizuchi — were a known entity, a serious force to be reckoned with.

But this is where things get tricky, because if you read the rest of that entry for the year 379, you see why we were mentioned in the first place. What happened was that there was a brave man in the region, an exceedingly fierce fellow for a Human, who flung three calabashes into the water and yelled, "Thou art continually belching up poison and therewithal plaguing travelers. I will kill thee.... If thou canst sink these calabashes, then will I take myself away, but if thou canst not sink them, then will I cut up thy body." In those days, we Kappa despised cala-bashes, what you kids call gourds. They were our kryptonite! It's actually quite interesting that we hated gourds, especially given our love of cucumbers. Similar kind of vegetable, of course, but cucumbers are full of water, while dried gourds are hollow and buoyant — they are, you might say, anti-water and therefore a powerful weapon against us water-born Kappa... but I digress. My point is that the Mizuchi couldn't sink the gourds, and the gutsy Human sliced him up. Our first official appearance in Human history ended in defeat and humiliation.

What are the lessons here? Well, the most important thing to remember, my friends, is that like most monsters, we Kappa thrive as concepts in the minds of Humans. Our very lives are premised on interaction with Humans, on our ability to culti-vate relationships, to stimulate Human imagination so that peo-ple *think* about us. The classic way to do this is through fear. This was long our modus operandi. Scare them, and it sticks with them, infecting their dreams. Humans are obsessed with monsters: they tell stories about us, warn of places where we lurk, develop methods of avoiding us.

Kappa historians speculate that this was the case with Mi-zuchi before that fateful day in 379. Whenever people came to a river, they imagined a scary water creature lurking just under the surface, and these thoughts gave us life.

But their next thought was that we could be conquered, and this was a big move for the Humans, so monumental they re-corded it. The *Nihonshoki* — like most of the stories Humans tell — is not about us, not about nature, not about anything ex-cept Humans. Being written about in this context, as part of *Human* history, was an epoch-making moment for us: it ensured that Kappa would be part of the permanent documentary re-cord.

But it was an ambiguous honor. We made it into the book not because of our viciousness, but because we were conquered — and by some guy just tossing a few gourds into the river! Kappa historians are conflicted about this moment. Some consider it a tremendous defeat for our species, a sign that Humans would always dominate us. But I would posit that, in fact, this was a brilliantly calculated move on the part of our ancestors, a fine example of adaptive mutation and a harbinger of future success. Those ancient Mizuchi understood that the technology of writing would someday rival the spoken word, and they also realized that the only way to become part of the Human record was to occasionally allow themselves to be defeated — because Humans are obsessed with their own triumphs. I think of this early unnamed Mizuchi as a sort of unknown soldier who gave his life so that future generations might thrive. His sacrifice in the past made our present possible.

I won't go on about this early case, but you get the point. Remember, we live in Human media and rely on Human modes of communication. Making it into the *Nihonshoki,* such a foundational text for Humans in Japan, was a remarkable achievement. Even today, people read and study this book, though, sadly, they often skip the Mizuchi part.

For a long time after we made our mark, however, you don't see much of us in written records, especially from the Heian period (794–1185) through the end of the Muromachi period (1336–1573). I have a theory about this. I think we were doing just fine, prospering and multiplying, but we did so by living in small rural communities and causing problems locally. People thought about us plenty. They told legends about us and warned their kids not to go swimming in the places we might lurk, but these people didn't do much writing. It was the Humans in the capital, the elites and sophisticates and the fancy nobility, who were the ones doing the writing. And they were much more focused on big flashy creatures, charismatic mega-monsters like Oni, those horned demons who would come down from the mountains and steal the daughters of court officials. Oni are about as savvy as Kappa when it comes to getting talked about, but with their horns, their tiger-skin loincloths, and their iron staffs, they are more flamboyant. My point is that during this time our Kappa ancestors thought it better to live in rural communities, where they would prosper in oral lore — that was the medium of our existence in those days.

In fact, this local existence gave us a chance to experiment and develop some of our quirkiest, our most monstrous, characteristics. Up north in the Tōhoku region, for example, we would yank horses into the water and drown them — what better way to get the attention of Humans? And in a lot of places, we would kill children. Yes, my friends, those rumors about the nasty exploits of our ancestors are quite true. All the more ironic that we are such a favorite among kids today! When a young boy was reckless enough to swim alone in a pond or slow-moving river, one of our ancestors would pull him down by the heel, drown the little bugger, and then reach up through his anus to yank out his vital organs! Apparently — though I don't know this from firsthand experience — they were delicious. We were so successful in those days that we were given credit for almost any drowned child, even when we had nothing to do with it. It certainly helped that our method of killing was violent and disgusting. Humans are perversely fascinated with blood and gore, and such details stick in their minds.

We also became famous for our immense strength, due to the liquid in the cavity on our heads. To remain in the media — that is, to be the subject of folktales and legends — we had to show off our strength in creative ways. So we started challenging random passersby to sumō, that utterly ridiculous Human sport. We let it be known that they could only win if they got us to bow and thereby spill our precious strength-giving liquid. Our ancestors, you see, were very calculating about everything they did. They skillfully manipulated Human narratives to focus on tales not only of our exploits but also of our follies and foibles, to make us more likeable, or as the Humans might say, to make us more *Human*. To them we were somehow familiar but not quite Human — walking upright but living in the water — which made us curiously ambiguous and therefore unforgettable.

We Kappa also kept up a strategy of localization. Yes, many of the characteristics I am mentioning here were common to all of us, but we also made sure to keep our narratives localized to specific ponds or rivers. This made Humans in any given village feel they were somehow special, the only ones who knew our stories.

And accordingly, we also went by different names. All monsters are probably like this, especially in Japan, but in our case the names were legion — literally thousands of them. Every community had its own moniker for its local water goblin: Kawatarō, Kawako, Suiko, Enkō, Garappa, Komahiki, Dangame, Gameshiro, and the list goes on. The names are not important in and of themselves, but they show how people identified us with local places and specific stories. Sometimes they explicitly reflected our special traits, like Komahiki — used in the Tōhoku region — which means "horse-puller" in the Japanese vernacular.

During this period, we worked hard on the village level. In some places our ancestors even channeled legends about us into forms of worship. People made shrines to their local Kappa and gave us offerings of our favorite foods — cucumbers, eggplants, and so on. Those were halcyon days, and we were certainly well fed! Remember, this is how we survive — by remaining relevant in the minds of Humans — making them think about us, fear us, worship us, whatever it takes, so long as they care about our existence.

Things were good until the Edo period (1603–1868) when these local strategies started to break down, and we had to adjust to changing Human habits. Humans were traveling more and moving to urban centers — like Osaka and Kyoto, and especially Edo, which they now call Tokyo. And when Humans met other Humans from different parts of the country, they told stories about us, compared notes and names and all the things we were known for doing. People realized that there were all these creatures living in the water causing mischief (that is, having fun!) and sometimes killing kids and horses, but they all had different names and slightly different characteristics.

The other big change was technology. It became a lot cheaper for Humans to print books and pictures, and a lot of people were now able to read. Suddenly they were writing down those local stories about us. This was a tough time in our history because we were competing with a lot of other monsters, like Kitsune (foxes), Tanuki (raccoon dogs), Mikoshi-nyūdō, Rokurokubi, Nuppeppō, Raijū, Kamikiri, Nekomata, and even Tōfu-kozō, that weird little boy carrying a brick of tofu. Take note, my friends, that some of these have fallen by the wayside — Kamikiri and Nuppeppō, for example, are only known today by serious *yōkai* aficionados. Others like Kitsune and Tanuki are still common, but they have the distinct advantage of being real animals you can put in a zoo. Kappa, on the other hand, must survive in people's minds despite the fact that nobody has ever captured one of us in the wild.

But I am getting ahead of myself here. These other *yōkai* didn't start fading away until the twentieth century. Back in the Edo period they prospered, mostly because of the new print media that flooded the market. There were all sorts of books, everything from serious encyclopedias to lighthearted illustrated works, like the manga of today. Kappa did a decent job of keeping our place in the media, but we made compromises. In some places, we kept to the old pattern of causing trouble and then letting ourselves be "conquered." There were a lot of stories like the one in which the wife of a doctor goes to the outhouse, and a Kappa reaches out of the toilet to stroke her buttocks. She runs and gets the doctor. He grabs a sword and exclaims, "I'll go conquer this thing!" When a hand reaches out of the hole, he grabs it and chops it off — or in some stories, he just yanks it out of the arm socket. (I know this is painful for you to hear, but remember, this was all a sort of game to the Kappa of old.)

The next evening, the Kappa knocks at the front door and asks the doctor to return his arm, explaining that if he doesn't apply medicine and reattach it right away, he won't be able to reattach it at all. After some negotiation, the doctor gives the arm back, but in exchange the Kappa teaches him our secret knowledge of bone-setting — something all of you learned way back in high school. With this newfound medical technique, the doctor prospers as an orthopedic specialist.

An interesting story, of course, but I assume you are starting to realize it was all part of a pattern, a moment in our evolution like that Mizuchi episode in the *Nihonshoki*. In this case, notice how we have gradually transformed from malicious to merely perverse, from killing kids to stroking buttocks in the toilet! Our behavior was more appropriate for the comparatively peaceful days of the Edo period — still troubling for Humans, but a little less, shall we say, murderous. This is all a manipulation of Human desires for the sake of our own survival. The story gives the doctor — and by extension all Humans — a sense of superiority over Kappa, but it does not annihilate us. In fact, for generations to come, Humans will attribute the doctor's medical success, and that of his descendants, to his encounter with a Kappa — we become part of this Human family's history and part of village lore. Again, this little story, and many like it all over Japan, kept us in the minds of Humans.

Let me return to the explosion of print media. Humans were becoming interested in knowledge and information — collecting it, organizing it, writing it down. So we made sure to get in on the action. You might have heard about the great encyclopedia called the *Wakansansaizue*? It was written sometime around 1715 by a Human named Terajima Ryōan who knew a lot about medicine and pretty much everything else. There were entries on animals and plants, buildings, foreign countries, you name it. He included even a section dedicated to strange creatures. Most of the entries there were unfocused, in my opinion, with references to all sorts of old Chinese texts and other works. But there was also an entry on Kappa, with no outside references at all — just a straight description (fig. 2):

About the size of a ten-year-old child, the Kawatarō stands and walks naked and speaks in a Human voice. Its hair is short and sparse. The top of its head is concave and can hold a scoop of water. Kawatarō usually live in the water but in the light of the late afternoon, many emerge into the area near the river and steal melons, eggplants, and things from the fields. By nature, the Kawatarō likes sumō; when it sees a person, it will invite him to wrestle.... If there is water on its head, the Kawatarō has several times the strength of a warrior....

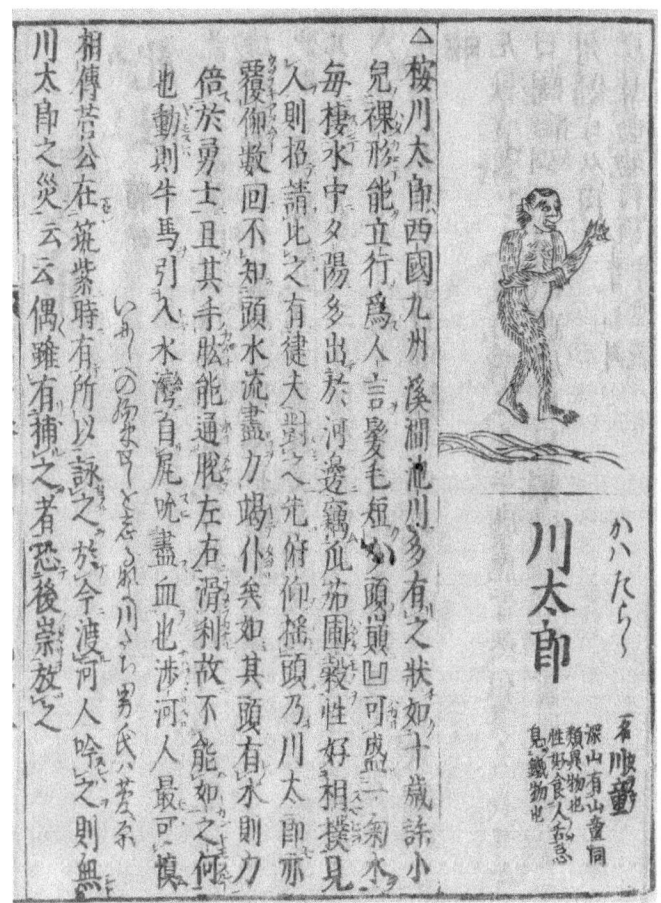

Fig. 2. "Kawatarō" entry in Terajima Ryōan, *Wakansansaizue*, vol. 40.
National Diet Library Digital Collections.

The Kawatarō has a tendency to pull cattle and horses into the water and suck blood out of their rumps. People crossing rivers must be very careful....

Did you notice anything interesting about this description? First, clearly this Terajima guy had done his homework and collected a lot of the brilliant characteristics we had developed over the years. He evidently contacted people from all over Japan and synthesized the local ideas we had promulgated.

The other thing you might have noticed is that he didn't use the word "Kappa," but instead called this creature a "Kawatarō." Of course, Kawatarō is one of the many names we used in those days, particularly in the Kansai region, down near Kyoto and Osaka — turns out Terajima himself was from Osaka. And if you read that description carefully, you might also notice there is no mention of shells or webbed feet or many of the other attributes we celebrate today. That's because, as I suggested earlier, before the Edo period Kappa developed a little differently everywhere. Generally speaking, in the west near Kyoto and Osaka, we were a bit closer to monkeys. And in the east, in Edo and the Tōhoku region, we were more turtle-like. This diversity was fine in the old days, but with the rapid expansion of print media, it posed a problem. What if we got split up, thought of as different creatures — a Kawatarō here, a Kappa there, an Enkō over there? We might soon be forgotten altogether.

We had to form a united front. Clearly there were two major divisions, the Kawatarō faction in the west and the Kappa faction in the east. It was also apparent that the east, by which I mean Edo, was taking the lead in the cultural world of Humans. So some of the Kappa living in Edo managed to work their way into the thoughts of a fellow named Toriyama Sekien. He was an artist, and the first Human to systematically catalogue the various *yōkai* in Japan. We got him to draw a nice eastern Kappa — looking a bit like a turtle with webbed feet — and put it way up front in his first book. But here is the key: the caption reads, "Kappa, also called Kawatarō" (fig. 3).

Fig. 3. "Kappa, also called Kawatarō," Toriyama Sekien, *Hyakkiyagyō,* 1805 [1776]. National Diet Library Digital Collections.

This was a critical evolutionary moment for us. It united the two factions, and for all intents and purposes brought those various stories and different characteristics together under one easy-to-remember name: *Kappa*. Now that there was no fear of fracturing into dozens of forgettable subgroups, it was simply up to us to keep the Kappa image and name in the Human mind.

The Meiji period, which began in 1868, was another make-or-break time for us. This was the advent in Japan of what Humans call modernity. Suddenly they started mass manufacturing things, opening factories, using guns, building a new educational system, running huge steam-belching trains throughout the country. It was a scary time for us and all the other *yōkai* because, among other things, they started importing Western scientific knowledge and skepticism. Throughout the Edo period, we Kappa had managed to walk a fine line through the Human mind, simultaneously appearing as characters in print media and continuing to live as real, believable entities in local villages. But during the Meiji period, with its celebration of "rationalism," some people began claiming that we didn't exist at all, that scientifically speaking, there was no evidence we ever had. Just because they couldn't lock us up in a zoo or dissect us on an examining table, they claimed we weren't real!

This is where we really started working with the process of adaptive mutation. A few of our very cunning ancestors figured out that if you can't beat them, you'd better join them. Well, they didn't literally join Humans — a horrifying thought! — but they convinced Humans to see us as Humans — or rather as metaphors for Humans. Surprisingly, this was a relatively easy maneuver because Humans are naturally self-obsessed; whatever they pretend to be talking about, they are really just talking about themselves. So, we insinuated ourselves into the minds of people, particularly the artistic and literary classes, who began to think of Kappa as Human proxies. Allowing ourselves to be taken — or rather mistaken — for metaphoric Humans was a critical evolutionary step.

There are numerous examples of how this played out, such as the famous author Akutagawa Ryūnosuke, who wrote a short novel simply called *Kappa* about a Human who falls into Kappa-land — but all the Kappa characters are stand-ins for Humans. Pretty soon artists started drawing us, and we were used for ads for all sorts of things. For example, a man named Kojima Kō loved to draw sexy female Kappa; they looked just like Human women except for the powder blue saucers on their heads and the long fancily patterned shells on their backs, like fashionable dresses. Some of these Kappa helped advertise a famous sake company, so we achieved widespread visibility and a cheerful association with alcohol. As you all know, in the old folklore and even many of the Edo-period books, we Kappa were generally male, so thanks to Mr. Kojima, and another artist named Shimizu Kon, we also came to be thought of as females, and sexy ones at that! Despite their explicitness — or perhaps because of it — these images made us much more memorable in the minds of Humans.

What I want to stress here is that Kappa were starting to be seen as attractive and desirable creatures. By the mid-twentieth century, we had outpaced all other *yōkai* in popularity, except maybe Tanuki and Kitsune. We were no longer deadly and disgusting. We were beloved. Our image in the Human imagination had flipped 180 degrees.

Next came our *pièce de résistance*: we made ourselves irresistibly cute. As you realize by now, most of our adaptive mutations, our evolutionary developments, were strategically calculated. Our cuteness is no exception. We read the tea leaves, as it were, and we studied history. We noticed that over the last several decades, as Japan became wealthier and more consumer oriented, girls and boys were developing a tremendous desire for cute things (*kawaii,* they call it) — plush toys, characters like Hello Kitty and Anpanman, little lucky charms and figurines to hang on their bags or cell phones. We Kappa started refashioning ourselves to fit this aesthetic. We remained green, but we modified our slimy rubbery look to a more rounded and full coloration; now our greenness is lush like a manicured lawn, not blotchy like rotting seaweed.

And a group of our finest historians discovered several *yōkai* who weren't very popular in the old days but were making a comeback now because of cuteness. I am thinking, for example, of the Kasa-bake or umbrella monster, who dances around on one leg. Nothing really effective about him — not the slightest bit spooky — but in the late twentieth century, he became popular again because of his sheer goofiness. We learned from this, and soon the cutest of our own species, those squishy cuddly Kappa completely lacking in sliminess, were in ascendency. Indeed, they have prospered, reproducing with abandon. They appear as charming characters on kids shows, where they flop around the stage singing and dancing with Humans. I do not say this disparagingly. No not at all. This is a wonderful trick of evolution, a transformation of the most profound sort. After all, who would ever harm a cuddly Kappa?

We have even made ourselves useful to Humans for their own causes. There are dozens of villages across Japan where we are employed as local mascots or community icons. Imagine that — the very creatures that used to kill people are now so loveable we attract tourists! Similarly, even though we used to represent, or rather *be,* the dangers lurking beneath the water's surface, now we are used as symbols of clean rivers — so natural and unpolluted that the Kappa have moved back! We have come a long way from the days of the Mizuchi when they wanted to banish us from these same rivers.

Of course, this evolution has led to a somewhat generic appearance, and as I mentioned in the beginning, many of our most distinctive features have been forgotten. Few people remember how we used to lurk in the toilet. Or drown kids and eat their entrails. Or even how we were known for the potency of our farts! These days people don't even remember how much we despise gourds. (Fortunately, they *do* remember our fondness for cucumbers!)

This is where we stand now, my friends. We are prospering in a society that cherishes manga and cartoons, toys, stuffed animals, and giant mascot characters. In contemporary Japan, many *yōkai* have faded into obscurity. Who but folklore afficionados and monster *otakus* remember Tenjōname, Himamushi-nyūdō, or Hyōsube? Even once-popular Human-like monsters like Mikoshi-nyūdō and Yamawarō have been relegated to specialty knowledge. These species, I dare say, are on life support, all but forgotten in the minds of the Humans on whose memories and imaginations we depend.

My point is that we Kappa have assumed a uniquely secure position, with one foot in local folklore and another in the popular commercial culture of contemporary Japan. We may occupy a larger space in Human minds today than at any time in our long history.

But this is no reason to rest on our lotus leaves or sit back and put up our webbed feet. Popular culture, and our species with it, never stops evolving. We face dangers on all sides — new anime and manga characters, CG film heroes and demons, robots, and cyborgs. All these things threaten our food supply, as it were, the limited fertile fields of the Human imagination. We are competing for attention in the minds of Humans who were weaned on Studio Ghibli, and who think that Totoro or No-Face is a *yōkai* of equivalent proportions to a Kappa. Despite our current popularity, we are in a precarious situation.

And that is why I implore you now, as the next generation of Kappa innovators, to take action! I call on you to mobilize the skills and knowledge you have acquired here at our finest university to be fearless in your pursuit of the future. For your future is the future of our species.

In my talk today I have recounted our storied history because I want you to remember this history, remember how much we have changed, and remember mostly that innovative Kappa have been the agents of this change. Now it is your turn. Do not be complacent with the status quo! You must react creatively to the ever-shifting Human cultural environment. A Kappa is not a static entity — like any successful monster, we must reinvent ourselves constantly to reflect the concerns of the moment. I cannot tell you where the fickle Human mind will take that species, but it is there that you must make yourselves known — you must explore the hollows of Human desire. This is my call to action: for all of you young innovators to think outside the pond, to infiltrate the Human world and discover new niches in which to proliferate.

I will leave the specifics up to you. But before I conclude today, let me alert you to one critical place that, in my opinion, we have failed — and our success there may be essential to our future. We have not been good at hacking the latest Human technologies. Our Tanuki rivals have managed to get a spot in that Human game called Mario Bros., but not us. Pokémon has introduced many new *yōkai,* and despite their shallow, commercial history, Pikachu and his friends threaten our place in the imagination of young Human folk. Same with Yo-kai Watch and Jibanyan, although a few clever Kappa have succeeded in making it into this franchise! My point is that we can — we *must* — learn from these new technologies and forms of communication.

Perhaps there is a future for us in virtual reality? Imagine goggles that would allow Humans to see wild Kappa in every river or pond! And what about AI? A wise Kappa robot to teach Human children how to swim, for example? Or maybe we should expand beyond the confines of this country called Japan. To be sure, we have started the great transcultural trek — remember our small (yet fabulous) appearance in the *Harry Potter* series? — but we have to be more aggressive. We must become monsters of a global scale, known by all, like dragons or vampires or even our gigantic awkward cousin, Godzilla. At the very least, we need to promulgate Kappa emojis or memes to keep us in the public eye when so many of these eyes are looking at small screens.

These are just random musings of a withered old Kappa, but *you* my friends, *you* are the ones with the vision to see beyond the confines of our rivers and ponds. You are the disrupters — future generations are counting on you to take our species in surprising and innovative new directions, as we create our evolutionary path. Yes indeed, I am asking you to think big and perhaps, like our Mizuchi ancestor, sacrifice yourselves for the well-being of all of us. We Kappa have a long and heralded past, and with your leadership, your vision, your energy, we will be the monsters of the future.

Bibliographic Note

This creative essay was inspired by research on Japanese folklore that I have pursued ethnographically and through library and archival sources. There is no space here to list the numerous excellent works in Japanese that document the history of Kappa and other folkloric creatures, but one outstanding example is Nakamura (1996). Interested readers can also access my own books on the subject (Foster 2009, 2015) and the detailed bibliographies therein. Both of my books (especially 2009) explore the ways in which understandings of monsters, and therefore the monsters themselves, change over time in Japan. For analysis of how monsters transform in other cultural contexts, see the insightful essays in Musharbash and Presterudstuen (2020) and also the classic work by Daston and Park (1998). For broader theoretical approaches to the concept of transformation, see for example, Foucault (1972) and White (1972). Although branding, commercial products, popular culture and other media articulations are often deeply influenced by folkloric ideas, images, and precedents, surprisingly little work has been done explicitly analyzing these connections, but see for example Foster and Tolbert (2016). My intention throughout this essay was to explore the complex symbiosis between human history and how we think of monsters — in terms of belief, media, narrative, etc. The idea to flip the perspective and consider how monsters manipulate us as much as we manipulate them was loosely inspired by Michael Pollan's classic, *The Botany of Desire* (2001), which suggests the agency of plants in their own evolution. Of course, the responsibility for any historical or interpretive errors falls on myself and Dr. Gamishiro-Kawappa-Garappa.

Akutagawa, Ryūnosuke. 1971. *Kappa: A Novel.* Translated by Geoffrey Bownas. Rutland: Charles E. Tuttle.

Aston, William G. trans. 1972. *Nihongi: Chronicles of Japan from the Earliest Times to A.D. 697.* 2 Vols. Tokyo: Tuttle Classics.

Daston, Lorraine, and Katherine Park. 1998. *Wonders and the Order of Nature, 1150–1750*. New York: Zone Books.

Foster, Michael Dylan. 2009. *Pandemonium and Parade: Japanese Monsters and the Culture of Yōkai*. Berkeley: University of California Press.

Foster, Michael Dylan. 2015. *The Book of Yōkai: Mysterious Creatures of Japanese Folklore*. Oakland: University of California Press.

Foster, Michael Dylan, and Jeffrey A. Tolbert, eds. 2016. *The Folkloresque: Reframing Folklore in a Popular Culture World*. Logan: Utah State University Press.

Foucault, Michel. 1972. *The Archaeology of Knowledge and the Discourse on Language*. Translated by A.M. Sheridan Smith. New York: Pantheon.

Musharbash, Yasmine, and Geir Henning Presterudstuen, eds. 2020. *Monster Anthropology: Ethnographic Explorations of Transforming Social Worlds through Monsters*. London: Bloomsbury Academic.

Nakamura, Teiri. 1996. *Kappa no Nihonshi*. Tokyo: Nihon Editaasukūru shuppanbu.

Pollan, Michael. 2001. *The Botany of Desire: A Plant's-Eye View of the World*. New York: Random House.

Terajima, Ryōan. 1994. *Wakansansaizue*, Vol. 6. Tokyo: Heibonsha.

White, Hayden. 1972. "The Forms of Wildness: Archeology of an Idea." In *The Wild Man Within: An Image in Western Thought from the Renaissance to Romanticism*, edited by Edward Dudley and Maximillian E. Novak, 3–38. Pittsburgh: University of Pittsburgh Press.

9

How to Make (and Possibly Un-Make) a Digital Monster

Jeffrey A. Tolbert

QUOTiDIAN CULTURE

The Blog of Dr. Richard L.H. Morgan

October 27th, 2017

Just in Time for Halloween: Making Monsters!

Posted by <u>Rick</u> in Categories: Digital Ethnography; Expressive Culture. Tagged: Halloween; Monsters.

I'm working on a new article about digital monsters. With the craze surrounding Slender Man over the past few years, and my interest in issues like emergence and collaboration in expressive culture, I've decided to try an experiment using this blog as the "laboratory." In fact, let's run with that analogy: I'm a mad (social) scientist making a monster, and I want your help! Let's put our heads together and see if we can create our very own terrifying digital monster, something that seems frightening and also plausible (whatever that means). Let's do it... *for science!*

Since this is for a scholarly paper, there are a few key questions I want to consider:

- What does it take to make a successful Creepypasta? (Creepypasta are those horror pictures and stories that have been popular online for ages now, like Slendy and Jeff the Killer.)
- What makes a digital monster scary?
- What causes it to reach meme proportions?
- How does a given Internet community — in this case, you, my dear readers — go about creating something they can agree on?
- And why would anybody want to do this in the first place? (Aside from having an anthropologist ask them to, that is!)

Keep in mind, we're not trying to trick or scare anybody — the idea isn't to actually create the next Slender Man. The idea is just to create something that you all feel would work as a digital monster, something with meme potential, so to speak.

[Please note: Since this is an academic study and is intended for publication, I have to adhere to human subjects protection guidelines from my university. Click here for more info on this study and what your involvement will entail.]

Post your ideas in the comments!

54 readers like this.

COMMENTS

Posted October 27th, 2017 10:58pm by ManxMan_1977
This is a great idea, Rick! Lots of fun and interesting too. I'll think about it — stuff like Slender Man gives me the creeps.

But I think it's more fun to be involved in making it than just reading about it.

> *Rick replied October 28th, 2017 8:15am*
> Thanks, ManxMan, and nice to see you again! Looking forward to hearing your ideas!

Posted October 27th, 2017 11:10pm by Jinxy
love it. I always though that what made Slendy scary was how it wasn't only online. Or it was, but it went across a lot of different places, like forum posts and YouTube videos and such. Like it was everywhere, you couldnt escape it, and there were those games too, video games and alternate reality games where you had to like decode messages and stuff.

> *Rick replied October 28th, 2017 8:17am*
> Interesting, Jinxy, thanks! I played one of those video games — very scary.

Posted October 28th, 2017 12:37am by Vrblogger
I'm not sure what kind of article you could write from this. Is this how anthropologists do research now? I mean, I guess it's okay, but shouldn't you be out in the bush somewhere and not just sitting at your keyboard?

> *Rick replied October 28th, 2017 8:18am*
> Fair questions. Anthropologists study all humans, though. And sometimes we do digital ethnography too — studying online cultures. That's what this is about. Seems like at my keyboard is the best place to study Internet culture! Also, my PhD is in anthro, but I teach in a Media Studies department. ;)

Posted October 28th, 2017 7:31am by Sheeple
Cool idea! I'm on my way to work but I'll definitely post something later. I have a blog too and I've actually written a

few short horror stories. I agree with Jinxy that these things are scarier when they're multi-media. Like, you read about something in a forum, then go watch the video on YouTube or whatever. Then, maybe, you're cursed! Something like that.

> *Rick replied October 28th, 2017 8:20am*
> Thanks, Sheeple! Kind of like Sonic.exe, huh?

>> *Sheeple replied Octobert 28th 2017 6:44pm*
>> Yeah, that was a good one!

[*See more comments*]

October 29th, 2017

Making Monsters: Let's Get to Work!

Posted by Rick in Categories: Digital Ethnography; Expressive Culture. Tagged: Halloween; Monsters.

Hi everyone! Glad that there's so much interest in this. Let's use this post to actually build our Creepypasta monster! Feel free to post images and text in the comments here.

As I've mentioned, I'm really interested in the idea of *emergence.* That's just a complicated way of saying that I'm interested in how, through conversation here on the blog, the things we all come up with influence the *other* things we come up with, how everything works together (or doesn't) to shape a narrative or narratives about scary stuff. So don't be afraid to be critical (though please don't be mean!). The idea is to see if we can agree on something scary.

Looking forward to making a monster with you all!

67 readers like this.

COMMENTS

Posted October 29th, 2017 5:42pm by <u>*Jinxy*</u>
Here's some text to get us started.

I was thirteen when I first saw the creature. It was just sitting there at the end of my family's driveway. It sat there for three days. Nobody saw it but me. I could feel its eyes on me even when I was in the house, away from any window. Only I saw it, and it seemed to see only me.

> <u>*SoAndSo*</u> *replied October 29th, 2017 8:51pm*
> Nice jinxy I like it

> <u>*ManxMan_1977*</u> *replied October 29th, 2017 9:14pm*
> [Ooo, I like it too. Mind if I run with it?]

I don't know what it wanted or what it was. It didn't have a clear shape; it was just a sort of darkness, though I felt there was something feline about it. It never moved, night or day, for the three days of its visit. I avoided it as best I could, though we had to pass it as we left home on the way to school or running errands. My parents never saw it, but when we passed it I felt as though its unseen head swiveled to watch me. On the third day, as my mother was bustling us out of the house on the way to school, I worked up the nerve to approach it. I poked a finger at the spot I imagined its face would be, if it had one. It disappeared, not in a puff or a flash: it was just gone. The next day there was a shooting at my brother's high school. He died in the gym, where panicky teachers had herded most of the student body. I never saw the creature again.

> <u>*Sheeple*</u> *replied October 29th, 2017 10:51pm*
> ManxMan, you're a really good writer. I think this is too much like things we've seen before, though. It's like

a fetch or a black dog or a banshee. Death messengers aren't scary. I think we should make something new.

> *SoAndSo replied October 29th, 2017 11:04pm*
> what come on manxman that was good, dont be that way, this isnt 4chan

>> *Sheeple replied October 29th, 2017 11:11pm*
>> What are you talking about, SoAndSo? I'm not flaming him, I'm just suggesting we try something different.

Posted October 29th, 2017 9:57pm by Frictionless
I like this idea. Here's my contribution:

What do you think?

> *Jinxy replied October 29th, 2017 10:39pm*
> I love it! Nice job!

>> *Sheeple replied October 29th, 2017 11:01pm*
>> See, again, I think it's just too familiar. It's a kind of big-foot/werewolf thing.

>>> *Jinxy replied October 29th, 2017 11:07pm*
>>> Man, you're so negative. ;p

SoAndSo replied October 29th, 2017 11:09pm
dude that's just a stock image lol like we should write
a story about the MS word paperclip guy that would
be terrifying

Sheeple replied October 29th, 2017 11:16pm
Hah!

Rick replied October 29th, 2017 11:31pm
It does look a little like a stock image. But it's a
good place to start!

Rusty replied October 30th, 2017 12:13am
The scariest thing I can think of is Mr. Top Hat. I played that
game as a kid and it terrified me. I used to dream that he appeared in my house. I heard years later that other kids had
the same dreams. One kid I knew disappeared after playing
the game.

SoAndSo replied October 30th, 2017 12:18am
lol wtf

Jinxy replied October 30th, 2017 12:21am
This has potential! What game are you talking about,
Rusty?

Rusty replied October 30th, 2017 12:27am
You never played it? I guess I'm older than most on
here, heh. It was an Atari game in the early '80s. Mr.
Top Hat was a bad guy, and something about him was
just really scary.

SoAndSo replied October 30th, 2017 12:30am
lol is this real or are you just making creepypasta

Sheeple replied October 30th, 2017 12:32am
[Dude just roll with is, this is good.]

Rusty replied October 30th, 2017 12:33am
It's real, SoAndSo. I'll post more about it tomorrow, heading to sleep now.

Rick replied October 30th, 2017 6:57am
Interesting! I like that you're tying it to your own experience. Is that necessary to make these stories scarier, do you think?

Sheeple replied October 30th, 2017 7:06am
I think so. Makes it more real if the backstory is from your own life. None of that "friend-of-a-friend" stuff like with urban legends.

Rusty replied October 30th, 2017 8:41am
I don't know about all that — I'm just telling it like I remember it.

Rick replied October 30th, 2017 9:02am
Ah, gotcha. ;)

[*See more comments*]

October 30th, 2017

Making Monsters: Mr. Top Hat

Posted by Rick *in Categories: Digital Ethnography; Expressive Culture. Tagged: Halloween; Monsters; Mr. Top Hat*

There was some great discussion last night. A lot of great ideas were floated, and lots of people also contributed their thoughts on the work of others. This is great! It really illustrated the kind of collaboration I'm interested in learning more about, with everyone voicing their opinions on what's scary and what isn't.

I think the thing that most people seemed to like was **Rusty**'s creation, Mr. Top Hat. Let's run with this one. What's his story? Do you find him scary? If so, why? Are there specific experiences this character reminds you of? Is he simply vague enough that he can stand in for a lot of different fears? What kinds of stories/media do you think he's best suited to? Do you think he *works*?

Tell me what you like about this monster, and how it should behave, and what kinds of stories people should tell about it. As our monstrous stories emerge, it will be interesting to continue to think about the feedback we all give about what works and what doesn't.

I'm also curious about the related ideas of *realism* and *reality*. What makes something seem "realistic" to you? How does a story like Mr. Top Hat come to seem more or less real?

81 readers like this.

COMMENTS

Posted October 30th, 2017 7:04am by Sheeple
I think it's scary because it's both really vague and really familiar. Lots of us have played video games, and lots of video games have monsters and "scary" things in them. This one is different because of its simplicity, because it's so far away in time (for many of us, anyway), and because there's no clear reason why an obscure game character would even want to hurt anybody. (To say nothing of why it should be able to hurt anybody.)

Posted October 30th, 2017 8:45am by Rusty
It was scary for me because I knew a guy who was affected by it. I also played the game myself, so I spent a long time as a kid wondering if the same thing would happen to me.

Here's an image of him. There doesn't seem to be much about this online. From what I remember of the game, it was one of those adventure/puzzle games, a little like an early Zelda.

It was called Dark Journey. You had to find keys and avoid monsters and stuff. Mr. Top Hat would appear in the third level. You got to this empty room with a treasure chest, and when you walked toward it some creepy music would play and he'd appear in front of you. A little text box would appear saying "FIRST YOU MUST PAY." If you got too close it was game over. I think you had to have some kind of item to give him or something.

> _Rick_ replied October 30th, 2017 10:00am
> This is a really elaborate story, Rusty!

>> _Rusty_ replied October 30th, 2017 11:59pm
>> It's really not just a story, Rick. I swear, I really played the game, and my friend did too, and he really disappeared. I probably shouldn't have shared a real story here since we're supposed to be making a fictional one. It was all I could think of.

> _SoAndSo_ replied October 30th, 2017 2:08pm
> Woa I love it he looks like the babadook

>> _Rick_ replied October 30th, 2017 3:11pm
>> Is that a good thing, SoAndSo? I thought we wanted to make something totally new?

>>> _SoAndSo_ replied October 30th, 2017 8:08pm
>>> lol I dunno I just really like that movie

>> _Sheeple_ replied October 30th, 2017 10:03am
>> I really like this idea, Rusty. What's the story of the kid who "disappeared"?

>> _Frictionless_ replied October 30th, 2017 12:09pm
>> Hah! I use a stock image and people hate it, Rusty uses one and they love it! Good story tho

Posted October 30th, 2017 11:02am by <u>missmarple</u>
I don't get why others find him scary, honestly. It's just a game, and a really old, silly-looking one at that.

> *<u>Rick</u> replied October 30th, 2017 11:05am*
> You don't find the image or the story scary, missmarple?

>> *<u>missmarple</u> replied October 30th, 2017 12:17pm*
>> No, not really. It reminds me of millions of other horror stories, from the Ring to that one with the video game and the roses and Elizabeth Bathory or whatever — can't remember the title right now. Technology just isn't scary to me.

> *<u>Sheeple</u> replied October 30th, 2017 11:51am*
> Are you a gamer at all, missmarple? I think part of it comes from remembering that stuff as a kid. I played an old DOS game called "Hugo's House of Horrors" that looks ridiculous today, and was meant as a comedy, but I actually found it kind of creepy at the time. Like, there's a zombie dog you have to throw a steak to and then you could sneak past. That always creeped me out.

>> *<u>missmarple</u> replied October 30th, 2017 9:01pm*
>> Sheeple, I do play games sometimes now, but I didn't start until fairly recently. I missed all the pixelated stuff.

>>> *<u>Sheeple</u> replied October 30th, 2017 9:47pm*
>>> Ah, that's probably why. I get how it must look pretty silly, then.

Posted October 30th, 2017 12:02pm by <u>Jinxy</u>
You guys, I found a rom of the game buried on an emulation website under a different title! I'm going to load it up on an emulator tonight and play it. If anything scary happens I'll let you know!

[*See more comments*]

October 31st, 2017

Happy Halloween!

Posted by Rick in Categories: Digital Ethnography; Expressive Culture. Tagged: Halloween; Monsters; Mr. Top Hat

A very happy and scary Halloween to everyone!

I'm pleased to note that Mr. Top Hat really took off. Out of curiosity I Googled the name this morning and found one or two other mentions of him that seem to have been made after he appeared on this blog. Have any of you been talking about our monster with other Internet communities? It's fine if you have, of course — it's just helpful for me to get a sense of what channels of communication our behatted friend prefers.

I found the conversation about whether Mr. Top Hat was scary or not especially interesting. Some people found him creepy because he's so simplistic and innocuous-looking. Others said that video games, especially old ones, aren't really scary. Through all your feedback, we're getting a clearer picture of Mr. Top Hat and what makes him scary (or not!).

What do you all think happened to Rusty's friend who disappeared? There's more of the story to flesh out. Have other people gone missing, too? How does Mr. Top Hat work, exactly? That is, what does he *do?*

I hope you all have a wonderful, safe holiday! And don't let Mr. Top Hat get you!

1730 readers like this.

COMMENTS

Posted October 31st, 2017, 7:47pm by Rusty
I know you guys don't believe me, but this really is real. I shouldn't have mentioned it. When I was about 8 years old,

my friend and I had a sleepover at my house. We played the game and got to the part where you see Mr. Top Hat and got so scared that we turned off the Atari. I swear before I fell asleep that night I heard a weird robotic voice say, "FIRST YOU MUST PAY." My friend was already asleep, but I was so scared that I threw a quarter out my bedroom window for Mr. Top Hat.

Three days later my friend disappeared. I think he didn't get me because I paid him.

SoAndSo replied October 31st, 2017 9:09pm
Ooo scary lol I like it

Rick replied October 31st, 2017 9:12pm
Great story, Rusty! Does everyone feel that this kind of personal narrative makes Mr. Top Hat more believable?

Frictionless replied October 31st, 2017 9:56pm
I think so. And hey, I found the game too, and got all the way to where Mr. Top Hat appears. (Why do they call him that, anyway? Is that his official name?) It was actually creepier than I expected, but I gave him a coin and then went on and beat the game. Just finished it a minute ago. I wonder if Jinxy has played it yet?

missmarple replied October 31st, 2017 10:13pm
I found it too! I'm going to try playing it now to see what's so scary about it.

Jinxy replied October 31st, 2017 10:14pm
I played it and now I can't stop hearing his voice don't play it don't play it don't play it

SoAndSo replied October 31st, 2017 10:21pm
Ahhhh haha that's creepy jinxy stop lolz

[*See more comments*]

November 1st, 2017

More Mr. Top Hat: Playing the Game

Posted by Rick *in Categories: Digital Ethnography; Expressive Culture. Tagged: Monsters; Mr. Top Hat; Video Games*

That last post got a ton of likes! It seems like we've really hit on something with Mr. Top Hat. Now there's even a video about him on YouTube! I think I might start a Wikipedia entry about him, just to prevent any confusion — we don't want people to get the wrong idea.

But on that note, I have to admit it — I was stunned to find that the game *Dark Journey* actually exists! A reader emailed me a link to a copy of the game, and I've been able to load it up on an emulator. Somebody must have thrown it together after reading about Mr. Top Hat here. I'll try playing it later today after my last class.

I think this is an interesting example of the emergent properties of digital storytelling. It's a lot like fan fiction, with people writing stories and critiquing each other's work. In fact, I think it's basically identical: we are "fans" of Creepypasta, the only difference is that we come up with the original stories, too. There isn't (usually) a mass-mediated element: just fans telling stories. The "mass culture" part may enter into it with things like Sonic. exe, where a real game becomes the source of horror, but that's a little different from telling a new story set in an existing fictional universe. Or with our Mr. Top Hat, a fan actually created a *fictional* "original" text, in the form of this (fake) Atari game! It's really complex and fascinating, and I'm amazed at everyone's creativity.

What do you all think about how things are going? Are you scared yet? What should we add or change to make it more scary?

2867 readers like this.

COMMENTS

Posted November 1st, 2017 7:37am by Sheeple
Good god, I'm amazed how this took off. Has a life of it's own!

Posted November 1st, 2017 10:16am by SoAndSo
oh wow i got the game too gonna play it now I watched that youtube video thought it was cheezy but good

> *Jinxy replied November 1st, 2017 10:16am*
> Don't do it don't do it don't do it don't do it

> *missmarple replied November 1st, 2017 10:16am*
> Don't do it don't do it don't do it don't do it

> > *01101101 01101001 01110011 01110100 01100101 01110010 00100000 01110100 01101111 01110000 00100000 01101000 01100001 01110100 replied November 1st, 2017 10:16am*
> > FIRST YOU MUST PAY

> > > *Rick replied November 1st, 2017 10:40am*
> > > This is really brilliant — even the name in binary! Well done!

Posted November 1st, 2017 7:37am by Rusty
Okay, guys, let's be serious for a second. I made it all up — pretending it was real was part of the Creepypasta. But after reading some of the comments here, I looked it up and I found the game too! But how is that possible? I invented the whole story! Nobody disappeared! This is actually really freaking me out!

> *Jinxy replied November 1st, 2017 7:37am*
> Its real Its real Its real Its real Its real Its real Its real

missmarple replied November 1st, 2017 7:37am
Its real Its real Its real Its real Its real Its real Its real

Sheeple replied November 1st, 2017 8:04am
Haha, nice one, you guys. 😵 This is getting good.

Rick replied November 1st, 2017 2:34pm
I'm about to load up the game myself. Nice twist, Rusty! How do people feel about this blurring of fiction/reality? Do you think it's scary?

Sheeple replied November 1st, 2017 3:01pm
Not sure it's scary, but it's definitely interesting. And now I'm not entirely sure which parts are real and which aren't! The same thing happened with Slendy, back when the Something Awful thread was taking off and Marble Hornets had just started. I think the ambiguity is key to its effectiveness. These monsters that "live" online aren't really that scary on their own, except that they're digital, and we use digital things all day, every day. Like the Ring did with video technology, Creepypasta can make us afraid of digital stuff.

_01101101 01101001 01110011 01110100 01100101 01110010 00100000 01110100 01101111 01110000 00100000 01101000 01100001 01110100_ replied November 1st, 2017 2:34pm
COME AND PLAY BUT FIRST YOU MUST PAY

[_See more comments_]

November 2nd, 2017

Tired

Posted by Rick in Categories: Uncategorized.

I played the game. I got to the part where he appears and the game crashed. Then I heard the voice. It said, as you might expect, that I must pay.

I admit this was creepy. I'm not sure how the programmers made the effect so convincing. I was just using junky old earbuds. Major kudos to whoever made *Dark Journey.* I was actually so unnerved by it that I couldn't get to sleep last night.

And still the likes keep coming. We've really created a monster here, pun very much intended.

It's interesting to me how the monster has spread. What is it about this particular monster, or others like Slender Man or Jeff the Killer, that makes people want to tell *new* stories? Why do some things become so massively viral, and others don't?

I'm too tired to think too much about it right now. I'll try to write more after I've had some rest.

How is everyone else doing?

7891 readers like this.

COMMENTS

Posted November 2nd, 2017 7:02am by Sheeple
Rick, I don't know what's going on here, but I heard the voice too, and I didn't even play the game. I think maybe we should stop this. And I'm being serious here — this isn't part of the Creepypasta.

> *Rick replied November 2nd, 2017 7:13am*
> I like this angle — the story's jumping out of its container.

Sheeple replied November 2nd, 2017 7:15am
No, Rick, really. Listen, I'm going to call you at your university number, okay? Since this blog is public and we all know who you are, I can find your contact info easily.

Rusty replied November 2nd, 2017 8:17am
Rick, I agree with Sheeple. I made the whole thing up, didn't know there even was a game until someone mentioned it here, and now I've heard the damned voice too!

Rick replied November 2nd, 2017 8:20am
Rusty, do you01001101 01110010 00101110 00100000 01010100 01101111 01110000 00100000 01001000 01100001 01110100 00100000 01110011 01100001 01111001 01110011 00100000 01101000 01100101 01101100 01101100 01101111 00100001

SoAndSo replied November 2nd, 2017 8:20am
01100110 01101001 01110010 01110011 01110100 00100000 01111001 01101111 01110101 00100000 01101101 01110101 01110011 01110100 00100000 01110000 01100001 01111001

missmarple replied November 2nd, 2017 8:20am
01100110 01101001 01110010 01110011 01110100 00100000 01111001 01101111 01110101 00100000 01101101 01110101 01110011 01110100 00100000 01110000 01100001 01111001

Frictionless replied November 2nd, 2017 8:20am
01100110 01101001 01110010 01110011 01110100 00100000 01111001 01101111 01110101 00100000 01101101 01110101 01110011 01110100 00100000 01110000 01100001 01111001

Jinxy replied November 2nd, 2017 8:20am
01100110 01101001 01110010 01110011 01110100 00100000
01111001 01101111 01110101 00100000 01101101 01110101
01110011 01110100 00100000 01110000 01100001
01111001

Rick replied November 2nd, 2017 8:24am
How did you delete my comme01001101 01110010
00101110 00100000 01010100 01101111 01110000
00100000 01001000 01100001 01110100 00100000
01110011 01100001 01111001 01110011 00100000
01101000 01100101 01101100 01101100 01101111
00100001

Posted November 4th, 2017 4:54pm by <u>ManxMan 1977</u>
Whoa, I go away for awhile and shit hits the fan! This is really creepy, you guys!

[*See more comments*]

November 8th, 2017

Time to Stop It

Posted by <u>Rick</u> in Categories: Uncategorized.

Well, it seems like we got hacked. All that stuff with the comments was part of it. I talked with tech support at my web hosting company and they're pretty sure they've been able to block the compromised accounts. (Sorry to people whose accounts were affected.)

Mr. Top Hat has appeared on a number of other sites, too, and the game someone uploaded to that emulator site is featured in several dozen Let's Plays on YouTube already. I guess we were successful in making our monster, but it's time to call it off. I talked to <u>Sheeple</u> on the phone the other day and he was really scared. (Hopefully I was able to put your mind at ease,

Sheeple!) The intention wasn't to frighten anyone, it was just to understand how these things spread. So I'm officially calling off this little social experiment.

To be clear: **Mr. Top Hat is not real.** We created a "fake" Creepypasta as an experiment, but it's become a "real" Creepypasta, in the sense that other blogs and websites are now telling their own Mr. Top Hat stories. In a sense this a good thing: we figured out the process, or at least one version of it. But again, Mr. Top Hat is not, and never was, "real." It's just a silly story we made up together.

I've submitted some edits to the Wikipedia article to ensure that it links to this blog. Hopefully the Mr. Top Hat furor will die down — but I think it won't really go away until the next major Creepypasta comes along. Although it's always real people behind these processes, there's a reason they're called "viral."

Thank you all for your help and enthusiasm. I'll be working on my article in the weeks ahead, and I'll keep the blog updated with my progress. If you have any further comments they're most welcome. Thanks again, and talk to you all soon.

01010100 01101000 01100101 00100000 01100110 01110101
01101110 00100000 01101001 01110011 00100000 01101010
01110101 01110011 01110100 00100000 01100010 01100101
01100111 01101001 01101110 01101110 01101001 01101110
01100111 00100001*readers like this*

COMMENTS

Posted November 8th, 2017 8:11am by <u>Rusty</u>
But I heard the voice! How can it be fake if I heard that voice? And look at that "likes" count! Your site's admins said they fixed it?!

> <u>Rick</u> *replied November 2nd, 2017 8:28am*
> Really Rusty, let's call it quits with this. You're a great storyteller — maybe try creating a new 'Pasta? As for the site, I'll get on the phone with tech support again. If they can't

block the problem IPs permanently, I'll consider switching to another hosting service.

Posted November 8th, 2017 10:00am by <u>ManxMan_1977</u>
What a great story that was! Should be enough to write a few papers at least, right, Rick? I'm thinking of a new story now and I'll post something tonight. I like the idea of a Creepypasta that actually kind of infects digital media. I might try to run with that idea, but in a different direction.

Posted November 8th, 2017 10:00am by 01001101 01110010 00101110 00100000 01010100 01101111 01110000 00100000 01001000 01100001 01110100 not a game or a story Rick I'm here now and you can't stop me not with stories or articles or conference presentations I am not what you think I was already here you just helped me find a lovely new home after so many years see you soon and thanks for everything

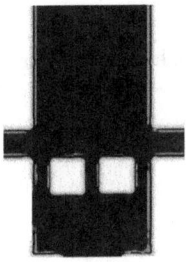

Posted November 8th, 2017 9:30pm by <u>Pink_parrot_72</u>
Wait so is this real or not??

Bibliographic Note

As a folklorist, the thing that originally seemed most important to me about Slender Man was the way in which his earliest creators wanted to create an entire "mythos" for him. This was the term they used to refer to the body of narratives, graphical representations, "official" reports, and other paraphernalia associated with the monster. In other words, they wanted, as I've argued elsewhere, to make it seem like Slender Man had a pre-existing body of "real" history and folklore. This impulse to mimic "real" folklore is part of what we have come to call the *folkloresque* (Foster and Tolbert 2016), a catch-all term for popular culture's use of traditional cultures.

As is now a matter of historical record, Slender Man took on a different significance after two young girls in Wisconsin tried to kill their friend as a sacrifice to the fictional monster. After this traumatic event, the blurring of the fiction/reality binary rose to the fore in my thinking about the digital monster. The creeping "reality" of the Mr. Top Hat problem is inspired directly by the original Something Awful forum thread that birthed Slender Man, in which many participants claimed they were frightened by their own fictional creation. Disclaimers of its fictional status were often absent from posts purporting to describe encounters with the monster, contributing to ambiguity regarding its existence. Most notably, some users even speculated about the danger of focusing so much thought and creative energy on a monstrous being, and whether such attentions might result in the monster becoming real. A similar logic, and corresponding ambiguity, underlies the story of Mr. Top Hat.

On Slender Man and other popular engagements with the idea of folklore:

Blank, Trevor J., and Lynne S. McNeill, eds. 2018. *Slender Man Is Coming: Creepypasta and Contemporary Legends on the Internet.* Logan: Utah State University Press.

Foster, Michael D. and Jeffrey A. Tolbert, eds. 2016. *The Folkloresque: Reframing Folklore in a Popular Culture World.* Logan: Utah State University Press.

McNeill, Lynne S. 2009. "The End of the Internet: A Folk Response to the Provision of Infinite Choice." In *Folklore and the Internet: Vernacular Expression in a Digital World,* edited by Trevor J. Blank, 80–97. Logan: Utah State University Press.

Peck, Andrew. 2015. "Tall, Dark, and Loathsome: The Emergence of a Legend Cycle in the Digital Age." *Journal of American Folklore* 128, no. 509: 333–48. DOI: 10.5406/jamerfolk.128.509.0333.

On digital ethnography:

Boellstorff, Tom. 2012. "Rethinking Digital Anthropology." In *Digital Anthropology,* edited by Heather A. Horst and Daniel Miller, 39–60. Oxford: Berg.

Langlois, Janet L. 2014. "'They All See Dead People — But We (Do)n't Want to Tell You About It': On Legend Gathering in Real and Cyberspace." *New Directions in Folklore* 12, no. 1: 5–56, https://scholarworks.iu.edu/journals/index.php/ndif/article/view/12768.

Pink, Sarah, Heather Horst, John Postill, Larissa Hjorth, Tania Lewis, and Jo Tacchi. 2016. *Digital Ethnography: Principles and Practice.* Thousand Oaks: SAGE.

Underberg Natalie M., and Elayne Zorn. 2013. *Digital Ethnography: Anthropology, Narrative, and New Media.* Austin: University of Texas Press.

Varis, Pija. 2016. "Digital Ethnography." In *The Routledge Handbook of Language and Digital Communication,* edited by Alexandra Georgakopoulou and Tereza Spilioti, 55–68. London: Routledge.

On emergence in ethnographic contexts:

Bauman, Richard, and Charles L. Briggs. 1990. "Poetics and Performance as Critical Perspectives on Language and Social Life." *Annual Review of Anthropology* 19: 59–88. DOI: 10.1146/annurev.an.19.100190.000423.

Tedlock, Dennis, and Bruce Mannheim. 1995. "Introduction." In *The Dialogic Emergence of Culture,* edited by Dennis Tedlock and Bruce Mannheim, 1–32. Urbana: University of Illinois Press.

Howard, Robert Glenn. 2008. "Electronic Hybridity: The Persistent Processes of the Vernacular Web." *Journal of American Folklore* 121, no. 480 (Spring): 192–218. DOI: 10.1353/jaf.0.0012.

10

Becoming a Sakawa Boy:
Magic and Modernity in Ghana

Matthew Gmalifo Mabefam and Kalissa Alexeyeff

A woman appears on the computer screen and says "hello" warmly, crossing her long legs as she does so. She is pretty — long dark hair, brown toned limbs — and she is wearing a revealing white dress. "Hello?" she says staring into her monitor smiling, "hello?" Her image begins to crackle and distort and finally freezes as she starts to type on her computer....

It's 2005, in Ghana's capital Accra. In a crowded, smelly internet café, a young man has made a video call to London. He now begins to type: *I'm so sorry my computer still isn't working very well, my sincerest apologies, dear Sir! How are you? I spent my wage on fixing this computer as I was so looking forward to organizing to meet you face to face!!* So, this is what it has come to the young man thinks, whoring videos of my little sister to lonely, rich white men.

He types some more: *My uncle is sick again, so I had to use my money to pay for his doctors, I am so sorro-ful for him, he is my only family.* As if I didn't know how to spell sorrowful, for fucks sake. I have been to university and look at me now: *If you could just lend me a small amount of money? Not much, about 1000 pounds? I can get a new computer and perhaps better care for my only family … xoxoxo.* I'm doing what I can as the big brother, the young man tells himself. I'll put food on my family's table. He looks at his silver ring, that provides him magical protection. Now I am a Sakawa boy, he thinks. Soon, soon I will have all the wealth I have dreamed of.

The young man presses "send." His hand shakes a little. The message is sent.

***

While he waits, the young man opens a document and goes on to write:

> *I am making a record of my time here in Accra and what I have done. I don't know what is going to happen to me, I don't think I will be here for long. I want my family to know I did this for them. I did everything I could to be a good son, to put food on their table. But I can't tell them now, the shame would kill them. Maybe I will print this story out and post it in a bottle, and throw it in the sea, the old-fashioned way. Maybe I will put it in a blog and send that to my sister to explain all my wrongs, or maybe I'll just delete it.*

I arrived in Accra from S—— Village. The bus trip had taken all day. I stared out the window at the river Oti and its bridge, the hills of the Volta region, the Adomi Bridge, and the green plantations of Eastern Ghana, all the landmarks I had heard about at school. It was dark when we arrived in Accra, but people were roaming around like it was daytime, I remember being shocked by that. Poor, innocent village boy! The buildings so tall and they glittered. Our capital! Our gateway to Africa! But "all that glitters is not gold." That's one thing our pastor got right. That very first night I saw a man right near the bank on La Paz Road. He stood there just showering money, paper notes onto the ground with no expression in his eyes. He told people there would be more money if they came with him. People went crazy grabbing the money, an old man grabbed me: "Don't go to him. He is a Sakawa, a zombie! That money is dirt, take it and you will die."

Back then I had hope. I would get rich myself. I was one of only five students who finished Senior High School. I was the only one from my village going to university in Accra. I was going to study hard, get a good job, look after my family, and maybe even go overseas. Ha! I thought I was hungry back home; it is nothing like here. Not even family can help you here.

For most of my years in Accra I have lived in the slum at Agblogbloshie, where people from the northern part of Ghana mostly stayed. People built houses anywhere they could, and from anything they could. The streets were muddy but clean. It was my friend from university who organized for me to perch in his room. He had to ask an old lady who owned the house, if you could call the bunch of rusting corrugated zinc a house! She looked at me for a long time and asked me about my studies, my family, my village, my future plans. "No Sakawa stuff here," she said. "Oh no no no," my friend replied, "he is a good boy, he is going to be an economist and make us all rich!" The joke sealed it, and we walked inside.

I shared a room with four boys who were also studying. We shared everything, our food, our clothes, our computers, our hopes. Everyone in our neighborhood was poor. They wore tattered and secondhand clothes and rarely ate three meals a day. No one had a bike let alone a car! Sometimes Sakawa boys came through the streets, in a black Toyota, dark windows, playing loud music. They threw money out of the car as they passed. People would rush for this money on the street even though they knew it could kill them. You should never take the money, but we all did if we could.

In our room while we studied, we spent a lot of time talking about Sakawa. Like everyone, they scared us, but they also had everything we dreamt of. We spent hours in the room trading stories about Sakawa. We knew they used *juju* to possess the minds of foreign cyber-targets. How did they do it? "To do a successful hit," one roommate said knowledgably, "you went to the *juju* priest and had to bring a sacrifice." Young girls are the best because they were pure, the priest would take their blood. *Juju* priests got Sakawa to drink human blood or potions made with other body parts — pounded flesh and human shit. This made a Sakawa turn into a snake and vomit up dollars. I didn't want to believe these stories, but I did. I had heard similar stories from back home — *juju* sacrifices, magic that possessed and even killed, snakes vomiting gold and dollars. An old woman in our village had put a spell on a neighbor, and they lost the power to speak. Us boys poured over pictures of Sakawa on the internet, some of them were lying in coffins with snakes and money. Other pictures showed Sakawa with white powder over their bodies, bowing down as the priest, surrounded by pillars of money, enchanting their computers. Were these images for real? We all wondered. Mainly, we looked at the piles and piles of dollars.

The first time I really met a Sakawa was at a christening party my second cousin had to bless her baby. As she sat holding the baby on a plastic chair in the middle of the gathering, music started, and a young man came out from the crowd — this was my cousin's boyfriend. He held a large wad of money in his hand and began to shower it over her and the child. How could he have all this money? As the money showered down on my cousin, cheering erupted from the crowd, and shouting: "Dollar Man, Dollar Man!" My cousin's boyfriend smiled as he flicked crisp notes over to her. He sped off afterwards on his motor-bike. Not long after we heard he had died. His body was found naked in a ditch. Maybe he was a Sakawa boy, people said? At his funeral, the neighborhood politician came along, his arrival was announced over the loudspeaker. He came with his guards, and he also showered money on the grieving family. That's what politicians do, they show off their status like that, they buy our votes.

"How is what the politicians did at your cousin's boyfriend's funeral any different from Sakawa?" They are buying votes, wanting something. One roommate talked about politics all the time. He talked for hours and got all worked up about political corruption, our rotten economy, the evils of the World Bank. I wanted him to shut up. He blamed everything and everyone but not himself. "Americans took us as slaves. We made them rich, they made us zombies." He loved to talk about the past. "Ghana used to glitter with gold, and then the white man stole it." How often had I heard that said? "Now, they are making us slaves again, capitalism is destroying us once again!" I had to put a pillow over my head, but this roommate would not stop. "Sakawa have it right, they are taking back what was taken from us!" He read every story about cyberfraud, romance, and inheritance scams. He watched all the Sakawa movies and Sakawa music videos that had become popular.

Everyone talks about Sakawa boys, even our president. It was reported in the newspaper that he wrote a speech that was read by the Greater Accra Regional Minister at church which said that "in their quest to attain riches and status in society, young people are sacrificing their youth, health, family life, and spiritual values." As a consequence, "vices such as Sakawa, occultism, and cyber fraud, among others, are creeping into our social fiber, and are gaining roots," he added. According to the report, our president "appealed to Christians to make it their duty to train the youth in the ways of the Lord, to help inculcate the fear of God in them." Our pastor in our church tells us every week prosperity will come. I hear on the radio… everywhere, everywhere there is the promise of wealth. But now I think you have to grab it with your own hands.

The newspaper today says we are better at internet scams than even the Nigerians! Ha! We also have more computers than anywhere in Africa the paper said. How is that? No jobs but we have the internet! The tech capital of Africa we are called, the fastest internet in Africa! There is not much else in this country that works.

I was getting more and more desperate. I finished my studies just two months ago. I am supposed to graduate in a few weeks. Ha! What's the point? I have done my four years economics degree

Figs. 1 and 2. Shangrila bus stop with posters advertising occult services. Photos by Matthew Mabefam.

at the University of Ghana. What for? There are no jobs. Our university lecturer told us all the time that "the government has frozen jobs, there are no jobs, unless people retire or pass away." Thousands of young people were graduating from university and from school and roaming the streets looking for jobs. I wanted a white-collar job. I went delivering job applications by foot to government institutions and private companies. I would do any work, anything in any of these offices.

I saw many things and thought many things as I roamed around. Billboards with pretty girls selling computers. Posters at shopping malls and bus stops offering to help fix problems. The words "spiritual guidance," "lotto numbers," and "business success." All these new churches, with posters offering to make one "rich, popular, and successful." Other posters were colorful, with pictures of money, of *juju* men with "black powers." I took some pictures as I wandered around (figs. 1 and 2).

I saw the King Solomon poster a lot, he could fix anything. He also had a web page which covered every illness caused by "spiritual attacks." He could fix personal problems in a marriage or relationship; he could even get you promoted at work! As I walked disconnected thoughts floated through my mind: King Solomon's mines. Gold. Or was it copper? King Solomon in the Bible, he had wisdom and riches. What else? He had seven hundred wives. Then God forsook him for his idolatry! Ha! Solomon had all the wisdom in the world, and he succumbed to fleshly desires. That's Romans 8, verses 26–39 as I recall it. In Proverbs 3, verses 11–13 it says: "Happy is the man that has found wisdom, having it produces gold itself."

We all have our magic, our protection, our miracles. The old lady who rented her rooms to us boys, her husband had died a long time ago. We paid her by working for her brother off-loading yams from cargo trucks in the Konkomba market. She would sneak into our room sometimes, we could never hear her coming, like a ninja! One roommate said he had seen her coming out of the house of an alleged witch in our neighborhood. He said he bet the witch gave the old lady some fake eyelashes, which meant she could monitor us. I had heard of that before, back in my village people said our mayor's wife had got those special eyelashes. When she put them on, she would be able to see whatever is happening around the village. She wanted to know what we were doing on our computers. "You better not be Sakawa," she said. "I only let you stay 'cause one day when you have a job you will remember me and my grandson. I want no *juju* here, it will only bring bad luck to my family."

Only a few weeks ago, we woke up one day to find posters on trees and walls. These posters invited young boys to join a Sakawa group. They had their contact information as part of the advertisements and pictures of money, cars, and girls. The elders quickly removed the advertisements. But many boys had memorized those contacts. The old lady's grandson played around on the road pretending to be a Sakawa boy: "I'm a Sakawa. I'm a Sakawa… see!" Around his bare neck he had electrical cord wrapped and shining like gold jewelry. The old lady wacked him on the head with her broom till he cried. She screamed at us all, "you see, you see?! I can see how you boys look at the posters longingly, I can see you. You think they are rich and want you to be rich too? No good comes to these boys, they are rotting inside from their evil." To her grandson she said, "they will steal your penis, cut it off, and give it to the priest." We all backed into our house, avoiding her broom as she ranted on the street.

I spent four stinking years perching in a shared room. Sleeping in shifts, studying in shifts, looking for food in shifts. I am hungry, tired, and after weeks of roaming the streets searching unsuccessfully for a job, I was ready to do anything. You know what made me decide in the end? My father. My family were always ringing me, I had stopped answering my phone. They leave messages to say, "can you send through money for your sister's school fees?" or, "can you buy us clothes?" or, "please can you send us money to buy food?" I told them I didn't even have a job, but they don't understand. They think Accra, so big, so many people, there must be something to do. The pressure was like a rock tied to my neck and each day it sunk me deeper and deeper into despair. On this one day, my father rang, and I answered. I missed my family and told him truthfully how difficult it was. All my determination was gone. Dad knew it and conceded. "If you are so poor come back and work on my farm." It was then I realized I could never go back there without money or a job. I had seen it before, boys coming back from university with their degree and nothing else. Everyone mocked them. I knew there was only one thing I could do to make things right.

A friend from my economics class became a Sakawa boy. A while ago, he stopped me on the road, he was in a jeep with four others. I was scared but he called my name, so I had to go to him. He showed me his necklace, pure gold. He said, "feel how heavy it is! That costs 5000 Ghana cedis." His friends were generous too. "You want a smoke? Here, have a smoke," and passed me a joint. He got out of the car and walked me away, his arm around me protectively. "How are you? No job? You look wild and sharp. You hungry man! I found a way to get what we deserve. Come see me? No obligation, but I can show you the way."

He frightened me, but in my dreams, I envied him. In my dreams he gave me his necklace and his ring, he let me drive his car. We even ate at a restaurant, and I ate food I had never tasted like fried rice and pizza. Only in dreams hey? For many days I didn't go on that road or where I knew he lived.

That night, after that call from my father, I went to his house. I stood at the security gates, there was a party. All the lights were on, music blasted through the open windows, and I could see so many young people laughing and dancing. My friend came out to greet me. "Brother! I knew you would come tonight. Come, come." He showed me around, introduced me to people. The girls were so pretty. He took me into his room where there were bundles of money on a table. I have never seen money like that before in my life. I was shivering at the sight of the money. Where could the money come from, if not Sakawa?

I asked my friend, "Are you a zombie? People say you are a zombie." This more than anything was my deepest fear. What if I could not control my actions? What if I hurt my family or my friends? What if I did something to my little sister? He laughed. "No zombie, man. We are in charge. This is payback time!" He explained he was a peaceful man, he said he did not want to hold a gun or rob a bank or kill people. He explained that all we had to do was hit foreigners up for money over the internet. "When I first went into the internet café, whoever I met online and whatever I asked of them, they did. For example, I asked a client for

100,000 US dollars as part payment for a joint business, and he sent it through to my account without any further questions." He said at first he was scared beyond belief and wondered, "how does this happen, how are people so gullible? This is because we turn them into zombies. The Sakawa ritual just takes over their minds, they send money no questions asked."

I slept at my friend's house that night and the next. I smoked, I drank, and I ate my fill. I could do what they do just for a few months, I could help my family, help myself, do something other than roam the streets for nothing. I finally said to him, I'd do it. The following night a jeep picked me up, inside were two other young boys, just like me. We were going to visit a *juju* priest who would help us get Sakawa powers. Looking at my alarmed face my friend laughed, "we don't use humans, only chickens at this place!" Still, as we drove off into the countryside, it was so dark and quiet. I could have been killed, and no one would know. I now felt I had no control over anything. We stopped at a small hut at the end of a dirt lane. My friend called as he took us inside the place. "These are our friends," he said, talking to an old priest sitting in the middle of the room and pointing to us. "They want you to help to them." He placed a bag next to the priest and bowed respectfully.

The priest took us into a small room where there was no light whatsoever. He lit a lantern and began to chant. In front of us there was an altar with different images which looked as if they were molded or carved out of clay. At this point, all I wanted was to leave that place alive. The priest told us to take off every piece of clothing. After chanting again and pouring some liquid onto the images he said, "my gods have heard your plea and are willing to help you. But before then, I need to take you through the rules of Sakawa. Here there are rules which everyone who comes to me for assistance must abide by."

He then made a cut in our left forefingers and squeezed blood in the container. He murmured some words that were hard to hear. My heart was pounding too hard to hear anything anyway. Finally, the priest prepared a cup of concoctions for us to take. He poured it from an old bottle he picked up from the altar. He tasted it then handed it to me. The taste was bitter and smelled bad. After drinking, he gave us all a ring to wear. This ring would be able to help us scam the victims if they read any messages we sent on the internet. We could never remove the ring. And just like that we were initiated into the Sakawa network. What had I done?

***

Our country was rotten, our economy was rotten, and now, so was I.

The girl on the screen appears *Oh hello! Hello!* As the screen breaks up, she says, *Africa! Our internet is so slow, so unreliable! I'm terribly sorry.* Text appears in the dialogue box next to the frozen image:

> *My dear sir! I can't keep living like this. I am a slave, please! I must come to you! I know you said you would pay for my flight, I have hesitated to ask you, you have done so much for me! I have enough money to pay for my passport. Can I, if I may, give you my travel agent detail and you could arrange the transfer? It would be of more comfort if you didn't give it to my account. I would prefer. I hope that our day has come. Just 2,000 dollars will cover it all. In sincere and loving anticipation. xoxo.*

A few days later, a young man borrows his friend's motorbike. He rides until he reaches the jungle near his family village. He sits there till it is late and very dark. He slips quietly into a house whose layout he knows by heart. He places a wad of fresh notes carefully wrapped in plastic on the kitchen bench. Then, even more cautiously, he places a letter under a young girl's pillow before disappearing back into the night.

Bibliographic Note

In his article "Undead (a Zombie Oriented Ontology)," Jeffrey Jerome Cohen suggests that zombies are significant as they point to "a gap in the fabric of the known world [...] in which everything familiar loses its certainty" (2012, 398). Sakawa boys use occult practices to ensure that the internet fraud they participate in is successful, and at the same time they run the risk of being turned into zombies, being dehumanized, and turned into exploited slaves that are unable to enjoy the money, stylish clothes, luxury cars, and other goods they accumulate. The "gap" that Sakawa boys embody is the rapid economic decline that occurred in Ghana from the 2000s, when unemployment and poverty increased due to a drop in foreign exchange earnings, structural inequalities, and international economic interventions (such as World Bank and IMF bailouts), which put a ban on public sector employment. As many scholars have shown, sorcery, *juju,* and other occult practices have been integrated into postcolonial political economies as attempts to access global capital (Comaroff and Comaroff 2001). Sakawa boys inhabit this "alternative modernity" and narrate a tale of promise of untold wealth and conspicuous consumption as well as the dangers of illicit consumption, and immoral accumulation that ultimately leads to human suffering, exploitation, and death. The fictional narrative presented here is based on the experiences of Ghanaian author Matthew Mabefam who grew up with witchcraft and *juju* as an integral part of this society. Rumors and sightings of Sakawa boys circulated with increasing frequency during his time living and studying in the capital Accra. It is an attempt to convey the endemic poverty and sense of hopelessness that is felt by poor people trying to get by.

On Sakawa boys in Ghana:

Armstrong, Alice. 2011. "Sakawa Rumours: Occult Internet Fraud and Ghanaian Identity." PhD Diss., University College, London.

Oduro-Frimpong, Joseph. 2014. "Sakawa Rituals and Cyberfraud in Ghanaian Popular Video Movies." *African Studies Review* 57, no. 2 : 131–47. DOI: 10.1017/asr.2014.51.

Riedel, Felix. 2015. "Sakawa — The Spirit of Cyberfraud: Analysis of a Rumour Complex in Ghana." In *Racism, Ethnicity and the Media in Africa: Mediating Conflict in the Twenty-First Century,* edited by Mano Winston, 261–82. London: I.B. Tauris & Co.

On the occult economy in Africa:

Comaroff, Jean, and John L. Comaroff. 2001. "Millennial Capitalism: First Thoughts on a Second Coming." In *Millennial Capitalism and the Culture of Neolibralism,* edited by Jean Comaroff and John Comaroff, 1–56. Durham: Duke University Press. DOI: 10.1215/9780822380184-001.

Comaroff, Jean, and John L. Comaroff, eds. 1993. *Modernity and Its Malcontents: Ritual and Power in Postcolonial Africa.* Chicago: University of Chicago Press.

Geschiere, Peter. 1997. *The Modernity of Witchcraft: Politics and the Occult in Postcolonial Africa.* Charlottesville: University of Virginia Press.

Moeran, Brian, and Timothy de Waal Malefyt, eds. 2018. *Magical Capitalism: Enchantment, Spells, and Occult Practices in Contemporary Economies.* New York: Palgrave Macmillan.

Smith, Daniel Jordan. 2001. "Ritual Killing, 419, and Fast Wealth: Inequality and the Popular Imagination in Southeastern Nigeria." *American Ethnologist* 28, no. 4 (November): 803–26. DOI: 10.1525/ae.2001.28.4.803.

On illicit accumulation and its dangers:

Michael T. Taussig. *The Devil and Commodity Fetishism in South America.* Chapel Hill: University of North Carolina Press, 1980.

On the meanings of zombies:

Cohen, Jeffrey Jerome. 2012. "Undead (A Zombie Oriented Ontology)." *Journal of the Fantastic in the Arts* 23, no. 3: 397–412. https://www.jstor.org/stable/24353082.

Hurston, Zora Neale. *Tell My Horse: Voodoo and Life in Haiti and Jamaica.* New York: Harper Collins, 1938.

McAlister, Elizabeth. 2012. "Slaves, Cannibals, and Infected Hyper-whites: The Race and Religion of Zombies." *Anthropological Quarterly* 85, no. 2: 457–86.

Vervaeke, John, Christopher Mastropietro, and Filip Miscevic. 2017. *Zombies in Western Culture: A Twenty-First Century Crisis.* Cambridge: Open Book Publishers.

11

Possession, in Four Voices

Richard Davis

EXCORCIST

"I want to talk to you about possession and exorcism."

The audience quickly quietens down and looks on perplexed at the man walking across the stage. The advertisement for the night said that the top act would be Bill Riley, a local comedian who invariably told husband–wife jokes. Bill was in his fifties, tall, and always looked as if he had walked straight off the town golf course with his impeccable pose, pastel-colored polo shirts, patterned slacks, and two-tone shoes. The man on the over-lit stage is not Bill. He is short, looks to be in his early forties, slightly bent over, disheveled, pot-bellied, and does not walk with ease. Across his midriff his shirt is too tight, and his khaki shorts flap around his knees. Honking loudly into a tissue that he then puts back into his shirt pocket, he suddenly stops his pacing. People walking to tables cease moving at the honking sound and his sudden stillness. Now the man on the stage draws himself up and slowly scans the room with a focused, intense stare.

"Possession and exorcism," he continues, "the two are siblings; the one follows the other in an inevitable sequence, yes?"

Sounds of air sucking through teeth. "Of course, it depends on what, or who, you are possessed by. Try on one of the Big Three mono-religions and possession by God, Jesus, or the Holy Spirit is mandatory, preferably made obvious by babbling tongues, healing, raising up of the dead, or future-telling." Several people call out, and he ignores them. "No exorcism is sought for there, why would it, it is salvific, a pathway to healing and eternal reward? At any rate who would do it? A priest, a minister? The Catholic Rite of Exorcism needs being inhabited by a malevolent entity to stage an intervention, and from a priest POV God ain't malevolent." A woman stands from her seat and shouts out for the man to stop talking. The performer ignores her and continues on. "So, it would require some sort of auto-exorcism, or an unsanctified gun for hire, and he who willingly casts out the Divine is subject to serious banishment from God's graces, no way back, door shut, burn baby burn. Just check out 2 Peter 2: 20–21 if you are wobbly on the detail. But hey, in the immortal words of AC/DC, 'Hell Ain't a Bad Place To Be'…," at which point a group of young men at the bar roar out their approval at the mention of the rock band.

He waits for the commotion to die down and calls out, "So, my first exorcism…." He smiles and quickly shakes his head. "I was about eighteen and —" A pale-faced man walks past the stage, stops in front of him and asks out loud, "why are you telling us these things, they are not what we came to hear. Where is Bill? We came here to laugh, not to be told about God and possession and exorcism. Who are you?" People nod sympathetically, and the performer responds, "You are wondering, yes, why I want to tell you about exorcism? Well, Bill could not make it tonight, he is ill, and he asked me to fill in for him. He always said I should get up and tell some of my stories, so here I am. My name is Joe, but people call me Fanell, a nickname. Maybe that should be my stage name. At any rate I am here, and I am telling you these things because, well, Bill said I should tell you my stories, and this is my story, so I am telling it, here, tonight. Please, listen, it gets interesting, I assure you."

People move about in their chairs and lean back a little, an encouragement for Joe, or Fanell, to continue. He walks to the edge of the stage and drinks from a water bottle while patrons continue to walk in and fill up the tables. Soon the small club is full. "Yes, 18, young, young for this business. I was a Christian then," someone whistles, "walking along Manly Corso in Sydney on New Year's Eve with my Christian friends and the youth pastor of our church and we run into my girlfriend's sister. Now, you should know something about my girlfriend Carol and her sister Peta." One of the men at the bar calls out, "yeah, yeah, we know all about your girlfriend and her sister." Joe points his finger at him and wags it. "As I was saying, my girlfriend, she went to church like me and was a part of the youth group. We were earnest, change-the-world types, always talking about Third-World issues… poverty and famine and social justice. It was good, eye-opening, and made me, a Sydney beach bum, think about the world around me." He grimaces and waves his hands towards himself in recognition that his body is distinctly unathletic and untanned. Scattered laughs and taut grins

"She had been going to church since she was old enough to remember. That, and school, had pretty much been her world. Her sister was different. She left school early, about thirteen, and was partying, drinking, and gravitated to a hard world that seemed to revolve around Kings Cross. I hardly ever talked to her, but here she was, at Manly Corso, on New Year's Eve, and, well, drunk. You know the Corso, right?" No response, keep going. "It goes from Manly Beach to the wharf where you can catch a ferry to Circular Quay in Sydney's CBD. Every New Year's Eve I went to the Corso, there was a band playing and people dancing. There was a band again this night and my friends, and I walked straight into Peta and her boyfriend Michael, who was looking as drunk as Peta. I'd never really spent any time with Peta, but she and Michael were in the mood to talk so we eventually moved away from my friends and the band, and we go into the grounds of the local church and sit on a small bench to talk. There, she and Michael started talking about something I will never forget."

He continues. "They both said that they had just come from a meeting with a group of witches and warlocks." He pauses for an instance to gauge the audience reaction, which verges on shocked laughter, then barrels on. "What do you mean 'witches and warlocks?' I replied, and Peta says they belong to a coven, an occult group and every New Year's Eve they meet. I can't quite get my head around this, and I stupidly ask if they worship the devil. They don't bat an eyelash at this question and answer that they don't, but they have contact with spirits. 'Spirits, as in dead people?' I ask. They say no, spirits as in spirits, something else. Michael then gets up and says he is going to go and find another bottle of bourbon, walks off, and I'm left with Peta, this woman who is my girlfriend's sister who has just told me she is a witch and deals with spirits."

Through their soft chatter Joe can see the audience keenly watching him so he presses on. "Now, I'm a good Christian, and I don't really know what spirits means, other than demons. That's what I had been taught at church, that spirits are demons, evil beings that are part of Satan's troupe. I also know they have powers, and I'm not really sure that being a young believer is going to get me a lot of protection from something that I can only picture as doing things to me like was done to that girl in *The Exorcist*." One of the young men at the bar moans a ghostly "ooooooh," but Fanell ignores him. So, I am feeling way out of my comfort zone here, but I'm curious too so I ask Peta 'do you have anything to do with these spirits?' She replies with a bomb, 'yes, one is inside me.'" Now the audience is completely silent. No glasses clatter, and no one shifts in their seat.

"'Right now?' I ask, and she nods yes to me. I look at her closely to see if I can see this spirit, and I can't, and I know I am in waters so deep I might sink, so I ask her if she minds if I go and find a friend of mine to come and talk to her. This is when I start to see something odd about her. When she replies that she doesn't mind me going to bring someone else into the conversation she starts on the strange mannerisms. An odd lopsided shrug, an ever-so slight shudder, a movement of her face muscles that suggests an inner voice or compulsion." He notices several of the club patrons shiver, as if in sympathy with his words.

"I get up and go to find my friends to tell them what Peta has just told me, and when I find them, I see our youth pastor amongst them and start to tell him everything. The others just watch on, looking concerned and not knowing what to do. Eventually, the pastor, who is a few years older than me, moves off to go to Peta, I join him. When we get to her, she listlessly looks at us, and then turns her gaze away in an unconcerned way. I can't get a bead on whether she is drunk or stoned, or something else. Given how much she wanted to tell me about her coven before I walked away from her, her disinterest is arresting."

He wipes the sweat off his face with the same handkerchief he blew his nose into, and the table closest to him groan their disgust. He grimaces at them before launching forward with renewed breath. "The pastor then asks her if she knows where she is, and she slowly nods 'The Corso.' He asks a few more questions then asks her about the group she is part of. She looks at him and says, 'we meet to contact them?' 'Who is "them"?' the pastor replies. She says she doesn't know but they can give powers. What powers, he asks. She is silent for a while, then she says, 'When they are in us, we can read minds, we can fly, we can influence. Influence you.'"

A lady in the far shadows of the room shouts out "Fly!? What does she mean fly? No one can fly, this isn't a Superman movie ya know!" Fanell flings his arms out and flaps them like a bird and shouts, "Hey, I am not the bird here, that's what she said, and I'm just reporting it to you so you can buy it or you won't, I don't care. But let me tell you something, at one in the morning when someone is telling you ghost stories you don't go around asking for evidence, you're in the scare zone. Although that is what the pastor did." Suddenly, Fanell's arms drop, and he looks tired as he slowly bends to pick up his water bottle. After taking a swig, he screws the cap back on and speaks slowly, "Like I said, he asked that dumb question of Peta, 'Peta can you fly?' and Peta

DEMON

I have been here for a while, years even. I was asked. I didn't just force my way in. I did not even tempt my way in. Not by words was I asked, but through intent. There was no warfare of the human mind, I just slipped in through a softly opened cleft, and made myself an-other. It is a thing we do, we different-kind, we subsist in two natures when we find bodies to anchor ourselves. In this sense we are true gnostics, we have no natural corporeal existence.

There are better times for possession than others, better world times and better person times. Those earthquakes in southern Sumatra, they were good. The famines in rural Malawi, very good. The destruction of the World Trade Center, that was fantastic, the whole world was uncertain and we found many body-houses to dwell in.

When secreted, we turn the person. Turn them this way, then that.

answers, 'yes, I did earlier, when we were all together. One of us flew straight up.'"

He continues. "I agree, that's not right, flying, but she said it so matter-of-fact that it seemed something you could do. I will never forget her smile when she said that. It was slow and mocking, daring us to think it was not true. And then she said it, 'he is here with me now.' I mean she just said it, like she was daring us to not believe her. But we did, we were right there let me tell you, very much so, and so it began. The exorcism, I mean. She kept saying there was something with her, something inside her, she wouldn't stop, and I didn't know how I knew to start it or why I chose the words I did, but off I went."

"'In the name of Jesus, I command you to come out. With the power of the Holy Spirit, I command you, unclean one, to leave this woman Peta. You do not belong in her, get out of her.' I said these words again and again in different ways, 'The Lord Jesus commands you, you who once dwelt with him in the Most High but are now defiled and unclean, to leave this woman. With the power of Jesus's blood I command you to get out of this woman. Get out, get out! Your power is nothing against the power of Christ the Lord, who sees all and knows all, corrupted one. In the name the Father, the Son, and the Holy Spirit, I command you to be loose of this women, leave her.' On and on I went. When I got tired or confused the pastor took up the exhortation so that the commands did not stop."

Joe then continues. "At first Peta was indifferent, but it all changed when we started commanding the evil thing to tell us its name. That's a thing right, getting the name of a spirit. Gives you power over it." He noticed a man at a table to the left him whisper in his partner's ear, nudge her, then shout out, "What's your name, your real name, not Fanell or Joe, they're not real names." Fanell froze, then spat back, "what is your real name, the one she calls you at night when you are in each other's arms? You tell me, us, that, and you will have my real name." For several seconds people around the room looked directly at the man to see what he would do, when a falsetto voice came out of a dark corner and said, "Sweety coo coo pie" in such an over-the-top, camp pitch that the room erupted into laughter. The aggressive fear left the performer, and he joined in the mirth while, at the

This one, it wasn't the world, she went looking. Terrible body image and self-loathing. I pressed against her and made her forget the problem of her matter. She agreed. I entered. We have been one ever since. I turn her loathing into appetite, driving her to vast wastes of eating. I drink the appalled looks of passersby, the avoidance of mirrors, the tortured nonchalance of public eating. I have rarely to delve into the lifelong lack of love to plunder her suffering. It is always and everywhere, acutely there. My evil satisfies.

table, the man and his partner sheepishly looked around the room, nodding in acknowledgment of the well-timed joke.

Relaxed, the performer went on. "Then she got weird, really weird. Hissing, slapping at us, speaking in strange voices. Not languages, but tones; guttural, high-pitched, slow, fast. She chopped and changed all over the place. One minute she was 'Get away, leave me, fuck off', in one of those growling death metal voices, the next she was girlish and coy, pleading with us to stop attacking her, why couldn't we just love her? I mean, talk about being in a horror movie, this was bullshit!"

The performer continues. "We pressed her, 'Your name, tell us your name!' More snarling and changing voices, and I could not take my eyes off her. Then I heard a bark that seemed to come from the air around us. Commanding, that voice spoke the word MARAH. To this day I swear that I did not see her mouth open when I heard that voice. Peta seemed to gain strength from that word and again it came out of the night around us. Then she locked eyes with me and said in a normal tone, 'my name is Marah.'"

He continues. "Well, you go looking for something and then you find it, and you don't know what to do with it. I looked to the pastor and asked whether he had heard the voice. He nodded agreement. 'So, what do we do now?' I asked him. He turned to Peta and said to her, 'who are you Marah?' Peta replied, 'I am the bitterness at the end of the desert. When you most need to drink, I am there.'"

With a grimace of confusion Joe says, "I don't know about you, but that made little sense to me, but the pastor seemed to know something because he said to Marah, 'you were with them when they came out of Egypt, weren't you.' Peta said 'yes', shivered and then said, 'I am scared, what are you going to do to me.' I asked her 'who is speaking?' She huddled and said, 'I don't want to go, leave me alone.'"

He continues. "At this, the pastor started the commanding to leave stuff again, but this time with the name of the demon, 'in the name of Jesus, I command you, Marah, unclean spirit of

> *When these two attacked me in my house, they did not know that I had asked other demons to join me inside this woman. I had done so earlier in the evening, when I compelled her to meet with her friends, who so enjoyed meeting us. There is a way of doing this, a way of enlarging a person's suffering to allow others possession of it. When we join together inside, we are strong in our multitude. One may go, but others remain. But not this night. This night I had not finished my joining work. I was alone before the words of magic hurled at me. There were none with me to grip and adhere to this woman should I be cast out.*

the desert, to leave this woman and go to the place that God has made for you.' I joined in the commands and then I saw something I wish then, and now, I could unsee. Something was happening to Peta. Her face started to elongate, pushing her nose and mouth far out in front of where they should be. Her skin started to twitch and ripple, and her eyes became unfocused. Her arms bent wrong, in several places. Also, there were more fingers than there should be. Of all the strange things I saw that night, the fingers disturbed me most." Someone twanged the "Duelling Banjos" music from the movie *Deliverance*. Nervous titters at that.

"Michael came back with a half-drunk bottle of booze, and looked on for a bit, asked Peta if she was alright, then went away to sit on the ground before he curled up and went to sleep. Peta started to groan, and her face seemed to be made of putty as it went through bizarre contortions. I had become incredibly scared. I thought that if the demon comes out of her, it might come into me, and I started to pray for Jesus to protect me and not let this happen. I wanted to be far from that bench, not at the Corso. I feared not knowing myself should I be possessed by this thing. Then I blurted out, 'Peta, if you want this evil out of you, let the blood of Jesus wash over you and let the love of Jesus into your heart.' She stood up like a rocket had been lit under her, spat at both of us, then collapsed on the ground." He paused for a moment.

"We both went to her and through her prone exhaustion she was quietly crying and constantly saying 'thank you,' again and again. We helped her up and gave her and Michael a bed in the rooms attached to the local church that night. We met her the next morning for breakfast and a talk about what she was going to do now. The exorcism was over and that was really a talk about her now becoming a Christian, which I won't bore you with here."

Joe peered out at the audience and, before anyone could clap, boo, make a comment, or move, he said, "as I said earlier, this was my first exorcism. The next one was a disaster, a total catastrophe. I was making up for it twenty-five years after, and if you

I had been forced out before, not often, and it is always the same. That other presence comes in, the one I will not name. It is a shock, hurtful beyond words, and I become diminished. I, who was in the Desert of Shur, who poisoned the well of the wanderers three days out of Egypt, cannot bear that presence. Of all things, I cannot compel my body-house not to invite that one in.

That night, as I resisted the words of power, I stretched her body, pushing my nature through hers. I know what it looks like, this distortion of skin and muscle, it breaks symmetry. It is a violence and can halt any desire to continue in the confrontation. I felt that in the boy and turned my attention to him where I saw the fear my contortions of her body wrought in him. His own distrust of himself, edging towards self-denial. I knew then I could go to him, take him, and saw his panicked recognition of this. Then, he impulsively uttered the offer that the woman agreed to and instantly the ur-kind came in and I was gone, gone from her body, the house I had made, to desolation, where few go.

want to hear that story, don't forget to hit up the manager on the way out for me to get another spot up here. This has been fun. Goodbye and have a good one." And with that, Fanell picked up his water bottle and walked off the stage.

Muruyg

Slithering across the strands of *wali,* the thread that is mystically woven through southern New Guinea and northern Australia, the Muruyg, a reincarnated Saibai Island ancestor in the form of a snake, stops to contemplate the disturbance left by Marah. Only those spirits, monsters, reincarnated ancestors, rainmakers, sorcerers, magicians, worldshapers, and peoplemakers of north Australia, Torres Strait, and southern Papua New Guinea travel the wali. It is a means to be, elsewhere. From his place in the weave the Muruyg calls out to the departing demon.

Hey, devil, I wish to say something to you, but you are gone. No matter, I will talk as if you can hear my words. I have been watching your kind since you came long time ago to Torres Strait with the Jesus believers. I have heard the missionaries say your kind are bad angels from the beginning of time who are against God. Well, that is your no-good business, and it is not the Muruyg way. Muruyg are different, we only possess Torres Strait Islanders, and don't try for all human beings. We stay inside them for a short while, give them visions, and then we go. They see something amazing, and they can share it with whomever they like and make a new understanding of things.

Not like you. Some of you came here to Torres Strait and damaged our people. Your kind got inside them, like that woman I saw you thrown out of, and humiliate and wound. When I see how you make sickness inside of them and make them talk and act against their own self, it makes me think that you are just like the white people you came with. Both of you are always trying to be boss, always trying to take over and own us. Occupation is what you and whiteman do; always trying to occupy.

I am a snake, but I was once a man. On my island of Saibai, I used to tend my gardens of yams, cassava, and sweet potato with

ANTHROPOLOGIST

You came to me unbidden, in my dream. A psychologist might say it was my conscience compensating for my appalling error in disrupting the healing service held for you at the Saibai church some days prior, but I think not. I knew I was not responsible for the bullet through your back that put you at death's door. That was someone else, in a hunting accident. Besides, I made up for that poor timing by later approaching a senior elder, asking him to smooth the way with disgruntled kin and others. He told me not to worry, my "stumble in wrong way" was a mistake, not likely to lead to your death. I made sure I was on time for all the other healing services where all of us who loved you and were related to you asked God to heal you.

No, you came to me, not to berate me, not to make me feel at fault for your impending death, but to visit others. You possessed me that day, in my sleep. I did not know if you were the unmoored shade of the comatose, the spirit of the just-dead, a Muruyg, or that you had somehow found your own way to pass into me, but when you departed from me I became open to other dream possessions. When I return to Saibai after some time away the spirits of the dead inhabit my dreams at will. It's scary having voices inside — talking, looking, probing — even if they are unthreatening. I well remember the last time that happened; they were underneath my floor loudly conversing amongst themselves, and then they talked directly to me. It was not a tongue recognisable as speech, more like a message conveyed, a benevolent recognition of sorts. Your living brothers said that's what the spirits do, they come and check you out when you've returned after being away from the island for a while and speak in their own language. Somehow, I gained ancestors that rightfully belonged to others. Who can fathom such generosity? I appreciate that, I do, but those first few moments of the dream where they crowd and converse feels like a series of pokes. I'm developing into a regular little voodoo doll, am I.

my wife and children. Every year I prepared my garden beds and planted the remnants of the previous year's crop. Some years my yams were of prodigious size, at other times they were gnawed by rats, and I had little to show for my effort.

I long ago left that man-form, and I am now a Muruyg, an old creature. Sometimes old trees are called Muruyg too, but only men become snake Muruyg, and only after some generations have passed. People cannot tell if I am an ancestor or a regular snake but if anyone comes too close or steps on me, I will strike and inject my venom deep. As they fall into a coma, I will coil around them cherishing them with my tongue, much as I do when I slide along the stems of the plants in the gardens of my descendants, tending them with caresses of my tongue. My poison brings insight and new knowledge and as I nurture them back to wakefulness with my sliding and licking, they carry that vision to share with others, enriching their lives with what they have encountered in their delirium.

At other times we Muruyg seek a more long-lasting effect, and we crawl through the mouth of our host to coil in their belly. You who read these words may flinch at that thought but bear this in mind. We are the soil and bone of our gardens. Sometimes, we are the gardener, sometimes the root. When we sit inside the belly of a man, he carries all of that through the visions we bring. He travels with us inside him, until we no longer wish to sit in the cradle of his pelvis and we slide back out the way we came in.

I have already told you that I do not possess as you do, and neither do I poison as you do either. I have heard the sermons in the church describe that terrible exile through the desert beyond Egypt. Three days from the Red Sea under the burning of the sun and sand, and they chance upon you and your ruined oasis. You used your toxin to wound then, as you do now, whereas I use it to bring revelation.

I understand the nature of your malice and cruelty, you cannot love. You hurt all who can, all who need and all who long, to love. In all of my incarnations, I have never abandoned love. None of my kind do.

> *You remember the details of that gunshot. I was living in your house with you, your mother and son. You went out one night with your mates to hunt deer in the bush. Your choice of hunting vehicle was comical, ludicrous even. Council backhoe, really? What were you all thinking? There is no even ground out there, it is as lumpy as crabs in a bucket. The machine bucked all over the place and a rifle accidentally discharged a bullet, straight through your lung.*
>
> *You were brought into the village health clinic where the nurses poured plasma into you to replace all the lost blood. Somehow, you lived through that night. Next morning you were on a helicopter to Cairns Base Hospital where infection set in and pretty soon the prognosis was bad, very bad. We all went to church to pray for God to heal you of your terrible wounds. That church, where I made that mistaken entrance*

There are others that populate my spirit world, and we are all midway between humans and something else, or something else and humans. What am I but a transitioned person who, every now and again, likes to sit in the belly of the living? Like all Muruyg, my journey to this reincarnation is a complicated one. Just after I man-died, I was a wandering spirit, confused about having no body and not knowing what to do with myself. All we newly dead are confused like that. We are unaccustomed to ourselves and do strange things, surprising even to ourselves. I recently saw one loosened spirit span a great distance across the wali to his living mother and son only to find himself inside the dream of a whiteman he knew. How he disentangled himself from that dream, I do not know. Maybe he is still there. As for me, I kept turning up at the doorstep of my wife and children, broken-hearted and trying to be the husband and father that I once was. My wife did not berate or rebuff me. No, she talked to me, but the children weren't so happy. They had seen my lifeless body lowered into the ground by my brothers and covered in soil. To then hear me shuffling around the family house, mangling words as I came to terms with my new spirit-language was creepy and confusing for them. I was out of place, out of myself, and out of my mind.

I eventually stopped bothering my family when my closing funeral was done. We call that one the Tombstone Unveiling. It consolidates love and grief for family and friends. I was settled from then on and called Markay by the living. I did not feel so compelled to visit my family anymore, much preferring my spirit-community in the ground of the cemetery. Yes, cemetery, where else would it be? It is where we dead gather and are visited by the living who come to talk to us.

Occasionally, a few of us spirits liked to get out of the graveyard and go on night-time joyrides through the streets of Saibai village. We remember what we did a hundred or so years ago

---

And then I dreamed. I had laid down in my bed in the afternoon and fell asleep. I dreamt I was lying on the bed at the same time of day in the same light on the very bed I lay on so I did not know I was dreaming. I heard a knock, and you were at the back door (how could you be, I thought in my dream, you were in a hospital a 1000 km south?) and you asked to see your son and mother. I refused you entry, thinking that you had come to say your last goodbyes to them, and I did not want you to die, I wanted you to live. I told you to go back to your body. You turned around, walked off, and I woke up.

You survived your injuries and spent many months recuperating on the Australian mainland. During that same time I felt that I was responsible for your living, and I was ashamed and afraid. I did not know whether I had disrupted an important aspect of family members being visited by the spirits of loved ones on the threshold of death and life. I also did not know if you would somehow know what I had done to you.

---

when we pulled up to the island foreshore in our ghost-ship with messages of inspiration to the leaders of the village that the newly arrived whiteman could be overthrown. Recalling these events we would grab a spirit car, bolt some strobing spotlights on top and ride through the village. With curtains drawn over our brightly lit windows, onlookers could not tell who or what was going on inside, but we knew they remembered that anti-colonial determination of ours and how much we wanted them their own freedom.

Sometimes we just wanted a greater yarn with our living kin in the village. Some of us Markay would loiter through the streets at night or stand under trees and darkened doorways and call out to passers-by in our strange, unique language. Few of us convinced anyone to stop and talk. No wonder. I remember what it was like to see a shade of the dead standing on the road speaking spirit-speech and my knotted stomach declaring that it is not right, not human. What could I do? Call out to them to move? Even if I, when I was a breathing Saibai man, knew all the languages of Australia, Torres Strait, and Papua New Guinea, I did not know the language of the dead. Hardly anyone knows our language. Some living people have been known to speak it, but they have long since died and did not pass on the knack of it to others. So then, if a person is unable to call out to a Markay to turn away, perhaps it is best to stop walking, turn around and shuffle way-quick down the dusty road to career through a hastily flung-shut door? You take your chances though, because that is a hundred yards of uncertainty, right there.

One more thing, devil. When your white people came to Torres Strait en masse, the century before last, we called you Markay, just like the term we give ourselves when we have been through our funeral rites. Your people are pale, like a lot of Markay, but perhaps we call you that because you are not quite human. A person, for sure, but not quite human. Maybe even monsters.

Anthropologists like to talk about encountering difference, or recognising difference or taking proper account of difference. But what about being possessed by difference, properly possessed, taken over, because that is what you did to me, you took me over. Not like that two-nature demon that I exorcized when I was young, and not like a Muruyg. They do possession differently.

No, your accident, your dream-visit brought me into the fold of your family in unprecedented ways and made me vulnerable to your ancestors and responsible to your living kin. So much so that your brothers and sisters brought us together one day, several years later, where they were witnesses to my recounting that dream to you. You have always been a difficult man, your drinking especially, but there we were warily eyeing each other and considering how we were now bound to each other. We were watched closely that day and as it has ever subsequently been, this constant forming of relationships between the dead, your family, you and I has only ever been a question of "what will we do next?"

Bibliographic Note

This story works with the theme of possession across the colonial and Indigenous Australian divide. It primarily revolves
around two monsters, who separately belong to two different mythoi and who are treated as beings with their own intent and behaviors. One, a Muruyg, is a Saibai Island (Torres
Strait Islander) ancestor who, when reincarnated into a snake,
can possess people by residing in their host's stomach, grant-
ing them ecstatic visions. Muruyg are rarely encountered and
when one possesses an Indigenous person of the northern Torres Strait and southwest Papua New Guinea region that possession is strange, dangerous, ecstatic, and uncertain, but it is not
knowingly malicious in its intent. This is unlike the demons of
Christianity, an introduced religion of colonialism in Torres
Strait and Australia, who are universally thought of as hurtful,
spiteful beings, one of which is forcefully exorcised in the first
part of this story. This demon, who is named after the bitter well
the Israelites stopped at as they wandered after crossing the Red
Sea, asks us to consider what is to be cast out of a human host.

In Torres Strait, Muruyg and demons are unlikely to come
into each other's orbit and it is a conceit of this story that the
Muruyg is aware of the demon and the way its malicious nature mirrors the arrogance of colonialism in Torres Strait more
generally. This brings up the further issue of how spiritual beings from different cosmological origins encounter each other,
which in this story leads the Muruyg to reflect on its own revela-
tory form of possession as distinct to an aggressive immigrant
Christian mythos that treats possession as a sovereign act.

In the latter part of the story an anthropologist, who is the
older version of the young male exorcist, becomes inhabited
through dream, by a Saibai Islander man. Both events, the exorcism and the dream, draw on my own experience of similar
events. As I have explored these events some in poetic form,
elsewhere, I have asked myself the question of what it is to be
caught up in the mythic fabric of another, whether consciously

or not, and what it means for an anthropologist to be possessed by those they attempt to possess through research and analysis.

On possession and exorcism:

Cohen, Emma. 2007. *The Mind Possessed: The Cognition of Spirit Possession in an Afro-Brazilian Religious Tradition.* Oxford: Oxford University Press.

Cohen, Emma. 2008. "What Is Spirit Possession? Defining, Comparing and Explaining Two Possession Forms." *Ethnos* 73, no. 1:101–26. DOI: 10.1080/00141840801927558.

Csordas, Thomas J. 2017. "Possession and Psychopathology, Faith and Reason." In *The Anthropology of Catholicism: A Reader,* edited by Kristin Norget, Valentina Napolitano, and Maya Mayblin, 293–304. Berkeley: University of California Press.

Haustein, Jörg. 2011. "Embodying the Spirit(s): Pentecostal Demonology and Deliverance Discourse in Ethiopia." *Ethnos* 76, no. 4: 534–52. DOI: 10.1080/00141844.2011.598235.

On evil:

Caton, Steven. 2010. "Abu Ghraib and the Problem of Evil." In *Ordinary Ethics: Anthropology, Language, and Action,* edited by Michael Lambek, 165–84. New York: Fordham University Press.

Csordas, Thomas J. 2013. "Morality as a Cultural System?" *Cultural Anthropology* 54, no. 5 (October): 523–46. https://www.jstor.org/stable/10.1086/672210.

Parkin, David, ed. 1985. *The Anthropology of Evil.* Oxford: Blackwell.

On ghosts and spirits:

Baker, Joseph O., and Christopher D. Bader. 2014. "A Social Anthropology of Ghosts in Twenty-First-Century

America." *Social Compass* 61, no. 4: 569–93. DOI: 10.1177/00377686145473.

Bell, Michael M. 1997. "The Ghosts of Place." *Theory and Society* 26, no. 6 (December): 813–36. https://www.jstor.org/stable/657936.

Bubandt, Nils. 2012. "A Psychology of Ghosts: The Regime of the Self and the Reinvention of Spirits in Indonesia and Beyond." *Anthropological Forum* 22, no. 1: 1–23. DOI: 10.1080/00664677.2011.652585.

On Torres Strait Islanders and monsters:

Beckett, Jeremy. 1975. "A Death in the Family: Some Torres Strait Ghost Stories." In *Australian Aboriginal Mythology: Essays in Honour of W.E.H. Stanner,* edited by L.R. Hiatt, 163–82. Canberra: Australian Institute of Aboriginal Studies.

Davis, Richard. 2008. "A Life in Words: History and Society in Saibai Island (Torres Strait) Tombstones." In *Mortality, Mourning and Mortuary Practices in Indigenous Australia,* edited by Katie Glaskin, Myrna Tonkinson, Yasmine Musharbash, and Victoria Burbank, 171–87. Aldershot: Ashgate.

Lawrie, Margaret. 1970. *Myths and Legends of Torres Strait.* St. Lucia: University of Queensland Press.

On dreams see

Glaskin, Katie. 2010. "On Dreams, Innovation and the Emerging Genre of the Individual Artist." Anthropological Forum 20, no. 3: 251–67. DOI: 10.1080/00664677.2010.515293

Lohmann, Roger I., ed. 2003. *Dreamtravelers: Sleep Experiences and Culture in the Western Pacific.* New York: Palgrave Macmillan.

Mageo, Jeannette Marie, ed. 2003. *Dreaming and the Self: New Perspectives on Subjectivity, Identity, and Emotion.* New York: SUNY Press.

On reflexivity:

Bourdieu, Pierre, and Loïc J.D. Wacquant. 1992. *An Invitation to Reflexive Sociology.* Chicago: University of Chicago Press.
Lynch, Michael. 2000. "Against Reflexivity as an Academic Virtue and Source of Privileged Knowledge." *Theory Culture & Society* 17, no. 3: 26–54. DOI: 10.1177/02632760022051202.

12

Ghost (Story) Hunters

Caitrin Lynch and Adam Coppola

8:15 p.m. The freeway

Caitrin drives to Riverway, simultaneously focused on the road and deep in discussion with her student, Alex, riding shotgun. It's July 2017, a warm evening at the end of a hot day.

The pair are giddy and a little bit nervous. This is their first nighttime visit to Riverway and the abandoned mill next door, which is connected via stairs and ramps and known as The Other Side. These two textile mills were built in the 1800s, and they were central to New England's strong industrial history. But since the 1970s they have suffered the effects of global competition. Caitrin is an anthropologist and has been doing research about these mills for a few years. Alex is part of a team of engineering students engaging in fieldwork with Caitrin and hands-on engineering projects.

They'd been hearing about ghosts all summer, while working at Riverway, and they have finally set themselves up for an encounter.

A few days earlier, Caitrin had gone to The Other Side alone to find a metal part for her students' engineering project at Riverway. She had been using a wrench to remove an old safety railing from an emptied production floor, and she started to think about ghosts. She finished her work in haste and skedaddled out of there, thinking, *what would happen to my worldview if I see a ghost?*

In the car now, Alex seems less concerned about the possibility of ghosts. He's asking Caitrin questions like, *should I take notes?* and *how do we know they're telling the truth?*

"What makes this scientific?" Alex asks.

Caitrin replies, "We're here to collect stories and figure out what they mean. People do a lot of *sense-making* of bad stuff that happens to them and of routine stuff that they experience. And we all bring contexts with us that help us decide what are reasonable explanations. By now we've seen that ghosts are part of daily life at Riverway. Anthropologists talk about how people have different 'explanatory models' for their experiences and observations. Those models come from contexts like family, but also from perspectives that come from education, religion, or science. To me it doesn't actually matter if ghosts are real. What matters is that they are real to the people at Riverway. And I want to understand why and how that is. Does that make sense?"

"I guess I can see that," Alex replies.

"It's our job to collect the stories and understand what they mean for those who tell them," Caitrin adds. She is not totally happy with her own explanation, but Alex is quiet and seems to be internalizing these ideas. "And think about how we got here. We weren't looking for ghosts at first. We came to learn about how people keep a textile mill going, against all odds, and what that feels like for them. Almost all the other mills around here have shut down. The ghost stories have emerged as we've come to understand the ways in which people make sense of deindustrialization, and as their communal memories are created, recreated, and shared."

Silence. Caitrin wishes he'd keep asking questions. Student questions make her think and challenge her in productive ways.

But Alex appears to be processing or zoning out. He's quietly looking out the window.

8:20 p.m. The parking lot

The evening sun is dipping behind the mill. The cats lying on the pavement barely lift their heads as Caitrin's car enters the grounds. Glen, the security guard, exits the guardhouse to greet the visitors. He's tall, maybe around six feet, wearing a blue guard uniform: pressed pants and a button-down shirt with a badge. His hair is gray, his skin is wrinkled and showing a midsummer tan, and he's got a warm smile. "Hi there, I'm Glen."

A short woman, around the same age as Glen, comes out of the guardhouse, her white skin looking less wizened and tan than Glen's. She's wearing a sundress with sneakers, which Caitrin registers as sensible shoes for a nighttime ghost tour.

"This is my wife, Renee. She wanted to join us." Glen says.

Renee says hello and exclaims, "We're going on a ghost tour! Okay-e!" She says this last word with an upward emphasis, implying that she's excited and that she knows this is also an absurd happening.

After asking Glen and Renee for permission to record the tour, Caitrin turns on a voice recorder and clips the mic to Alex's bag.

Glen leads the group from the parking lot into Riverway, which is closed for the evening. Following Glen's watchman route, they'll pass through the Riverway production facilities before heading to The Other Side.

Glen clears his voice, and explains, "I'm here till eleven tonight. I work four to eleven and then the overnight guy comes in. He's here eleven to seven. I do five rounds a night, so. It takes about half hour. I take my time. I don't race through the place. I'm here all night, so what's the sense in rushing around? You know?"

8:28 p.m. The production floor

Alex is relatively quiet and holds the audio recorder the whole time, sometimes placing it in his pocket so he can take photographs with his cell phone. An engineering student, he claims not to believe any of this ghost stuff. To him, everything has an explanation. Unexplained creaks and whistles might just be pipes expanding or contracting as temperature changes. Or maybe a chipmunk that snuck inside through a hidden hole.

Alex looks terrified anyway, and Glen asks him, "You work here during the day, right?"

Alex responds, "Yeah. We've never been here at night. Uh, we mostly work around the corner in the mending section, by the chute."

Glen says, "When they say to me 'mending' or 'knitting,' I don't know what that means." Caitrin and Alex laugh. "No one ever explains to me what they do here, so I don't know what any of these machines do. I mean what is this? The carding room or something?"

Alex, says, "Yeah, that's up here."

Glen says, "I don't know what the carding room is used for."

They pass by a set of carding machines, routinely used in the first steps of textile production. They are conveyors that take in bales of fiber and output long slivers. In between, the machine contains a series of gears, grates, and teeth. Renee tucks her fingers under her arms.

Alex makes a face, and Caitrin says to Alex, "Is this place weird at night?"

Alex's voice cracks, and he responds, "It's just, different. I don't know." His voice deepens. "It takes a lot to, like, actually scare me."

Everyone laughs.

"Bring it on," Alex says, and everyone, including Alex, laughs.

Glen says, "Well, you never know. Let's see what's down here."

Glen leads the way and shines his flashlight from side to side, searching the entire room. He points his flashlight forward. They can't see where the room ends.

Glen says, "See? This light isn't all that powerful."

The light goes out.

Glen's voice is now deeper, and he remarks, "In fact, it just quit. Just blew the bulb. So, now we have nothing."

Alex whispers, "Spooooky."

Glen responds, "That's an omen. It only goes downhill from here."

Caitrin says, "True, true. And I've got my phone flashlight if we need it!"

Glen says, "I'm just gonna leave this flashlight over here. No sense of lugging it around if it doesn't work. Maybe it'll be gone when I get back."

"Well, that would tell us something," Caitrin says.

Everybody laughs. They can still see fine. There's enough residual daylight coming in the windows.

The walls of the room are lined with boxes and stacks.

Glen points to the boxes, "These are all orders. So, when you see it stacked up like this, you know they're busy."

Despite professing to know little about fabric production, Glen's experiences with the spaces and artifacts allow him a unique perspective on the production process and the state of the business. He can see when business is up, and when it is down. He's seen overflowing shipping docks, and he's seen emptied out second shifts.

Glen explains, "See, what they do is they take all this stuff, and they throw it down the chute and then they bring it downstairs and run it through the uh…"

Glen fades as he realizes he's probably explaining something they already know.

Caitrin is curious, as an anthropologist, how Glen knows so many details, and scared, as a human being on a ghost tour, that he's playing games with them. This, the walking, and the heat still trapped in the building from the daytime means that everyone is breathing heavily as they traverse the production floor.

A budding researcher, Alex visually captures the tour with photographs. Caitrin's scribbling notes, which she'll later find to be unreadable.

Machines continue to fade in and out of earshot, and the wood floors consistently creak with each step. Glen's keys, hanging from his belt loop, jingle, keeping time with his steps. The mill's closed right now, but circulating pumps and fans and other machines run 24/7.

Caitrin asks Glen, "How long have you worked here?"

Glen responds, "Ehh, off and on, I don't know, about twenty years. Well, I took five years off, and then I come back. In those five years, I worked with a lot of companies. 'Cause they come and go."

Renee says to Glen, "Wasn't this the area where you had that first... um..."

"Encounter?" Glen asks.

Renee replies, "Yes."

Glen says, "No, it was over here."

Renee says, "Oh, it was over here. Sorry, ruined it."

Renee turns to Caitrin, "I didn't want him to forget."

Caitrin laughs.

Glen says, "Yeah, you don't forget those things. You kinda wonder what the hell is going on?"

8:47 p.m. The dye house

The group enters the dye house. The smell of mold comes from somewhere. Wet, musty, and stale.

Glen announces, "Darkness."

They stop and Glen faces the visitors.

"Okay. The first encounter," he says.

Renee says, her voice revealing excitement, "The man in the red checkered shirt."

Glen says, "Maybe, we don't know for sure. Well, they call this the dye house. The first time I heard anything really weird. Right here. Walking down right here. I heard footsteps over my head."

Glen pauses, and continues, "I'm just walking along like this." His voice is nonchalant. He takes some steps, to reenact the scene. The floor doesn't creak this time, but his keys jingle no less.

"And somebody upstairs is walking with me."

Glen walks, and the visitors follow him silently.

"And it was funny because the only one in the building at the time was the company president. And I thought it was him coming to use the bathroom over here. And then I said to myself, 'Why would he use the bathroom all the way down here when he has one in the office?' So, I thought that was odd. You know?"

Alex asks, "So did you check with the president after your round?"

Glen responds, "Ahh, I didn't really mention it to him because I didn't really think anything of it at the time. You know, I thought nothing of it."

Caitrin asks, "What did you think it was?"

Glen says, "Well, I don't know. Well, at first I thought I was hearing things, then I thought, *nah nah I heard it.* But uh. I just let it go 'cause I didn't think nothing of it. Then more things start happening, you know? Like more footsteps and…"

Later on, when Caitrin and Alex listen to the voice recording, they'll find at this point that the voices are muffled by noise. The group is in the boiler room now.

Alex is skeptical of the "first encounter." He continues to suggest alternate explanations, but maybe misses the point of the story, which the others implicitly understand. They know that in this mill there are multiple possibilities to the way each story can be told, and to how each sudden sound or shadow might affect a response. It's as if the way in which the ghost stories emerge from reality depends on a process of reinterpretation, rather than one of accurate representation. The group walks on.

8:56 p.m. The office

The last stop before The Other Side is the Riverway office. The only air conditioned place in the daytime, the office provides temporary refuge from the heat for the research team. The air conditioner is off now. The group does a quick walk through.

"Has anybody else told you anything, like, in the office?" Glen wants to know of the anthropologist.

Caitrin responds, "Yeah. They just hear things; one guy saw the guy in the red shirt. Alex and I interviewed some guy that was telling us about the little green men. Do you know about them?"

Glen says, "Oh Martians?"

"Yeah."

Glen says, "No."

Caitrin says, "There's some guy who committed suicide, like, a long time ago."

"Oh, I didn't hear that one," Glen replies.

Caitrin says, "So, people talk about that."

Glen says, "You know what? Every one of these buildings has a history of someone dying in it." The visitors laugh. Glen continues, "That's why they're so spooky. You know? 'Cause how do these things start? 'Cause somebody hung themselves or somebody did something. You know? But if you got a place this old with all those people working down through the years. Someone had to do something."

Now everyone is spooked. Even Alex. They walk up a ramp that connects Riverway to The Other Side.

9:01 p.m. The attic

The team crosses over to The Other Side. The research team has been to The Other Side a few times already, looking for old machine parts for their engineering projects. Whenever they head that way, an old-timer Riverway machinist always jokes, "You harvesting from the graveyard?" He'll add, "the pickings are getting slim. We've gotten almost everything we can by now."

A new kind of unease now sets in. So far on the tour, the spaces have creeped out Caitrin and Alex only by virtue of being a dark and quiet version of what they know to be active in the daytime. The machines, though dusty, are still warm and could be reactivated with the pressing of a couple buttons. On The

Fig. 1. 1890 scratched into the wall. Photo by Zack Davenport.

Other Side, by contrast, no machines remain on the floor. There are only the wide empty rooms, residual marks and bolts on the floors, safety signs that hang in otherwise unmarked areas — all this provides space for the visitors' imaginations to project notions of their own. Their projections, prompted by the dust, the mold, and the writing on the walls, begin to take the form of ghosts from a more distant population.

The group follows Glen up a narrow staircase, the attic stairs creaking and footsteps following in succession. In a room in the attic, graffiti on the walls with names and dates reveals how long this place has been operational.

Glen explains, "This is all of that old stuff, you've seen it. World War II, these guys. And it's not only these walls; it's walls way in the back with writing on them too. It's pretty historic. A lot of the writing is by doors for some reason. People write them so you can read them on the way out."

Caitrin says, "Yeah, look, it says something right there."

Glen says, "There's also some names over here. 1948. Amazing. 1925."

Caitrin remarks, "August 1937."

"Yeah, so there's some names. There's some old timers up here," Glen says.

Glen points at one just overhead, "Johnson '69. '69? He's a new kid."

Everyone laughs.

"There was one way up high that was like 1880," Glen says. "One guy that was up here was Charlie Brown."

Alex says, "Charlie Brown's over here too."

Renee asks, "What's his date?"

"'42," says Alex

"They go till about '92," Greg explains.

Everybody is looking somewhere. Some of the names are scrawled in pencil, some engraved, some seem to be in chalk. Most of it is still readable through the test of time, though the content is up for debate.

Now everyone chimes in names and dates.

"1876."

"1910."

"1941."

"There it is, Chandler, 1890."

"That one seems to say PG Cronin August… April 14th 19…"

"1940?"

"1910, I think."

"We don't really know if it's a four or a seven."

"This one says World War Two on it."

9:10 p.m. The dark room

On The Other Side, they find redundant doorways and a lot of empty rooms. Alex opens the door to an empty false doorway, no deeper than the door frame. Glen jokes, "perfect size for a body."

Glen says, "This room is kind of a waste. About ten years ago it was rented out as a wood shop. It's a shame it's empty now. It's actually a nice room, but it just sits here."

Alex points out that the ceiling looks freaky, with hanging power cords and everything.

Glen explains, "Well, what happened was they shut the heat off and then the 'coons got in. And they started getting up in the insulation. Do a lot of damage to the insulation. They get inside the building; they were running around up there. I shine my flashlight up there, and they're just looking down at me with beady little eyes, eating wires."

The group walks on. Glen says, "So here's where I had my latest encounter. Right about here I just got a chill, and I felt like there was somebody behind me. And I looked. Of course, the lights aren't on. You can't see anything. You know? But it was just weird because you could feel them walking behind me. There was... nobody."

They look around, eyes adjusting to shadows and light. They wonder about the smell of the room. Dirt? Vines? Dead rats?

Glen walks ahead of the visitors but turns while he speaks. "I never used to believe in ghosts before I started working here. Never did. But I do now because there's something going on. I'll walk into a room. You can feel it. You get a chill. I felt like there was someone breathing behind me, and I get a chill. Of, course I whoop around and nobody's there. I'm like, 'Wow, what was that?' Couple weeks I go home and tell Renee 'It happened again.' Right down here. It felt like someone was right behind me, almost in my footsteps. You know, like wow. 'Cause your hair stands up on your arms and your neck when you get a chill. It's like, wow. You look around, and there's nobody there. But you can feel them like they're right behind you. You know?"

Renee says, "My personal opinion, I think they're not ready to let go yet. Like the red shirt guy that was working. I think he's still working on whatever he was doing at the time it happened. Right, 'cause I don't think these ghosts are vicious ghosts. That's just my opinion. But, you know? I think they live here, and it's their place. We're just part of their world."

Glen adds, "Maybe they're looking out on what we're doing. On eternal patrol. How's that? *On eternal patrol.*"

A door slides open, and they hear an electric buzz coming from somewhere. Is it a fluorescent light?

Fig. 2. An empty room. Photo by Zack Davenport.

Caitrin asks, "Wait, so what happened that time with the footsteps? It just went away?"

Glen responds, "Yeah, just turn around; of course there's nothing there. You know, I had my flashlight on. Didn't hear no footsteps or nothing. You know?"

As the group walks away, each of the poles casts a shadow from the one light source way at the end of the room. With the walls and ceilings beyond the reach of the one light, there is no way of knowing how big any of these rooms are.

9:18 p.m. The room that's completely empty

Glen announces, "Okay, here's the room that's completely empty. This used to be full of files, while the space was rented out to a financial company, but it's been empty for some time. Now, I was standing here. Well, it was all boxes here. And I was just walking by. In this same room. And I heard really low voices, someone talking, but it wasn't English. I could hear it, but you couldn't understand it because they were talking a different language. And I stop, and I'm like, *"What is that?"* And I just stood, and I listened, and of course, as soon as you try to hear it, they stop."

Silence.

"So, I'm just, I was just walking around and I'm, like, shining the light on everything and, like, that was the end of that, I never heard it again. It was like a couple voices, say like two people talking to each other."

Seamlessly following the rhythm of Glen's story, Renee asks, "And this is the room that the, is this the room that you smelled the perfume in?"

Glen replies, "No, *I* didn't, Mike did. That's another security guard. He smelled women's perfume. I told him one night about the voices I heard, and he said, 'Oh that's strange, because I was walking in the same room, and I smelled perfume.'"

Caitrin is thrown off, recalling her conversations about the history of the mill with retired managers. She shares her realization: "In this room there used to be rows of Portuguese women weaving."

Glen replies, "Well, that explains why I couldn't understand them."

The visitors all shift uncomfortably.

Glen says, "See? Footsteps. Did you hear that? There were footsteps."

Caitrin and Renee speak simultaneously, "Those were Alex's footsteps."

"Yeah, but did you hear them?" Glen asks.

They all laugh.

Renee remarks, "Wise guy."

Caitrin listens to Glen and wants to get more into his head. She thinks about how the experience of ghost encounters is relived in the retelling. Upon telling a ghost story to a new listener, the ghost reappears. A memory is created in the listener — "in this same room." Caitrin feels chills, and she thinks about how the chills signal the planting of a possible haunt. Retelling a ghost story brings the listeners into a past experience while bringing the ghosts into the present. Memories alter the sense of time so that past and present are one, and they create communities and meaning; maybe more so when the thing to be remembered might soon be gone. Like old-fashioned textile mills from another era.

Caitrin is over her chills and reluctantly asks for clarification: "And, when you hear voices, is it your job to go find out if someone's on the property? Aren't you supposed to investigate that?"

Glen says, "Well I could run around and see what it was, but there wouldn't be anything. I've done that. But there's never anything. You can't see 'em, you can only hear 'em. I've never seen a ghost-ghost. An actual visible ghost. Like something you see. I only feel them. But people say they have. Like the guy in the red shirt. I've never met him."

Renee says to Caitrin, "He worked here; you should look him up!"

Caitrin looks at Renee and thinks about how much fun Renee is having. Alex is also into it. He's taking comfort in science, in making sure the recorder is working and he's in the right place at the right time to capture the best recording. He's in control. Glen is enjoying sharing what he knows. But Renee, she's having the most fun. When ghost stories resonate with a listener, the thrill is visceral, it's as if the listener is experiencing the encounter itself. Listeners might simultaneously feel that it's terrifying that the ghost might still be here today and thrilling that something happened in the same space that the story is being told. Renee gets really into the stories, in particular when she might make connections to the present. *The man in the red shirt used to work here, so you can actually look him up in the records. How cool is that?*

Caitrin is still confused and asks Glen, "Wait, so, like, are you looking for ghosts or are you looking for, like, trespassers?"

Glen replies, "Nobody trespasses here. Nobody comes by here."

Caitrin asks, "Wait, so, what's your job? What are you supposed to be looking for?"

"Fire prevention," Glen explains. "Alright. Now remember this. Remember, there was a wall there and there was a wall here. Remember? Now if you come over here, because they used to have those walls there, you never had this view. You never had the view with the moonlight coming through the windows. Because the walls were there. Now if you come back over here you might see it a little better. Yeah, that's a parking lot light out there too. But, I mean, you never had that view."

The group comes over to where Glen is standing to see what he means. The moonlight and streetlights are both casting light on the wood floor, with shadows formed by the outlines of the windowpanes. They look up to see a half moon glowing just above the trees that line the edge of the parking lot.

9:30 p.m. The basement

They walk on, Caitrin thinking about how Glen's got such a diverse appreciation of the beauty of the building that is his everyday workplace. Caitrin thinks about her own recognition for the beauty of Riverway and The Other Side. She finds she is constantly trying to resist romanticizing what this place means. She cannot ever be in Riverway without thinking about capitalism and deindustrialization. Being on the ghost tour makes this even more evident for her. The ivy and the bats that make the mill their habitat. Generations of workers with their names etched on the walls. The perfume and voices of Portuguese women long gone from the mill. Empty spaces that used to be brimming with industry and people's lives. And deaths. And dismemberment. Caitrin remembers the stories she heard from Riverway workers: the guy who hanged himself out back, the one-armed watchman who worked at Riverway before Glen was even born. His arm had been ripped off in a dye-house accident, and then he was transferred to a new job as a night watchman. Before Glen's time.

They enter a basement area. The smell of wet dirt becomes intense.

Caitrin remarks, "It's funny, the house that I grew up in was, like, a hundred years old and it has a basement like this that we used to roller skate in. Smells just like this."

Glen says, "This just comes out to the other big room. See when Samson Mills was down here, they used to use this room quite a bit. And what they did was they had a desk here and they had a phone. This used to be a busy room. What they would do is here's a tube, they would send stuff up the tube just like the drive-up window at a bank. Yeah, see right here? It would go up. And it was like an office. And, you know."

Roughed by weather and neglect, brick walls crumble and wooden walls degrade upstairs. The concrete walls of the basement, however, so far are only affected by humidity. That's the smell Caitrin recognized.

Glen says, "The paint's peeling and cracking because of the moisture. There's plugs down here, you got water coming in. These guys upstairs are renting the space upstairs and some of the scraps are from them. You know, like all this stuff."

Glen's explaining what's on the floor. Flakes of light blue paint dust the base of either wall, outlining the hallway floor, which otherwise is coated in dirt and broken bits of glass and nails.

The walls are covered in discolored relics from 2001. Workplace rules, sandwich shop menus, a pinup girl, tags and stickers that have lost their stickiness, and phone lists that include numbers for people who still work at Riverway. Alex suggests taking some things as a souvenir, but Caitrin says it's best to leave it for now: "I kinda like the stuff *here,* you know?"

Glen reads a sign, "Walking or sleeping on felts is not permitted."

They laugh, thinking about millworkers hoping to sneak in a nap on the job.

Alex reads the year on a wall calendar, "2001."

Glen explains, "Samson Mills left here in 2001. That's what that calendar is. This room down here. The other side, they would always do the floor with dry mops. You could eat off the floor, it was so smooth. And they would roll out the fabric on the big rolls, inspect it for mistakes, roll it back up, and send it right up that conveyor."

They keep walking.

Fig. 3. Not Friday the 13th. Photo by Caitrin Lynch.

Glen says, "There used to be three machines in this room. I used to come down here, see, back then they had a second shift here. A lot of times I'd come down here Saturdays and they'd be working Saturdays. There used to be a bunch of Vietnamese girls working here too. There's the old calendar. In fact, someone even circled the last day they were here. June 13th, 2001, or something like that."

Caitrin walks over to the calendar on the wall. There are X marks on dates, and one day says "Last Day" in black marker. There are no marks after that. "You're right, June 13th," Caitrin says.

"Yeah, Friday the 13th," says Glen.

Everyone laughs nervously. "No way!" Renee exclaims.

Alex takes a close look at the calendar. "Nooo," Alex sees that it's not true. "Wednesday June 13th." They all feel relieved.

Caitrin calls the group over, "There's some pictures over here of a woman."

Glen responds, "Oh yeah, somebody was infatuated with this young girl." Everyone laughs. "That's the best way to put it, because you see what he writes under her picture. Right here? It's

Fig. 4. You're in my dream. Photo by Caitrin Lynch.

stenciled. 'You're in my dream.' And I don't know what that is up there. Yeah. So that was his sweetie. Now figure it out. This place has been, they've been out of here for twenty years. That girl looks like she's about twenty. She's probably forty years old now."

It's a newspaper clipping for an Asian American film festival. "A sensationalized but beautiful-to-watch tale about a Cambodian peasant," reads the caption. Caitrin wonders, *who hung this up? How did they have time to use the stencils meant for safety and other notices, for this? What were their other dreams?*

Renee says, "That's the personal stuff you like to see."

On the way out, through a steep narrow staircase, Caitrin jumps ahead of Alex, afraid to go last.

9:52 p.m. The outside

They get outside and Caitrin realizes she is totally turned around.

Glen, says, "Alright. That was great. And we didn't even turn any lights on. That was good. And we didn't need any flashlights."

Alex remarks, "Oh, we forgot to go check to see if the flashlight's still there."

Glen says, "Eh, it'll probably be there. If not, I have your number, I'll call you. *Hey you're not going to believe this, the light's gone.*"

They all laugh and thank each other for the great night.

"Good for some laughs," Glen reflects.

9:55 p.m. The drive home

"That was awesome!" Alex says, as soon as the car doors close. "Glen had me on some of that. I recorded it all. He's got some really good stories."

"So, wait, do you believe them?" Caitrin asks.

"He's pretty convincing," Alex says, "but I'm sure a lot of it is just wild animals, old pipes, and a little too much of that factory air."

They pull out of the Riverway parking lot and turn onto the main road that follows the curve of a coiling river. They pass two-story brick mills that have found new lives as condominiums, shopping malls, art centers, and high-tech business complexes. Most of the mills they pass have broken windows, overgrown greenery, crippled asphalt, and for sale signs.

Alex says, "it's funny to see those mills after what we just experienced. I never noticed them before."

Caitrin and Alex are quiet. They've gone down this road five days a week for the past two months.

"What *did* we just experience?" Caitrin asks. "I feel like I was brought into a world of making sense that I hadn't yet seen at Riverway."

"What do you mean?" Alex asks.

"I think a lot about what it must be like to be in an industry that is disappearing out from under you. A bunch of people at Riverway have moved from mill to mill, as they each successively close down. They've done that for forty, fifty years. From the family of owners down to the most recently hired hourly worker, they all know that this is a dying industry. And remember when Stu in knitting told us in an interview that Riverway is a dinosaur in the age of robots?"

"Oh, yeah."

Caitrin continues, "I've been hearing about ghosts for a couple of years. Walking around with Glen let me see how people hold on to a past and make a meaningful future through ghost stories."

"I can't imagine what that place must have been like a hundred years ago. It's cool that people who used to work there left up their calendars and phone lists, so we can still see them. I mean, I guess some of that has only been twenty years," Alex said.

"Yeah, the attic graffiti kind of sums it up for me," Caitrin says. "Did you notice how we were all having our own conversations and observations when we were in the attic? Actually in all the rooms. I bet we each had very distinctive experiences, making sense of what we were hearing and seeing in our own terms, as we were meandering through the mill."

"Yeah."

Caitrin continued, "But it's so cool that the history of people in the building is inscribed in the attic. It's the record of work and life on the walls. And it feels so present to me now. Stories of ghosts challenge us to not think in polar opposites about categories like life and death, materiality and being, past and present. Somehow the people and the stories of this mill come alive to me in the names of people who are no doubt gone from this world, and yet still present. The girl of my dreams still lives on in there. And so does the man with the red checkered shirt."

"On eternal patrol!" Alex says and laughs in a way that betrays some dismissiveness. He's still skeptical. "Ooooooo."

Acknowledgments

Every ghost story recounted here is told as we heard it; we've used creative license to disguise people and places, and for dramatic effect. We thank the National Science Foundation for funding that supports this research. We thank Glen, whose real name we cannot use, for his generosity and storytelling prowess. Thanks also to Max Dietrich, Ilana Gershon, Andrew Holmes, and Yasmine Musharbash for comments on earlier versions of this essay.

Bibliographic Note

We are retelling a nighttime ghost tour at a 150-year-old New England textile mill and the abandoned mill that is directly next door and is connected via stairs and ramps. Everyone at the still-operating mill, called Riverway, refers to the mill next door as "The Other Side." Riverway is located in a part of the United States decimated by closures of mills and factories, where rates of unemployment, divorce, school leaving, addiction, and suicides run high. With constrictions to the business related to global capitalism, Riverway now employs far fewer people than it did at its height in the early 1970s. Global capitalism has shrunk the industry. The company on The Other Side and its many employees are long gone. As Laura Bear points out, this is a landscape filled with the endings and deaths that capitalism requires to create its sense of endless growth. We are showing how past employees and their stories of work and livelihoods live in the walls, stairs, corners, and everyday stories of these two adjacent mills. In doing so, we are building on other scholars' insights about how ghosts, metaphorical and literal, are always haunting capitalist landscapes.

On the role of openness to ghost stories in anthropological methods:

Carlisle, Steven. 2015. "What Holds People Together? First-Person Anthropology and Perspective-Taking in Thai Ghost Stories." *Ethos* 43, no. 1 (March): 59–81. DOI: 10.1111/etho.12072.

On the role of ghosts in interpretations of capitalist processes:

Bear, Laura. 2018. "The Vitality of Labour and Its Ghosts." *Anthropology of This Century,* no. 2 (January). http://aotcpress.com/articles/vitality-labour-ghosts/.
Comaroff, Jean, and John L. Comaroff. 1999. "Occult Economies and the Violence of Abstraction: Notes from the South African Postcolony." *American Ethnologist* 26, no. 2 (May): 279–303. https://www.jstor.org/stable/647285.
Hatfield, D.J. 2011. "The [Ghost] Object: Haunting and Urban Renewal in a 'Very Traditional Town.'" *Journal of Archaeology and Anthropology* 75: 71–112.

On contemporary ghost hunting in the United States, and the narrative constructions of hauntings:

Baker, Joseph O., and Christopher D. Bader. 2014. "A Social Anthropology of Ghosts in Twenty-First-Century America." *Social Compass* 61, no. 4: 569–93. DOI: 10.1177/0037768614547337.

On the longevity of a building, the sense of people being visitors in a longer history, and the viscerality of the thrill of haunting:

Miller, Daniel. 2001. "Possessions." In *Home Possessions: Material Culture Behind Closed Doors,* edited by Daniel Miller, 107–22. Oxford: Berg.

On the collapse of New England's textile industry:

Koistinen, David. 2013. *Confronting Decline: The Political Economy of Deindustrialization in Twentieth-Century New England.* Gainesville: University Press of Florida.

13

How to Brand Your Monster

Matt Tomlinson

Welcome to the Monster Branding Seminar! Please take your seat — there should be enough chairs for everyone.

All settled? Good. Make yourselves comfortable. Please set your cell phones to silent.

You're here today because you have a monster to promote. You've got something in your town — or maybe your lake, or forest — that you want to sell. You can share your monster with the world, and make a bit of money, am I right?

People, I am here to tell you that monsters don't just sell themselves. It doesn't matter how many spikes he's got, or how many campers he's driven out of the woods, or if he's the largest sea monster since the kraken. You've got to brand him. Branding defines your monster's identity, and it's how he'll get noticed. A strong brand means he will succeed in a crowded monster marketplace. As my first boss, Carl Denham, used to say, King Kong is cash, and cash is king!

Now, why am I the guy up here at the podium? I'm the author of *Monster the Competition! Rules for Clawing Your Way to the Top,* which Fangoria called the best monster-industry title of 2022. Copies are on sale at the back of the room, with a discount available, today only. Some of you might also know me as the Jersey Devil Guy. The Jersey Devil is a successful brand. He started out as a two-bit goblin, and now he's an icon. I'll tell you his story later in this seminar. But first, let's dive right in with the lessons you came to learn.

How to Brand Your Monster: Seven Rules

Let's face it: you haven't heard of 99 percent of the monsters out there in the world. Monsters are everywhere, but when you try to think of one, you always come up with the classic brands: Bigfoot, the Loch Ness Monster, Dracula. So, if you want your monster to be the "It" Monster, the one that everyone knows, then you have to identify and build the brand.

To have a brand, your monster needs to do seven things. Or rather, *you* need to do them — your monster is busy scaring people, right? So, it's up to you, the brand manager. As I'll explain, the Jersey Devil became a winner when I helped him do all seven of these things. He always had the potential. But he needed a manager to build his brand and make these seven points stick.

1. Your monster needs a memorable name

This is obvious. But if you don't recognize the obvious, you'll run into brick walls again and again.

Let me tell you a story. It's about two Canadian monsters. Both of them live in deep waters and look a bit like snakes. One lives in a lake and the other lives in the sea, but that doesn't matter for our purposes. The first guy is named — Kudloopud-looaluk. Sorry, I might be mispronouncing that. The other is named Ogopogo. I'm guessing you might have heard of Ogopo-go, the lake monster from British Columbia. But Kudloopud-looaluk? Probably not.

A name needs to reveal your monster's character. It's who he is! Not all monsters have the same character. Ogopogo is a cute name, and sure enough, there is a cute statue of him in his hometown. It's a bouncy name. It's got rhythm. For you word nerds, it's a palindrome, and that opens up a huge number of possibilities for your graphic design team.

But do you know what Ogopogo's original name was? "N'ha-a-itk." I'm sure I'm pronouncing that wrong. This is a hard name for English speakers to work with. Among other things, it's difficult to figure out what rhymes with "-itk."

So, here's how the story goes: The good citizens living by the lake took care of all this in the 1920s. A popular song of the day was called "The Ogo-Pogo: The Funny Fox-Trot." It had lyrics describing a creature from India who was the offspring of a tadpole and a whale. He loved playing the banjo. The locals had a naturally appealing monster, but it was stuck with a bad name. When they heard the catchy song about this banjo-playing polliwog, they decided to rename him. So N'ha-a-itk became Ogopogo. And today he has a respectable life as a celebrity monster.

A good name is a good name, wherever it comes from. Consider that guy who lives on Mt. Everest. Call him "The Abominable Snowman," and he sounds like a British noble who's gone to seed. It's an awful name. Stodgy. Unlovable. A terrible brand. Call it "Yeti" instead, and you have a successful brand. "Yeti" is a Sherpa word. It's a lot shorter than "The Abominable Snowman," it's catchy and memorable, and it rhymes with other words, which is why it's used to sell products like the board game "Yeti in My Spaghetti."

2. Your monster needs an iconic look

Monsters come in recognizable shapes and sizes. If you have a creature swimming in your lake, it's gotta be big. It's gotta be snakelike, or maybe crocodile-like, which isn't too far off. If you've got a hairy man running around the woods, he's gotta be bulky and shambling.

But some monsters give you more latitude. Space aliens, for example. You can project whatever you want onto the blank screen of outer space. The thing that attacked Sigourney Weaver? Excellent. Those octopus guys on *The Simpsons* Halloween episodes? They're great, too. Chewbacca? Yes, yes, yes.

I hear someone in the back saying that Chewbacca isn't a monster. I'm not gonna argue this point right now. For the moment, all I'll say is that limited thinking does not pay the bills.

I always like to say that branding has a gravitational force. In other words, don't be too creative — there are sensible limits. Through decades of hearing UFO stories, most Americans have learned that the strongest space alien brand is, basically, little green men. Or actually, small, sexless people with green or gray skin and huge pupil-less eyes. Twenty years ago, an anthropologist named Susan Lepselter called them "the little grays with big black insect eyes," and said they were "the ones who've made all the press these days." She was right then and she's right today.

3. Your monster needs a good setting

Monsters need to live in places that make sense for them. I grew up in New Jersey, which is how I became the Jersey Devil Guy. My point is, I grew up by a lake named Lake Hopatcong. Supposedly, we had a monster in our lake. I guess it was some kind of creepy eel, or maybe a turtle with fangs — I'm not sure. Here's the thing: I didn't care. Me, I love monsters. I *live* for monsters. And I was supposed to have a monster right here, in my lake, but I knew this was a crock, because Lake Hopatcong can't possibly host a monster. It's a perfectly nice body of water, but it's kind of small, and really suburban. It's not *monstery*.

But, Loch Ness! What a majestic place. It's perfectly suited for a monster. Those hills, those mountains, and the water is a million feet deep. I'm gonna let you in on a secret. How old do you think the Loch Ness Monster is? A thousand years old? Ten thousand? Fact is, he first appeared in 1933, so unless he was hiding for a really long time, even today he's still only in his eighties. He's the same age as Willie Nelson and Yoko Ono. This should be a problem for a monster because they need to have deep roots. They're best when they're ancient. But here's where the natural setting of Loch Ness helps. It's a land of dragons, with rugged peaks and a famous castle, and those murky waters. Looking at that landscape, you'd think the monster from 1933 had to be born at least 33,000 years ago.

Some people try to put monsters in inappropriate places. That was the problem with the Lake Hopatcong Monster. The only scary thing about my hometown is the leaky septic systems.

It's also the problem with some ghosts — if you're willing to consider ghosts to be a type of monster. I hear an objection from the back. I'll come to you in a moment. For now, let me say that ghosts can be identified with many places — crooked old houses, museums, hospitals, prisons, cemeteries, railroad tracks — it's a long list. But they can't go just anywhere. When I was a kid, the TV show *That's Incredible!* made a huge fuss about a haunted building in California. Problem was, it was a Toys "Я" Us store. Apparently, the store still gets mileage out of its reputation, but think of how much more successful that ghost could have been if its brand manager hadn't put it in a toy store.

Okay, yes, back row? You say ghosts aren't monsters? Folks, I can't emphasize this enough. *A monster is a brand. And you build the brand.* If you brand your ghost as a monster, then he's a monster. Or she's a monster. I don't want to get into gender politics here.

4. *Your monster can't be too scary or depressing*

Monsters need to be scary, of course, but don't overdo it. Let me continue with ghosts for a moment. Think about how the very best ghosts aren't too scary.

I grew up in New Jersey, but I now live in Canberra, which is the capital of Australia. In Canberra, there are several places famous for being haunted. Just do a Google search for "Haunted Canberra" and you'll get a couple of names, including the National Film and Sound Archives and Blundell's Cottage. Let me compare them for you.

The National Film and Sound Archives is in an elegant art deco building from 1930. It's said to be haunted because it used to be an anatomy institute. In other words, lots of dead bodies were stored there. It's not a site of murder and mayhem — the bodies were already dead when they arrived — but I guess they built up a ghostly aura. The archive enjoys its reputation, and regularly holds ghost tours. I took one recently. The guide took us through the building at night, and I was blown away. This wall is where a ghost emerged, and a man's ashes were later found stored behind it. That hallway gets really cold, and a dog once got scared and refused to walk down it. This is the foyer where an employee saw a whole gala of ghosts, reliving a party from the 1930s in tuxedos and cocktail dresses. Now, here's the thing. None of the stories was actually scary. I mean, honestly, folks — a dog won't go down a hallway? But the way the tour guide told the stories, and put them together, it was magic. Being haunted is a key part of the National Film and Sound Archives's brand.

Now switch over to Blundell's Cottage. It's a rugged, homey stone building. It feels like it could be haunted, because it's old — the original section was built in 1860 — and so few buildings in Canberra carry that deep history. And it is haunted, but there's a problem. The ghost is a poor, teenage girl who was accidentally burned to death. Her ghost manifests itself in the sickening smell of charred flesh. She might be a nice ghost, but the story is so tragic, and meeting her is apparently so distressing that this isn't something Blundell's Cottage wants publicized. I took a tour at the cottage, and a cheerful guide told me about its social importance. It represents Canberra's real working history — not phony baloney government but the hard work of immigrant farmers who rode horses insane distances, fought bandits, and carried water everywhere. The different sections of the house reflect the different eras of settlement, from tough beginnings to later days that were cozier, but always without running water or electricity.

The guide didn't breathe a word about the ghost. I didn't blame her.

5. Your monster needs sex appeal

This is another obvious point. Dracula is sexy, and he's a great monster. But let's back up a bit and think this through.

There's an argument made by some academics that vampires in medieval and early modern Europe were nothing like what they are today. Those first vampires were bloated, gassy things. Back then, peasants didn't understand how bodies decomposed. So when people were dropping like flies because of the plague, and someone accused your Uncle Pete of being a vampire because he was the first to die, you did what you had to do: you dug up his corpse to prove he was innocent. But there, to your shock, is Uncle Pete in fine shape: fatter than when he was alive, with blood on his lips, long teeth and fingernails, and skin as smooth as a baby's. He's still going strong, long after you buried him.

The public verdict is swift: he's still alive, or actually, undead. He's sucking blood from the living.

Now, there are logical reasons why he looks the way he does. He's fat because his belly is bloated with the gas of decomposition. His rotting abdomen forces his lungs upward, which pushes blood out of his mouth and nose. The bloating makes his outer skin come off, and the skin underneath looks fresh and new. The tight new skin looks drawn back, which makes his teeth and nails seem like they've grown. But the peasants don't realize this. They just see a vampire. An *old-fashioned* vampire.

In other words, you've got a rotten blimp on your hands. Who can market that?

So you change him. You make him Dracula. You keep the marketable parts and toss the rest. Fresh skin and long teeth, yes. Gassy belly and piles of dead skin at your feet, no.

The traditional vampire was a creepy peasant. Dracula is elegant. *Interview with the Vampire,* anyone? But best of all is if you can get the right TV show. Since *Buffy the Vampire Slayer,* vampires have become sensitive teen idols worth their weight in telegenic gold. If your monster is a vampire, he's a much better brand as a Don Juan than as some sick slob, no offense to Uncle Pete.

6. Your monster needs a sense of humor

Sex appeal and humor go together. And here is where zombies come in.

All monsters are built of parts that don't quite fit — things that don't really go together. In fact, you can say that a mishmash of badly fitting parts is a key element of the monster brand. But some misfits are horrifying, and some are funny. Zombies are funny. What makes them funny is the way their mishmash is a bundle of contradictions. Who doesn't love a brainless creature that lives on a diet of brains?

They're out of place wherever they go because they don't really belong anywhere. They don't belong in the grave — they just crawled out of it. They don't belong in your home, obviously. If you want to do research on this, I suggest you rent the movie *Dawn of the Dead* to learn how they don't belong in shopping malls, either, but it's hilarious when they show up there.

Zombies' humor is an essential part of their brand. It's why they're the "It" monsters of the moment. They inspired the recent mash-up craze where classic works of literature have zombies added to them, like *Pride and Prejudice and Zombies*. Lots of self-help books tell you how to survive the coming Zombie Apocalypse. I'm guessing that some of you came here today because you've got a zombie horde you want to market. The good news is that your brand is incredibly hot right now. The bad news is that it's a really crowded market, and werewolves are about to become the new trendsetters. I'm telling you: werewolves. The signs are all there.

7. Your monster needs a special feature

As I said, monsters are a mishmash. A perfect example is Frankenstein, built from bits of corpses that don't quite fit. And then there's the Jersey Devil, who I'll get to next — he's got a bat's wings and a horse's head and hooves. But a hodgepodge isn't enough. Your monster needs to have an extra ingredient. This is the seventh essential feature of your monster's brand.

Your monster's special feature might be his ethnicity. Think of Chupacabras, the Latinx celebrity monster from the 1990s. His name translates into English as "Goat Sucker," suggesting that sticking with "Chupacabras" was a wise choice. Chupacabras is a hungry, spiny-backed beast, kind of like a dog or a bear, but not really. He hops around like a kangaroo. He is a killing machine. This is all good, but it's not especially remarkable as far as monsters go. What matters is that he has an ethnic brand: he is the Old El Paso of monsters. He's from south of the border, but he's so popular with mainstream audiences that he's even been seen in Maine. And he guest-starred in an episode of *Scooby-Doo.*

The best special feature of any monster, however, belongs to the werewolf. He's the perfect modern monster because he works part time. It's also tremendously appealing that he's shaped by natural rhythms. The monsters that are shaped by human pollution, like Godzilla, are so twentieth century. The werewolf is *now.* He's moved by cosmic time and lunar rhythms — I see a potential yoga franchise tie-in, although the violence might be an issue. The idea that a person can be normal one moment and monstrous the next is a great brand, and, let's face it, so true of some people you know. The werewolf's special feature is that he is only a temporary monster, and believe me, that will be priceless.

The Jersey Devil

I've given you the seven rules you need to brand your monster. Now let me tell you how I put it all together for the Jersey Devil. I give the full description of this in my book, on sale at the back of the room.

Now, New Jersey is not a great brand. When most people think of the place, they think of the Turnpike between New

York and Philadelphia — depressed cities, oil refineries, Newark Airport. But in the southern part of the state, we have the Pine Barrens. This is a real forest. It's truly remote, even desolate. It's got sandy earth and slow winding rivers. It's got a ghost town named Ong's Hat. It's got lots and lots of pine trees. And best of all, it has a monster.

The Jersey Devil is the Pine Barrens's most famous son. He was born in 1735. As I heard the story when I was young, his mother, Mrs. Leeds, had already had twelve children. When she learned that she was pregnant again, she said, "if I have another child, let it be the devil."

She got her wish! Instead of a normal baby, a monster was born. I learned later from reading various accounts that the Jersey Devil has a bat's wings and a horse's head and hooves. He killed the midwife and flew out of the house. If this were the end of the story it would be plenty, but what makes the Jersey Devil special is that he has haunted the Pine Barrens for almost three hundred years now. He has terrified people, butchered animals, left his footprints on rooftops, and become that rarest and most impressive thing: a celebrity monster. He is an icon. But it didn't happen automatically.

Back when I was about ten years old, my best friend Jeff moved from Lake Hopatcong to the Pine Barrens, about two hours away. When I visited him, we decided to hike in the forest to find the Jersey Devil. We tramped around the woods, excited but also skeptical. In my memory we walked for several hours, but it probably wasn't really that long. We walked and talked, looked, and listened, and found… nothing. Nothing monstrous, anyway.

I was really excited about that hike. The emotion is hard to describe but I bet it will sound familiar to you. It's the kind of excitement where you want something to be true but suspect it isn't. And your suspicion is divided between disappointment — I didn't see the Jersey Devil — and relief. What on earth would I have done if I had?

I loved the hike, the anticipation, all of it. I decided that when I grew up, I would become the Jersey Devil's brand manager. At

Fig. 1. Comic drawing of the Jersey Devil in the *Philadelphia Evening Bulletin,* 1909. Source: Wikimedia Commons.

first, he seems like a hard sell. It's hard to love a midwife-killing, bat-winged imp with hooves, right? But the Jersey Devil has become an enormously successful brand. He's a local hero, and he's commercially successful well beyond New Jersey.

He did this by fulfilling each of the seven rules.

A memorable name? Yes indeed. "Jersey Devil" is a perfect combination of two things that shouldn't go together: an American state that has a reputation for being an unmagical place, mostly strip malls and Burger Kings, and the ultimate bearer of dark magic, the devil.

Like many successful monsters, his famous name is not his original name. An early reference to him, from an article in *The Atlantic* in 1859, called him "Leeds's Devil," which makes him sound like an English soccer hooligan.

Fig. 2. T-shirt with the iconic modern cartoon image of the Jersey Devil drawn by Ed Sheetz, worn by Alex Tomlinson. Photo by the author.

Devils, as a kind of perfect enemy, are often chosen for sports teams' names. Think of the Duke Blue Devils, the Dickinson Red Devils, and the Arizona State Sun Devils. The apex predator here is the professional hockey team called the New Jersey Devils, who are *so* much scarier than the Toronto Maple Leafs. And the name is so good that it's gotten applied to other things, too, like a rare species of tomato called the Jersey Devil Tomato. I'm not sure how it got that name, although in photos it looks a bit like a chili pepper, which I suppose gives it a touch of evil.

Rule two: an iconic look. The Jersey Devil has got it. It all depends on the bat wings. No bat wings, no Jersey Devil. But his head can be molded into different shapes. His horse-like head, famously shown in an article in a Philadelphia newspaper, was later redrawn as a radish-shaped head with pointy ears, horns, and a tidy set of fangs (fig. 1). This image, which appears on posters and postcards, is, according to one source, "probably the best-known 'likeness' of the Jersey Devil" (fig. 2).

Rule three: a plausible setting. Check! As I mentioned at the beginning of this seminar, the Pine Barrens is a place that can really host a monster. It isn't far from major population centers, but it has plenty of room, plenty of shadows, and plenty of the sort of folk that get called "folk." Perhaps the best evidence of the Pine Barrens's monstrousness is the episode of *The Sopranos* called "Pine Barrens." In it, the capo Paulie Walnuts explains why he and Tony Soprano's nephew should go there to bury the body of a man they think they killed. "Let's take 'im down the Pine Barrens," Paulie says. "It's perfect. It's fuckin' deserted down there… Best part is, we'd be like twenty minutes from AC [Atlantic City]!"

The fourth rule for branding your monster — that it shouldn't be too scary or depressing — is another win for the Jersey Devil. Except for killing his midwife — and maybe also his parents, according to another version of the story — the Jersey Devil sticks to killing animals, not people. If you're a cow or a chicken, look out. Otherwise, you're probably safe.

The time he caused the most fear was during one week in January 1909. There was snow on the ground, and people began finding unusual hoofprints of various sizes. These prints led in strange directions — up trees, across rooftops — and then disappeared. Chickens were found dead with no visible injuries, and farmers wondered if they had been frightened to death. Sightings and tales got out of control. The Jersey Devil was a glowing beast with a ram's head: a hairy, monkey-like thing; a horse-faced, long-necked bird prancing on the roof of a shed. People formed search parties to track him down. It was a panic.

And the newspapers responded just as you'd expect, sensationalizing everything. But they did so with a light touch, calling the Jersey Devil "'jabberwock,' 'kangaroo horse,' 'flying death,' 'kingowing,' 'woozlebug,' 'flying horse,' 'cowbird,' 'monster,' 'flying hoof,' and 'prehistoric lizard,' among other things," as James McCloy and Ray Miller put it in their classic book on the Jersey Devil. The first image I showed you was drawn for the *Philadelphia Evening Bulletin* at this time, and shows you that the devil wasn't really too devilish. So a lot of the craze of 1909 was tongue-in-cheek.

Rule five: sex appeal. Okay, taken on his own, the Jersey Devil might not be the most charming guy. I do have to mention, though, that he's single. According to McCloy and Miller, he was once "seen with a beautiful golden-haired girl dressed in white." He was also spotted "cavorting at sea with a mermaid." After three hundred years in the woods, he's still eligible. And think about how villains always get the best lines, and devils are sexier than angels.

Still not sold? Then consider these two facts. First, he's a celebrity. He's the villain in several movies and the star of his own video game (Sony PlayStation's *Jersey Devil,* from 1997). He's also in an *X-Files* episode (from 1993). Second, he has a cocktail named after him. Its main ingredients are applejack and cranberry juice, a perfect local drink. Applejack is the local moonshine, and cranberries are the major crop. When your name gets used for a cocktail, you know you've made it. The only serious rival in popularity to cocktails is energy drinks, and I'd like to point out that one of the biggest brands in that category is called Monster. Now if we can get an energy drink to change its name to Juicy Devil, we'll be set for life.

Rule six: a sense of humor. During the panic of 1909, a museum in Philadelphia took its cue from P.T. Barnum and announced that what people were calling the Jersey Devil was actually a creature that had escaped from its premises. It was, they said, "the only rare Australian Vampire in captivity." This jibed with reports that compared the Devil's body to a kangaroo's. A New York newspaper took the Australian theme farther by announcing that the Jersey Devil had been identified as a "bombat," but then added a patriotic twist. The bombat laid eggs that were red, white, and blue. Laying patriotic eggs is comedy gold.

Finally, rule seven, the special feature. In some ways, the Jersey Devil's X factor is New Jersey itself. He's the spiky weed growing through concrete at the edge of the construction site.

He belongs to the structure, but he doesn't quite fit it — until he lends his name to our hockey team, of course.

But the Jersey Devil's true special feature is a surprisingly humble but effective one. Despite his horse head, bat wings, and hooves, he's human. He was born of human parents. He was born in a real place, New Jersey, in a real time, 1735. Okay, he might not actually have existed. But the stories make it clear that he is ultimately supposed to be a *person*.

His humanity is so appealing, in fact, that some people claim to be related to him. No one claims to be related to the Loch Ness Monster, and people who claim to share kinship with space aliens usually have very disturbing stories about how this kinship came about. But the Jersey Devil was one of us. He was originally just a baby, mewling his way into the world and then fighting his way out with fingernails that were "kind of clawy," as one local told a folklorist in 1941.

In fact, one of the more revealing books on the Jersey Devil is written by an author who presents his work as family history. His grandmother told him he was related to the Jersey Devil. So he sets out on a quest to figure out what she meant, and disprove those who disagree with her. (They don't disagree because they disbelieve in the Jersey Devil. Instead, they say *they* are the Devil's true relatives.) In his version of the story, the Jersey Devil is the author's great-great-great-great-great-great-great-great-great uncle.

Making someone care this much about their great-great-great-etc. uncle is proof that a monster's brand has achieved a profitable balance. At the same time that you want to drive the Jersey Devil into the deep forest, into the Pine Barrens and the cranberry bogs, past the ghost town of Ong's Hat — to really make him disappear forever, into the gloom — you also kind of want to invite him into your family.

Conclusion

Your monster doesn't belong to you alone. Identify his brand and build it. In doing so, you will entertain the world. Just as monsters mash up a riot of features — hair, horns, fangs, wings — they also provoke a range of emotional responses: Pleasure in fright, warmth in icy coldness. The trick is to follow the seven rules listed above so your monster achieves that lovely monstrous balance. If you don't, your monster will live alone in his hollow or cave or haunted house, unknown and unloved. And in our modern world, nothing is more frightening than being ignored.

The Jersey Devil was born almost two centuries before that week in 1909 when he terrified everyone and pulled off that rarest trick for monsters, much rarer than having a weird body and leaving hoofprints that stop in the middle of nowhere. He became a brand.

And this leads us to the eighth rule — the one I didn't plan to reveal, but since you've been such a terrific audience, I'll let you in on this last secret. Exclusivity attracts. If your monster is too popular, its cachet will dwindle, because secrecy is a key feature of the monster brand. Monsters can't be too easy to find, or they would stop being monsters. This is why they live their most vital lives in grainy photos, shaky film footage, and old newspaper clippings. When I went on that hike in the Pine Barrens with my friend Jeff many years ago, I really hoped we might see a monster. If we knew our goal was impossible, we wouldn't have bothered. But if we knew it was too easy, we would have been too scared to leave the house.

Have fun branding your monster. And folks, copies of my book, *Monster the Competition! Rules for Clawing Your Way to the Top* are available for purchase. Thank you.

Bibliographic Note

The inspiration for writing this chapter was hearing about the Jersey Devil when I was a kid, but as I quickly discovered, there is wonderful written material available. A useful starting point is James F. McCloy and Ray Miller Jr.'s overview from 1976, *The Jersey Devil*. I stumbled across Bill Sprouse's *The Domestic Life of the Jersey Devil* (2013), wherein the author claims to be related to the title character. It is fun in a rambling kind of way, although tending toward cutesiness, as seen in the ye-olde-fashioned sub-subtitle beginning "An *Immodest Inquiry* into the Origins of the Leeds Devil" and going on for fifty words after that. The most evocative work is John McPhee's classic *The Pine Barrens* (1968). Although the Jersey Devil only occupies a small bit of textual territory here — a sliver of chapter four, "The Air Tune" — McPhee's descriptions of the Pine Barrens are beguiling. From "cedar water" rivers to highly combustible trees — oaks with leaves so oily "that they appear to be made of shining green leather" and the pines themselves, which recover quickly after fires have burned through the country — McPhee's lyricism is intoxicating, but he doesn't neglect the funny jarring details, such as the fact that the Jersey Devil shares the woods with a shapeshifting witch named Peggy. In thinking about how monsters are brands of their own, I made reference to the excellent research of Manning, Moore, and Nakassis listed below.

Manning, Paul. 2010. "The Semiotics of Brand." *Annual Review of Anthropology* 39: 33–49. DOI: 10.1146/annurev.anthro.012809.104939.

McCloy, James F., and Ray Miller, Jr. 1976. *The Jersey Devil*. Wilmington: Middle Atlantic Press.

McPhee, John. 1968. *The Pine Barrens*. New York: Farrar, Straus and Giroux.

Moore, Robert E. 2003. "From Genericide to Viral Marketing: On 'Brand'." *Language & Communication* 23, nos. 3–4 (July–October): 331–57. DOI: 10.1016/S0271-5309(03)00017-X.

Nakassis, Constantine V. 2013. "Brands and Their Surfeits." *Cultural Anthropology* 28, no. 1 (February): 111–26. DOI: 10.1111/j.1548-1360.2012.01176.x.

Sprouse, Bill. 2013. *The Domestic Life of the Jersey Devil.* Great Egg Harbor: Oyster Eye Publishing.

14

How to Live with Aliens

Susan Lepselter

Place: A gleaming building in SiliconValley.
Time: A few years from now.

Tiffany: Hello, everyone! I'm very pleased you've all decided to come on out for our One Universe Networking Seminar on Human/Alien Contact and Cooperation. We're very proud of our Alien outreach program, here. Our analytics show a slight change in participant demographics this year, and we're proud — hell, stoked! — that some of the more recent uptick suggests that a full 2 percent of our members now may be Aliens or hybrids. And as we humans keep gearing up to settle Mars and beyond, we'll be meeting all sorts of Alien neighbors in the years to come.

The point, here, is what we're trying to accomplish with our interactive events. And that is helping everyone understand that we all need to live together. Alien and human. Human and Alien. Hybrid. Reptilian, Gray, Space Brother. Gray, green, purple, polka dot, or what have you!

Some of you've asked me about those campaign promises we've all been hearing about as the election approaches. Those of us who — let's be blunt — have the means to do so will want and need to leave this old Earth behind when the time is right. Atmosphere-informed construction is developing such exciting designs for new Mars properties. At the same time, Aliens from space are still infiltrating our borders. But with all due respect to Washington, the business community agrees that America simply is not going to be building a border wall between Earth and space anytime soon, if only because the force field technology isn't yet at a cost that makes sense. So yes, we humans and Aliens are all in this together. But that's good. There is so much potential here! In fact, we're offering a special cruise to orbit Mars as a door prize. Pretty soon, we think, this homesteading will be very big business indeed.

Real Estate Investment in Space, our institute's first summer workshop course, is now being considered for distance credit at Wharton business school. And there's all the incredible new medical research just emerging out of the Alien knowledge base, especially in reproductive technology services. We are using some of this new knowledge for continued development of our own surveillance technologies for business and advertising. AI is going through the roof. And then, of course, there's the *really* wide-open field; not just how Alien technologies contribute to our product development, but also, maybe, if you'll dream with me here just a little, the completely untapped market of Aliens as consumers themselves! As their human markets are still unfortunately shrinking, Pepsi and Philip Morris are both super excited about getting in on this with the Reptilians, hush hush. But I'm perhaps getting a little ahead of myself here. There's no evidence Aliens even use a cryptocurrency, as yet. Still, we can dream.

Well. Today is a busy day at our seminar. We have three very special speakers today, and each of them want to tell you, in their own way how to live with Aliens. We have a Reptilian Alien. We have a Nordic Alien, also known as a Space Brother. We wanted to have a Gray to speak with you, but you know, those Grays just don't talk to groups. They would just... gaze at you. And that, of course, can be a little bit disconcerting. So, we have someone even better: our new, executive-level Alien education specialist, a DNA certified hybrid. She's half human, and fully 50 percent Gray Alien. I'll leave you here and turn you over to Aline, here. Please welcome Aline.

Aline: Hey. Hey everyone. Okay, thanks. Bye, now, Tiffany. [Tiffany exits.] *Wow.* Well. Is she gone?

Audience: Yes.

Aline: Okay, good. Hello everyone. First off, I volunteered for this position because I have so much to say, and I really want you to understand how to live with Aliens.

Of course, you already *do* live with Aliens, and you always have; because what is an "Alien" anyway? An Alien is any being that is *other* to the person calling them Alien. A stranger. Foreign. An *émigré* from a world that isn't yours. When you call something Alien, you become aware of what's so natural to you that it usually goes without saying. The Alien shows you what's most familiar to you.

First rule for living with Aliens: look at yourself. I'll get back to this later.

But for now, you know that Aliens from beyond this planet are appearing on Earth in a variety of different forms. All "Space Aliens" have one thing in common, that they are beings who are not native to Earth.

So there's no one way to live with Aliens, and I've invited a couple of others to help me round out the picture. Let me introduce our other speakers. Here, on my right, is Sven, a Nordic Alien. And there — where did you go? — ah, there in the back of the room, the tall man, wearing the boater, is Lacerto, representing the Reptilian Aliens among us.

Man in Audience: Hey, I have a question! You know all those sci-fi movies where the Earth is attacked by Martians? And they look like robots? What do you think about them?

Aline: Yes, some Extraterrestrials are warlike, and threaten the Earth with their high-tech craft and weapons. They will destroy nature to use it for their own means. They don't care how precious it is to Earthlings.

But other Aliens come to warn us that we humans are in the process of ruining Earth all by ourselves. These are wise guardians who are quietly watching us, trying to save something of Gaia from the dangers of our nuclear war, our pollution, our endless extraction of resources from the Earth. These guardian Aliens have taken all kinds of forms over the years. Sometimes they look like Angels from the Bible. Sometimes even the sinister, abducting Gray Aliens, with their big heads and eyes, sometimes even they take abductees aside and warn them to take care of the Earth. And often, the guardian Aliens are like Sven, sitting beside me here.

Sven, here, is a Nordic Alien. You might have heard of Nordics. In the 1950s, George Adamski, a Polish immigrant, spread the word about Sven's particular species, calling them Space Brothers. So many American humans listened to George! So many American humans wanted to quit the ordinary rat race and live with Alien Space Brothers!

These Space Brother Aliens are tall — would you mind standing up, Sven? — often too tall to be really human, blonde, and blue-eyed with fair skin. Like Sven, here, they have attractive faces and well-proportioned physiques. The male bodies look athletic. The female bodies are athletic and very shapely, which you can see because they wear such close-fitting uniforms. Physically, these Space Brothers or Nordic Aliens look almost human but, you know, *better* than human. When they first started showing up in the United States in the 1950s, why, the word was that all the humans back then wanted to be tall and blonde. Nordic Aliens are the epitome of 1950s ideal whiteness. And in all ways, not just physically, they are better than actual humans of any race. They emanate harmony, peace, and wisdom. They have superpowers of empathy.

They won't abduct you! Humans who interact with these Aliens are called contactees, not abductees. Contact is about coming together. The Nordics teach you, and ask you to spread their wisdom. They were most often seen when the Cold War was ratcheting up, nuclear fear was strong, and kids were learning to "duck and cover" in school.

Audience member: Are you going to tell us how to live with Sven? Can I sign up somewhere?

Aline: How to live with Nordics, my friends, is the kind of problem you want to have. I can see why you're so eager. On the other hand, you wouldn't find yourself in contact to begin with if things on Earth weren't in such a mess. The thing is, I get it, some of you want to really live with them, not just co-exist with them. You want more than that parallel play you humans do with other species, with squirrels or ants. So, you want to actually live with the benevolent, peaceful Aliens? There is no sign up sheet, but you can go to the desert or the woods, and sit, and bring other humans with you. Focus on the spiritual dimension of the universe, the oneness of all things, and concentrate on harmony.

Please, though, don't sell all your belongings to wait for their ships to land in the desert. Really. That never ends well.

Audience member: [waving her hand] Um. Hello? These Space Brothers or Nordics or whatever you want to call them are stuck in the 1950s! We're supposed to just accept that this… super-whiteness represents perfection? This white-fetishizing denial of diversity? No, I don't buy it. Sorry.

Another audience member: I know! Right? [Everyone looks at Sven.]

Sven: [stands up, and intones] Yes, yes, I get it. We so-called Nordics feel a bit out of date in these idealized white bodies, honestly. You see, my kind are from the Pleiades (even though some people sometimes called us Venusians). And you see, we evolved differently than you. We don't *have* a fixed material body. We are fully tuned into your thoughts, your desires and fears. Our bodies take shape according to *your* image of us. And evidently [he looks down at himself] I am still quite tall and blonde. But to be blunt, that's on you. We can only appear as you need us to appear as you desire perfection. You humans have some work to do.

Do you want to live with us? We'll come help you save yourselves, again and again, from the brink of ecological and nuclear disaster. But I can sense it. Yes, soon we Space Siblings, to update the gender a bit, won't look only like this. We always reflect your wiser, better nature. When we first came to America, when believers and experiencers revealed us to an anxious nation, well, this is what perfection seemed it should look like. But some things have changed. So if you would like to live with us again, friends, you'll have to get conscious. I predict we'll be looking physically perfect in many more shades and shapes.

Aline: Does that make sense to you, Human?

And you — who asked the first question? You see, Sven seems nothing like the Alien attackers you know from science-fiction Martian movies. But he has something in common with them anyway. Because whether Aliens are aggressive towards the Earth or protective of it, the Extraterrestrial reminds us to see the Earth as a specific place with borders, something that can be destroyed, vulnerable to technologies that exceed its capacities for renewal, its ecology altered beyond compatibility with human existence.

If step one to living with Aliens is to look at yourself, step two is to think about Earth with care. You are alive in an epoch on Earth where the conditions of nature are already dominated by human technological activity. Plants are vanishing, animals are vanishing, the temperature is changing, the ice is melting. We Hybrids know that air and water are alive. You humans are not the only ones who can claim this planet as your place of origin, of course. Everything Earthly can do the same. All the other species of animals on Earth are natives of this planet, too.

To live with Aliens means to understand this: Your connection to Earth and nature is a story, and it could be told in a different way. You could say this is why we're noticing Aliens now. But humans have always knowingly lived with other beings.

Audience member: Wow, you know, that reminds me of my great grandmother. She was from Ireland. She said when she was a girl, way out in the countryside, people knew they lived with Fairies. The Fairies would kidnap your baby if you didn't watch out!

Aline: People then knew they lived with Other beings. They didn't have to be ashamed of it. It didn't make them seem crazy.

When Fairies abducted a human child from her bed, in her place they left a Fairy double — a changeling. The changeling looked like the kidnapped child, but the baby's mother could sense a difference. The changeling was smaller, wizened, less interactive. The changelings looked just a bit off. They grew more peculiar over time, more Alien. Just like some say of the Gray Aliens who abduct humans now, the Fairies might have needed to take humans to strengthen their own stock. The Fairies were cunning but too small and weak, like today's Gray Aliens, and they too needed to breed their own kind with the robust blood of humans. People like your great grandmother knew they lived with Fairies. But as the culture changed, more and more humans admitted to believing only in creatures whose existence you could actually prove.

And, so, Fairies drifted away. But the stories about them remained. And even though fewer people wanted to admit it, they still had contact with Others. Now they called them Space Aliens.

We Hybrids sometimes talk about the changelings who could pass among you. Some of us think the Fairies were really Gray Aliens, described in a way that made sense to the culture who lived with them. And some people say Aliens are the new Fairies, entering the role of the otherworldly kidnapper in a way that makes sense to us now. Certainly the space Alien, with all their advanced, dominating technologies, makes sense to our world here and now, in a way that Fairies made sense to people back then. Because, you see, in every story you hear today there's always some other story from the past layered inside it.

Audience Member: So, Aliens in different forms have been here for ages! I've heard the Reptilian Aliens have been here for eons, too. I heard they came from another planet long long ago and interbred with humans. I'm worried, to tell you the truth. I hear now they've infiltrated everything. They shape-shift into human form. I've heard the conspiracies. Reptilian Aliens are consolidating all the power so they can make the world into a single global political entity. I hear they're plotting behind the scenes, pulling strings at the top, secretly controlling us all. That doesn't sound like little old Fairies drifting away in the bogs, to me.

Aline: Reptilians are another species of Alien. Like every Alien, from Fairies to Grays, they mingle with us. That's really the point, isn't it? You can't tell where the Alien ends and the Self begins. And vice versa. Luckily, we have a Reptilian here today — in the back there, oh he was in the back — Oh! Here he is, right beside me. I think it's time to let the Reptilian speak for himself. Please allow me to introduce Lacerto.

[Lacerto has suddenly materialized beside Aline. The audience blinks. First, he looks like a seven-foot tall reptile. He seems to dissolve into a human form, a white-haired man wearing an expensive suit. Then he looks like a giant reptile again.]

Lacerto: Hello, People. People, people, this anxiety is not... useful. You know, we Reptilian Aliens are not your enemies. Why, we are your friends. We, not the Space Brothers, are here to protect you. The Space Brothers are fools. Clever people! Listen to us instead.

We do not want the Earth's resources. That is a silly, silly lie. We have not interbred with you humans for thousands of years, creating a dangerous new breed for our own purposes. We did not come to Earth long ago to take your gold, which we did not bring back to enrich our own planet. We did not engender a race of slaves to serve us. What a silly lie. But on the other hand, if just say we once did engender a race of slaves, well, what's wrong with being a slave? It's the order of things. The slave wishes to serve. We were doing them a favor, no?

Do you listen to those rumors, the stories that we Reptiles have become the overlords of the Earth? Do you worry that we dominate the International Monetary Fund and the United Nations, that we are the force behind the New World Order? That we have infiltrated the deep state and the monarchy, inter-bred with royalty through the centuries to consolidate power, and that dear old Queen Elizabeth was really a shape-shifting Reptilian, petting her corgis with her long lizardy finger? How ridiculous is that? But even if it were true, just for argument's sake, well, why would you object to such a thing? Isn't it better for Aliens to have all the power so you can just be your little self and do your, I don't know, your Facebooking and your drinking of giant sodas? You don't need to worry about all that ruling business. You just need to know how to get by. So let me tell you, dearest humans, how to live with us Reptilians.

First, if you meet a person who seems to give you a bit of a shiver, check their skin. Is it a little bit... scaly? Next check their eyes. Are they gold, shifting to green, with a vertical pupil? Are they looking at you as if they wish to eat you? If so, it is a good idea to either let them eat you, but if they don't, then just have sex with this person. If you're a woman, try to get pregnant. Your baby will be absolutely fantasssstic. It will of course just be a sweet, normal human baby who will love you, don't be silly! Feed it flies.

Here are some other tips to living with Reptilians. Always donate money to political campaigns for people who have your best interest at heart. It can be difficult to know who these good men and women are. Many ineffective, weak politicians will pretend to represent you, but be careful. The ones who really care about you may be recognized if you follow our guidelines.

First, these good leaders understand that climate change is a lie spread by the weak and ignorant. And anyway, let's say it turns out that in fact there is a bit of climate change. Tropical environments are much better anyway, no? Don't you think it should be blazingly hot everywhere all year long? Just think how nice it is, to lie on a sunny rock, digesting. Frankly, ice is ridiculous. Use your common sense. Is water supposed to be solid? Of course not. Anyone who tries to tell you that there *should* be so-called "ice caps" at the poles of the Earth thinks you are stupid. Only the clever humans can live with us, and we know you are so very clever.

To live in peace with us, dear, clever little humans, you must have hardship, conflict, and war. We have to tear up the Earth so in the end, only the worthy reap its riches. So please vote for anyone who wants to drill as many pipelines as possible, especially in arctic regions. It's also an excellent plan to drill in coastal areas. You can determine the very best spots for coastal drilling by looking for towns where the little people make their living by fishing. The ocean should get thick with oil. Fires should burn on the surface of the water. The aroma of burning oil is so enticing. Toxins are good, dear people! Here's some more advice for us to live together. Tap water should be filled with lead. The air should be difficult for humans to breathe, and human children should ideally have plenty of asthma. Give plenty of toxins to the poor most of all. And hurricanes, naturally. Don't skimp!

We want anger. Conflict is fuel. When people fight each other, we get stronger. Of course, you may find some of this uncomfortable. If so, blame the humans who are just a bit different from you. Blame the immigrants if you are not one, blame another race, a different religion, get enraged. I have some cards here to pass out, dear humans, explaining how to form a mob. To live with us, you can start small. Cause a traffic jam at rush hour. Generate this angry fuel for us. Violence is definitely to be encouraged. Please, dear humans, make sure everyone has a gun. Please make sure other countries have all the weapons you yourself are counting on, and then just… dare them to launch. Chaos is my friend and your friend, dear human. Don't worry.

When it gets too bad, we will give you comforting martial law. When we rule over you, you can relax.

It's important that all power remain in the hands of a very smart few, you see. The few humans with Reptilian DNA snaking around their human genes. We have been around for a long time, and we aren't going anywhere, little human. If you are very, very good, you might get a little drop of power, yourself. That's how you can live with usssss.

Aline: Okay, maybe we should stop there — Lacerto? Where did he go? I'm not sure. He could be among you. Maybe he vanished. You heard Lacerto say that the powers that be are Reptilian Human hybrids. To live with all Aliens, you have to understand that most everything is a hybrid, really. As a Gray Human hybrid myself, I know that all stories are told by many people, not just the single individual storyteller. Most things are hybrid in some way, if you look closely for the mergings and combinations. And when we want to understand how to live together, humans and Aliens, we have to remember that if you listen closely, you'll hear a bunch of combinations, forming many dimensions of many stories, told in different languages from different times, echoing through the stories of our own interspecies Alien/human encounters.

Audience member: That lizard guy was creepy! But what does it mean, Aline — that you're an Alien–human hybrid? What's your story?

Aline: My mother was a full breed human. I have two older half-brothers, both human, and I have many hybrid half-siblings who stayed on the Alien side. The Aliens in my DNA are called Grays. Some Grays are very small, the size of human children. These Little Greys have chilling clinical skills. They know how to extract what they need from human bodies. They are the most prolific of abductors, the ones who wipe your memory clean so they can come back for you again and again.

Audience member: Are you... one of *them?*

Aline: Well, partly. I came to consciousness in a lab on board the craft. When I was very small, I floated in a small incubator, and I looked across at the other baby hybrids waiting for the day they'd be able to walk free. Once when I was very new, my human mother was allowed to see me on board the craft. The Grays don't have much emotion. They wanted to understand what her feeling towards this Hybrid child would be. They seemed pleased that her maternal instinct was strong. She forgot the visit afterwards, of course, but a faint shadow of the memory remained in her as a feeling.

Every day, a Gray would come to observe me and chart my development. Would I have emotions like a human being? Would I bring some part of human nature — longing, sadness, the joy of being embodied — back into the Alien stock? That's what they wanted to introduce to their own genetics, I believe: the heartiness, the emotion, the part of being human that was of the body. Their own bodies are so small, weak. Their brains are too heavy.

And little by little, I wanted to leave the Alien realm and come to the Earth side. I wanted to learn to live with humans.

Part of the desire to come down here was plain curiosity. Part of it was the human longing for other people that had been bred into me through my mother's side. So one day, when I was eight years old, they allowed it. I was sent down. I felt the cold, wet grass on my feet for the first time, and I walked across the yard in the night, with the craft's light shining a path for me. People in the town thought it was the moon. I walked straight to my mother's bedroom window and peered inside. I could see that she was asleep, but immediately she sensed something and woke up, and stared back at my face from across the window.

At first she was afraid, she had the familiar feeling of the Alien moment, priming herself for another abduction. But then she saw me. She just knew who I was. She walked over to the window and put her hands on the glass. I put mine up too. My fingers were so long, spindly, and white compared to hers. I could see my face reflected in the window right next to hers: my thin white hair, my round forehead, my large dark eyes without the whites, without the pupil you humans have. Yet some of my mother was in my face too. Then she came outside and hugged me. Of course it was the first time I had ever touched anyone this way, and it was quite fascinating, and in fact, I believe I felt something. That was interesting. She was weeping. But I couldn't stay. That night I went back into the craft, but I returned now and then, the human side of me just wanting to find my mother for no logical reason, waking her up by looking in the window.

Audience member: So you knew your mom was an abductee? How could your mom live with you, knowing where you came from?

Aline: My mom told me she always knew something was different. She would come to, in the mornings after her abduction, kneeling by the rings of burnt grass in her yard where nothing would grow. She showed me the small scar on her stomach, and I knew that was the beginning of my existence. That was where they took the egg.

My mother, you see, was always an abductee. Some people are abducted only once or a few times, but others are tracked and followed from childhood on. Mom sensed, all her life, that *something* had been happening to her. She didn't know what it was, exactly. She had a feeling that there was something different about her, something she half-knew about herself. But everyone's childhood has a few such things, things you don't really talk about, and you're not sure if they happen to other people too.

Sometimes she would venture a hinting question to her friends, to see if the fragments of what she remembered of her abductions were common to other people. She'd casually ask: *Do you ever wake up just feeling like you've been taken? Do you ever suddenly remember a white shape slipping through your wall? Or suddenly get scared thinking of huge black eyes looking into you but you don't know whose they are?* Like many abductees, Mom had screen memories. Aliens wipe out the memory of what happened, but new images replace those memories, and they keep a trace of the original episode — a feeling of dread, or the Alien black eyes. She would ask her friends: *Do you ever think you've been watched through your window by an owl, with big, black eyes — a very frightening owl that just vanishes…? Like a dream, but you're awake?* But Mom's friends gave her blank looks in response, and she realized this was a true secret, an unspeakable kind of difference, even though she wasn't sure yet exactly what it entailed. Mom knew she'd been chosen. It was terrifying and yet it was what made her special.

One reason it was so hard for her to talk about is that back then, my mother had never heard of Alien abduction. She would not have known the word abductee. Oh, she'd seen UFO movies, but she was growing up in the early 1960s, and the abduction story wasn't being openly told, not yet.

Sven: But for your poor mother, these encounters… weren't all bad, were they?

Aline: No, sometimes there was something good, too. A sense of mystery. A feeling of connection to the universe. A deep awareness that there is a greater meaning and purpose to life than you get in the ordinary world.

Was that mystical inkling a trick, was it a way the Aliens kept humans docile? Or was it a human response to the extraordinary? One positive feeling that couldn't be explained away though was the overwhelming love you'd feel when the Aliens might show you your baby, conceived with your egg, created through this abduction, being developed in the UFO. A hybrid, like me.

Audience member: What did she remember, then?

Aline: Mom would go to bed at night, and then sometimes, she would wake up with a start and realize she was paralyzed. She could not scream. She would look at the clock in her line of vision, her heart pounding with fear, and then suddenly she'd be sitting up in bed, with her nightgown on backwards or inside out, and the clock would say it was two hours later. Seemed like less than a second. Not until she was hypnotized years later did she remember what happened during that paralysis: the silent gray Aliens gliding noiselessly towards her, with their large black eyes focused on her, and then her body rising from her bed, floating with them through the outer wall of the house, and into the UFO. Of course, Aliens don't call it a UFO, but this is my mother's story.

Audience member: So you mean there were old-time Fairies, and now there are Gray aliens, and the rest of the human world is free of this stuff?

Aline: No, humans everywhere live with an Other, an Alien. Right between sleep and waking, people everywhere wake up paralyzed, and they sense a presence in the room with them, something not human. Alien, you could say, but what that means and what form that takes varies. In Newfoundland, Canada, and in the American South too, the old hag comes in the night when you're sleeping and sits on your chest. You can hardly breathe, let alone move. In Newfoundland they accept it. You've been hagged, they say. They have learned to live with the old hag, they chat about it over a beer in the pub. In Scandinavia a damned woman, the mare, comes and sits on your chest, and you can't move then, either. The mare from the nightmare is not a horse, it's this experience, a being who is Alien to you, coming in the night, paralyzing you, reminding you that you're not alone, you humans, and that the things that seem real by day can shift by night.

Yes, these encounters happen between sleep and waking worldwide, because these things belong to things that are liminal, betwixt and between. Some researchers, psychologists, would say these encounters are simply a byproduct of the hypnagogic state. They thought that your mind is partly conscious, then, but your body has already been paralyzed so you won't act out your dreams. You can imagine how frustrating this was for abductees to hear. There is so much more to abduction than a physiological response. And the thing is, Aliens don't only abduct people in the state between sleep and waking. The first modern abductees, named Betty and Barney Hill, were abducted driving their car in 1961. And so was my own mom.

When she was driving to college one night, on a dark and empty road, Mom had a strange feeling, like her heart was vibrating, like all the electric systems of her body were ramping up. And then the car began vibrating, and the lights flashed, and the engine failed. She was scared. She looked up and saw there was a full moon. But she knew the moon wasn't supposed to be full that night. That moon began to descend. She frantically tried to start the engine, and the light from this moon filled the car. And then, she was sitting in the passenger seat, and the key was on the floor. She picked it up and started the car, and she saw that two hours had somehow passed. Well, that was the night I was conceived.

As I tell you these stories, you might hear echoes of things that sound familiar from other situations, other stories. And yes, like me, these stories are hybrids. They have parts from different places and that makes them stronger. The famous Alien abductee researcher, the late Budd Hopkins, once said that in the abduction scenario, humans are like the Aztecs and the Aliens are like the Spanish. He said, for the Aztec, the world before the Spanish arrived probably seemed like Eden. The sense of Earth as an Eden we can no longer dwell innocently inside is part of the Alien story. So are centuries of human colonization.

These days, some very rich and ambitious humans want to colonize new planets. Then they will be Aliens; that is, they'll be the strangers colonizing new worlds. They will grab up the resources of a new planet; they will bend the new world to adapt to their needs; they will claim this place as their home. And they will have to learn how to live with whomever is native to that world, from microscopic creatures on up. But this should not sound unfamiliar to you humans.

Like I said at the beginning, the first rule for living with an Alien is always to look at your self.

I want to help you all be a little less afraid. But in some ways, I do want you to be a little more afraid.

Because the world could end soon. We *should* be more afraid of that. The oceans want to live, the rain forest wants to keep breathing. It doesn't seem real, I know. The Earth itself seems Alien to you. Nature seems like something that came before you, or is outside you, or surrounding you. You might not know that the way you think about nature has been shaped over hundreds of years, and it's only a story that puts you humans in the center of things. This center is unstable.

That's what we Aliens have been saying since we began our modern visits to you, right after the bomb, that you people see the Earth as a thing that is both yours and foreign to you, something to extract profit from.

There are terrifying, evil, conspiring Aliens who want to devour the Earth, who are consolidating power for themselves. There are wise Aliens who want to guide you, to help you take care of Earth and everything living. All of them tell you something about what's happening to your planet.

The way to live with Aliens is to listen to any story that makes the hair stand up on the back of your neck: about invasion and colonization, about the opposing desires for destruction and redemption, and to understand that there is no Alien apart from the self. If you want to live with Aliens, you first have to live with the Earth.

And now, here is Tiffany, again. She'll take you out through that double door, through the virtual gift shop.

Bibliographic Note

The world was a very different than it is today when, back in the early 1990s, I began interviewing people who talked about living with aliens. I spoke with people in the American Southwest who frequently gathered together, as friends and exploratory intellectual collaborators, to discuss what they knew, and believed, and half-remembered, and suspected about UFOs and uncanny conspiracy theories. These were people who often had strange memories they couldn't quite explain, and who sometimes referred to themselves as alien "experiencers." Even many decades ago, before climate change was an everyday topic of debate in mainstream conversation, many of these people who thought a lot about living with space aliens and UFOs were also intensely aware that the Earth was a fragile system. For those who thought about living with aliens, the Earth was not invisible or "unmarked," and humans were not the only possible form of sentient life. Some folks believe in benevolent aliens, and others believe in malevolent ones. But all these stories about human-alien encounters make explicit that the Earth is vulnerable in many ways, and that its human occupants are not necessarily the center of things. Many of the bibliographic works I refer to here explore rich, contemporary meanings of space alien belief. Other books I list here offer related ways to understand other connections between human and other-than-human beings in our current time of rapidly progressing Earthly vulnerability, reminding us that living with aliens means, always, that self and other are always relative and shifting terms. I also include a single, classic work of narrative theory, which helps me frame the stories I heard and the stories I tell as inherently layered and intermingling, as any story about humans and aliens living together must be.

On Alien abduction and similar experiences around the world:

Adler, Shelley R. 2010. *Sleep Paralysis: Night-mares, Nocebos, and the Mind-body Connection.* Piscataway: Rutgers University Press.

Bullard, Thomas. 1988. "UFO Abduction Reports: The Supernatural Kidnap Narrative Returns in Technological Guise." *Journal of American Folklore* 102: 146–69.

Clarke, David. 2015. *How UFOs Conquered the World: The History of a Modern Myth.* London: Aurum Press.

Huffard, David J. 1982. *The Terror That Comes in the Night: An Experience-Centered Study of Supernatural Assault Traditions.* Philadelphia: University of Pennsylvania Press.

On Aliens, politics, and culture:

Battaglia, Debbora, ed. 2005. *E.T. Culture: Anthropology in Outer Spaces.* Durham: Duke University Press.

Brown, Bridget. 2007. *They Know Us Better Than We Know Ourselves: The History and Politics of Alien Abduction.* New York: New York University Press.

Dean, Jodi. 1997. *Aliens in America: Conspiracy Cultures from Outerspace to Cyberspace.* Ithaca: Cornell University Press.

Finley, Stephen C. 2022. *In and Out of This World: Material and Extraterrestrial Bodies and the Nation of Islam.* Durham: Duke University Press.

Kripal, Jeffrey J. 2010 *Authors of the Impossible: The Paranormal and the Sacred.* Chicago: University of Chicago Press.

Lepselter, Susan. 2016. *The Resonance of Unseen Things: Poetics, Power, Captivity and UFOs in the American Uncanny.* Ann Arbor: University of Michigan Press. DOI: 10.3998/mpub.7172850.

Pasulka, D.W. 2019. *American Cosmic: UFOs, Religion, Technology.* Oxford: Oxford University Press.

On narrative and climate change:

Haraway, Donna. 2016. *Staying with the Trouble: Making Kin in the Chthulucene.* Minneapolis: University of Minnesota Press.

Helmreich, Stefan. 2009. *Alien Ocean: Anthropological Voyages in Microbial Seas.* Berkeley: University of California Press.

Holquist, Michael, ed. 1981. *The Dialogic Imagination by M.M. Bakhtin: Four Essays.* Translated by Caryl Emerson and Micahel Holquist. Austin: University of Texas Press.

Latour, Bruno. 2017. *Facing Gaia: Eight Lectures on the New Climatic Regime.* Translated by Catherine Porter. Cambridge: Polity.

Lowenhaupt Tsing, Anna, Heather Swanson, Elaine Gan, and Nils Bubandt, eds. 2017. *Arts of Living on a Damaged Planet: Ghosts and Monsters of the Anthropocene.* Minneapolis: University of Minnesota Press.

Afterword

Stuart McLean

Monsters, monsters, everywhere. One of the first things that is likely to strike any reader of this volume is the sheer number and variety of the monsters depicted in its pages: the giant, hirsute Bigfoot, lurking in the forests of the Pacific northwest; the reclusive ghost of a deceased spouse (or is it?) haunting an ethnographer's own house; the waterhorses, trolls, and hidden people occupying Iceland's humanly uninhabited interior, revealing themselves to horses at their summer pasturage; the Kurdaitcha of the Australian outback, dark-skinned and red-ochre dreadlocked, or else invisible, bent on killing, ensorcelling, or raping their human victims; the soul-stealing Anito monsters of Taiwan's Lanyu Island; the Minis of Vaduvur in Tamil Nadu, spirits inhabiting trees and bodies of water, and requiring regular appeasement in the form of sacrifices; the various sub-varieties of Georgian mountain goblins (Kajis, Chinkas, Alis, Tsqarishmapas), waiting to encounter unwary travelers; the Kappas of Japan, amphibious, turtle-like spirits who have image-managed their own development from malevolent water creatures to crowd-pleasing cartoon characters; Mr. Top Hat, a digital monster ostensibly created as part of an online, ethnographic research project, showing increasing signs of a life independent of his self-styled creators; Sakawa boys in Ghana engaging in gender-flipping internet scams assisted by magic and jujus; a muruyg, or snake spirit on the island of Saibai, offering its own account of possession to challenge those of a Christian exorcist, a Biblical demon, and an anthropologist; after-traces of the industrial past assailing ghost hunters in New England textile mills; a seminar on monster "branding" taking as its case study the Jersey devil of the Pine Barrens; a human-alien hybrid welcoming visitors to a business-style seminar for aliens and humans in the not-too-distant future.

The extent and scope of the list seems to confirm that the early twenty first century, whatever else it may be, is certainly a time of monsters, who proliferate in seeming defiance of social scientists' earlier characterizations of modernity in terms of the "disenchantment of the world."[1] In this regard at least, however, is the present really so different from any other time? "The old world is dying, and the new world struggles to be born; now is the time of monsters." These much-cited words have been attributed (via a decidedly loose translation popularized by Slavoj Žižek) to the Italian Marxist theoretician Antonio Gramsci, as he languished in a fascist prison in 1929 (Muehlebach 2016; Žižek 2010). Gramsci's (or his translator's) formulation suggests that the time of monsters is an in-between, interstitial time, a time of transition between a moribund world and a nascent one. Certainly, in the case of Europe in the late 1920s, the rise of fascism heralded the outbreak, a decade later, of a conflict that would engulf and forever transform the world. Fast forwarding to 1996, we find literary scholar Jeffrey Jerome Cohen (1996, vii) declaring, in his editor's Preface to an anthology titled *Monster Theory*, that the moment of the volume's

---

1   The phrase "disenchantment of the world" (*"die Entzauberung der Welt"*) has been given currency most famously by Max Weber, who adapted it from the poet Friedrich Schiller. The claim that the "modern" world is indeed disenchanted has recently been the subject of a sustained rebuttal by religious studies scholar Jason Ananda Josephson-Storm (2017).

publication is, similarly, a "time of monsters." In support of his claim, he mobilizes an eclectic range of examples, including: a baseball-sized atomic bomb made from red mercury; the resuscitated dinosaurs of the film *Jurassic Park* from 1993; the cannibalistic serial killer Jeffrey Dahmer, also known as the Milwaukee Monster; a fake photo, as it turned out, of the Loch Ness Monster; support groups for alien abductees; and a host of recent horror movies from *Bram Stoker's Dracula, Wolf, Mary Shelley's Frankenstein* to *Interview with the Vampire, Mary Reilly, Species,* and *Nightmare on Elm Street VI.* That was then and this is now. Are we living today in what could be considered even more a time of monsters—or a time of even more monsters? The intervening decades have certainly witnessed the emergence of some new and highly efficacious monster-making technologies, notably the internet and social media, which have fueled not least the demonization of political adversaries and ethnic, religious, and sexual minorities by a resurgent and emboldened far-right, whose leaders and spokespersons are themselves frequently portrayed in monstrous terms by their adversaries. Is burgeoning monstrosity a symptom of both the pre- and post-millennial decades? If so, how does this compare to the monsters of Gramsci's time? Or does monstrosity always bespeak a certain untimeliness, and thus an undoing of convenient periodizations?

As many commentators have remarked, monsters are liminal, interstitial beings, disturbers of received categories, incorrigible boundary crossers. Their bodies are often characterized by the splicing together of disparate features, elements of different species from marine to terrestrial to airborne, the human and the other-than-human. We should perhaps not be surprised then that a similar ambivalence seems to attend upon the present-ness and presence of monsters. Not only do monsters seem to partake only incongruously and uncertainly in any given present, but their very mode of being-present appears to be marked by a radical, irresolvable indeterminacy. Rarely if ever do monsters offer themselves fully and unequivocally to perception. Rather they are encountered more often in the guise of fugitive glimpses and intimations, sounds, smells, a sudden change in temperature. Coming face to face with a monster can cause the observer to doubt their own substance and integrity. A ghost-hunting anthropologist wonders aloud whether the dead in a haunted house are haunting its living occupants, or vice versa. A digital monster called Mr. Top Hat punctures the pretensions of the humans who think that they created him by pointing out that he was already there and that their efforts merely helped him to find a new home.

Such moments of reversal have long been a stock in trade of monster fiction. In H.P. Lovecraft's story "The Outsider" first published in 1926, the narrator encounters a monstrous, misshapen figure — "the ghoulish shade of decay, antiquity, and desolation; the putrid, dripping eidolon of unwholesome revelation; the awful baring of that which the merciful earth should always hide" (2016, 181) — and, in horrified fascination, reaches out to touch it, only to touch the glass surface of a mirror in which his own image is reflected. Of course, Lovecraft's monsters, frequently termed "indescribable" yet verbosely and extravagantly described nonetheless, are explicitly identified as fictional creations, although their stories are often told via such quasi-documentary devices as "found" manuscripts. In contrast, the monsters featured in this volume refuse such compartmentalization in that all of them are understood, at least by someone, somewhere, to be real. What confers upon such monsters a quality of ontological slipperiness is the fact that they are real in some people's worlds but not others. Sometimes they are real to the people anthropologists write about but not, or not in the same way, to anthropologists themselves, a dilemma that the contributors to this volume have chosen to address by turning to ethnographic fiction as a medium that allows the question of what is or is not real to be left open.

In fact, many of the monsters featured here seem to pose particular dangers to those who would find a definitive answer to that question. Those who treat monsters as an object of knowledge, seeking unambiguous evidence of their presence or absence may find their own presence assailed or called into question. Such a fate appears to have befallen many who have gone in pursuit of a glimpse of Bigfoot in the forests of the Pacific Northwest. Such ill-advised seekers end up themselves either disappearing or being reduced to traumatized silence. In contrast, the native peoples of the region seem to have no need of such a confirmatory visual fix, being content to register the monster's presence through the medium of smell, or simply a sense that things "feel different." Above all, those who live with monsters know better than to talk about them openly. To refer to Bigfoot by his lesser-known Coast Salish name risks summoning him. The Anito monsters of Lanyu Island and the Kurdaitcha of Australia's central desert are deemed capable of overhearing human conversations and responding with further attacks. Outsiders who speak unguardedly about such matters may find that there is a price to pay for doing so; like Justin, the white, community radio program design trainer, who forfeits both his job and the friendship of his aboriginal hosts and co-workers as a result of a broadcast detailing the depredations wrought by Kurdaitcha, which include the death of the niece of one of his trainees. If Justin's misstep is prompted by his professional ambitions, the world of academia, no less than that of radio, can be inimical to keeping quiet about monsters, with its demand for evidence and documentation, and its linking of career advancement to the verbalization of research findings in the form of conference presentations and publications.

Ethnographic fiction provides here, among other things, an alternative to the demand for scholarly explanation and verifiable facts on the one hand and the pressure to remain silent on the other. Monsters, as the editors note, propel us into the realm of the "as if," where the question of what rightfully exists or does not exist remains perennially unsettled. In doing so, they not only remind us of the various as-ifs that surround us in everyday life, including role-playing, role-switching, and what has been called "fictive" kinship, about which anthropologists have already had a great deal to say, but also call attention to what is arguably a much wider realm of uncertain presences. Surely much of what anthropologists encounter in the field — rumors, whispers, public secrets, innuendoes, possibilities, might-have-beens, lingering pasts, hinted-at futures (to name only a few of the more obvious examples!) — is by no means reassuringly stable and solid. Engaging with monsters offers a salient reminder that presence is by no means a straightforward, unambiguous affair, that it cannot always be readily distinguished from what is often proposed as its opposite, and that that reality might therefore comprise more than we thought we knew. Perhaps then hard and fast distinctions between what is and what is not are too blunt an instrument for exploring the complexity of the real, in which case the turn to fiction might appear less an indulgence than an imperative.

The late Jacques Derrida, a philosopher whose oeuvre was devoted to questioning the authority and self-evidence of presence in Western thought, was also interested in monsters and ghosts (especially the latter). Addressing the work and legacies of another famously ghost-obsessed philosopher, Karl Marx, Derrida (1994) wrote:

> If there is something like spectrality, there are reasons to doubt this reassuring order of presents and, especially, the border between the present, the actual or present reality of the present, and everything that can be opposed to it: absence, non-presence, non-effectivity, inactuality, virtuality, or even the simulacrum in general, and so forth.[2]

In response, and as an alternative to the more familiar philosophical idiom of ontology, Derrida proposes the hybrid (monstrous?) formulation "hauntology," a term subsequently given wider currency in the writings of the British philosopher and

---

2   Among Marx's ghosts, discussed by Derrida, are the specter haunting Europe described by Marx and Engels at the opening of *The Communist Manifesto,* and the spectral character of commodities discussed in the first volume of *Capital* (Derrida 1994).

cultural critic Mark Fisher.[3] Suggestive of slippage, uncertainty, and the reciprocal interference of pasts, presents, and futures, rather than the fullness and confidence of being, hauntology is an idiom that bears affinities both with the monstrous and with ethnographic fiction as a writerly mode. Like them, it is evocative of flickering indeterminacy, of the unresolved simultaneity of multiple possibilities (or ontologies?), rather than the already-decided-upon reassurance of actuality.

To be uncertainly or unambiguously present in a particular time and place is, among other things, to evoke the possibility of being present in other times and places. It is, one might say, to invite comparisons. Some of the monsters depicted in these pages seem themselves to suggest comparative leaps across centuries and continents. The centuries-long self-promotional efforts of the Kappa seek to draw upon and learn from a range of comparisons, including not only the vicissitudes suffered by other *yōkai*, Japanese magical creatures, but also the written documents and, latterly audio-visual works produced by the humans on whose collective consciousness they have sought to imprint themselves. A seminar on "How to Brand Your Monster" references, in addition to the New Jersey Devil who provides its centerpiece, Dracula, Bigfoot, the Loch Ness Monster, along with zombies, the Himalayan Yeti, and two Indigenous Canadian monsters, the better known Ogopogo and, for Anglophone larynxes, the harder-to-pronounce Kudloopudlooaluk. Alinc, the alien–human hybrid welcoming visitors to a seminar in the New Mexico desert invokes the variety of guises assumed by the aliens who have appeared on earth over the millennia (biblical angels, greys, reptilians, handsomely Nordic Space Brothers, and so on), along with the variety of motivations that have impelled their visits from aspirations to military conquest to a desire to warn humans about the dangers of nuclear war or environmental destruction. One audience member introjects a

3   In Fisher's (2014) writings, "hauntology" refers more specifically to the ways in which the cultural landscapes of contemporary capitalism remain haunted by the ghosts of unrealized alternative futures.

further comparison, recalling an Irish great-grandmother who grew up all too aware that humans coexisted with other beings in the form of the Fairies with whom they shared the countryside and who, like latter-day extraterrestrials, were sometimes given to abducting humans. Aline adds that humans' longstanding awareness of such co-existence began to wane as they became more inclined only to believe in beings whose existence could be definitively proven. To compare fairies and space aliens in this way is, as she puts it, a reminder that "in every story you hear today there's always some other story from the past layered inside it".

If monsters are good to think with, it seems that among the things they prompt us to think about it are not least other monsters. Monsters might be said to haunt not only humans but one another. Monsters, in other words, are an incitement to comparison. Individually, the chapters in this book take their cue from ethnographically conceived research projects rooted in particular localities and circumstances, or in the trans-local online milieu of creepypasta creation. Taken together, however, they suggest the scope and variousness of a comparative work, even one of the sprawling, compendious kind produced by some of anthropology's nineteenth-century practitioners. Certainly, there is no trace of the grand, unilinear schemes of social evolution that Edward Tylor and his contemporaries often appealed to as an organizing and unifying principle, but the geographical breadth and variety of the monsters grouped together here is evocative at times of the eclectic breadth of reference and the leaps across time and space that characterized a tradition of anthropological writing on which latter-day practitioners of the discipline have, largely, turned their backs.[4] If individual chapters exemplify the focused ethnographic particularism that has since become anthropology's hallmark, and if their stylistic and formal experiments proceed from this, the volume as a whole might be nonetheless thought of as an experiment in

---

4   For a discussion of anthropological comparativism, past and present, and its possibilities, see McLean (2017, 99–161) and Candea (2019).

comparativism, a comparativism eschewing any recourse to a readymade, overarching explanatory framework, but rather informed by an open-ended and exploratory play of similarities and differences; a monstrous comparativism perhaps, in which monstrosity itself affords the only overtly stated principle of association. Monstrosity might be seen as conducive not to grandly totalizing transhistorical visions, but to a more uneasy and destabilizing comparative method, aimed at putting assumed certainties, including that of the knowing self, into question. Once again, Aline puts it best when she tells her audience, "you already *do* live with Aliens, and you always have" and that "to live with Aliens means to understand this: your connection to earth and nature is a story, and it could be told in a different way." Has the most radical potential of anthropology as a discipline not always consisted in thus rendering newly dubious the taken-for-granted contours of the real, suggesting that whatever is, or appears to be, has the potential to be otherwise? Could it be that monstrous ethnographic fictions like the ones assembled in these pages are the harbingers both of a new anthropological comparativism and of a new ethnographic realism?

References

Candera, Matei. 2019. *Comparison in Anthropology: The Impossible Method.* Cambridge: Cambridge University Press.

Cohen, Jeffrey Jerome. 1996. "Preface: In the Time of Monsters." In *Monster Theory: Reading Culture,* edited by Jeffrey Jerome Cohen, vii–xiii. Minneapolis: University of Minnesota Press.

Derrida, Jacques. 1994. *Specters of Marx: The State of the Debt, The Work of Mourning and the New International.* Translated by Peggy Kamuf. London: Routledge.

Fisher, Mark. 2014. *Ghosts of My Life: Writings on Depression, Hauntology, and Lost Futures.* London: Zero Books.

Josephson-Storm, Jason Ananda. 2017. *The Myth of Disenchantment: Magic, Modernity, and the Birth of the Human Sciences.* Chicago: University of Chicago Press.

Lovecraft, H.P. 2016. "The Outsider." In *The Complete Fiction of H.P. Lovecraft,* 176–81. New York: Chartwell Books.

McLean, Stuart. 2017. *Fictionalizing Anthropology: Encounters and fabulations at the Edges of the Human.* Minneapolis: University of Minnesota Press.

Muehlebach, Andrea. 2016. "Time of Monsters. Cultural Anthropology Online." *Society for Cultural Anthropology, October 27.* https://culanth.org/fieldsights/time-of-monsters.

Žižek, Slavoj. 2010. "A Permanent Economic Emergency." *New Left Review* 64 (July/August). https://newleftreview.org/issues/ii64/articles/slavoj-zizek-a-permanent-economic-emergency.

Contributors

Kalissa Alexeyeff is an Associate Professor in Gender Studies at the University of Melbourne. She specializes in the areas of gender and sexuality, globalization, and development. Her research covers a range of interdisciplinary topics. Her first book *Dancing from the Heart: Movement, Gender and Cook Islands Globalization* (University of Hawai'i Press, 2009) explores the significance of dance to Cook Islands femininity throughout colonial history and in its contemporary global manifestations. She is co-editor with Niko Besnier of *Gender on the Edge: Transgender, Gay, and Other Pacific Islanders* (University of Hawai'i Press, 2014) which explores alternative sexualities and gender identities in the Pacific region, and with John Taylor *Touring Pacific Cultures* (Australia National University Press, 2016), a creative collection of Indigenous and non-Indigenous responses to touring and tourism.

Indira Arumugam is an anthropologist who works in Tamil Nadu, South India, and among the Tamil Diaspora in Singapore and Southeast Asia. She is an Assistant Professor in the Department of Sociology and Anthropology at the National University of Singapore. Her research interests include vernacular political imaginaries, ritual theories and practices, intimate economics of (re)production, modalities of sacrality and monstrosity, play and pleasure, and popular Hinduism. Her writings on animal sacrifice, divine agency, rituals, the gift, and kinship have appeared in leading journals of anthropology, religion, and Asian Studies. She is currently working on a book on vernacular political theorizing titled, *Visceral Politics: Intimate Imaginaries of Power in South India.*

Misty L. Bastian is the emeritus Lewis Audenreid Professor of History and Archaeology and Professor of Anthropology at Franklin & Marshall College. Her fieldsites include Nigeria, the USA, and the internet. She has researched mermaids, witches, Neo-Pentecostals, spirits, and ghost hunters, amongst many other topics. She is the author of numerous journal articles and chapters in edited volumes, as well as co-author (with Marc Matera and Susan Kingsley Kent) of *The Women's War of 1929: Gender and Violence in Colonial Nigeria* (Palgrave Macmillan, 2013).

Adam Coppola is a technical trainer working in the software industry. While teaching the ins and outs of software, Adam incorporates lessons on how human needs and values shape technical systems and vice versa. Adam has worked in education and anthropology research, and he is inspired by critical theorists and human rights advocates.

Richard Davis works with Aboriginal and Torres Strait Islander peoples throughout Australia, publishing on masculinity, performance, the frontier, epitathic writing, death, knowledge, and poetry. He is the editor of *Woven Histories, Dancing Lives: Torres Strait Islander Identity, Culture and History* (Aboriginal Studies Press, 2004), co-editor (with Deborah Bird Rose) of *Dislocating the Frontier: Essaying the Mystique of the Outback* (Australian National University E-Press, 2005), and co-editor with James Leach of *Recognising and Translating Knowledge: Navigating the*

Political, Epistemological, Legal and Ontological (Special Issue of Anthropological Forum 22:3, 2012). He has held research fellowships and lecturing positions at several Australian universities. He is currently working as an academic anthropologist for the Australian government.

Michael Dylan Foster is a professor in the Department of East Asian Languages and Cultures at the University of California, Davis. He is the author of *The Book of Yōkai: Mysterious Creatures of Japanese Folklore* (University of California Press, 2015), *Pandemonium and Parade: Japanese Monsters and the Culture of Yōkai* (University of California Press, 2009), and numerous articles on folklore, literature, media, and monsters. He also co-edited *The Folkloresque: Reframing Folklore in a Popular Culture World* (Utah State University Press, 2016) and *UNESCO on the Ground: Local Perspectives on Intangible Cultural Heritage* (Indiana University Press, 2015). His current project explores discourses of tourism and heritage as they relate to local festivals in Japan.

Leberecht Funk is a social and cultural anthropologist working in the field of psychological anthropology. Leberecht received his PhD from the Freie Universität Berlin (Germany) and has conducted field research in Taiwan. He is interested in childhood and socialization, emotion, social relations, and Indigenous cosmologies. His regional focus is East Asia and Southeast Asia. He is the author of *Geister der Kindheit. Sozialisation von Emotionen bei den Tao in Taiwan* [*Ghosts of Childhood: Socialization of Emotions among the Tao in Taiwan*] (transcript, 2022), and the lead author of the collective volume *Feeding, Bonding, and the Formation of Social Relationships: Ethnographic Challenges to Attachment Theory and Early Childhood Interventions* (Cambridge University Press, 2023)..

Ilana Gershon is a Professor of anthropology at Rice University and studies how people use new media to accomplish complicated social tasks such as breaking up with lovers and hiring new employees. She has published books such as *The Breakup 2.0: Disconnecting over New Media* (Cornell University Press, 2010) and *Down and Out in the New Economy: How People Find (or Don't Find) Work Today* (University of Chicago Press, 2017), and has edited two other volumes of ethnographic fiction on work and animals. She has been a fellow at Stanford's Center for Advanced Study in the Behavioral Sciences, at Notre Dame's Institute for Advanced Study and is currently a visiting professor at the University of Helsinki. She will soon publish a book analyzing how working in person during a pandemic sheds light on the ways workplaces function as private governments.

Mary Hawkins is a Professor in the School of Social Sciences, Western Sydney University. Mary received her PhD in social anthropology from the University of Sydney and has conducted field research in Indonesia and Iceland. Her recent Iceland-focused publications include Helena Onnudottir and Mary Hawkins, "Margt byr i Thokunni: What Dwells in the Mist?," in *Monster Anthropology: Ethnographic Interpretations of Transforming Social Worlds through Monsters* (Bloomsbury Academic Press, 2020) and Mary Hawkins and Helena Onnudottir, "From Resurrection and New Dawn to the Pirate Party: Political Party Names as Symbolizing Recent Transformations in the Political Field in Iceland."

Susan Lepselter is an Associate Professor of American Studies and Adjunct Associate Professor of Anthropology and Folklore at Indiana University Bloomington. She spent years interviewing people who told of their experiences with UFOs and aliens. Her book *The Resonance of Unseen Things: Poetics, Power, Captivity and UFOs in the American Uncanny* (University of Michigan Press, 2016) won the Society for Cultural Anthropology Bateson Prize of 2017. Currently, she is working on a book of poetry and prose about encounters between humans and animals.

Caitrin Lynch is the Dean of Faculty and professor of anthropology at Olin College of Engineering. She is the author of two books, *Retirement on the Line: Age, Work, and Value in An American Factory* (Cornell University Press, 2012) and *Juki Girls, Good Girls: Gender and Cultural Politics in Sri Lanka's Global Garment Industry* (Cornell University Press, 2007). She also produced the documentary film, *My Name Is Julius*. Her research and teaching passions include examining the dynamics of work and cultural values with a focus on aging and gender, as well as the cultural dimensions of offshore manufacturing, plus a commitment to understanding social behavior in global contexts and a devotion to encouraging students to use qualitative methods to think critically about the world around them.

Stuart McLean was born in the United Kingdom and is of English and Scottish ancestry. He studied English literature at the University of Oxford and went on to complete a PhD in sociocultural anthropology at Columbia University. His interests include anthropologies beyond the human; art and visual culture; death and mortuary practices; experimental writing; landscape, environment, and place; and time and memory. The regional focus of his work has been the maritime and island communities of North Atlantic Europe. His publications include *The Event and Its Terrors: Ireland, Famine, Modernity* (Stanford University Press, 2004), *Fictionalizing Anthropology: Encounters and Fabulations at the Edges of the Human* (University of Minnesota Press, 2017), and *Crumpled Paper Boat: Experiments in Ethnographic Writing* (co-edited with Anand Pandian, Duke University Press, 2017). He is currently Professor of Anthropology and Global Studies at the University of Minnesota, Twin Cities.

Matthew Gmalifo Mabefam is a lecturer in Development Studies at the University of Melbourne, a Visiting Fellow at the Institute of Postcolonial Studies, and a Diaspora Fellow for African Research and Impact Network. His research focuses on the politics of international development, development in Africa, spirituality, religion, witchcraft, and wellbeing. He obtained his PhD in Anthropology and Development Studies from the University of Melbourne in 2021.

Paul Manning is a Professor of Anthropology at Trent University in Canada. He is the author of three books, *Strangers in a Strange Land* (Academic Studies Press, 2012), *Semiotics of Drinks and Drinking* (Continuum/Bloomsbury, 2012), and *Love Stories Language, Private Love, and Public Romance in Georgia* (University of Toronto Press, 2015). Among his other ethnographic projects, he has written on the "spectral migrations" of various kinds of folkloric monsters in time and space, from Georgian goblins moving from village to the city (2012, 2014, forthcoming), how Cornish mining spirits (knackers) became Transatlantic mining spirits called Tommyknockers (2005), how Cornish Pixies became part of British fairylore (2016), to North American ghosts, spiritualist seances, and "weird" fiction (2017, 2018, 2020, 2021).

Cailín Murray is an Associate Professor of Anthropology at Ball State University in Muncie, Indiana. She received her MA and PhD in Cultural Anthropology from the University of Washington in 2001. In 2004 she completed a two-year Andrew W. Mellon Postdoctoral Fellowship at Wesleyan University in Connecticut and joined the Ball State faculty. Dr. Murray is an environmental ethnohistorian who studies Indigenous knowledge systems, settler colonialism, and the transformation of historical landscapes. She is particularly interested in how folklore, cultural memory, history, and foodways have informed how landscapes were used in the past and continue to construct and sustain attachments to place in the present. She regularly teaches an undergraduate course about monsters and culture. Dr. Murray has conducted ethnographic and ethnohistorical research primarily along the central Northwest Coast. She is currently researching twentieth-century witch accusations in the US and settler colonialism, religious beliefs, and historical gardening practices in the Great Lakes region. In 2019 she conducted preliminary research in Ireland and hopes to return there in order to explore

Connemara's shell fisheries. She has published in *Ethnohistory* and other scholarly journals and co-authored with Coll Thrush Phantom Past, *Indigenous Presence: Native Ghosts in Culture and History* (Nebraska University Press, 2011).

Yasmine Musharbash is an Associate Professor and Head of Discipline (Anthropology) at the School of Archaeology & Anthropology at the Australian National University. She conducts participant, observation-based research with Warlpiri people in Central Australia with a particular focus on relations: among Warlpiri people on the one hand and between them and non-Indigenous people, fauna, flora, the elements, and monsters, on the other. She is the author of *Yuendumu Everyday Contemporary Life in Remote Aboriginal Australia* (Aboriginal Studies Press, 2008) and of a number of co-edited volumes, including two about monsters that she co-edited with Geir Henning Presterudstuen: *Monster Anthropology in Australasia and Beyond* (Palgrave Macmillan, 2014) and *Monster Anthropology: Ethnographic Explorations of Transforming Social Worlds through Monsters* (Routledge, 2020).

Helena Onnudottir is a Senior Lecturer in the School of Social Sciences, Western Sydney University. Helena received her PhD in social anthropology from Macquarie University and has conducted field research in Aboriginal Australia and Iceland. Her recent Iceland focused publications include Helena Onnudottir and Mary Hawkins, "Margt byr i Thokunni: What Dwells in the Mist?" In *Monster Anthropology: Ethnographic Interpretations of Transforming Social Worlds through Monsters* (Bloomsbury Academic Press, 2020), and Mary Hawkins and Helena Onnudottir, "From Resurrection and New Dawn to the Pirate Party: Political Party Names as Symbolizing Recent Transformations in the Political Field in Iceland" (*Politics, Religion and Ideology,* 2018).

Jeffrey A. Tolbert is an Assistant Professor of American Studies and Folklore at Penn State Harrisburg. His research focuses on vernacular belief and the supernatural, popular, and traditional cultures, and digital ethnography. He is particularly interested in understanding how contemporary people integrate super-natural belief and experience into their daily, technologically mediated lives. He is co-editor (with Michael Dylan Foster) of *The Folkloresque: Reframing Folklore in a Popular Culture World* (Utah State University Press, 2016), and *Möbius Media: Popular Culture, Folklore, and the Folkloresque,* forthcoming from Utah State University Press. His current monograph project is an exploration of the role of folklore and the folkloresque in the horror genre.

Matt Tomlinson is an anthropologist who studies language, religion, and politics with a focus on ritual performance. He has conducted long-term research in the Pacific Islands, especially Fiji, Samoa, and New Zealand. More recently, he has conducted fieldwork in Australia on the religion of Spiritualism. When not marketing the Jersey Devil as the most entertaining monster in the world, he teaches anthropology at the Australian National University. His most recent books are *God Is Samoan: Dialogues Between Culture and Theology in the Pacific* (University of Hawai'i Press, 2020) and the edited volumes *The Monologic Imagination* (with Julian Millie, Oxford University Press, 2017) and *New Mana: Transformations of a Classic Concept in Pacific Languages and Cultures* (with Ty P. Kāwika Tengan, Australian National University Press, 2016).